LANDFALL

HUGH FITZGERALD RYAN

hughfryan@gmail.com

Landfall

© High Fitzgerald Ryan, 2020, 2013

Published by Shennick Books

Print ISBN   9798697288061
eBook ISBN 9781839781223

'The eagles took to the Atlantic, while the
vultures fell upon Ireland.'

STANDISH O GRADY

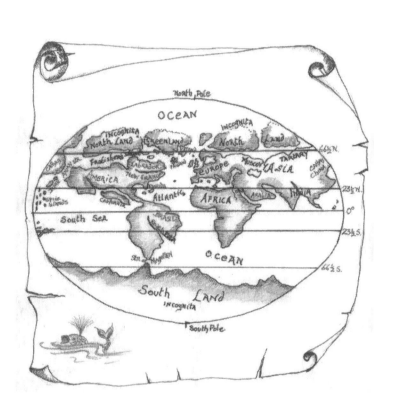

Prologue

During the bloody years of Queen Elizabeth's reign, England lived in a state of constant vigilance. There were enemies within, prepared to deliver the realm into the hands of the Pope or worse still, into the hands of King Philip of Spain. There were those who wished to turn back time, to demolish the newly established Protestant religion, as her father had so comprehensively crushed the old, Catholic order. The ruins of abbeys and monasteries, laid low by King Henry, were everywhere, reminders of what once had been.

Engorged with plunder, Spain's empire sprawled across the New World. Gold made everything possible. King Philip's fleets ruled the Atlantic. It would be no great matter to land armies in England or send an invincible armada into the Thames to fillet London like a Billingsgate haddock.

It was a time for courage and ruthless discipline. Dissent was treason. The heads on London Bridge made clear the fate that awaited all who questioned, or seemed to doubt the authority of the Queen. Punishment was instant and hideous in nature.

A new energy and new confidence suffused many aspects of English life. Explorers and adventurers sailed to far-flung and unknown lands. Privateers and pirates rifled the holds of the Spanish treasure fleets. The sea proved, yet again, to be England's bastion. Poets and the play-houses brought lustre to the language and to its literature. An empire came into being and wealth flowed through London's Royal Exchange. War with Spain became a constant fact of life.

But always there was the matter of Ireland, the oldest colony, the thorn in England's side for four turbulent centuries. The Irish lived in nominal and tenuous allegiance to the Crown, but ancient loyalties to chieftain and clan were more powerful. The myths and legends of millennia of conquest and re-conquest blended with stubborn adherence to the Catholic faith. The conquering

Anglo-Norman families of the 12th century were subsumed into the native culture to the point where they became distinguishable only by their names, from the wild Irish of the forest and mountain fastnesses. Only around Dublin and certain walled towns, did English law hold sway.

When rebellion flared in Ireland, both 'Old English' and 'Wilde Irish' looked to Spain and to the Pope for assistance. For Elizabeth's Lords Deputy, brutal military repression, famine and summary justice were the only ways to prevent Ireland becoming a threat to the very survival of England itself. Wholesale replacement of the native people by loyal English settlers, appeared to be the surest means of returning Ireland to obedience and allegiance.

> 'But if that country of Ireland whence you lately came, be so goodly and commodious a soyle as you report, I wounder that no course is taken for the tourning thereof to good uses and reducing that salvage nation to better government and civility.' E.S.

The White Bear

1575-1580

Chapter One

"You see, Master Dee," continued Lord Burghley, "in my own father's time the world was no more than half the size it is now."

He paused on the sloping spiral path, steadying himself with a silver topped cane.

"There were no Americas. No Christian man had sailed to India, Cathay or Sepangu. They were more legend than reality. Nobody had even rounded Africa." He smiled, making a play of mopping his forehead with a linen handkerchief. "And now you come to me with a plan to make the world even bigger. Have we not problems enough as it is?"

He regarded his companion with tolerant amusement. He was interested, nonetheless, in what John Dee was suggesting. Although he was younger than his lordship by seven or eight years, Dee, at forty seven, with his long robe and flowing white beard, was the very picture of an ancient wizard out of a fairy- tale. He had a well-founded reputation for learning in all the sciences and languages, ancient and modern. He had cast a propitious horoscope for Elizabeth on the day of her coronation, something she had never forgotten. He was regarded with apprehension, by ignorant people, as something of a sorcerer but his reputation for kindness and general goodness protected him from danger. If he had a fault, it was that he trusted people too easily and too much.

The same could not be said of William Cecil, First Baron Burghley, Lord High Treasurer and chief adviser to Her Majesty, Queen Elizabeth, for most of her long reign.

Dee cleared his throat. "But think of the wealth, my lord. The gold of the Indies. The silks and spices, with no interference from the French or the Spaniards. It would be an English ocean all the way to the Great South Sea." He paused, his enthusiasm getting the better of him. Let the hare set.

"Let us walk to the top and sit for a while, Master Dee. Let us contemplate this new world of yours."

They climbed onwards, upwards by the spiral path, until they reached a little rustic temple at the top of the mound. They sat on a stone bench and took in the view. "Do you like my garden, Master Dee?" asked Burghley. His breathing eased. He stretched his legs out before him like a child and clicked his shoes together.

"It is very fine indeed, my lord," nodded Dee. "Very fine indeed."

They looked down at the intricate patterns of clipped box and yew, lines of low hedging intertwined and knotted like a manuscript of old. The colours of summer and autumn had deserted the neatly tended beds. The vines and roses of the arbours, exposed to the winter's harshness, showed their leafless sinews.

"I had this mound constructed in order to gain a place of quiet and contemplation. From here I can see all the world."

Dee regarded him curiously, waiting. "All the world, Master Dee. Do you take my meaning?"

"Not entirely, my lord."

Burghley pointed with this cane. "This is the world. This is my world, the spires, the palaces, the river, the bridge. This is London. The world comes to us."

They sat in silence. Lights showed in some of the windows of Burghley's home, Exeter house. Beyond, loomed the Savoy on the other side of The Strand. Through gaps in the houses glinted the Thames, with the lanterns of the watermen glowing like fire flies. Further downriver in the violet haze of a winter afternoon, the smoke of the innumerable cooking fires hung over streets and laneways. Out of the haze loomed the massive bulk of Saint Paul's Church, with its truncated, square tower. There were the dim needle-points of Saint Laurence's, The Dutch church, Mary le Bow, Saint Peter's, Saint Helen's, Saint Dunstan's and many more, a city devoted to God. The towers of the Exchange spoke of commerce; the cupolas of The Tower spoke of temporal might.

"Listen," said Burghley softly, raising his hand. From the fields by Covent Garden came the cries of geese by the little lake. "My winter visitors from the north land." He smiled. "Perhaps they know the route your sea explorers should take."

"Perhaps they do, my lord" replied Dee. "Perhaps they do." He liked the conceit, surprised by this fanciful notion in a man famed for his practical and pragmatic approach to all matters.

"Understand me, Master Dee. I am a man of affairs. I have heavy responsibilities and enjoy a measure of success. I have few passions but I hold them dear."

Dee sat in silence. He felt a twinge of fear at the thought of receiving confidences from the most powerful man in England. It might put some unlooked for responsibility on his shoulders. He might fail this man in some unanticipated way. Burghley might come to regret confiding in him. He might see it as a weakness in himself, a weakness to be expunged by procuring Dee's silence in some hideous and ruthless manner.

"You seem surprised, Master Dee. Did you think me incapable of passion?"

Dee spread his hands noncommittally. "My lord," he murmured, wondering if more were expected.

Burghley laughed softly at his guest's awkwardness. "Gardens, horticulture, architecture. These are some of my passions. I like order in my world. I shall buy those fields and that little lake from my good neighbour, my lord of Bedford. He does not know this yet, but he will agree. They always agree. I shall extend my gardens and the geese will visit me every year. They will bring their wild and raucous music into the city."

"You are a poet, my lord," said Dee lightly.

"It is the excellent foppery of the age. Everyone must be a poet. Everyone must be thrusting his rhymes and his hexameters on people of quality, in the hope of patronage. No, Master Dee, bring me no poets. Bring me sea captains, by all means. Bring me merchants and adventurers and men who know how the world works; men who can take a prize or direct an army; men who can write a readable history, a book of science, of mathematics; men like yourself, Master Dee."

John Dee inclined his head, acknowledging the compliment.

"But in God's name, bring me no poets"

Burghley clapped his hands together, rubbing them to dispel the chill. Dee noticed that he wore no gloves. There was soil under the fingernails, as if the great lord could not resist pulling a weed as he strolled in his garden, or picking a stone from a flowerbed.

"You spoke of several passions, my lord. I would learn from you what they are." Perhaps he had gone too far.

"Very simply told, my friend," replied Burghley.

My friend, thought Dee. Friendship with great ones is like a vortex, into which less weighty beings can be drawn down and down to their doom. He knew the story of Nicholas of King's Lynn, who sailed north two centuries before and how he had seen great gulfs and swallowing sinks, where mighty currents raged between lands of eternal snow. Beware, beware of too great a familiarity.

"Simply told, my friend. My good wife, my family and most of all, my service to my Queen."

John Dee nodded in acquiescence and understanding. It was not his place to comment.

"If the light were better and our eyesight keener, we might make out London Bridge. If our hearing were sharper, now that the noise of the city is dying down, we would hear, at this time of low tide, the cascade beneath its arches."

"I have heard it, my lord."

"It is a dangerous bridge, but a necessary one. Dangerous to the unwary boatman and dangerous to the traitors whose heads adorn it".

"Indeed, my lord." He remembered as a boy, shooting the bridge in a wherry. He had laughed as the boat plunged the height of a tall man, and shot through an arch. Onlookers cheered the dexterity of the watermen and the glee of the young passenger.

There were heads on spikes, black and wizened warnings to miscreants and traitors. There was one head, the watermen told him, the one that stayed incorrupt for months, the head of a saint. Thomas More, a man who had defied his king. The watermen had crossed themselves furtively and bent again to their oars. The thole-pins creaked as they fought the swirling waters.

The head was still fair, alone among the blackened and eyeless skulls. Did he imagine now after all the years, that a light surrounded it, high on the spiked bridge? He held his tongue. More was a traitor who defied his king. It was necessary that he should die.

"Yes, indeed," murmured Burghley, rising from his seat. "These are my passions, Master Dee. I like order in my garden and in my home. Most of all, I like order in the realm. Things must be done correctly. I shall see your maps and globes and your adventurers, but please," he chuckled again, "no poets."

He took John Dee by the elbow, as if deferring to an older man, and conducted him down the spiral path of his little mountain. The smell of damp rose from leaf mould. A gardener stirred a reluctant bonfire on the other side of a hedge. Smoky swags drifted against the dying light. Somewhere in the gathering dusk, the geese called to one another.

***

Michael Lok, director of the Company of Muscovy, a seafaring merchant adventurer in his own right, sat back from the table, enjoying the conversation of his companions. A keen angler, he understood how to deploy dubbes and flies to land his quarry. He laced his fingers together and leaned his elbows on the arms of his chair. Candlelight from two candelabra illuminated the maps spread out on the table. The light glowed red in his glass of wine. He noticed that the stem of the glass was slightly crooked. Nonetheless the circular disc of wine stood level, like a binnacle. He was at peace. The arduous voyages of his youth were behind him. The anxiety of setting forth on the sea and on business, the long night watches in all weathers, had given way to prosperity and a comfortable middle age.

Yet as he listened to John Dee and his friend, Martin Frobisher, discussing navigation, he felt an old stirring in his heart, a desire to cast off the cares of life on land and pit his strength, possibly in a last battle, against the elements. He felt a certain envy of Frobisher, a sturdy dark-skinned man with an air of impatience about him. Lok knew from long acquaintance, that Frobisher was quick in friendship but no less quick to quarrel. He had a reputation for great physical courage and an intense loyalty to those who served under him.

Handled judiciously, Frobisher would be the ideal man to lead an expedition to the Great South Sea. Lok determined to commission a ballad on Martin Frobisher the Privateer. He could make Frobisher a public hero, a veteran of many a victory over the French and Spanish on the rolling Atlantic. In fact, he mused, I could write it myself, a string of stock phrases linked to a rousing tune, with a table-thumping chorus.

A popular hero would loosen the purse-strings of venturers and investors. A route to The Indies via a North-West Passage would become a cornucopia, disgorging an endless stream of wealth into the coffers of the Muscovy Company. Frobisher was the man to encircle the world by sailing westwards and returning from the east. It would be like tightening a drawstring about the Arctic regions and scooping their riches into England's net.

"If you will come to me here at Mortlake", John Dee was saying. "I can impart to you all that I know of cosmography, navigation and the most useful maps for your purposes."

Frobisher frowned. "I am not in a position to pay for your tuition. I am at present without a ship. I am already indebted to my friend here for lodging. Dee waved away the objection.

"A trifling consideration. I am suggesting merely some scholarly embellishments to your great practical experience. It would be a privilege to contribute to a venture that has already gained the approval of Her Majesty." He leaned to peruse the out-spread map, moving one of the candelabra to weigh down a corner. The map exhibited a desire to spring back into its wonted cylindrical form.

"As we can see, the geographers deduce that here in the region of the Pole, there must be an open ocean, free of all ice."

Dee pointed to the Arctic, imaginatively depicted, yet leaving a clearly discernible passage between the extreme north of America and the Pole itself. "As salt water does not freeze, the ice forms only along the coast. Get through this ice barrier and the way to The Indies will lie open to you."

Frobisher grunted. He was not so sure. He had spoken to whalers and to fishermen who had braved the fisheries of the New World. Yet the passage lay in much the same latitude as Britain's Northern islands. He rubbed his short black beard. It would not be so simple.

He looked at Michael Lok. Lok was not interested in hearing about difficulties. His eyes were shut. Frobisher surmised that Lok was listening to the music.

In her private quarters John Dee's wife was playing a virginal. It was a well-known piece, *The Battle* by William Byrd: the low, measured beat of the marching footmen, the clash of opposing forces, horse and foot, the trumpet, the flute and drum, faster, more urgent. The music rolled, reverberating around the house. Lok's fingers drummed on the arms of his chair. He knew that Dee's wife had insisted on her own private apartments as the price of moving into his mother's house. The slow, sombre notes of the burial of the dead, the sonorous horns, the funeral beat. No glory there. Joan, his first wife had played such an instrument. Lok loved the virginal, the beauty of inlay, the extraordinary cleverness of the plucking quills, the rise and fall of the jacks. There was one at home, but his many children had battered it almost into silence. It would be folly to replace it at this stage. Possibly in a few years.

The music stopped abruptly. Lok opened his eyes. He thought of his lost Joan and her unruly brood. Frobisher was on his feet.

"We have intruded for long enough, Master Dee," he said, picking up his bonnet. "We can go down by your stairs and hail a boat."

He liked to be on the move. He would be a restless scholar. They made their farewells. It was obvious that Dee was anxious to return to the maps. He rose and bowed to his departing guests. He heard the outer door closing, but already his mind was on the northern ocean and the puzzle of the ice.

15

***

On the morrow the Queen came to a house of mourning. A cold March day it was, with a carping wind blowing upriver from the East, a wind with the salt of the North Sea in it and a chill that penetrated well padded tunics. She came to consult her scholar, her astrologer and good friend, John Dee, a friend who never asked anything for himself.

John Dee had risked his very life in showing her the horoscope he had cast for her sister, Queen Mary. It told her when Mary would die. It was treason to show such a thing and treason to ask. It was their guilty secret. She found him standing at the river stairs, waiting to greet her. His servants had heard the rhythmic thump of oars and had come running in panic, their feet pounding in the corridors, to tell him that Her Majesty the Queen was approaching at some speed. Her royal standard streamed from the jack. Ten watermen pulled on the oars. Gentlemen stood to attention in front of the canopy, holding their long halberds. The curtains were closed against the wind.

The helmsman swung the craft out of the fast-moving current and laid it expertly alongside the stairs. Watermen leaped ashore to secure the barge fore and aft. The curtains on the starboard side were drawn back and the Queen stepped easily onto the lower stairs. John Dee went forward and dropped on one knee. He took her outstretched hand and put it to his lips. He felt the touch of gold and jewels, made cold in the stiffening breeze. She bade him rise.

"I find you all in mourning, Master Dee," she began. "What does this betoken?"

"Majesty," he replied, "I am at a loss. I am not prepared for this honour." He shook his head in confusion. "It is my wife, you see. My poor wife!"

"Dead?" enquired Elizabeth. "Indeed I am dismayed to hear of your sad loss."

"Yes, Majesty. She died last night in the midst of her music. She was playing, you see. We could hear her and then she stopped. I paid no mind." He hung his head. "My apologies, Majesty. I have kept you standing here in this wind. I pray you come inside."

Elizabeth flinched. She had a dread of disease. She hesitated. "I will not trouble you in your time of sorrow. Let us walk up to the church and shelter from the wind." She gave a wan smile. "My father had it moved back from the river bank. If he had not, we should have been sheltered on this spot."

Dee smiled a little smile in acknowledgement of the pleasantry. Her father, King Harry for reasons known only to himself, had indeed uprooted the church of Saint Mary the Virgin and all those interred therein, and moved it and them back to what he considered a safe distance from the riverbank. As head of the church he had regard for the safety of its property.

Dee's black scholar's robe fluttered about him. The pearls in Elizabeth's elaborate coiffed hair danced in the wind. There was a healthy rosiness to her cheeks, visible even through the layer of make-up. She leaned against the stones of the church wall, holding her elbows in her cupped hands, hugging herself for warmth.

"I know that today you are distraught with grief, my good friend." He felt no twinge of apprehension at the word. Her sympathy was genuine. "Today you must mourn and for a while longer, but know that your queen has need of you always. Let this be some comfort to you. When you are reconciled to God's will, come to me and tell me of this great expedition to The Indies. Tell me what legitimate claims I may make on new lands in the frozen reaches of the globe. Tell me how I may bring the true scriptures to ignorant and savage people."

Dee felt a stirring of gratitude towards her. Indeed his mind was already filled with answers to her questions. She knew him well. She had thrown a line to him in his hour of need. She knew how devoted he was to his wife, how he would miss her smiling company, her steady advice and the music that had filled his house with happiness. But also she knew that his mind would never be at rest as long as there was knowledge to be gained, mysteries to be unlocked or plans to be pushed forward. Like a salmon swimming upstream, John Dee's mind strove towards the light.

"I am yours to command, Majesty," he murmured. She extended her hand and again he knelt to her.

She returned to the stairs. Her ladies held her train as she stepped down and boarded her barge. The watermen cast off and the craft swung into the Tideway. The thicket of oars descended into the water. The watermen pulled as one. The royal standard snapped in the wind.

John Dee stood immobile at the top of the stairs, watching as the craft swung around Chiswick and disappeared behind the willows and alders of the riverbank. The glowing standard disappeared last of all. Soon there was only the faint thump of the oars to show that the visitation had taken place. He contemplated the melancholy duty that lay ahead of him that day and guiltily, he realised that the Queen's commission was already working in his brain. There was a Welsh prince who had reached the New World, centuries before the Spaniards or the French. There was an Irish monk. A case could and would be made. He checked himself. The wind ruffled the withered sedge along the verge of the river. It whistled through the willows that overhung the rushing stream. He shivered. It was the right sort of day for a funeral.

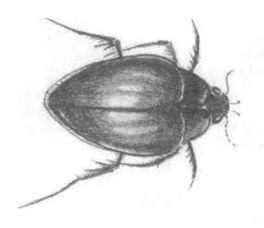

Chapter Two

Michael Lok looked at the night sky. A new crescent moon hung in the south-east. It held the faint disc of the old moon in its embrace. It was probably an omen. He resolved to consult John Dee on its significance. He gazed at the glittering constellations. Master Dee understood what they stood for. He could read the Zodiac and show how it shaped the fate of every living being. It influenced the fate of nations and empires, foretelling their rise and fall. There was little that he did not understand.

There was a hint of aquamarine in the eastern sky but still the stars glistened. He knew the working stars as any mariner would. He was familiar with the lodestone and how it cleaved to the North Star, but the mysteries of the constellations required explanation by keener minds. He felt that they looked kindly upon him at that particular time.

Pledges were coming in for the great voyage. The Queen herself pledged five hundred pounds. Ships were building. Frobisher had ignited the imagination of the nation. He had learned to smile and make a graceful bow, bending his stocky frame as nimbly as any courtier. He was cheered at the playhouses and at Paris Garden where the bulls were kept. Players enacted his many, now legendary, triumphs over the dastardly Spaniards. His success was prayed for in the churches. Frobisher was as secure an investment as could be found. Michael Lok had underwritten the cost of the voyage to the tune of twelve hundred pounds, engaging his house and property as security. All was in place for a successful summer voyage.

Lok wished that he might go along. He wished that he might be there to turn a page of history. This would be the voyage that would tilt the balance in England's favour. In future the treasure ships would dock at Bristol and Deptford, rather than at Cadiz. The merchant princes and grandees would build palaces to outshine those of the Catholic powers of the south.

He marvelled at John Dee's breadth of knowledge and the fine brain that could deploy that knowledge in legal argument. He had heard him explain to Her Majesty at Greenwich, why the voyage of her predecessor, Prince Madoc of Wales, in the twelfth century after Christ, established her prior claim to the New World. If law meant anything, then she, as Madoc's heir, was entitled to all lands since discovered and yet to be discovered, the Meta Incognita, as she herself had named them. As with a child's lucky bag, bought at a country fair on a holy day, she already owned she knew not what.

John Dee dismissed as irrelevant the Papal settlement between the usurping Spaniards and the Portuguese. The Pope's writ did not run in the Northern Ocean. It dwindled to nothing in the high latitudes. She had a duty to bring the Reformed Faith to the infidels of the Arctic and the Indies, before they might be contaminated by the aggression and rapacity of the Catholic powers.

He spoke of the rise and fall of the great empires of the past. They had risen through courage and good fortune and mainly through the willingness of powerful leaders to grasp every opportunity. Elizabeth liked what she heard. She nodded. She looked at Frobisher. She could use men like him. If rumour and gossip reported right, Frobisher might well have hung in the mud at Wapping, exposed to three tides, until his body swelled into a monstrous scarecrow, thence to be taken to Tilbury and left to dangle on that windy point, a warning to all passing seamen. That could have been his fate. Life is like the roll of a dice or the turn of a card at primero. She knew herself, how random life can be.

She knew that Frobisher had denounced the unregenerate Irish traitor, FitzGerald, the Earl of Desmond. Fitzgerald had tried to subborn Frobisher into spiriting him out of London to resume his treasonable activities in Ireland. She knew from reliable sources, that Frobisher had waited, dressed as an oysterman, a boat at the ready to whisk the Irish traitor downriver with the ebbing tide. But FitzGerald had not turned up. An Irish failing, she was assured. Frobisher, with the kind of brass neck she admired, turned his loss to profit of a sort and denounced his would-be passenger.

She caught Frobisher's eye. She knew her man and he knew that she knew him. In a way, they needed each other. He was her pit-bull terrier, awaiting her orders and his opportunity.

John Dee was the advocate. Michael Lok had the money. The Queen gave the signal. The planets were agreeable. The tide was swelling. All was propitious.

Except that all was not entirely well. Michael Lok's wife, Mary, the second woman to govern his house and his ever expanding family, twelve at the last count, was not convinced. With a lack of vision, probably to be excused in the mother of a large family, she saw bread on the table as being more important than dreams of empire among the floating islands of the Arctic and the swarming millions of the Indies.

She went out into the courtyard to where her husband stood, deep in his reverie. Since he had been received by the Queen he was like a man inspired. He spoke of a golden future for themselves and for the realm. He tried to communicate to her the majesty of John Dee's vision.

"What are you doing out here, my husband? This damp night air will make you ill."

She touched his shoulder. He turned to her, startled at first, but then he smiled.

"I am looking at the pilot stars and at the moon, on which England's fortunes depend."

"There are many who seek inspiration from the moon. If you go down by Bedlam you may hear them crying out to her," she chided.

He laughed softly. "Ah, woman, you do not understand. You should attend more to Master Dee when he dines with us."

"Master Dee! Master Dee!" she responded sharply. "Have you no ideas of your own? Are you in thrall to this sorcerer? You are worth twenty of him. Will you throw it all away for a dream?"

He laughed again and put his arm around her shoulder. He rocked her gently, drawing her close. She turned her face away.

"What of your present business? The gentlemen of the Muscovy Company are not happy.

That much was true, he admitted. When they dined with him there were frequent disputes and raised voices. Some of them would leave early, flushed with ill-humour and Michael Lok's best claret. She often met them in the front hall, clapping on their hats, fine beaver-hats from Russia, stumbling over scattered toys and squabbling children and muttering under their beards.

She preferred the company of the children, however noisy, to the acrimony of the dinner table.

"Shopkeepers and clerks," he snorted. "I am proposing a new company, The Company of Cathay." He pronounced it as if expecting a fanfare, the Company of Cathay, tah-rah!

"I shall transfer the pledges for this voyage to my new company."

"Can you do that? Will you sever your links with the gentlemen of Muscovy?"

"I shall cast them adrift," he proclaimed. "They will wallow in my wake. My tide is rising with the moon." He laughed, delighted with the idea.

"And we are to live then on pledges and promises?" He paid no attention.

"You know, I think I am something of a poet." He was pleased with his rhetoric.

"Wallow in my wake. That's good. Wallow in my wake is good. I must tell that to Master Dee."

Mary looked at the moon. She shivered. Pledges and promises from great ones, instead of a regular income from the snowy wilderness of Russia. She could see the grey disc of the old moon held in the embrace of the crescent. Where she came from, that was said to be a sign of foul weather. She said nothing. Her children would have to live on pledges and promises.

"But you are cold," he said at last. "I have kept you here, listening to my blather." He was contrite. Those were matters beyond a woman's comprehension. It was unfair to try her patience. She would understand, when his ships came home, wallowing to the gunwales with the wealth of the Orient. Now that would be wallowing of a different kind.

The satisfaction warmed him. He drew her shawl about her shoulders and took her face in his two hands.

"You shall see," he smiled, amused by her worried expression, the brows drawn close together by needless anxiety. "This tide will lift us both. The gentlemen of Muscovy may howl at the moon, like Russian wolves."

He bent and kissed her gently on the forehead. She closed her eyes.

***

The gentlemen of the Company of Cathay ate no less than those of Muscovy. They enjoyed their wine also, but there was less argument at the table. She took to joining them, gradually falling under the spell of their enthusiasm. She was fascinated by John Dee, by his knowledge of so many subjects and by his gentle consideration for her lack of understanding.

"The philosopher's stone," he was saying. "You may ask what it is." He spoke with his mouth full, as if there were not time enough to accomplish all that had to be done. He took a draught of wine. He thought deeply for a moment. "*Lapis philosopicus*. It is a stone, yet not a stone. It is a spirit, a soul and a body and yet not a body". He paused again to refresh himself.

Mary frowned. Already this was beyond her comprehension.

"If you dissolve it, it is dissolved. If you coagulate it, it is coagulated. If you make it to fly, it flies."

She frowned again. He saw her confusion and waited.

"So you have found this stone, Master Dee? I should like to see it."

John Dee laughed tolerantly. "I have sought it these thirty years, but alas! dear lady, I have not yet found it. I have men working day and night in distilling and smelting, in heating and cooling, but still it eludes me." He spread his hands.

"So the properties of which you speak are still in the realm of speculation."

Michael Lok looked at her, surprised by her forwardness. He shook his head, warning her to be silent. She would not.

"When I make a pie or a pudding, such as the one you are addressing just now, I measure my ingredients, the fruit, the suet, the spices, the flour. I know the time of cooking. I know the outcome."

"Ah yes," replied Dee, unfazed by her directness. He took a spoonful of the pudding. "But you overlook the essential ingredient; your own skill, your instinct for excellence, the unmeasured pinch of salt or spice. There are many who can measure and weigh but they lack your gift of bringing all together in a pudding as excellent as this. This is your individual genius. This is what I seek in my work."

Mary blushed at the compliment. The gentlemen reached for more pudding. They inclined heir heads towards her. Michael Lok smiled with sudden pride.

"It is the elixir of life," declared John Dee.

She was not sure whether he spoke of the mysterious stone or of her pudding. She felt in her heart that he spoke the veriest nonsense, but she held her tongue. Their collective fortunes rested now on faith, faith in the cosmographers and their speculative maps, faith in the pilot stars and on the spark of genius in Captain Martin Frobisher.

***

Perhaps, mused John Dee in lighter moments, things were less complicated than he imagined. Perhaps the elixir of life was water, water in its many forms. We cannot go a day without water. Boil it and it flies away. Cause it to coagulate on a winter's night and it becomes as hard as any stone. It refreshes the weary labourer and bears goods up and down the river. Apply it to seeds or seedlings and they flourish. It rises from the ground. It falls from Heaven. Perhaps the truth is simpler than his philosophy.

There was a horse-trough outside his front door. A servant drew water from his well and filled it every day. He saw to it that the trough was kept clean. He liked to loiter there on occasions, talking to travellers, gleaning news from far-away places. It was carved from a single block of granite. Some said that it was a coffin, dislodged from its place under the floor of the church, when King Harry caused the whole building to be up-rooted; that it had contained the bones of a Romish bishop; that the king had put it to better use. Others averred that it was a stone carried to that spot in the time of the great flood, when God sent a deluge to wash the world free of sin; that the king had merely directed masons to hollow it out for the benefit of his devoted subjects.

In the water of the trough John Dee saw his reflection. He saw the sky and the flying clouds. He drew back. His reflection was no longer visible. Did it still exist? He moved forward and there he was again. He knelt low and descried the houses on the other side of the street. The whole world is mirrored in the water, if you can position yourself to see it. It was a puzzle.

A beetle fell from somewhere above. Its impact made concentric rings on the surface. He moved to scoop it out before it might drown, but it evaded him, extending two long legs and rowing down into the depths, with the spasmodic movements of an oarsman. It turned and dived. It surfaced again and moved across the mirror of water. He scooped it out and set in on the rim of the trough to dry. He stooped again and watched it closely. A man passing by smiled and shook his head. Master Dee again. Ah well! He did no harm. The man lingered a moment.

The beetle shuddered. It opened its striped carapace and fluttered the white petticoats of its wings. With a flick, it took to the air, pausing, weightless for an instant, before slanting away out of sight.

John Dee stroked his long beard. This beetle was master of the elements of earth, air and water. It was more clever than the most learned man in England. There was so much to learn.

Flick! There it was again in the water, rowing down into the abyss, twisting and turning as if with a terrible urgency.

"Colymbetes, the swimmer," Dee said aloud.

It was the title of a book in his library. It was a word from the Greek, in a treatise by a German professor of linguistics. He might just have said 'swimmer' or 'the art of swimming' in his own language but the Greek word suggested sunshine, white sand and azure seas, a more attractive prospect than this murky Thames. Nevertheless, he resolved to try it. Forget the book. "You will be my master, Colymbetes," he said softly.

He extended his arms and imitated the beetle's jerky stroke. He flexed his knees like a frog. He peered intently into the water.

The watcher moved quietly away to a greater distance. It was said that Master Dee could see strange matter in reflections. It was known that he had a skryving-mirror, in which he saw angels and demons, who told him of what is to come. It was a patten of mysterious, polished stone, carried home from Mexico by some adventurer. It was dark, from the bowels of some fiery mountain and from the blood of human sacrifice. All the meaning of life was in that stone, but only Master Dee could read it, people said. They gave him too much credit.

The watcher felt a chill of fear tickle the back of his neck. Perhaps Master Dee was conjuring the long-departed bishop from his granite tomb. He scurried away, but looked back from a safer distance. The sorcerer was still executing his strange, hypnotic dance by the coffin of the dead Papist. The watcher crossed himself and quickened his pace. There are things that no Christian man should enquire into.

Chapter Three

Admiral Martin Frobisher stood on the bridge of his flagship, *The Ayde,* a royal warship of two hundred tons, seventy three feet long, with a beam of twenty two feet. With five guns on either side, she was a match for anyone. With *Michael* and *Gabriel* and one sturdy pinnace, manned by four experienced hands, he was confident that summer would see them safely through the Straits of Anian and autumn would find him most likely, at the court of the Great Khan.

He had it on good authority that the eternal daylight of the Arctic summer would melt the ice ahead of him, opening leads and channels to guide him on his way.

He was impatient to leave, to catch the tide and surge downriver with the ebb, past the palace at Greenwich; past Blackwall, with unhappy Tilbury on his port side, past the low-lying lands of Kent and Essex; past salt marshes clouded with white birds; out and away into the freedom of the sea. He wanted to feel the deck rising and falling under him and hear the rigging taking the strain.

He was impatient to see the gentlemen of the Company, with their wives and families, safely over the side. He had all their good wishes for a safe and prosperous voyage, good wishes for his health and for the health of their considerable outlay of gold.

His blood was up, as if he were closing on an enemy ship, or preparing to scoop up a prize. He was sick of the land and of bowing and scraping to merchants and their scribbling clerks.

He was sick also of the great people, the lords and earls who bought part of the New World for fifty or one hundred pounds, with £10 paid up front and the rest to follow. He knew the lists by heart. There was the Lord High Treasurer, good for £100; Mr Secretary Walsingham, £100. Walsingham would expect a return on his money or Heaven help the man who squandered it. Young Phillip Sydney, a fifty pounder, (£10 deposit), was charming all around. There was the great Earl of Leicester followed by an obsequious young man, a hanger-on, in plain language. Leicester at £150 (£30 deposit) was talking down to Michael Lok. There was something about Lok that made Frobisher smile. He was a man who seemed to invite plunder. He had the eager enthusiasm of an inept card player. He pushed forward in every situation to furnish money; to pay for entertainment; to invest in visionary schemes. Frobisher surmised that Lok was already reaping the rewards for his thousand pounds. He was the only man in England who had equalled the Queen's investment. He had stepped to the edge of a precipice. The Queen could take a fall but this man who sought almost to outbid his monarch, could not. Here he was, beaming with pride, mixing with men who held the welfare of the realm in their hands and paying the bill for wine and ale. Here he stood, on the deck of a small wooden vessel that carried his fortunes and the welfare of his family away and away into the far northern seas; a vessel that might pop like a hazel nut between the floating mountains of ice. Frobisher shrugged. Perhaps they were two of a kind. He was venturing his very life in those same seas in the hopes of similar gain, admiral of all new lands and seas, with one percent of all profits derived from all trade, for himself and for his seed, forever. It was a prize worth striving for.

"Captain Frobisher," Mistress Mary Lok interrupted his thoughts.

"Madam," replied Frobisher, warily. He sensed that she was not wholehearted in her support for this voyage. Yet he respected her common sense, something he had witnessed at Michael Lok's generous table.

"Captain Frobisher," she continued. "I wish you Godspeed and health and a safe return."

He sensed her sincerity. She was the only one not to wish him profit as well.

"I place myself in the hands of Almighty God. If our cause be just, He will bear us up."

"Hmm," she murmured, pursing her lips in a vain effort to conceal her reservations.

Frobisher surprised himself in his concern for her anxiety.

"If I may surmise, Madam, you do not endorse this venture with the same eagerness as your good husband."

"What am I, Captain Frobisher? What does my opinion count in such company?" She waved her hand towards the throng of dignitaries. "When the flags fly and the drum beats, I am still but a mere woman, fearful for her family."

Again Frobisher surprised himself.

"I am but a rough sailor, madam. I follow orders. Your husband is a wise and prudent man. I shall do all in my power to serve his interests and those of the Company." He made a small bow. "And yours too of course."

He had learned to play the gallant, but this was no play-acting. He felt a stirring of annoyance with the sunny optimism of Michael Lok. He vowed that he would do all he could to protect this plain speaking woman. But deep down, he feared in his soul, that if the occasion demanded it, his savage nature would cast her and her family to the wolves. It saddened him to think that he might never know the warmth of his own hearth and a good and loving woman. He wished to be away from the conflicting feelings brought on by shore life. Gales and tumbling waves, blizzards and growling ice, the wild savages of the Arctic, would present fewer problems.

"I shall pray for you," she said softly, moving away. He looked up at the fluttering flags and pennants, the symbols of his authority and of England's power.

"Captain Frobisher." It was the young man who followed the Earl of Leicester, a nervous young man with a slight, but persistent, cough. It was obvious that the wind sweeping down the river, a fair wind but chilly, despite the sunshine, was not to his liking.

"Edmund Spenser, continued the young man. "At your service."

Frobisher regarded him tolerantly.

"Sir," he replied, inclining his head slightly. The young man wore a short, pointed beard, somewhat in the Spanish style, a thin, carefully cultivated beard, as might befit a student. His eyebrows seemed permanently arched, imparting an air of superciliousness.

A shrewd judge of a man, Frobisher surmised that this Edmund Spenser was a young man on the rise, a man of vulpine cunning, who climbed in the world by wit and by making himself agreeable to those who might be useful. There was something of the fox about his features and his quick, darting eyes.

Spenser smiled. "I am a poet, sir. I am inspired by the epic nature of your undertaking."

"Indeed, sir," replied Frobisher. "A poet! Should I have heard of you, sir?"

"I but begin to labour in the field, Captain Frobisher. I have not yet found my grand theme. Perhaps you will furnish me with one."

"Ah yes, of course. The field you say"

"A metaphor, sir. We poets see ourselves as shepherds, in the manner of Virgil and Theocritus. We tend our flocks and tune our oaten reeds." He coughed.

"I see," replied Frobisher, stroking his moustache. "Oaten reeds." He would not play this young man's game. He knew that he could not match him in classical allusion or literary discourse, but if he had to endure his patronising air for another minute, he would smash his face in with his fist and throw him into the water, Earl of Leicester or no Earl of Leicester.

The young man, sensing Frobisher's mood, drew back. He took off his bonnet and made an elaborate bow.

"I wish you every success, Captain Frobisher," he said, this time without the air of condescension.

"Your servant," said Frobisher, inwardly amused at the idea that he might be the subject of a great epic. He watched the young man going back to his fashionable friends. That lad will do well in this world of climbers. It was time to be away. He turned to his boatswain instructing him to pipe the guests over the side. Oaten reed, indeed. Just what he needed. He laughed softly, thinking ahead to his epic struggle.

***

Elizabeth liked to sit by the window, watching the river traffic. She loved the way the river struggled with the tide and how the boats bucked and darted about like schoolboys released from their studies. The great ships dipped their flags in salute to her royal standard, as if conscious that her eyes might at that very moment, be upon them.

Greenwich palace was her real home. It was the place of her birth and that of her father. Although she knew the dismal history of her mother and carried her image in a locket, she had no memory of her. She knew that her father's moods could change as suddenly as a squall on the river. She could imagine his voice echoing in the corridors of this, his favourite palace. It was at Greenwich that he had conceived his vision of England as a great naval power. At Greenwich he realised how vulnerable he was to a concerted attack from the sea. The Spaniard could sail to his very door and disembark his troops on the palace steps. Since that time the shipwrights scoured England's forests for oak trees, straight and crooked to supply planks and knees for England's navy and for the many trading vessels that ploughed the seas.

She watched the stately barges and the russet geometry of their sails. She looked upriver. They were coming, three elegant ships, with one small pinnace bringing up the rear, like a small boy struggling to keep pace with his older brothers.

She felt a surge of excitement. Perhaps these ships would tilt the balance of power in the world. Perhaps they would deliver to her the empire that John Dee foretold. She wondered. The cares of empire would disturb her security. They would stretch her resources. Empire would put everything on the hazard.

Nevertheless, there would be spoils. She stood up, taking a white handkerchief from her sleeve. She drew the windows wide and waved her handkerchief. The May breeze ruffled her hair. The handkerchief fluttered.

The ships replied. Smoke billowed from the open gun-ports and then came the sound, a rolling thunder, reverberating on the surface of the river and echoing away into the distance. The flags dipped and rose again. She waved like a young girl. These were her champions. The world was there for the taking.

Her ladies, alarmed by her sudden animation and the bright flush in her cheeks, moved to close the window, but she restrained them. She stood watching as the ships put about, rounding the point to the north, setting more sail for the broad run to the sea. She stepped back from the window. She dabbed her brow with the handkerchief. She was conscious of her racing heart beat.

***

Edmund Spenser was feeling vaguely discomfited by his encounter with Frobisher. He consoled himself that Frobisher was an uneducated man, little more than a pirate, although protected by letters of marque. Spenser mentally audited his own achievements to date. In the company of Phillip Sidney he resented his own more humble origins. Son of a relatively prosperous merchant tailor, he had been educated through the generosity of relatives. As a sizar in Cambridge he had earned his keep by performing menial tasks for the sons of the nobility. That still stung. Although he counted himself more gifted than most of his fellows, he was sixty-sixth in his class of seventy when he took his Master of Arts degree. He was convinced that his modest lineage had counted against him with his tutors.

With his friends Gabriel Harvey and John Young, he was at the forefront of the movement to give to English poetry the status and the stateliness of the great Roman poets. Privately he was satisfied that he was the movement. Harvey could be a boring pedant at times. Young, a kindly teacher, was destined for distinction in the Church. Young, now Bishop of Rochester, had been in a position to afford some help to Spenser, by appointing him his secretary.

Still Spenser was impatient. It was an undemanding post, giving him ample time to develop his poems of the Kent countryside. He knew that by his gifts, by the seductive sweetness of his verse and with its crystalline perfection, he would soon come to the notice of the Court.

There he would climb by his own efforts. The Court was no more than a score of miles away, but it was a world away from that provincial city on the straggling Medway.

"You are low, my friend," said Sidney, breaking into Spenser's self-pitying reverie. "Let us go to Bull's house and taste some ale. You can tell me your troubles."

"Ah, too long to tell," murmured Spenser.

"Let us walk along together. Perhaps we could take a boat up to the city and go to watch my uncle Leicester's players."

"I am in no mood for players," grumbled Spenser. Sidney laughed.

He conducted his friend through the low door of a noisy ale house. Spenser looked around. It would not do for the bishop's secretary to be seen consorting with raucous watermen and dock labourers.

They sat at a table in a corner. Sidney called for ale and oysters. His good humour began to lift Spenser's spirits, while the ale loosened the poet's tongue.

He confided to Sidney the tedium of his existence. He spoke of his plans for a great poem and how it would lift him onto a higher plane. Sidney's generous soul was touched. He understood his frustration.

He took an oyster from the platter and tilted the shell into his mouth.

"Ahh!" he sighed. "It is the taste of the ocean." He swallowed with an expression of pure bliss. "When I eat oysters I want to be at sea. I can taste the spray and the salt borne on the wind." He pushed the platter towards his companion. Spenser declined. Food from the sea did not agree with his stomach. "You should try them, my friend. They are the perfectest food for young and old."

"Why so?" queried Spenser.

"They are the food of Venus. Did she not spring from a shell herself?"

Spenser gave a wan smile. "I have been disappointed in love before and will not risk it again. I need no food of Venus."

Sidney laughed aloud. "Ah yes, the fair Rosalind. You still pine for her."

Spenser shrugged. He would not reveal that his Rosalind was no more than a weaver's daughter, a mere summer dalliance. She turned way from his eloquence, preferring the attentions of a lively young farmer. Spenser was reluctant to admit, even to himself, that at times he could be a dull dog and pompous with it, despite his youth. Rosalind became an excuse for a poem of loss and love unrequited.

Sidney had been thinking. "I have a plan," he said. "My uncle Leicester knows you for a learned and discreet man. He has need of men of circumspection and vision. We will go to him immediately. I will give you a character and he will be sure to give you employment. He holds poetry in high regard. Perhaps you can provide him with plays for his company."

Spenser demurred. "I could not write for the playhouses." Sidney laughed aloud. "It is beneath you."

"No, no," replied Spenser. "I lack the skill. I think in verse, in allegory. I cannot create characters for the stage. The groundlings would throw winkles at my characters." For the first time he laughed, although it was at his own expense. "They would cry 'halt' at my verse and call for clowns and tumblers."

"Perhaps they would," conceded Sidney. "No, we will go to my uncle Leicester and find more private employment. We will at some point, produce you at Court, where you may dazzle Her Majesty and her retinue."

He spoke with ease of the Court, little knowing the effect he was having on his companion. Spenser felt as it the sun had emerged from behind a great, grey cloud. He felt the warmth of its beams. He felt like a voyager casting off on a voyage of discovery. He raised his tankard and drank a health to Sidney and to the future.

Chapter Four

John Dee inspected his workshop early in the morning. The processes fascinated him. It was as if he were watching Creation itself. He watched the men measuring particles of metals and ores into his crucibles. He pondered how the bellows, adding nothing but air to the good beech charcoal, could make the coals glow to white heat. At grave risk to his long white beard, he leaned close to see the metals moving, subsiding like melted butter, seething as liquid and flowing in the form of glowing serpents, into the moulds. The men grunted and sweated as they carried each crucible to the moulds. Somewhere in there were the seeds of gold.

Somewhere in the glass alembics, lay the elixir to cure all ailments, to bestow wisdom, understanding and immortality on whomsoever might release the secret. He watched the slow drip from the retorts as various murky liquids became crystal clear. Sometimes the fumes caught in his throat. Sometimes he imagined that he got a faint smell of malt.

He directed the men to keep doors and windows open. He resolved to get a good chimney, a proper brick-built one to carry off the smoke and the vapours. The men were unusually diligent, three good lads. They were inspecting the liquid that issued from a long copper coil. They were laughing. Dee was pleased to see them enjoying their work. He turned a blind eye to their little sideline.

"Good lads. Good lads," he said, moving on to the next experiment. He coughed. He felt the need to step outside into the fresh air. He pondered. Perhaps the true elixir of life is air. Air makes the clouds to move. It turns black coal to white fire. It lifts birds into the sky and carries ships across oceans. From the moment of birth to the last rattling breath, we draw in air. Music emanates from tubes filled with air. But what of the creatures that live in water? He determined to try an experiment.

He went into his house, emerging in a little while in a long, white, night-shirt. He carried a length of rope. He called the men from their tasks and led them down to the river stairs.

"Leave all for the moment, gentlemen. I need your assistance."

The men were laughing and joking in unusually high spirits. He tolerated their mirth, accepting that it must have been funny to see their master in his night attire at this hour. He tied the rope about his waist and gave the free end to his assistants.

"Now, Colymbetes, be my master," he said, stretching out his arms.

The men looked at one another in sudden alarm. Dee hurled himself into the fast-flowing river. He disappeared under the surface.

The men dashed to the brink and peered into the brown water. They could see a faint white shape below. The rope went taut. Suddenly Dee came to the surface, flailing about and trying to yell. He sank again. The men swore and hauled together on the rope. They dragged him ashore and stretched him, lifeless, on the lowest step. The night-shirt clung to his skinny body in a ridiculous manner. His member, unexpectedly long and vertical, lifted the fabric like a tent-pole, a comical gnomon. His beard and hair were lank.

The men swore again in great dismay and turned their drowned master on his side. Undoubtedly their negligence would be blamed. Their punishment would be severe. Their hilarity evaporated.

Dee twitched. He convulsed suddenly, expelling a great quantity of water. He gagged and coughed. He got up on all fours. The man patted him on the back. He wheezed for breath. He retched and struggled to speak. He sat up on a step, putting his head low and leaning his elbows on his bony knees. One of the men pushed his head down, causing him great discomfort and alarm. He waved him away.

"I think I understand," he gasped, pleased with a revelation of some sort. "Colymbetes must carry air in his wings. Under his carapace." He nodded in satisfaction. But then, but then. How can he dive so deep? Would the air not keep him afloat?

One of the men ran to the workshop and returned with a flask of the clear liquid.

"Take a sip of this, Master," he said gently. "It will restore you."

Dee did as directed. The liquid burned inside him with a pleasing warmth.

"The water of life, Master," said the workman.

"Indeed, yes," replied Dee. He took another sip. "I think we may be close."

His natural good humour returned. "I must consult my book and my water-beetle."

The men smiled, pleased to see him back in the land of the living. There would be no need to explain to Her Majesty that they had inadvertently, mislaid her good friend and mentor in the Tideway of the swirling Thames. They passed the flask from one to another and sat for a while, enjoying the view.

Thereafter John Dee swam almost every day. He learned to fill his night-shirt with air as he entered the water, raising the hem and flapping to capture his invisible prey. A bubble of shirt might spring up to transform him into a floating hunchback. Sometimes he reclined on his back with a great white belly above the surface. He moved his arms and legs as the book directed. He swam like a dog, or sometimes like a frog, but he could never extend his arms behind him, in the manner of the water-beetle. All the while a servant standing on the step, held the end of the rope, watching over his master and hauling him ashore when Dee tired of his exertions and began to drift downstream.

Dee loved to put his head under the water. He could see little more than a yellow light and yellow arms and legs. He was almost blind, but he delighted in the sounds of the river, the reverberation of his own breath bubbling up and the never ending rush of the stream. Why did the air within his lungs not serve, after a count of twenty or twenty five? Why did he feel panic rising within him after so short a time? Was there anything as wonderful as the first mouthful of clean air at the surface?

His servants wondered about this Colymbetes. They knew that their master communed with spirits, or so it was rumoured. Perhaps this Colymbetes had granted him the power to stay afloat in the rushing river. It was not a matter to be enquired into too closely.

Still the learned man wondered about the countless millions of fishes in the sea and in the rivers. Why should the air, so vital to all creatures on land, be fatal to them? No, air was not the entire answer. Neither, he admitted after his recent experience, could water be the perfect elixir. The workmen made more of their water of life. He quite liked the effect it had on him, taken in moderation. It cleared his head and warmed his innards. It gave him a sense of all things being possible. He made it the basis of many of his cures and tonics. They were much in demand. He was not a man for strong spirits, avoiding the cognac of the French and the detestable ginebra of the Hollanders. His aquavit was clean-tasting and comforting. A nip or two after his morning swim, made the world look brighter.

***

The world was looking brighter too for Edmund Spenser. The publisher, William Ponsonby, on Sidney's recommendation, took his manuscript to Stationers' Hall in Ave Maria Lane, close by Paul's Church. There it was registered and licensed. Arrangements were made for printing. It was the calendar of a year in the life of Colin, a shepherd. It was dedicated to the noble and virtuous Gentleman, most worthy of all titles, both of learning and of chivalry, M. Phillip Sidney. Spenser was given to understand that he would have to be patient. There were other poets in the queue ahead of him.

That same virtuous gentleman was as good as his word. A promise of employment from the great Robert Dudley, Earl of Leicester, raised hopes of a move from provincial Rochester to more exciting prospects in a wider world. Leicester had instructed him to make himself familiar with affairs in Ireland. It was made clear to him that he would find himself frequently travelling to that unhappy land. In his daydreams he saw himself as a future proconsul, bringing peace and civilisation to a colony torn by strife and rebellion

Leicester also intimated that he should find himself a virtuous and steady wife. It was time, the great lord hinted broadly, to subordinate the childish pursuit of poetry to a study of civil matters. Poetry, he advised, could be an ornament to life but the real business of a man was politics and the amassing of wealth and thereby, influence.

Inwardly Spenser did not agree. There were many ways by which poetry could influence the world of politics. Even the vulgar street ballads, a rough form of poetry, admittedly, could sway the minds of the common people. He had learned already that the wild Irish chieftains maintained their own personal poets, not merely to entertain, but to commemorate and glorify their great deeds. The mighty Elizabeth was not averse to praise. Spenser was confident that he would ascend in the world as much by the steely perfection of his verse as by diligent service in the rain-sodden bogs of Ireland.

He went again to the printer, one Hugh Singleton of Creede Lane, near Ludgate at the sign of the golden tunne.

"Ah, young man," Singleton greeted him. "You come again." He could understand the young poet's impatience to see his work in print. Printing, to Singleton, was as much an art as a business. Any fool with a quill and a pot of ink, could dribble his thoughts onto a sheet of paper, but the printer gave ideas their real validity. Not until the lines stood out in black ink, with the military precision of uniform lettering, would people take them seriously, even the author himself.

The art was in the woodcuts and floral embellishment. It was in the calculating of each page, the folding, the binding and cutting of the edges, the embossing of a fine calf leather cover, to produce a book fit to be handled by the Queen herself. It was a wondrous thing, a book, but of course, it takes time.

"I can show you some of the wood-cuts," he offered. He took some trial plates from a shelf. Spenser peered closely, touching the raised images. Black ink came away on his fingers. He saw shepherds of an elegance that he had never seen in the rough north country of his forebears or in the rolling Kentish Weald. Here grazed docile sheep and placid cows. There were dancers and cupids under a tree. There were tidy farmsteads and a great city of towers and spires, beside a tranquil river. A workman laid his axe to the base of a tree.

"I have only three as yet," said Singleton apologetically. "Pressure of work."

Spenser was mollified. "You have caught my world perfectly, good sir. I long to see all twelve plates."

"In good time, sir," replied Singleton. He beamed upon the young poet, lacing his fingers together in front of his leather apron. His hands, dyed by his trade, were those of an Aethiop. He wore small, round eye-glasses. He understood Spenser's hunger. He relented.

"I have set some type. You might like to see it. It is a fraction of February. It is a trial, of course, not necessarily the finished work." He indicated a frame partly filled with type.

Spenser leaned close again, trying to make out his own words in reverse. Singleton smiled. "It takes a lifetime to learn to read the mirror," he said, proud of his craft. "Here, try this." He wiped an inky pad over the lettering. "Now press your hand down hard upon it."

Spenser did as directed. He looked at his palm. As if by magic, his words returned to him, the words of the old man, to the ardent young shepherd:

'All that is . . . . . . will be lost.' There was a gap where the hollow of his palm had failed to make contact with the cold metal. 'lent to love.' An old man approaching winter, feeling the nip of frost and the stiffness in his joints: 'all that is lent to love will be lost.'

It was if the old man, Thenot, he had called him, were speaking to the one who had created him. It was indeed strange that this creature of his imagination, had taken on a life of its own through the medium of the mirror writing. The old man, the offspring of his brain, was three times the age of his progenitor. Yet he would live in black ink, long after his creator had … It was a prospect to dizzy the brain. It was not a process to be hastily cobbled together or turned out in a smear of printers' ink. He would learn patience and give the children of his brain time to emerge into the light.

"I am gratified, sir," he said, with a new-found diffidence. "You will accomplish everything in your own good time. I am grateful."

Singleton bowed gravely. "I shall do you proud, young sir. Your work deserves it. You will be my boast in the years to come."

"I must go abroad for a while," said Spenser, divulging no details. His mission was too important to be spoken about openly. A great trust had been laid upon him, by Leicester, a task touching on the safety of the realm. It could not be the subject of idle chatter. "I shall attend upon you when I return."

"It will be ready for your inspection, good sir," replied Singleton, fired with new resolve. He was eager to see how the shepherd's year might turn out.

From the tranquillity of Singleton's premises, Spenser stepped out into the racket of the street. He walked briskly down Ludgate and westward into Fleet Street, disturbed and not a little moved by the wretches gathered outside the prison and the cries of the inmates of that grim institution. The wailing carried to his ears even over the noise of the market. Vendors cried their wares at him: 'What d'ye lack, sir?' Beggars plied their clappers at every corner. Carriages jostled for space. Agile water-carriers, balancing jugs on their shoulders, dodged through the throng, rarely spilling a drop. There was laughter from taverns. There were bills giving notice of exhibitions of curiosities and monsters from all parts of the world. London life in all its vibrancy and squalor, was all around him. The wailing of the poor wretches stayed with him as he made his way towards The Strand.

An idea began to form in his mind, an idea wonderful in its simplicity. Too many people were trying to survive in too little space. Both moral and physical health, were put in peril by the struggle to maintain life itself. It would be better to remove great numbers of them and settle them as industrious subjects in the empty lands of the New World or in places such as Ireland. There they would develop the habits and virtues of industry. They would give good example to the native people by their loyalty and labour. The beggar slouching by the tavern door, could become a sturdy yeoman. Even the whores, translated to green fields and verdant woods, with pure streams of crystal water flowing by the cottage door, would leave off their sinful ways. They would have an opportunity to raise families of healthy, God-fearing children, as had been done in the olden days, in the days when Chaucer smiled upon England and its people. He thought of the wood-cuts and the ideal world of the shepherds. With good authority to guide them, those people would be blessed. He determined to raise the idea with Sir Henry Sidney, as soon as he arrived in Ireland.

Chapter Five

The days grew longer and colder. Although it was June, frost formed on the rigging during the short, luminous nights. They had gone beyond the limit of sixty degrees of latitude, as set by Ptolemy to be the furthest extremity of the habitable world. Frobisher was aware that the Muscovy sailors had reached similar latitudes in the warmer seas of Europe, without encountering ice. They were the fortunate ones, wafted by kindly south-westerlies, to the trading ports of the White Sea. Or so he had been told.

He blew on his hands. The brass of the astrolabe was cold to his touch, three pounds and ten shillings worth of mathematical precision, as pointed out by Michael Lok. Three guineas for twenty compasses of divers sorts. The man was a nuisance but necessary nonetheless. Frobisher smiled grimly. He squinted his eyes, the better to see the flicker of white on the northern horizon. The low sun picked it out against a background of glowering, slate-grey cloud. The light imparted an orange tinge to the menacing barrier. This would be his first real test. Beyond that ice lay the Straits of Anian and open water. Beyond that again, lay the palm-fringed islands of the Great South Sea and the untold riches of the Indies.

But first there was that grey mass of cloud descending from the north. The wind was picking up. The swell was rising, lifting and rolling the ship beneath him. He shifted his weight from one leg to the other, following the roll of the ship. White- caps whipped by. Sea birds fled before the approaching storm.

He gave the order to shorten sail. He signalled to his fleet to keep in touch, if possible. He could make out, far behind him, the mast of the pinnace, the merest twig in the immensity of the ocean, with its handkerchief sail, a straw in the wind. He feared for the four men, knowing in his heart that they were doomed. Four good men. He prayed that the Almighty might spare them. Spare them for their own sake and because the pinnace was essential to his purposes. It was a selfish thought. In the random way of storms at sea, he admitted, his own ship with some five dozen mariners, might be the first to founder, while the pinnace might well slip through the straits to the sunlit seas beyond. They were in God's hands. The sun was obscured. The world darkened about him. The storm struck.

It was as if some mighty force resented their intrusion, as one might flick a louse from a sleeve. All their endeavours seemed pointless and puny. The ship hung on a sea anchor, as the storm vented its fury. A scrap of sail on the mizzen kept her bow to the wind. The watch huddled in the waist, out of the driving hail. The rigging shrieked above them. They hunched together in cloaks and quilted doublets, trying to keep their footing amid the sloshing water. It surged over the rails or spouted upward through the scuppers, with each wallow of the vessel. They swore. They cursed. They prayed.

Just before dark, in a lull between gusts of blinding hail and sleet, they saw, away to starboard, the topmast of *Michael* snap like a twig. The ship was no longer visible behind the melting, cascading, ever renewed mountains of foam and black, tumbling water. They cowered hour after hour, powerless to influence their fate.

As dawn broke Frobisher felt the wind relenting. His ship was still afloat. The masts were still intact, the rigging taut and firm. His crew, frozen and slow moving, were still alive. He gave thanks to God for their deliverance. The sea-anchor tugged, reminding him that they had carried backwards during the night. He climbed a little way into the rigging. Even in his mittens his fingers refused to answer. He hooked his hands around the ratlines and looked about. The lunge of the ship sent him swinging out over the surging ocean. He looked down. Slush and fragments of ice drifted by.

The pinnace had vanished. *Michael* was nowhere to be seen. The water was curdling about them. There was a dark speck between them and the rising sun. It must be *Gabriel* with her masts intact. Frobisher squinted against the glare. The wind was veering to the north-east. *Gabriel* was making sail. The sun rose out of the ocean in all its splendour. He climbed down again. He looked at the grey faces of his crew. He ordered the fire-box to be lit again, anticipating with relish, a can of hot soup. The men shuffled and swung their arms, slapping themselves on their sides, restoring dormant circulation. They stamped their feet in their sodden foot-ware. They made their obedience to their captain, watching him closely.

Frobisher smiled. "Good lads. Good lads, all," he said. "Now for the Indies." They raised a feeble cheer. It was enough to be alive.

***

Sir Henry Sidney was in tolerant mood. The weather was fine. Much of the country was notionally at peace, although the Irish chieftains and nobles still managed to find cause for quarrel amongst themselves. Divide and conquer. It was still a good rule of thumb.

He indicated to Spenser that he should sit. He turned the package of sealed letters in his hands, fingering the red wax. He put it aside. Through the open window came the sound of soldiers drilling in the castle yard. Dublin was full of soldiers. The fife and drum resounded constantly in the narrow streets.

"My lords Burghley and Leicester would have me go about like a gad-fly, stinging the Irish into rebellion." He exhaled in exasperation. "Do you know what Stukeley says you will gain in Ireland?"

Spenser shook his head. "No sir, I do not."

Sidney laughed. "Hunger and lice. That's what Stukely says. Now there is a gad-fly if ever there was one."

Spenser had heard a little of Thomas Stukely. There were ballads about his exploits. Even the Queen laughed at how he had greeted her with over familiarity, as a potential fellow monarch. Instead of having him hanged for his manifest knavery, she had given him a ship and one hundred men to set himself up as a king in Florida, Frenchmen and Spaniards not withstanding. She believed, it was said, that given sufficient rope, Stukely would hang himself. She was probably right.

"Hunger and lice," repeated Sidney. "You must come with me when I go south into Munster. I have to go there regularly to keep a lid on things. You are a friend of my son, you say."

"Indeed sir. He has been most helpful to me in my affairs. We share an interest in poetry."

"Ah yes. A man of many parts is my son." He stroked his ginger beard.

"Ah Stukely," he murmured. "Do you know that he is in Rome? He wants to lead an army of Papal troops to set the Pope's son up as king of Ireland. God help the Pope's bastard, if he finds himself king of this benighted island." He laughed aloud.

Spenser smiled diffidently. He thought of his woodcuts. It might be a bit soon to propose a settlement of Ireland with the sweepings of London's streets. There was much to be learned. Colin Clouts by Liffey stream, herding his flock in the hills of Wicklow. Tuning his oaten reed. He kept silent.

"Washingham keeps me well informed. We will be ready for Stukely and for His Holiness if he decides to pay us a visit. Oh yes. Yes indeed." He picked up the package of letters and undid the ribbon. "I thank you, young man. I shall see that you are comfortably lodged. Play your cards right and you may do well in Ireland."

Spenser was dismissed. He rose and took his leave, with due deference. He was taken with this Lord Deputy. Ireland, he imagined in his optimism, was in good hands.

'The countrie, Arcadia, hath ever been had in singular reputation, partly for the sweetness of the ayre and other natural benefits, but principally for the well tempered minds of the people.' P.S.

***

Frobisher made good time westward, picking his way between drifting masses of ice. *Gabriel* followed close behind. The men marvelled at the floating rafts of ice and at the creatures that hauled out of the water, to bask in the sunshine. It was a world of blue and white.

They lowered the ship's boat and took seals at will, dispatching them with pikes and axes, astonished by the tameness of the animals. The seals gazed at them with large innocent eyes. The ice was splashed with scarlet. The meat was good.

Whales rose from the depths, as if surveying these intruders into their icy world. They accompanied the ships for a time, diving with an undulating motion and then surfacing in a spout of spray. They seemed to regard the sailors with vaguely amused detachment. Occasionally they rubbed their encrusted hides against the ships' sides, to the general alarm of the sailors, but mainly they kept their distance, revelling in their strength and the grace of their movements.

Some days there was no ice. At times Frobisher wondered if he might have turned south by mistake during the brief hours of darkness. He knew that his compasses were apt to behave strangely in the polar regions. John Dee had expressed it in colourful terms. The lodestone, he suggested, became delirious with joy at being so close to its home. Like a puppy greeting its master, it wagged its tail and skittered about.

Frobisher checked his astrolabe. His latitude was sixty two degrees and fifty minutes. Longitude was a matter for conjecture. The lines come closer and closer together, just like the segments of an orange, until they meet at the Pole. At the Pole there is no longitude. He sailed by cross and staff and by instinct.

There was a cry from the crow's nest. The lookout was pointing to the north-west, or as near to the north-west as made no difference. Frobisher went aloft. Away to starboard there was land; low rounded hills with caps of snow; grey rock, streaked with slashes of white; ice around the shore, as he had been given to expect, but to the west a glorious expanse of open water.

Somewhere, away to port, lay America. By some miracle of navigation and sheer good luck, the fabled Straits of Anian lay open before him. He felt a wild surge of joy and vindication. This was more than recompense for the loss of the pinnace and the ship, *Michael*. Everything comes at a cost. The world is not conquered without risk. Empires do not rise and fall by some abstract destiny. They are made and lost by struggle, by courage, by blood and most of all by luck. Frobisher was always lucky. In the stormy Atlantic and in the Narrow Seas, he always found his prey, the merchantman fleeing from the pursuer; the Spaniard slinking home with the plunder of the Americas, home to a bloated empire, a country drowning in its own wealth. This however, was the greatest prize of all.

The man with the lead sang out ten fathom, with sand in the tallow. The omens were good. Wind and tide were with them. Frobisher became conscious of the increasing strength of the tide. It was, he surmised, that the waters of the Atlantic were forcing their way through the narrow strait into the ocean beyond.

He climbed higher and into the crow's nest. The look-out moved aside, to make room for his captain.

"Land to port, Captain," he said pointing to the south. There was indeed, a low line of snow topped hills, inching above the horizon. America! Meta Incognita, where no Christian man had set foot. The speculations of cosmographers were correct.

"Well done, Nicholas," said Frobisher. "God bless your eyes."

He felt the ship trembling far below, surging along in a tide-race. He became conscious of the sound, a sound of home, the cascade at London Bridge. The rigging thrummed in harmony. The leadsman called twelve fathom, with more sand in the tallow. A pod of whales spouted as if in salute, wishing them safe passage. The tide was rising at an astonishing rate.

The day was long. The low sun hung in the west. Everything ahead appeared in silhouette, black shapes and glinting water. He took in his topsails and spritsail. He moved more cautiously. *Gabriel* followed at a distance, but keeping pace. More land rose up ahead of them. Land now on both sides and dead ahead. A dark suspicion began to cloud Frobisher's optimism. Perhaps he had missed the straits. Perhaps he was in a long narrow bay.

Perhaps the sea gods were playing a game with him. No, he told himself, somewhere behind those folds of hills, the straits lay hidden, angled away from his line of sight, concealed by a trick of light.

"Six fathom," cried the leadsman. "No sand."

Twilight was coming on. A chill of apprehension assailed the captain. The wind was onshore and the tide was falling. He gave the order to take in sail and let go the anchor. The ship hung on her chain in the swift-moving ebb. Gabriel hove to, nearby. They took stock of their situation.

The brief night was lit by strange streamers of light, drifting veils of luminescence in the great silence. The sailors gazed upwards in wonder and no little fear. Some had heard of this strange sight. They said it was a good omen. Others prayed, and longed for home. The sun lurked just below the northern horizon. The drifting veils faded and the sun appeared again, bleary eyed through a bank of fog.

The sailors peered at the distant shoreline. What they had imagined was snow, in the dying light of the previous evening, was in fact the droppings of countless numbers of sea birds, covering every ledge and outcrop of the steep cliffs. They could see flocks of geese grazing the weed of the boulder-strewn foreshore. The cacophony of bird sounds came to the sailors as a welcome cry of land. They thought of hunting and roast goose.

The ships lay in four fathoms. No sand in the tallow. Frobisher decided that he should pull back to deeper water before those huge tides might strand him. Then he would send the ship's boat ashore to see what this strange land had to offer and, most of all, to give thanks to Almighty God. The words of the Reformed Religion would be declaimed aloud for the first time in the land of America. Moreover, he would take possession of this new land, legally and validly in the name of Her Gracious Majesty, Elizabeth, rightful successor to Madoc ap Owain Gwynadd, that wandering man of Wales.

Chapter Six

Spenser climbed to the wooden firing-step. His feet sounded on the stout oak planks. Everything about Dublin and its castle spoke of power, of governance and stability. He peered through an embrasure. The sun was warm. White clouds floated over the mountains, casting fleeting shadows on green woodland, brown bog and purple heather. The mountains receded in diminishing planes of blue. It was a scene made for valiant knights on quests for adventure and honour. Perhaps in those mountains there dwelt giants or dragons.

Closer to the city smoke rose from the villages of industrious farmers, hard-working folk who tended their crops and gathered their families around the hearth at night for prayer and story telling.

"You are dreaming, young sir." It was the voice of the Lord Deputy, breaking into his reverie.

"I was indeed, my lord. I was thinking of how pleasant it would be to ride through the Greenwood on such a day and stand on the peaks of those sunny mountains."

"To listen to the shepherds piping their tunes and singing of love?" Sir Henry was smiling.

"My very thoughts, my lord."

"Ah yes. A pleasant thought for such a day as this." Sir Henry paced away, then turned again to Spenser. "Be sure to bring gold or you will return footsore and naked, if you return at all."

"Why should that be, my lord?"

"You have much to learn, young sir." Sir Henry shook his head. "When you bring my replies to Leicester and Walsingham, tell them that those villagers there, those industrious peasants," he pointed to the ploughland and green cornfields, "those loyal subjects, under the walls of Dublin, pay black-rent to the OByrnes and OTooles of the mountains, wild Irish chieftains, if ever I saw any."

He looked at Spenser with a degree of satisfaction, on seeing the young man's surprise.

"Who are these people? Are they not over-awed by your forces?"

The Lord Deputy looked down from the wall. The city gate stood open.

Carts, and pack horses came and went, carrying goods from the port and firewood and peat for the city. Men in long mantles trudged beside their cattle. Their hoods were thrown back, displaying long beards and unkempt hair.

"Your Irish men, young sir," said Sir Henry. "Essential to our survival, but not to be trusted within the walls."

Spenser watched the scene below with a quickened interest. "They are unarmed. What is there to mistrust?"

Sir Henry laughed softly. "Everything," he replied. "That mantle," he went on, warming to his subject, "it is his main garment in all weathers. It is his shelter and habitation. It is the place of concealment for weapons and plunder. With the hood up, it is his cloak of invisibility."

"Then make it illegal," replied Spenser. "Insist on English dress."

Sir Henry laughed aloud. "Young man," he said, slapping Spenser on the back, "I compliment you. You go straight to the nub of the issue."

Spenser flinched, unaccustomed to such robust familiarity. Sir Henry continued. Spenser was conscious of an edge of irony in his tone.

"When you report to my lord of Leicester, you may tell him that I have decreed that henceforth the wild Irish must dress as Englishmen and speak our tongue. They must conform to our religion and renounce the Pope."

Spenser was silent, conscious that he had spoken out of turn. He coughed awkwardly. It was a nervous cough that troubled him frequently.

Sir Henry was aware of the younger man's discomfiture. He placed a hand on Spenser's shoulder, this time more gently. He patted him on the back.

"You are correct, my boy. All that you say is already the law. It has been so for more than two centuries." He shrugged, smiling ruefully. "The trouble lies in enforcing it." He shrugged again.

Spenser caught his breath. "But..." he began. He fell silent.

The Lord Deputy sighed. "There is a rhyme about me. I fear it will end up on my tomb. 'O Sydney worthy of triple renown, for plaguing the traitors that troubled the crown.' What do you think of that my young poet?"

"It is a serviceable rhyme, my lord," said Spenser warily. "I am sure it is no more than the truth."

Sir Henry bowed, accepting the compliment. He turned again to look over the countryside between the city and the mountains. "The traitors," he mused. "Why traitors, I often wonder. I shall ride out again at harvest time, to burn their grain and drive off their cattle. I shall leave my fine castle, with flags flying and a great deal of fanfaronade, to bring starvation to the people of the forests, the mountains and the rich pastures of the South. When I return the aldermen will line up to greet me. The good citizens of Dublin and these loyal peasants, you see yonder, will cheer my progress. I shall festoon the gate with the heads of Irishmen." He sighed and, putting his hands behind his back, he paced again. Spenser waited.

"But still they will pay the black rent to OByrne. Still the Irish will pull their hoods about their ears and lurk in the forests until spring, singing songs of the greatness of their chieftains."

Sir Henry stood for what seemed a long time, starring into the distance. He returned to himself.

"My friend," he said with a degree of apology. "I have detained you too long. I have reports prepared for the Court." His mood lifted. "I understand that you are to be wed. I wish you joy. Come here to Ireland when you are a family man. You could do well here, an astute young fellow like you. Land. That is the key to loyalty. Get yourself some land. People it with loyal Englishmen. Rise in the world."

Spenser thought of his unspoken plan for Ireland. Sir Henry was a man of vision. He bowed.

"I take my leave of you, my lord and I thank you for your kindness. I shall think about what you say."

"Do that and commend me to my son. Let him not dwell too much on poetry."

Spenser bowed again. "My lord," he murmured. He went down the sounding steps into the street. He looked back. Sir Henry was still standing at the parapet, looking out at Ireland. The high clouds soared about his head. A knight in arms, worthy of triple renown, for plaguing the traitors who would starve through the winter and watch their children waste away, until such time as they might learn the meaning of true allegiance. Triple renown... burn the house down. A tawdry jingle. Ireland might yet provide his great theme.

He turned his thoughts towards London, to his forthcoming nuptials and to his bride, Machabyas Chylde, a woman of some considerable means.

***

Michael Lok was in despair. Ruin was staring him in the face. Penury was sitting down before his walls, ready to mine under his fortress and bring the ramparts down. He could not look at his wife and family without feeling the sweat of fear prickling his moustache. His children would have to beg for bread in the streets. He felt no appetite for his wife's cooking.

The gentlemen of the Company, conscious of their debts, abruptly stopped calling. They had all heard the news. Frobisher was lost. The ship, *Michael*, battered and leaking, had returned, after a perilous crossing, itself little more than a piece of flotsam, pounded by westerly gales in the Narrow Seas. It lay at Plymouth, or so the rumour had it, awaiting repairs. It was in Harwich. It had been taken into Leith by Scottish privateers.

Wherever the unhappy vessel lay, Lok knew that his chances of recovering his outlay from the venturers, were threadbare indeed. When he accosted them, in the street or in the Exchange, their eyes slid away from him, and stared into vacuity, into the void. They began to smell the stench of failure.

It was said that Owen Griffyn, captain of *Michael*, was a treacherous Welshman, who had left his admiral and general, his friend, to perish amid the frozen seas. It was said that he had deserted Frobisher and sailed home to claim the glory of discovery for himself. He was a coward, hiding in Yarmouth, ashamed to show his face in London.

Lok determined to hire a gentle horse and ride to Yarmouth to shake the truth out of the craven Welshman. Or might it be Great Yarmouth, not the Yarmouth on the Isle of Wight? He knew not which way to turn.

John Dee came to see him. He brought the balance of his subscription.

"They are men of honour, my friend," he advised. "Be patient. They will keep to their word."

Michael Lok was not so sure.

"They will pay, I assure you," continued Dee. "You have dealt plainly with them. Do you doubt the Queen's Majesty? Would she renege? Would Leicester or Walsingham go back on their word?"

Michael Lok felt the tight band of fear around his heart slip a little.

"Breathe more deeply, my friend. Exhale slowly." Dee assumed the air of one of his many professions, the gentle physician. "That's better. Now let us review the situation." He fumbled in his satchel and produced a long-stemmed clay pipe. "I have brought you some tobacco, a sovereign remedy for the nerves. It is good for expelling the rheum and the cold and moist humours of the body."

"Tobacco?" For a moment Lok forgot his fears. He had never smoked the strange weed, but had seen evidence of its efficacy in expelling the rheum, especially in the vicinity of the apothecaries and merchants who traded in it. Loungers in the street, puffing on their pipes, paused frequently to hawk and cough, expelling their rheum at great risk to unwary passers-by. The merchant in him wondered if there might be an opportunity, if a reliable sea-captain could be persuaded . . . brought him back to his predicament.

John Dee had by now, ignited the contents of the pipe bowl. He puffed several times. The tobacco glowed red, then faded to black and then reddened again. A sweet smell pervaded the room, a sugary, buttery smell, very agreeable to the nose. Dee exhaled a misty cloud of smoke. He sighed and passed the pipe to his friend.

"Try it," he urged.

Michael Lok examined the pipe. He sniffed the contents. He frowned.

"Go on," said Dee. "It will do you good."

Lok drew on the pipe. Cool smoke flooded his senses. It tasted of the New World. It caught his breath. He coughed and wheezed for air. His eyes watered. He laughed. He laughed for the first time in weeks. He coughed again and spat into the fire.

"You see," smiled Dee. "It has already begun to work. Now let us consider."

Michael Lok sat back in his chair. He gazed into the fire. He always kept a fire in his living-room, winter and summer. It made him feel safe. It made him feel that his children could be warm and dry. It kept the mists of the river at bay on gloomy days. Focus, the old Romans called it, the centre of the home. As if from a great distance he heard the murmuring voice of his friend, the wise and learned man, the magus, the reader of maps and of the heavens. He drew on the soothing pipe.

"I have confidence in Captain Frobisher. We must not let ourselves by affrighted by rumour. Where is the evidence? Does Captain Frobisher not remind you of a bear? In his strength, his inflexible sense of purpose, his great courage?"

"Indeed," nodded Lok. "A bear. A great bear."

Frobisher had many attributes suggestive of a bear. His courage was legendary. His fights at sea had become matter for ballads.

"Exactly," beamed Dee. "A great bear. I have cast an astrological chart for him. His dominant element is water. He is the consummate mariner. He was born at Martinmas and takes his name from that same saint. These are signs, my friend. The region he now explores is the true home of the pilgrim geese. The goose is the symbol of Saint Martin."

Lok's wife, Mary had entered the room. She caught the drift of the conversation. She coughed. The two men looked up from their seats. She looked at her husband in surprise, noting the smouldering pipe.

"You talk of signs," she said abruptly. "I sat behind Captain Frobisher, last Martinmas, in church. There was no sign about his head. No light. He is not marked for death."

Michael Lok raised his eyebrow. "That sounds to me like a Romish superstition, wife." He was annoyed by her intrusion into the affairs of men.

She shrugged. "It has always worked for me." She remembered Martinmas. The children singing and waving coloured rags. Captain Frobisher had no qualms about eating her fine roast goose. He was the essence of good cheer, well prepared and fortified for the onset of winter. John Dee resumed the thread of his discourse. Mary fell silent.

"He travels in the regions of Ursa Major and Ursa Minor, the Greater Bear and the Lesser. Does the Great Bear not point at the Pole star? These are the stars that will protect him. Hmm! Hmm!" He gazed into the fire.

Lok found comfort in the words. The stars would protect his champion. Frobisher took his Bible with him wherever he went. He had survived the perils of the Torrid Zone and the disease-ridden coast of Africa. He had survived the infidels of the Barbary Coast and the horrors of a Portuguese prison. He had triumphed at sea. He had overawed the Irish along their Southern coast.

"All will be well," went on Dee. "It were unreasonable to expect him to reach Cathay and return in a matter of months. We must be patient."

Lok drew on the pipe. He realised that he had been monopolising it. With an apology he handed it back. Dee reamed the contents out onto the hearthstone with a little pen knife. He handed it back.

"Keep it, my friend. I shall leave you some tobacco. I have a good supplier, a Frenchman." He tapped the side of his nose with his forefinger, smiling conspiratorially. "He obtains it from Spain."

They smiled together, two men of the world, knowing how the world works.

Michael Lok looked at his wife, a simple, unlettered woman. Her words had brought him comfort.

The Welshman was no traitor. He was no coward. He had brought his maimed ship home, without loss of any crewman. She lay at Deptford in sore need of repair. But who would pay? Michael Lok's fear assailed him again. He puffed more furiously than ever as he saw his fortunes going up in smoke. He prayed. He prayed.

***

Get ye up unto the high mountains, thought Frobisher. It is from the high mountains that men talk to God. From the mountain top he would see the straits. He struggled upwards, his men clambering behind him. He braced himself with the staff of a halberd. He never enjoyed walking. His natural element was the sea, with the deck heaving beneath him. He looked back.

His two ships lay at anchor, silhouetted against the low sun, mere cockleshells, toys in the immensity of the wilderness. He thought that he could descry low black shapes moving on the gleaming surface, a score or so of porpoises or whales. It was impossible to tell. The shapes slid away, disappearing behind a headland. There was one creature he was determined to capture, a whale or porpoise with a single horn, fully two yards in length, a unicorn fish. He wanted to bring that horn to the Queen as evidence of the wonders to be found in her new territory. It was childish, he knew. He wanted her praise and admiration almost as much as he craved the wealth that would come to him from the venture. He wanted to be her captain of captains, to dwarf all other contenders.

"Sir, Captain," came a shout. "Come and look at this." It was Nicholas Conyers, the Cornishman. Conyers, fleet of foot, a wrestler, with the keenest eyes on the ship. He was pointing at the ground beneath a rocky ledge. Frobisher made his way over to him. The men were examining the ground and kicking at scattered bones. There was a patch of blackened earth. People had made fire in this place. They had butchered animals and birds.

Frobisher felt the hairs rise on the back of his neck. He sensed that eyes were watching them, even at that moment. He peered about at the rugged landscape of boulders and sparse, blasted sedge. He gripped his halberd.

"Stay together," he commanded, "and keep a sharp lookout."

Below him he could see the longboat canted over on its side. Two men lounged beside it. They needed to be alerted. The longboat was vital to their safety. He sent Conyers to warn them. The Cornishman went skipping and plunging down the incline, enjoying the adventure, anticipating the surprise on the faces of his ship-mates when they learned that they were not alone in the Meta Incognita.

Frobisher watched as the longboat pulled back into deepwater. He stood on top of the hill. To the west there was no strait. There was no gleaming ocean beyond. They had found merely a bay, a blind alley. It would be necessary to retrace their course, to find a way around this high, black land. There must be a way. There is always a way.

He felt the bile of disappointment rise inside him. Every day the log was paid out behind the ship. Every day the line was hauled in. Speed and progress were computed and marked on the chart. He liked to move forward. Like the salmon striving for its birthplace at the stream's headwaters, it was his instinct to move forward, to seek, to find. To retire defeated, to retreat, was to tangle the line of his life.

Nevertheless, it was God's will. He took out his Bible. The men bared their heads and knelt.

'Yea, though I walk in the Valley of the Shadow of Death'. He intoned the familiar words.

They were comforted. They built a cairn to signify to all who might see it, down all the years to come, that this land, as far as any eye could see, belonged to England and to Her Gracious Majesty.

This gave them strength and resolution. Frobisher pointed to the east.

"I name that island Resolution and over there Warwick Island and Queen Elizabeth Foreland. Note this. That distant speck you see, shall be Lok's Island, for my good friend and generous patron, your paymaster, Michael Lok. Now let us give three resounding cheers to let whoever hears us know that we stand on English soil."

The men threw their caps aloft and give three wild "huzzas". Their voices came back to them, fractured by the cliffs and the tympanum of the sea, receding and receding into the empty wilderness. The men in the longboat far below, looked up and waved their caps in reply. Away in the distance the porpoises appeared again.

Back on the shore, Frobisher observed the flooding tide. There was something menacing, savage, about the way the water advanced, prowling between the rocks and boulders, reaching towards the dry land, surging in narrow channels, as if impatient to reclaim what it had lost to the ebb. Lank patches of wrack and weed took new life, swaying back and forth in the current. A scum of mud and dust lined the edge of the tide, always the sign of the coming flood.

He noted the urgency and force of the rising waters. Somewhere, he was convinced, two great oceans contended for supremacy. It was up to him to find their place of conflict, the place where they came together to push and tug like Cornish wrestlers. He beckoned to the, now floating longboat to come inshore and take them off.

"They are men, sir." It was Nicholas Conyers, breaking into his thoughts. "Men sir, not porpoises."

Frobisher was instantly alert.

"Men?" John Dee had spoken about the legends of Pygmaei, the Hyperboreans, eaters of fish, men with heads growing out of their chests, out under their arms; all fantastical stories; cannibals, eaters of raw meat. Yarns told by travellers, tales distorted and exaggerated by time.

"Men, you say?" He looked about, squinting into the light. "I see nothing."

"Aye sir," insisted Conyers. "They look like they have grown into their boats. They seem to have no legs. They move like insects sir, with wings. Like dragon-flies, sir."

Frobisher laughed. "You have been reading books, Nicholas Conyers. Tall tales."

Conyers shook his head vehemently. "I swear, sir. I witnessed it with my own eyes."

"I have regard for your eyes, young Nicholas. If what you say be true we must look about us. We must speak with them. They are now subjects of Her Majesty. We must deal justly with them."

He felt for the first time the responsibility of Empire, a balance of care on the one hand and power on the other. Perhaps in this new land they might start off on the right course. These legless, winged creatures could some day, become Englishmen.

From what he had seen of Ireland, it had all gone awry. The Irish could never accept the benefits of true allegiance. Befuddled by superstition and Popery, loyal to wild and lawless brigands, they preferred annihilation to orderly assimilation. In Ireland it was always a fight to the death. Here in the clear, cold Arctic, Frobisher determined to start with a clean slate. Whether two-legged or winged, Englishmen would possess and hold the Straits of Anian. The benefits would flow exclusively to England.

The longboat rose and fell on the swelling tide. It lifted his spirits. There was no sign of the winged people. The longboat buffed against the ship's side. He climbed aboard. His eye at a glance, took in the rigging. It was a particular gift of his to see instantly, anything that was out of place or unsecured.

He went up onto his bridge. He hooked his thumbs into his belt. He was home again.

Dusk was closing in. The days were shortening. He called to Gabriel, anchored a cable's length away, directing them to be alert for intruders. He went below to write up his log.

The seven bells woke him in the soft light of the Arctic dawn. He heard scuffling and raised voices. The savages! The infidels! They had come in their little boats to attack the ship. He seized his sword and dashed up on deck.

In the low waist of the ship two men were fighting, struggling together, exchanging blows, casting their eyes about in the hope that someone would separate them before too much damage could be done. Corneyles Rich the dour Dutchman, a sailmaker, was struggling with old John Wilmot, trying to snatch some object from him. Wilmot snarled and clutched the object close to his chest. He turned this way and that, like a child denying his opponent any grip or purchase.

The Dutchman lost his temper. He put his hand to the dagger at his belt. Frobisher roared at them to stop. The antagonists froze in shock. They had never heard him raise his voice like that. They looked at him wide-eyed.

"Draw that dagger Corneyles Rich and you lose your hand. I will tolerate no brawling on my ship."

The men were in no doubt. They stood apart. The sailmaker looked at his right hand. It was his livelihood. He would be no more than a shambling, mutilated beggar, sheltering in hedgerows or doorways, a husk of a man. His legs shook in fear of his captain's fury.

"Give it here, John Wilmot." Frobisher stretched out his hand. He gestured impatiently. "Give it here."

Wilmot made no protest. He held out the object of the quarrel, a piece of rock about the size of a small loaf; black as sea-coal but speckled all over with flecks of white. The specks glinted in the morning light. Frobisher held the rock, turning it this way and that, studying the iridescent specks. The two men watched his reaction.

"What is this?" demanded Frobisher.

John Wilmot swallowed hard. "Gold, sir," he murmured. His voice caught in his throat. "Gold, Captain Frobisher." Louder this time.

The watching crewmen crowded about. They jostled one another to get a better view.

Frobisher hefted the lump of rock. "So, Corneyles Rich, you would be a rich man?"

The Dutchman shuffled awkwardly.

"Where did you find this?"

"I found it, Captain," interjected Wilmot. "Yesterday, when we was standing by the longboat."

"I saw it de first, Captain," protested the Dutchman. "It is mine."

"When you were standing by the longboat?"

The two men nodded guiltily.

"So the country people might have crept upon you, while you were seeking your fortunes? They might have stolen our longboat, might they not?"

The men were silent, their eyes fixed still on the piece of rock.

Frobisher ran his finger along the rail. There was a thin rime of frost on the wood. Frost glittered on every rope and stay. Time was running out.

"You are fortunate to escape a flogging. If this be gold, it belongs to our sovereign, Queen Elizabeth. If any dispute this, they will hang. I shall look into the matter and make my decision. Our purpose here is to seek for the Passage, not to die wealthy men among the heathen cannibals."

The men laughed awkwardly. The choices were stark, to press on to the sunlit ocean or starve in a frozen wilderness, with enemies behind every rock. Frobisher was their best hope, not dreams of gold and a life of idle luxury.

Chapter Seven

Lord Burghley did not invite Spenser to sit. He looked him up and down. He extended his hand for the letters. Spenser bowed and delivered yet more reports from Ireland.

The Lord High Treasurer cracked the seal. He glanced back at Spenser with mild curiosity and then immersed himself in the missive. Spenser looked around. The gardens were soft and lush with the colours of late summer. Gerhardus the Herbalist, famed for his skill, was examining the well-tended fruit trees. It seemed an idyllic occupation. This Hollander lived his life by the cycle of the year, untroubled by the wars in his own country, the rapacity of French and Spaniard. He was indifferent to the depredations of Irish rebels. What plans the Pope might have to set his bastard son on the throne of Ireland, troubled him not at all.

He excised cankerous growth from a tree and destroyed it by fire. He kept his lawns trim with a whispering scythe. His edges were straight. Where there were curves they were graceful, as accurate as the curves drawn by any mathematician or architect with light-stepping compasses. The sun-dial measured his working day.

Spenser took in the view from the top of his lordship's mound. Here was a man who held the destinies of great ones in his hands. He sent armies to make war. He held the purse strings of the realm. All this from the top of his little mountain.

'As Cocke on his dung-hill, crowing cranck.' The line came to him unbidden. It was the shepherd Diggon Davie, from the, as yet unpublished, *Calendar*. September. Diggon despising the stick-in-the-muds. He had seen the world. Spenser smiled.

"You smile, sir." Lord Burghley's eyebrows arched.

Spenser was jolted from his thoughts.

"You find something to amuse you?" Lord Burghley had little tolerance for giddiness or levity. For a moment Spenser was thrown.

"Your garden, my lord. I smile in delight. Would that the world could be so perfect and," he bowed slightly in deference "and so well tended."

Burghley accepted the compliment. His tone softened. "I read here that you are to be trusted; a man of judgement; indeed something of a poet. Should I have heard of you?" Those eyebrows again.

"The fault is mine, my lord. That question always irked him. Should I descend from my lofty eminence to concern myself with the doings of such gnats as you? Gnats have their feelings too, their hopes, their music, by the downward-rolling streams on summer eves. Yea, gnats can bite also and afflict the great. Virgil himself was stung to poetry by a gnat.

"We must see what can be done." Burghley tapped Sir Henry's report. "I can use a man with a good pair of eyes and skill with words. I want you to travel with him on his next progress. Write what you see. Be free with your words. Give me your poet's perspective on Ireland. There is matter there for an ambitious man like you."

Spenser felt a spurt of alarm. This was an opportunity. Burghley had read him well. Poetry might be a bridge to advancement, but words once committed to ink, cannot be withdrawn. To write frankly might be to court danger. There were more perils in Ireland than quaking bogs and blood- thirsty rebels.

'He that strives to touch the stars oft stumbles at a straw.'

It was Thomalin, his shepherd of July, upbraiding the goatherd who pastured his flock on a rocky height. Spenser's head was filled with words. But words are not enough to support a new wife and the child to come. Machabyas had means, but not means enough to support a man on the rise, a gentleman of influence and authority. Perhaps even a great proconsul of Ireland. It rested on a throw of the spotted dice.

"It would be my privilege to serve you my lord."

"In serving me you serve Her Majesty. Bear that always in mind. Make that your theme. Now go." He smiled for the first time. "And watch your footing, or you might take a tumble."

Spenser was dismissed. He went carefully down the spiral pathway. He made his way through the garden. He noted the neat flower-beds, the burgeoning herb garden, the trees laden with ripening fruit, the fruits of success. He knew now what he wanted.

***

Frobisher had specifically ordered the five men not to set foot on shore. They were to take the longboat as far as the rocky outcrop. If they saw signs of habitation they were to return immediately to the ship. But where were they? They had rounded the headland, contrary to his orders and the rocky landscape had swallowed them, leaving no trace, not even the longboat.

He fired off ordnance. He took a search-party ashore. He left gifts on top of rocks in prominent places, in the hope of winning the goodwill of the country people. He saw a great herd of the native deer flowing over the rocky terrain, great shaggy deer with antlers festooned with velvet. The herd passed, a turbulent, muddy river, pouring down from the heights and flooding the low land by the coast, always moving, tossing, urged on by some mysterious compulsion.

He saw chevrons of geese, uncountable thousands, all heading south. He saw the strange seals lolling on the shingle, enormous moustachioed creatures with two protruding tusks. The moustachios gave them a gruff, good-natured expression but the men were wary of the tusks.

He began to understand how people could live in this bleak and blasted country, even in winter, but he could not find them. He left signs, five pebbles with human features scratched on them.

He left a note in a bottle urging his men to make some answering sign. He left mirrors and iron nails, a promise of great rewards, should the savages restore to him his crewmen.

Failure closed about him with the first light dusting of snow. Frost crackled underfoot in the low sedge and wiry grass. He returned to his ship. He looked at his charts. He had found precious little, a few speculative lines suggesting a bay with no discernible egress, except by the way he had entered; a few islands, arbitrarily named for patrons and shareholders; Queen Elizabeth Foreland, standing sentinel at the entrance. Nothing to show for his pains but the loss of Michael, a pinnace and some good men. A wild-goose -chase. Nothing to look forward to but disgrace and recrimination.

He picked up the black stone. It was like a fragment of the winter sky, specks of stars set in a black firmament. He turned it in his hands. His heart began to race. Perhaps the brawling sailors were right. Perhaps fortune had stepped in to rescue him. The Northland might well be rich in other things besides skins and blubber. He took a hammer and smashed the stone into fragments. The gold ran right through. He knew little of mining or metallurgy, but he knew that he held in his hand the key to unimaginable wealth, wealth far beyond the dreams of any Conquistador. He began to plan. There was little time left.

A mining party went ashore with pick-axes and hammers. They found gifts of fish and dried meat. They left goods in exchange and each morning the goods were gone. Gradually the people began to appear, broad, squat men with narrow eyes and a knot of black hair over the forehead. They appeared suddenly from among boulders and stood at what they considered a safe distance. When Frobisher approached them they melted away. He made five effigies and set them on a small rise. He rang a handbell, but to no avail. His men were lost to him.

August slipped away. Ice was forming along the shoreline. It floated in the bay. It was time to escape winter's grip and flee southward to home and comfort. There was ore enough in the holds to pay the crews handsomely and stimulate interest in a second and possibly even a third expedition.

He gave the order to raise anchor and set a course for England. He spread sail in a light westerly. The ship began to speak to him. It lifted on the tidal swell. Suddenly the winged people were all around them, propelling their skin boats with great speed, chattering and pointing. Their boats, thought Frobisher were like the shuttles of looms, pointed at both ends, totally enclosed on top, save where the paddler sat. Even he was enclosed by a kind of apron, designed obviously to make the whole craft water-tight. Like shuttles, the boats darted back and forth, light as spindrift on the rapidly rising tide. The people seemed to derive great amusement from the hairy faces of the sailors. They pointed and laughed. They held out their hands in expectation of further gifts. Frobisher shook his head. He leaned from the waist of his ship and held up five fingers.

"Five men," he called. "I want my five men."

The savages drew back, checking their little craft with a flick of a paddle.

Frobisher held out the hand-bell. He tinkled it gently. The sound echoed from the icy shoreline, the sound of a Christian missionary in an arctic wasteland. A savage drew near, wary as any bird. Frobisher smiled. Ting! Ting!

"Come on, my friend. Take it." The bell tinkled. "Take it," repeated Frobisher softly. "Take it." Ting! Ting! Delicious music. The ship rolled towards the little skin boat. The savage sat, a prisoner in his craft. He rose on the swell, almost level with the gunwale. He reached for the bell. Frobisher let go. The savage snatched at it as it splashed into the deep. His boat grazed against the planking.

In an instant Frobisher had him by one arm and the back of his hood. The ship rolled away, lifting both man and boat. By main force Frobisher heaved him from the water, boat and all and hurled him onto the deck. In an instant the savage, gibbering in terror, was pinned to the deck by sturdy hands. His companions turned with a great lamentation and sought the safety of the shore.

"Now, you villain," snarled Frobisher. "Where are my men?" He grasped the man by his coat. The savage stared at him.

He bit down hard and spat his tongue onto the deck in a gout of blood. He stared defiantly at the Englishman.

"Secure him below," ordered Frobisher. "If I cannot trade him for our shipmates, at least I can exhibit him in Fleet Street." Fury gripped him. "Take him below."

The ships hove to again and dropped anchor. They waited for three days. Each morning the men chopped ice from the blocks and rigging. There was no communication from the shore. Time had run out. They hoisted sail again and with a fair following wind, they left Frobisher's Bay behind them.

'And yet as ghastly dreadfull as it seemes,
Bold men presuming life for gaine to sell,
Dare tempt that gulf, and in those wandering stremes Seek waies unknown, waies leading down to hell.'
E.S.

***

Spenser was proud of his journeys to Ireland. He had crossed the sea in both smooth and stormy weather. He admired the life of the seafarers, sbut it was not for him. It fired his imagination. It called forth lines of verse, but he could never be a sailor, an explorer of foreign lands, a privateer. In a day- sailing to Ireland he had experienced the exhilaration of standing on deck, with the wind sliding off the sails, threatening to snatch his bonnet from his head. He had however, endured the misery of sickness when the ship wallowed in the swell, slopping from side to side, until his gorge rose uncontrollably and he was subjected to the misery and humiliation of a trip to the rail. The sea was perhaps better apprehended in flowing lines of verse. He blew on the new ink. He put down his quill.

"I must away to Ireland again," he said, as if as an afterthought.

"Again?" queried Machabyas.

Her constant questioning irritated him. He had important work to do, affairs of state. She was heavy with child. It did not improve her appearance.

"Yes," he said evenly. "It is my opportunity. I have important work there."

She sniffed. "May I not come with you, husband? Do you not wish to be near me when our child is born?"

Indeed he had no such wish. That was a matter for midwives and wet-nurses. It was not a world he wished to inhabit. He felt no ill-will towards Machabyas. She was a good woman, he granted, a good soul. She deserved the best of care, but she was not a suitable consort for a man of adventure.

"Of course I do. I wish for nothing more, but Ireland is a place of danger. I must move about there, as my masters decree. It would be no fit place for you and for our precious child."

He picked up his pen. He frowned.

'And Proteus eke with him does drive his heard
Of stinking Seales and Porcpisces together . . .'
E.S.

Porc pisces, pig fish. "Hmm." What strange creatures inhabit the deep. He made a note in the margin; 'the shepheard of the sea.' He liked the phrase.

"What did you say, my dear wife?"

"You were not listening. I said that we will be just as much in peril here in London, from filth and pestilence."

He sensed her hurt and anxiety.

"I promise you that I shall find us a place in Ireland, where we can live happily and raise a flock of children."

She was mollified. Why did he always express himself in terms of herds and flocks? She smiled inwardly. Her husband was no country man. He would be a poor farmer, lost as he was in dreams of fame and ideas above his station. She drew closer to the fire and thought of the child within her womb.

'There fruitfull corne, faire trees, fresh herbage is
And all things else that living creatures need.'
E.S.

He took up a pen knife and began to pare a fresh quill. He was wondering if the learned Welshman, Gerald, spoke true when he said that all venomous reptiles died in mid-passage on the way to Ireland.

***

'Bring John Dee with you and come in haste to Deptford. Frobisher'

Michael Lok stared at the note. It had arrived in the middle of the night, a message from beyond the grave. It was Frobisher's hand. How could this be? He could not have found the straits. All hope was lost. There were no spices or silks, just a crew of gaunt and hungry men who would demand their wages. He could hear already, raised voices in the street and clubs hammering on his door. Sweat broke out on his brow.

"Oh Jhesu," he groaned. It would have been preferable if Frobisher had indeed drowned with all hands. There would have been loss, but at least no violence. He would have to hire men to guard his door. More expense. More vittle.

"Oh, Christ," he groaned, rubbing his beard. Curse Frobisher anyway. A bad penny.

"Well, God be praised," exclaimed Mary. She held the candle close to the piece of paper. She peered at the writing. She had difficulty with letters.

"John Dee," she said. "It must be important."

"Of course it is important. It is important that we are all but ruined."

"Send for Master Dee," she directed. "He will know what to do."

"John Dee. John Dee. Is he a wizard? Can he conjure coin from the depths of the earth?"

"Stop walking about like a lost thing and send for John Dee. Take a boat to Deptford at first light."

It was a plan. Dee would know what to do. Did he not advise Her Majesty? There would be no violence in the presence of Master Dee.

He sent a servant with money to engage a waterman. Frobisher must have come upriver on the rising tide.

"Yes, yes," he said aloud. Mary handed him a glowing tobacco pipe. She found that it had a wondrous calming effect on him.

"You must take some breakfast before Master Dee arrives. You cannot go on the river without something warm inside you."

He blew a cloud of smoke. "We shall sweep down upon him with the ebb. We shall demand explanations. He has not fulfilled his contract." He envisaged himself shooting the rapids of London Bridge. He could see John Dee's white beard streaming in the cold October air. They would take Frobisher off guard before he could wipe the sleep from his eyes.

***

The watermen put them ashore at the Old Swan Steps, insisting that they should not risk the bridge on such a tide.

"You will find another boat below the bridge, my masters. Do not linger in the streets."

There was no need to tell them that. Even at that early hour there were people abroad, dark shapes in doorways or lurking on street corners. There were a few carts trundling towards the fish-market. Michael Lok gripped his stout staff and pulled his cloak about him. John Dee chatted amiably, speculating on what Frobisher might have found. He wondered about the stars and how the lodestone might have behaved. He talked about the great expanse of clear water around the Pole. He was as excitable as a child on his way to the circus.

Michael Lok held his staff before him. The ferrule rang on the cobbles as he strode. He held his arms out from his sides, making himself bigger, more menacing, not a man to be trifled with.

They came to the bustling steps at Bellyns Gate. Boats nosed their way in to discharge their cargoes. Fishwives shrieked. Porters hefted dripping baskets of silvery fish. The two men engaged a wherry man to take them down river. A bleary October sun rose out of the mist. The river traffic glided to and fro. The world was awake.

Chapter Eight

"Sometimes," said Sir Henry Sidney, "I despair of this country. You saw what happened today." He swilled some dregs of wine in his cup. He pushed his plate away, his meal unfinished. Spenser was silent. He had no appetite for either food or wine. A mother covered in the blood of her foster son, screeching to heaven for revenge.

"Where are we, young man?"

Spenser frowned. "In Lymbericke, my lord," he replied warily. The Lord Deputy knew well where he was. "In King John's castle."

"Aye, in a castle, with armed men all around us. It is ever thus." He gave a dry chuckle. "We are the rulers of this land, yet we fear to poke our noses beyond the gate."

"But, my lord, you have shown how this land may be governed. You have established shires and officers to administer them. You have sent for good Englishmen to farm the land."

The Lord Deputy snorted. "And they piss themselves with fear every time a bird flies up from the trees or a dog barks. There will be no husbandry until the Irish come in and accept the Queen's peace."

Spenser coughed. He knew how that could be effected, but this was not the time. The old Saxon system, where every man knew his place in his village, where the Headman kept order, answering to his lord. His lord answered to the King. The King protected his people. It was like a machine, a system of levers and pulleys, lubricated by loyalty and duty.

"They will come in, my lord," he assured Sidney. "You have shown what happens to those who subvert the law. They will come in, out of fear."

"And hunger, perhaps." Sidney was not so sure. He had given to the Irish both laws and treaties. He had burned their harvests and taken their herds. Neither approach seemed to work.

On this day he had executed the notorious and incorrigible rebel, Morrogh O Brien, a man who claimed descent from ancient kings. He had humbled this O Brien before his people, hanged him, disembowelled him as a butcher would a carcase, struck off his head as a warning to all who might entertain treason in their hearts. It was the only course.

But then that infernal woman had intervened. She dashed from the crowd and snatched the severed head from the hangman. She began to drink the blood. She licked it from the beard and from the veins of the neck. She nuzzled the head as a dog might worry a bone. She wailed and called to the crowd. It was reported by those who knew, that she had been foster- mother to O Brien; that she had nursed him as an infant and loved him as he grew to manhood. She screeched to all who could hear, that blood as noble as his should never touch the ground. Rough hands had taken the head from her, but still she wailed, that strange haunting *keen* that made the hair rise on the scalp.

Neither man could put her out of his mind.

"Are you a lover of the playhouse, young man?" asked the Lord Deputy.

"Not as such," admitted Spenser. "I am versed in the Classical writers of course."

"Ah yes. I thought that would be the case. You should go to the players. They teach us about life."

Spenser had an instinctive aversion to the playhouses, the vulgar crowd on the ground, ladies in their seats, nudging and ogling, the guffaws at every bawdy allusion. It was no wonder that these players were numbered with rogues and vagabonds.

"The players, my lord?"

"We are all players, my young friend. We strut. We speak. We try to influence the minds of those about us. The players teach us to feel, to fear and to weep. We learn to care for humankind."

Spenser was silent again. He had witnessed the most brutal cruelty that day. He had seen a woman, doubtless of some breeding, behave like an animal. Sir Henry read his silence.

"You saw my play today. I had a stage and a scene, this great castle. I had a cast of many hundreds, armoured knights, infantrymen, snorting steeds. My intention was to move the people to obedience and fear. But this madwoman, this distracted mother, stole my drama. She stole my audience. Who will remember my theme? They will remember her. People who were not there will remember her, through stories and ballads. I shall be King Herod, booed and pelted from the stage." He drew wet circles on the table, with his cup, circles and arcs catching the light. "In truth, I pitied her myself."

He grunted a low, ironic laugh. "You should go to the theatre, my boy. You would learn much."

Spenser demurred. "They will come in, my lord. When you have cut off all the heads of treason and rebellion, when the winter covert is thin, they will creep forth from their woods and forests to learn the ways of peace."

"When our castle walls creak under the weight of rebel heads, the Irish will learn to love us." Sidney shook his head. He reached for the bottle. Spenser declined another cup. He felt decidedly queasy. He wanted to be alone with his papers. He excused himself. A page lighted him to his chamber. He had no stomach for writing. Poetry seemed such a trivial matter. Out there in the darkness, the head of the rebel looked down from the castle wall. Somewhere in the town the distracted woman keened her child, her lost king. Spenser lay down on the straw, but he could not sleep. He could hear the ceaseless rushing of the river washing the feet of the great fortress. He wondered how it would be to take a little boat and go with the river, westward into the vast ocean, following the sun to a newer, cleaner world.

***

In the bleary sunlight by the captain's stern window, it certainly looked like gold. It weighed as heavy as gold. It drew mens' eyes as avidly as any gold.

Michael Lok could not take his eyes off it. He could barely restrain his joy. There was an aura around Frobisher's head, but it was not yet Martinmas. It was the aura of the hero, the explorer of hidden seas, the true adventurer.

Frobisher, on the other hand, was matter-of-fact, impatient to carry the business to the next stage. Already, in his mind, he was planning next year's expedition; miners; soldiers to protect the workers; condemned convicts who could be left to work over winter and earn their pardon through toil in the unending night.

John Dee, as the acknowledged expert, was grave and deliberate. He had a lens which he held to his eye. It gave him the appearance of an unbalanced Cyclops with one enormous eye and one small one. His hand shook as he scrutinised specimen after specimen. His hand was like that of a man with incipient palsy, or that of a man straining to keep his excitement in check, straining to preserve a professional detachment.

The fourth man at the table looked from one to another. He was a dark-skinned, unsmiling, man, dressed all in black, save for the white ruffed collar and white lace cuffs. He wore a tight-fitting skull-cap. He was weighing the man as much as he weighed the ore. Francis Walsingham, Secretary of State, did not give his trust lightly. It was he who had brought armed men to secure the ship. None of the others knew how he had divined the need for secrecy, even before the ship had docked. They knew better than to ask.

"Well, Doctor Dee?" said Frobisher after a while, with the tone of a man awaiting a long-overdue diagnosis. The doctor had consulted the auguries, the stool, the humours, the waters, whatever in Hell they did in their obscure arts. This man was an alchemist. It was time. Frobisher drummed his fingers on the table, hoofbeats bearing his destiny.

"Well, Master Dee?" he demanded, his voice rising a notch. "Give us your opinion."

"Ah!" replied the wise man. "Ah, yes! Difficult to be sure, in this light." He rose and went to the window. The sun's path lay on the water, golden fish flickering on the surface of the sliding river. "I would need to make a trial of the ore."

"What is your first impression?" demanded Frobisher. "Is it not clear to you, sir? This is gold. Do you not see how rich this ore is?"

John Dee flinched from the steely edge in the captain's voice. He wanted to believe that this was true gold. Yes, it was most likely gold, very high grade gold, perhaps white gold, but gold nonetheless. Yes. Yes. "It is gold." He declared. "Yes, indeed, gold."

Frobisher's fingers stopped their gallop. Michael Lok gave a long, sibilant sigh of relief. Francis Walsingham sat upright, looking from one to the other. These were fearful men in their different ways. He could see the hunger in their eyes. They would need to be watched, guided, controlled. He spoke for the first time, softly and with careful emphasis.

"Very good, my masters," he began, "now this is what I propose." He noted their surprise. "On Her Majesty's behalf, of course." There was no discussion. The matter was to remain a secret. Samples would go to the assay master of the Tower. The mariners were to be paid off and all bills cleared by Michael Lok on behalf of the Company, pending the collection of arrears and outstanding investments.

'Paid by Michael Lok . . . paid by Michael Lok . . .' The sweat came again. He scarcely registered that he and John Dee were appointed Commissioners for the smelting of the ore. He could see, but not hear, Frobisher's thick fingers drumming again, a pirate's fingers, the fingers of a brawler, a killer. 'all bills to be cleared by Michael Lok.' The ship stirred under him, feeling the tug of the river. Rigging creaked overhead. He heard boots on the deck overhead. He needed to go to the rail and vomit his fears into the swirling stream. He needed his pipe.

He could take his threadbare credit to the bankers, to the investors, but what could he offer as collateral? A ship full of gold? That would loosen the purse strings. But now that could not be. Walsingham knew better than anyone how quickly the French and the Spaniards would pick up the scent of gold. His spider-web of contacts throughout Europe worked in both directions.

"So, gentlemen," Walsingham was concluding, "if this secret gets out, as it may well do," he looked from one to another, "sailors ashore and all that." He gave a bleak smile, a concession to normal life, to ordinary humanity, "say that this ore is from Ireland. It is time that we got some advantage from that misfortunate island." He grunted and stood up from the table. "You have your tasks, gentlemen. Captain Frobisher, you will appear at Court. And bring that savage Indian. Clean him up a bit. I understand that he stinks. Her Majesty will be diverted to meet one of her new subjects from this wondrous land."

He took his leave. The boatswain's pipe shrilled. The three men looked at one another in silence.

Frobisher spoke, the man of action, prepared always to take the fight to the adversary.

"Well, my friend Michael, you now have the authority of Walsingham behind you." It was a fact. "There are none who will welsh on their obligations to Her Majesty." It was a glimmer of hope.

"As for you, my good doctor." Frobisher was deploying his forces, stealing the weather-gauge, cutting out his prize, "you will find men of skill, subtle men, well versed in the alchymical arts, who will prove our gold beyond all doubt."

There could be only one acceptable result. They would find gold, but first they would eat breakfast, fresh bread, meat, eggs, fruit, glorious to the taste, after months at sea. Michael Lok had little appetite. The crew ate well, doubtless at his expense. All on board, with the exception for the poor cannibal confined below, added to the tally.

***

The caliban, as the crowd called him, was a huge success. The queen demanded a demonstration of his little boat, at Greenwich. Although not in good health, he performed as required, in an enclosure formed by longboats and wherries. Frobisher was taking no chances of his escaping. The caliban turned, pirouetted, reversed, plying his double paddle like a dragon-fly's wings. John Dee thought of his colymbetes, his swimming teacher in the water-trough. Alas, poor colymbetes. One morning there was a fat frog in the trough, smiling a smile of smug contentment. The frog had speed and power, but he lacked the grace of the jewelled insect. John Dee was sad for his little friend but he did not punish the frog for being a frog.

There was a cry from the crowd on the river bank. The caliban had disappeared. There was nothing but the shining hull of his craft. There was a little turmoil in the water and the savage appeared again, like a seal surfacing for air. He did it again with a flick of his paddle and again, to the delight of his audience. It was as if he showed his skill in a gesture of contempt.

The crowds came to see him displayed at the Bell Savage Inn on Ludgate Hill. He drew bigger crowds than did the players, five and six hundred at a time, jostling among the horses to get into the inner chamber. They wondered at the ingenuity of his boat of skins. They gazed at this Indian, Tatar, or Samoyede, as some insisted, this caliban eater of raw meat. He could not speak, the story went, because he had cut out his own tongue. Sometimes, seated on his stool he drew a string from his boot with, attached to it, what appeared to be a sliver of metal. More probably bone or ivory. He would sit on a stool in contemplative silence. They watched him hold the string aloft, allowing the sliver to swing and turn until it settled, always pointing in the one direction. Some said it was a lodestone but that could not be. The caliban was from a race that knew nothing of science or metallurgy. The caliban coughed incessantly. He would roll the string around the sliver, slip it into his boot and sit impassive, in silent contemplation.

When Captain Frobisher appeared, he was cheered to the rafters. This was a man who had taken the world by the scruff of the neck and shaken it until it disgorged its wealth. He knew something of metallurgy too. It was the worst kept secret in London.

Gold finders were working their bellows in several parts of the city, night and day to prove his wealth. Nevertheless he came every night to count the house and take his share. For the moment the caliban was his gold mine.

***

"Captain Raleigh," said Sir Henry, "you must take twenty of your Devon men and convey Mr. Spenser to Cork. I fear that he is sick of Ireland and this incessant rain. Put him on a ship for England."

The young captain nodded. He was a year or two younger than Spenser, something of a dandy in his attire, with a pearl ear-ring dangling from his left ear lobe. His dark eyes matched in colour, his Spanish style beard. There was an air of pent-up energy about him, a man in a hurry.

"I shall, my lord and with your permission I shall over-winter there. I do not have to be in England until the spring. I have certain plans."

"I am sure you have, Captain Raleigh. I am sure you have. But mind that your men keep the peace or you shall answer for them."

"They are dogs, my lord but I shall keep them on a short leash."

The Lord Deputy smiled. "See that you do. The peace is a delicate plant. Take good care of my friend, Mr Spenser. He is not in the best of health. The events in Lymbericke have cast him down. He is more a poet than a soldier, you see. We must cherish our poets. It is they who determine whether we live on in the esteem of men or whether we be condemned as fools or scoundrels."

Raleigh's interest quickened. He was something of a poet himself, brusque and to the point, but to some extent in awe of the practitioners of high-flown diction and complex Latin metres. In these matters he felt himself quite the rustic, but he was prepared to learn.

"Wrap him up well. Let him see the splendour of the country in all its autumn colours. Perhaps he will look more kindly on Ireland. As for myself, I must go towards Kilkenny to put manners on Black Tom Butler. He hates my gizzard but he has the ear of the Queen. I must be diplomatic."

"He knows only the diplomacy of the sword, my lord."

"Ah, young man, you must learn patience. I hate the bastard but I need him as you need your hunting dogs. Now go in God's name, and take that serious man with you. He is anxious to get home to his new child, a boy or girl child, he does not yet know."

"My lord," replied Raleigh, taking his leave, impatient to get his men to horse, interested to hear what a poet might have to say about the country and the condition of Ireland as he saw it.

At first, Spenser was a tiresome companion, harping on about government and how Ireland should be pacified. He had a theory that one hundred thousand well provisioned troops, deployed in strong garrisons about the land, ten thousand of them cavalry, would be sufficient to hold the country and allow it to develop in peace and prosperity.

The Queen should pursue a French alliance, even a marriage, in order to wrong-foot the Spaniards and drive a wedge between the Scots and their French friends. Plain as a pike staff.

Raleigh snorted. "I was in France. I saw the massacre of the Protestants. I heard the bells ringing. Protestant England would never wear a French marriage."

Spenser was annoyed. He was not used to rebuke. His views were the result of long and serious consideration. They should be taken as such. He gathered his riding cloak about him and urged his horse a few paces head. Raleigh shrugged.

The rain stopped. The grass sparkled in new sunshine. The woods blazed with colour. Smoke rose in the forest. Harness jingled. A soldier whistled. Spenser turned to his companion, all his petulance forgotten.

"Do you not see us as knights embarked on a great quest, through an enchanted forest?" He smiled. Some of the stiffness went out of him.

"Knights? Not yet. Some day perhaps. What I see is plentiful opportunity for ambuscade. I see a half-ploughed field. I see no herds or people, just evidence of them hiding away, watching us, no doubt."

"All quests are fraught with danger," said Spenser lightly.

Raleigh responded to his mood. He did not see his companion as one to back him in battle or to enter the lists in armour to fight for a cause, but he interested him nonetheless.

Raleigh raised his hand. The column came to a halt behind him. Horses snorted and lowered their heads to crop the long grass by the wayside.

Three men were approaching, three men dressed in the Irish style. They rode without stirrups and carried long javelins over their shoulders. Raleigh rode forward to meet them. Spenser watched.

"What men are you?" demanded the leader, speaking in heavily accented English. "Where do you go?" Although heavily out-numbered, he spoke with authority.

Raleigh looked at the surrounding woods. What might they hide?

"We are men of the Lord Deputy's force. We are about his business. I will thank you to stand aside."

"You are on my land, sir," replied the stranger. It would be courtesy to ask permission to pass over it."

Diplomacy. Keep the peace. "Your pardon, sir" said Raleigh. "I humbly ask your leave to go about our business. That which is the Lord Deputy's business is also that of Her Majesty."

The stranger scratched his long moustache. "Indeed," he mused.

"Your name, sir?" enquired Raleigh. It was beginning to irk him that his journey was being delayed by three ill-kempt ruffians.

The leader pondered the question. He smiled. "I am Maurice, Lord Roche, Viscount of Fermoy, an Englishman like my ancestors, who came here four hundred years ago."

Raleigh was silent. It must be some kind of an Irish joke. Spenser drew near.

"You are surprised, young sir" said the oddly attired Englishman. "We Roches are the People of the Rock. We came from France with the Conqueror and afterwards we came to Ireland. Everywhere we go we build our castles on rocks. We become one with the land."

"But," began Raleigh, "your attire?"

The man laughed aloud. "When I am in England, I dress as an Englishman. I have been there to plead my case against accusations of treason. When I am at home, I dress like this. I am an Irish chieftain. That brings responsibilities. You may pass, but you must not molest my people."

Raleigh nodded. "We will purchase whatsoever we need."

"That is acceptable," said Lord Roche. He spoke to his companions in the Irish tongue. They turned their horses and galloped away towards the woods.

"What did you say to them?" Raleigh eyed him suspiciously.

"They have gone to tell the people to come out. There is work to be done before winter comes upon us."

Spenser was pleased. He could see how his plan would work. Whether Irish or English, this man showed how good authority, used lawfully, could transform the land. He watched a man leading a horse out of the bushes. The man hitched the horse to a previously abandoned plough and resumed where he had left off.

A woman was driving a cow towards a cluster of low buildings. The cow lowed, ready for milking. Children drove some geese, gleaming, white birds against the dark brown and gold of a hedge-row. The sun shone. The geese waddled.

"Come to me at Castletown," said Roche. "Ask anyone the way to Mad Maurice's castle." He laughed again, a warm, friendly laugh. "That's what my people call me." He turned his horse and waved. "You may pass." He galloped away across a field of stubble. A line of horsemen, twenty, thirty, more, detached themselves from the shadow of the woods. They looked towards the English cavalry, then formed up behind their lord, their chieftain, whatever they called him. Raleigh watched for a while, then moved his column forward, on a diverging path, south-easterly, avoiding any occasion of conflict.

At night they saw fires on the hills and distant mountains. "Booleys," offered Spenser. "Sir Henry explained it to me. They keep their cattle on the high ground during the summer. Universities of treason and revolt, he says. They sing their songs and tell stories of ancient kings and victories over the Sassanach. They come down again filled with pride and looking for fight. They come down for All Hallows with their animals and their grievances."

"Fortunately it will be winter by then. That will soften their cough." Raleigh was practical as ever. "How are you feeling by the way?" He had forgotten that he was to take especial care of the poet.

"Well, well," said Spenser, touched by his solicitude. "This sunshine is doing me good." He looked into the middle distance. A comely castle, with a high keep, caught the afternoon sun. It glowed white in the lowering light, a fairy castle, a castle fit for a princess.

"I like that castle," he said, blurting his thoughts. "Fit for a princess."

"It may yet be yours, if you play your cards. Take life on the hazard. This land is a powder cask. Someday it will blaze out again in rebellion. There will be rich pickings for men who keep their heads." He laughed. "Remember that we are on a quest. Who can say where that may lead us."

The castle gleamed, silver turning to gold. Spenser could not take his eyes off it.

In the morning the clouds huddled over the distant mountains. Their undersides put Spenser in mind of udders, dangling, engorged, ready to discharge a relentless flow on the mountain tops. It began to rain again, a relentless steely downpour. The horses sloshed through mud and the flooded inch-fields along the river bank. The river swept angrily along, carrying debris and branches. It plucked at the willows along the banks, seeking to dislodge them from their hold. There was no way of crossing that brown and treacherous spate.

They took shelter in the ruins of a deserted priory, within sound of the rushing water. The hand of King Harry had reached this far. The nave and chancel were unroofed. Only a long cloister had survived the maul and sledgehammer of the Reformers. The choir was bereft of holy chant.

They sheltered in the cloister, with the wind whistling through the gaping windows. The horses stood disconsolate, with drooping heads, their manes and tails like cascades from mountain streamlets.

'An hideous storme of rain,' a knight and his lady seeking shelter. It was an image to delight and inspire. The reality was not so alluring.

A shape rose from behind a tomb, an old woman, her nakedness covered only by a few tattered rags. Her limbs were as sticks, her hair long and tangled. Her eyes burned. She held out her hands towards the men. A cat brushed against her ankle. It wound itself around her legs. She said something in a cracked and wheedling tone, something unintelligible, but her meaning was clear.

Raleigh fumbled in his pouch. He took out some bread and held it out to her. She hobbled towards him and reached fearfully for the bread.

"Take it," he said, anxious to be rid of her. Perhaps she was a witch. Perhaps she had the evil eye. He had heard that Ireland was filled with tales of magic and witches, spirits in trees and stones, forts held by fairy people on the hill-tops. All nonsense.

She snatched the bread, as a wild bird, prepared for danger, might take a crumb. She turned away, cramming it into her toothless mouth, ashamed of her degradation before these silent men. She had seen how some crossed themselves, while others avoided her gaze, fearful of having their souls drawn out of their bodies. She retreated to her scant shelter behind the tomb. The men shuffled awkwardly. They heard her singing softly a strange and plaintive lay, whispering like the wind in the ruined walls or the river bending the water flags. They were anxious to go, rain or no rain. Raleigh signalled to them to lead their horses out from the ruins. They left silently.

They paused on a height over the ruins and looked back.

"Where is your cloak?" demanded Raleigh, noticing for the first time that Spenser wore only his leather jerkin.

The feather in his hat hung down, as bedraggled as his horse's mane. His breeches and hose were soaked.

"What have you done with your cloak?"

Spenser looked at him guiltily, like a child caught out in mischief or foolishness.

"I know what you did. You gave it to the witch. Did she cast a spell on you?"

He was angry. Spenser was his responsibility.

"No she did not. She is no witch. I gave it to her out of gratitude."

"You are a fool. You will die of cold or ague. What gratitude do you owe to a derelict beggar woman, a hag like that?"

"She gave me a gift," replied Spenser. He wiped the rain from his face with the back of his sleeve. He coughed.

"A gift? A curse more likely."

"She gave me a poem," said Spenser gently. "A poem of youth and age, of dignity and loss, of mutability, of things that were and are no longer."

They rode in silence, deep in their thoughts.

"Here," said Raleigh after a while. "You are undoubtedly mad. I understand that Castletown lies in this direction. We must make our way thither and throw ourselves on the mercy of our new friend, Mad Maurice, for the comfort of a roof and a hot meal. He would not refuse a fellow mad man."

He looked at Spenser again. The poet was smiling. He had indeed received a gift.

***

"You understand," said Mad Maurice, the Viscount Fermoy, wild Irish chieftain, whatever, "I must be cautious. It is no dereliction of hospitality to insist that your men may not enter my castle bawn. They may camp below at the bridge and welcome. They will not be molested. Your and your ailing friend will be welcome in my house."

"Ah," said Raleigh, stroking his moustache. He looked at Spenser, soaked and pale. The fellow was obviously in some distress. He coughed, long shuddering spasms that took his breath away. Raleigh looked about sharply, noting the men on the barbican over the gate and the tower house beyond.

"Come inside and warm yourselves," continued Maurice. He pushed the gate wider; spider and fly. "No harm will come to you in the company of a poet. I understand that poor nithering man is a poet."

Spenser nodded wryly. He felt utterly wretched, not caring if these Irish fell upon him, dragging him from his saddle and cutting him to pieces with their bright swords. All he wanted was to lie down and sleep.

"We are in Ireland, sir" went on Maurice, "no one would offer insult to a poet. No one would dare." He laughed. Boils and carbuncles, disgrace and mockery would be the fate of any who insulted a poet. "They have the power," he added. "They have the power."

It was tempting; hot food, a fire, dry straw and a roof overhead. It was an opportunity also, to spy out a castle, to see an Irish chieftain, by nature a potential rebel, in his natural milieu. Who knew when such knowledge might come in useful? Raleigh accepted, directing his men to go down to the mill near the bridge and mind their manners.

"I will come to you presently," he said to his sergeant, "and keep your eyes open." He still felt a touch of apprehension, despite the viscount's hearty invitation. Maurice reached up, extending his hand.

"An Englishman's word," he said.

An Englishman? There was something comical about the notion, an Englishman in an Irish mantle, trimmed with wolf-skin. Raleigh took the proferred hand.

"We are your guests sir and gladly." At that point he would have given his soul for a hot meal and a blazing fire at his back.

Mad Maurice pushed the gate wide. His two guests climbed stiffly from their saddles and entered the castle.

***

The caliban died. Frobisher's income stream dried up. He directed the host to exhibit the body for as long as possible, but the stench drove the spectators away, even from the stable yard.

After three days, the unfortunate infidel was carted away and buried in Moorfields. Some said that the heat of London in October killed him, although everyone else complained of the cold. Others said it was diet. As an eater of his fellow men, his constitution could not adjust to bread and gruel. Some more sensitive souls suggested that he died of sadness and a broken heart. They averred that the little blade which he dangled on a thong, was in fact a piece of lodestone; that it pointed always to his home under the North Star. They said that he had feelings, just like any other human creature. This of course, was ridiculous in one so base, indeed impossible. Neither did the infidels know metal. Although they lived in a land filled with gold, they knew nothing of smelting or of the power and luxury that wealth could bring. It was only right that a wise and powerful queen should govern them and use the riches of the land for the general good.

God blast him, one way or the other, thought Frobisher. He was obliged to go to Michael Lok for a loan to tide him over. Dulls the edge of husbandry. Borrowing, that's what John Dee maintained. Sententious fool. Like some character from a comedy. Dulls the edge. He took the caliban's splinter of metal from his pocket and tested the edge with his thumb. Definitely not flint. John Dee would certainly have a view on it.

He contemplated returning to his lodgings and pleasuring the widow Hancock. She was willing enough and warm in his bed on a cold night. She was a good cook too. As a God- fearing man, it troubled him that he was prone to excesses of the flesh, but as a Scorpio, he accepted that he had both good and bad days. He shrugged.

Frobisher found Michal Lok in close conversation with John Dee. There was an air of excitement about them. Lok rose and greeted Frobisher warmly. Dee got to his feet and shook the captain by the hand.

"News indeed, Captain Frobisher," he beamed.

"The gold?"

"The gold, indeed. Now sit down and let us tell you all."

Frobisher drew a chair in to the table. He looked from one to the other. These men, the Commissioners for Smelting, held the keys to the treasure chamber. He waited.

Michael Lok began. "We have appointed the most skilled and cunning refiner, Gian Baptista Agnello, a gentleman of Italy. His preliminary tests show high levels of gold in the ore." His eyes gleamed. "You realise what this means. We must have more expeditions."

Frobisher nodded. He was already thinking ahead. Leave in late Spring and mine all through the bright Arctic summer. The shareholders would fall over each other to buy a piece of the venture. He bared his strong teeth in a wolfish grin.

"My friend, Sir William Wynter, has conducted some proofs at his house in Lambeth," Lok continued. "He calculates three ounces of pure gold to every hundred pounds of ore. Three ounces!" He paused to let the significance sink in.

Frobisher felt a stab of apprehension in his gut. Sir William Wynter, sometime admiral of the Queen's navy. How had he muscled in on the act? Perhaps he was plotting to supersede him and take command of a great treasure fleet. No, by God, that would never do.

John Dee divined his thoughts. "Have no fear, Captain Frobisher. Sir William is with us. He speaks all praise of you."

"There are one or two naysayers," said Michael Lok. "Mr Williams, the assay master in The Tower, suggests that it may be marcasite, not gold." He snorted in derision. "One or two others." He dismissed them with the back of his hand. He lowered his voice almost to a whisper. "Agnello has offered to purchase the ore in secret for thirty pounds a ton. Do you think that he would pay that for fools' gold?" He scoffed at the absurdity of the idea. "We may forget about Mr. Williams and his ilk."

"I will go to The Tower and beat him senseless. I'll see that he changes his tune." Frobisher clenched a fist.

Dee shook his head. "That would not be wise, my friend. He is a man of some influence. Let us stay with Sir William. He has the ear of Walsingham."

Frobisher nodded, admitting the wisdom of this course. He would have relished the physical release, the crunch of fist on bone, the destruction of an enemy, but for the moment, a tussle with the widow Hancock would have to suffice.

"I trust your lodgings are satisfactory, Captain Frobisher. I have paid six months in advance." Lok was counting coins onto the table, gold and silver. "This is an advance of course, not a loan."

"Not a loan," echoed John Dee. "Dulls the edge of husbandry. That's what I always say. Neither a borrower nor a lender be." He nodded several times, acknowledging his own wisdom. "Loan oft loses both itself and friend. Ah, yes! Ah, yes!" He gazed at the little stack of coin. "That's what I always say."

Frobisher took the sliver of metal from his pocket. "Look at this," he said, handing it to Dee. "Tell me what you think it might be."

Dee came back from his reverie. He took the blade and turned it this way and that. He tapped it against the blade of his penknife. It adhered to the steel. He plucked it away and let it clink again.

"It belonged to the infidel," Frobisher volunteered. "The caliban, as the people called him."

"Strange. Strange." Dee was puzzled. "It is definitely lodestone. Unworked, but sharp nonetheless. Very strange. I will talk with you when you have some leisure, Captain Frobisher, about the Arctic lands."

"I shall wait upon you, sir," said Frobisher, inclining his head. "I shall look forward to that." Conversation with John Dee was always enlightening but such discussions tended to go on a long time. For the moment however, he had gold in his purse. He wanted wine and hot food. He wanted to bear down on Widow Hancock, come alongside, grapple her close, board her and take her as a legitimate prize.

He took his leave and strode through the darkening streets, suffused with a fierce joy, vindicated, carrying already in his purse, more gold than the poor caliban had earned for him in a fortnight.

Chapter Nine

The first thing Spenser saw, when he opened his eyes, was smoke swirling around a vaulted stone roof high overhead. It was sucked upwards and away by an opening in the stonework. It was like an inverted cataract. It made his head swim.

He closed his eyes again. His teeth were chattering. His body shook. He was aware of warmth. Absently he realised that his clothes were missing, that he was naked under a rough woollen blanket or cloak. He could smell the wool and the fur around his head. The fur was damp from his hair. "The *créatúr*! The *créatúr*! It was a woman's voice. She was towelling his hair. His mother, he assumed. It was a long time since she had washed his hair. She had a great respect for soap and water. As the wife of a merchant-tailor, she appreciated the value of a good appearance. She was speaking, but he could not make out the words. The sound seemed to come from a great distance, from a long time ago.

He opened his eyes again. It was not his mother's face. She had changed. Behind her head and far above her, the smoke swirled and roiled in the vault of the roof.

She raised his head and held a cup to his lips. The contents were warm and spicy. He sipped.

"Aha!" he groaned, shivering convulsively. Some liquor, for such he judged it to be, dribbled from the corner of his mouth. The woman wiped it away. She rubbed his shoulders and upper arms, through the rough cloth. She laid him gently down and turned him on his side, facing a fire. He felt the heat on his face.

"The *créatúr*!," she said again, tucking the cloth around him. "Leave him be."

He heard the hum of voices and the sounds of people dining, knives on boards, pans, a dog snuffling in the rushes, the crunch of teeth on bone, laughter.

The scholars were at Commons. He should be up, waiting upon them. They would be impatient for bread and ale.

'More ale here, Spenser my lad. Look sharp about it.' He hated them for their good-natured condescension. A long hall from the kitchen. A feeble joke. He was there for the long haul. They respected his intellect. In some ways their condescension was the revenge of lesser minds. He was the scholar, the poet. Some day he would astonish them. Some day they would seek to scrape his acquaintance. The dishes rattled.

His friend Gabriel was holding forth as he invariably did, about the superiority of the Classical poets. "Any poet worthy of the name, should shape his language to the metres of Virgil."

They had argued this, late into the night, Gabriel pompous and sententious. "No, no, no, Edmund. If we are to achieve anything that will resound down through the ages, we must emulate the Romans."

There was no choice. Chaucer was mistaken, gifted admittedly, but misled in his choice of language and form. Granted, Chaucer had led them a merry dance, but up a blind alley. Drone, drone. Gabriel was banging on.

Spenser slept. He heard the tread of hob-nailed sandals, the Romans coming again, trampling across poor Chaucer's world, scattering the native poets to the woods and to the rocks. You are mistaken, friend Gabriel. No, no, no. Some day he would astonish them all. 'More ale, boy and look lively there.' The dream faded into the glow of the fire.

He felt the warmth on his face. He kept his eyes closed against the light. He loved the North Country, the hills, the streams, the woods. It was difficult to read in the bright sunlight. The pages dazzled. He was a person of some consequence, the young scholar, the poet, one of the Spensers. It was a good feeling. People noticed him. The Spensers were prosperous, his uncle a draper and merchant, a benefactor to his bright young nephew, the dreamer, who would rather sit reading under the summer bough, than learn an honest trade. The uncle, although he had little, held learning in great respect.

Spenser knew that he was dreaming. He was not in the North Country with the sun beaming down on him. He was somewhere else, with strangers, with light dazzling his eyes.

He could see the girls in the bleach fields. They were lifting and turning the long swathes of linen, stretching and shaking the cloth, so that the wind caught it. 'Whump, whump'. They stood among the billows, laughing, aware of the scholar and his book. They were naiads, nymphs of streams and springs, disporting themselves in the waves. Immortals. Servants to Artemis, the chaste, the huntress. They drank from sacred springs. They foretold the future.

They lowered the sheets to the grass. Snow in summer, clothing the fields.

"What do you read?"

He remembered her so well, Rosalind, the daughter of the hand-loom weaver.

"A book," he stammered.

She laughed. He could still hear her laugh, down the years.

"A book! I can see that. But what does it say?"

He tried to close the book, to put it aside, to charm her with witty talk, to dally with her like a shepherd in a poem. She was barefoot. He could see the outline of her limbs through her summer smock. She placed her toe between the open pages. He gazed at her little foot, her sunburned ankle. Confusion overcame him. Spell bound. They were alone. He tried to draw the book away. He took refuge in his scholar's dignity.

"No," she insisted, pressing down on the page with her foot. "You shall not have it until you read to me."

"All right," he consented, anxious to be rid of her, suddenly terrified that she would go, skipping after her companions, laughing at his awkwardness.

"What shall I read?" he asked.

She laughed down at him, a tinkling, musical laugh. "How should I know? I have no letters. Here, let my toe decide." She lifted her foot from the page, letting the book spring shut. He made to snatch it again.

"No, no. I must choose."

He watched in fascination as she opened it again. Her toes were damp from the dew. A blade of grass was stuck between her great toe and the next. Her second and third toes were slightly webbed. A water nymph.

"Now read," she commanded.

He took up the book. "Oh no," he said blushing.

She sat down beside him and wrapped her arms about her drawn up knees.

"Oh yes," she insisted. "You must read what I picked out."

He coughed awkwardly. Surrender, come what might.

"You are blushing," she accused. "What does the book say that makes you blush?"

"Well then," he replied. He was older than she. He assumed the grave tone of a schoolmaster.

"It is Horace, writing to Chloe. Now that she is of marriageable age, she should not fear the sight of a man."

She looked at him with amused interest.

"I have never feared the sight of a man."

He made no comment. He coughed again.

'You shun me, in vain dread, like a fawn trembling in heart and knee.

But I do not follow you like a savage tigress or Gaetulian lion,
To tear you to pieces.
Therefore leave your mother,
Now that you are ripe for a husband.'
Q.H.F.

"Well anyway, that is the general gist of it?" 'Ripe,' ready to be plucked, to be enjoyed. He swallowed hard.

She sat for some moments in silence, rocking gently from side to side.

"What does he really say? Like a fawn. What is that in his language?"

"*Hinnuleo similis.*"

"*Hinnuleo similis.* Like a fawn. I like that. So he says that she should leave her mother; that it is time to find a husband. What do you say, scholar?"

He was again thrown into confusion.

"It is only a poem," he mumbled.

She plucked a long seed-head of grass and brushed his cheek. She stood up.

"You will read to me again. I must go now. Come here again. I want to know what happens."

He made to explain that it was not a story, but she had already gone, skipping between the sheets, a fawn in a field of snow.... *Hinnuleo similis.*

He sat for a long time, holding the book. His forefinger was still on the page, but he read no more.

It was a dream, a sunlit memory. He could smell straw. He heard the dog crunching on a bone. The dream fled from him. He reached out, trying to draw it back.

"Ah, the *créatúr,*" said the woman's voice again. She dabbed his brow.

Sometimes the voices made sense. Raleigh sang a song, in a strong baritone voice, a song of his own devising.

"If I ever have a son," he declared, "this song will keep him on the straight and narrow path.

'And they be these: the Wood, the Weed, the Wag:
The Wood is that that makes the gallows tree;
The Weed is that that strings the hangman's bag;
The Wag, my pretty knave, betokens thee.'"

The sense of his song was that all three grow free and untroubled, until the day on which they meet.

"'But when they meet, it makes the timber rot,
It frets the halter and it chokes the child.'"
W.R.

Silence. Spenser sensed the sombre mood. It was a stark, uncompromising song.

"Well then," said their host, "may we live good Christian lives, in true fealty and may God preserve us from the hangman."

"Amen," said Raleigh, soberly. "Amen to that."

After a long silence, he spoke again. Spenser listened as attentively as possible. The dog was snuffling about him, an enormous scraggy animal, a Gaetulian lion. He plucked at his mantle. The Gaetulian lion was subdued by a cloak thrown over his eyes. This hound had kindly eyes.

"But why this enmity between Black Tom and the FitzGeralds of Desmond?"

This was the nub of the problem, thought Spenser, local chiefs fanning their hatreds into outright rebellion. Break them all, as horses are broken, to the saddle and to the plough.

"Who knows?" replied the viscount. "Some grudge, begun perhaps in the Conqueror's camp at Hastings. Maybe it goes back to Normandy. Who knows? Five hundred years is nothing in terms of an Irish grievance."

Give them provender. Keep the reins taut. Train them to work. It all made sense. He would write it into his report. He would mention also, that she had thrown a veil over his eyes. He could not see her but he could feel the urgency of her hands on his body. He could smell the clean linen on his face. He heard her speak. He rolled on top of her and possessed her. The linen fell from his face to hers, covering her features like a lacy shroud. They lay together naked under the green boughs, as shepherds and their maidens were wont to do.

The readings stopped. She avoided the places where they had met. He haunted the woods and meadows. She came seldom to the bleach fields, but it was a small village. Everything came into the light.

"I am with child," she told him straight out. She held a bundle of linen in her arms, as if for protection. He was no Gaetulian lion.

"I am to marry Tom, the franklin's son. He will give me a good life."

"But . ." he expostulated, "what about . . . ?"

"The child?" She smiled, putting her head wistfully to one side. "Tom will live for me and the child. It is better this way. You will live for your books. You will be a great man. I shall be a farmer's wife. It is better this way."

He could not deny her argument. A scholar could not support a wife and child. A great man could not marry the daughter of a hand-loom weaver. This nymph was wise. She could indeed foretell the future. He would keep her with him always in verse, forever young, *hinnuleo similis*.

He stood up shakily, holding the mantle around him. His clothes were dry on a pole before the fire. He dressed methodically and felt more secure. Maurice beckoned him to join them at the table.

"You must get some meat on your bones, young man." It was the woman who had nursed him through his fever. She was not his mother of course, but matronly in her manner. "You have been gone from us for a night and a day. Now you must drink this."

She poured water from a bottle and handed him a cupful.

Maurice laughed. "This is my wife's cure for all ills, the waters of *Baile an Draoi*. You must do as she says. She has watched over you all this time and will not rest until you are well again."

Spenser took a cautious sip. It savoured of salt, with a back taste of iron.

"The town of the wizard, the wise man. You might say, the magus. Have you ever met a magus, Mr. Spenser?"

A strange question. He drank again, at the woman's urging. He shuddered at the bitterness of the iron, the irony, old memories, heartburn. He reached for some meat and found his appetite again. The woman nodded approvingly. He inclined his head to her in unspoken gratitude.

"I was explaining to Captain Raleigh, that there is no way of crossing the Blackwater, not with this weight of water leaning on her. There are no ferries. You cannot ford her. You must go around her, until you come to Youghal. There you will find a ship for England." Maurice spoke of 'her,' the nymph of the river. Perhaps he too was a poet. "For your kindness, I beg that you keep the *clóca mór*, the mantle. It will keep you warm until you reach home. But, mind you, do not walk abroad in it in London or you may be taken up as an Irish rebel." He laughed at the notion and passed the wine.

Spenser liked the mantle. It made him both conspicuous and invisible by turns. Some assumed that he was a prisoner of the handsome young captain with the troop of horse, a wild Irish ruffian. Where there were Irish, no-one gave him a second glance.

In London his wife gave him a new baby boy and a warning: "You cannot walk about the streets in that thing. People will think you an Irish caliban."

He laughed aloud, overjoyed to meet his son, a child of his own, son of a great man, or at least, one who was soon to be a great man. Not the son of a franklin or low-born weaver's daughter.

They called him Sylvanus, a child of the Greenwood, a boy destined for great things, a castle of silver and gold in a new country. When he went to report to Lord Burghley and Lord Leicester however, he left the *clóca mór* at home.

Chapter Ten

"The tests proceed very well indeed," declared Michael Lok. He smiled at his guests, venturers, directors of the Company, Captain Frobisher himself. They were in good fettle, well fed men, men who appreciated the good things of life. They knew how to plant the seed and reap a rich harvest. They knew how to direct the labour of others to their advantage, to mutual advantage. The labourer, the seaman, the soldier would have no living at all, were it not for such astute and far-seeing men.

"But what of the Passage, Captain Frobisher? Do you think that you will find it this year?" The questioner waited. A small, quiet man with the watchful eyes of a vole. He looked from one face to the other, seeking support. Frobisher took a long draught of ale.

"The Passage," he mused. His voice rumbled.

"Yes, sir," resumed the questioner. "You must remember that we ventured our money on the discovery of the Passage." He swallowed nervously. "The discovery of the gold is a splendid thing, but where do we stand? Do we, the venturers, have a legal right to a proportional share of the gold?"

It was a thorny point. In terms of the route to the Indies, Frobisher had failed utterly. Their money had sunk in the icy seas of the Arctic. It was gone many fathoms below the drifting ice. Nevertheless there was a euphoria surrounding the gold. Fortune had turned her wheel to their advantage.

"So where do we stand – legally?" The man was persistent. Frobisher felt a pulse throbbing in his temple. Was he being accused of fraud, or worse still, failure?

"I lost five good men on that voyage, sir. My first duty is to return and rescue them. After that we shall see about the gold."

There was a murmur of voices around the table. Heads turned, one to another, heads on white ruffed collars, like heads on plates.

"With respect, Captain Frobisher," the man continued, "our interests are not the same as those of your men, or indeed your own. You ask us to alter our terms, to put up money for a rescue mission. I ask again, where do we stand?"

Frobisher was silent. He was in the company of clever men, men versed in accounting and calculating. It was not his world. He had always struggled with letters and ciphering. He had enough learning to chart a course, but his world was one of action. It was a world where honour and courage counted for more than book-learning. He tensed, waiting for his adversary to come to him.

Michael Lok spoke up. He poured some wine and passed the bottle on.

"Gentlemen," he began. "Let me put your minds at rest. Captain Frobisher has succeeded beyond all expectation. As circumstances change, the Company must adjust its course. For the future we must concentrate on this new-found wealth, this El Dorado of the Arctic. All will have a share, in proportion to their investments. I guarantee that. I give you my word." The listeners were mollified. "We are embarked on a great venture. A new age opens up before us. This gold will make us invincible, will make England invincible. You are privileged to be in at the start of a new Empire."

His voice trembled. He was only beginning to appreciate the enormity of what lay ahead. The Queen would come to rely on his business acumen. He could be the equal of Walsingham, even Burghley, a man of destiny. He let his words sink in.

"We are fortunate to have a man of honour, of courage and loyalty at the head of our venture. Captain Frobisher is engaged to sail again to these far lands. He leaves in March. Collecting ore will be his primary concern. The Passage must wait." He smiled again. "Soon the Company will have money enough to make the ice split before us. Our ships will burst into the Arctic Ocean. Everything is possible." He paused. Frobisher raised an eyebrow. He made no comment, addressing himself to his food. He had seen that wall of ice.

"I have several refiners competing to assay the gold. Each one outdoes the others in his predictions. The most skilled men from Germany and Italy. I have every confidence in their abilities." He looked around the table. No dissenting voices were raised.

Frobisher felt good. He was warm and sated. Michael Lok's wife was a superb cook. What would it be like to have such a cook on board his ship? With food like that inside them, his men would smash through any ice. He sat back and stretched his legs under the table. Michael Lok was reminding his guests that their pledges were now due. In fact not a few were in arrears. The captain pondered the wisdom of going himself to collect the outstanding sums. On second thoughts, Michael was a man of greater diplomacy and tact. Better to rest, to build up his strength over the winter. His task would come later.

***

Lord Burghley fingered the tooled leather of the cover.

"It is a handsome piece of work," he conceded. "I shall read it at my leisure."

He placed the book to one side of his brocaded table. He picked up a goose quill and began to pare a nib.

"I have many things to occupy me. Poetry is not at the top of my list."

"I have the honour to be named in the dedication." Philip Sidney spoke softly, watching the Lord Treasurer's reaction.

"Ah!" said Burghley with the ghost of a smile. "You have a vested interest in the work." He took the book again and opened it at the title page. He nodded.

'To the noble and virtuous Gentleman, most worthy of all titles both of learning and cheualrie, M. Philip Sidney.' I see. Unstinting in his praise."

"Mr. Spenser does me too much honour," murmured Sidney.

"But why do you bring this book to me? It is well known that I have little time for the poets."

"My Lord," persisted Sidney. "I come to speak to you of Mr. Spenser. I believe him to be our Petrarch, our Virgil. I know enough of poetry to see that he will be the glory of our age."

"Besides of course, Her Majesty," said Burghley with a little touch of asperity.

"But that is my point, My Lord. England stands now on the threshold of a golden age. It is now that we need our poets, to sing this empire, to build it in the hearts of men."

Burghley raised his hand, stemming the flow.

"Enough, enough, Sir Philip. Enough of your rhetoric." He chuckled tolerantly. "I follow your drift. Now what is your suit? What do you ask for your friend and admirer?"

"Two things, my lord. Firstly that you place this book into the hands of Her Majesty."

"So I am to run errands for you, am I?"

"Not so, my lord. But coming from you, Her Majesty will appreciate the importance of this volume. She is daily beset by poets and authors, to the point of tedium. You will give the book an air of distinction."

"I must read it first."

"Of course, my lord. I venture to suggest that you will find it rewarding."

"And secondly?" Burghley raised his eyebrows.

"My father speaks highly of Mr. Spenser. He found him to be an astute observer in Ireland."

Burghley nodded assent. "I have read his reports. He sees himself as something of a strategist. There is merit in some of his ideas, but he is, at bottom, a poet, not a man of affairs. He needs to be annealed in the smithy of war."

"An excellent phrase, if I may say so, your lordship,"

"So what do you ask?" Burghley moved a roll of papers. He was anxious to spread them out and peruse the contents. "Do you want to get him a command in Ireland?"

Sidney shook his head. "Mr Spenser is no soldier, my lord, and never will be. What I ask is a post which will give him an income and time to develop his art."

"I see. I see. What would we not give for such a post? A wage devoid of duty or labour?"

"Think of it as an investment, my Lord."

"I am bedevilled by investors, young man. Every jackanapes wants to be rewarded with estates in America for the outlay of a few guineas, a shipload of gold for twenty pounds." He sighed.

"This one will pay back, my lord. It will gild our palaces and towers with resplendent language. It will inspire generations as yet unborn. It will make the English tongue the glory of the world."

Burghley smiled again. "You have the gift yourself, young Sidney. No need to cry your wares so loudly. I hear you. I will see what I can do. You may leave it with me."

Sidney rose from his chair. He bowed. "I am grateful, my lord."

"Yes. Yes," said Burghley, undoing the ribbon on the roll of documents. "Just a word of advice to your friend, Mr. Spenser."

"My lord?"

"The coat. Advise him to lose that execrable garment. We cannot have our English Virgil traipsing about the streets looking like an Irish savage."

"My lord, I will," said Sidney, bowing again. Burghley was already immersed in the bundle of documents. He dipped his quill in the ink-pot and tapped it on the rim. He made a marginal note.

Burghley wrote to his friend Nicholas White, seneschal of Carlow and Wexford. White was an astute observer of all things Irish. He would be happy to oblige his lordship with regard to obtaining a post for the rising poet. 'This Mr. Spenser,' wrote Burghley, 'will be the glory of our age. His name shall live forever.

Take him with you on your progress. Make a soldier of him, if you can.'

Burghley smiled at the idea. White was an advocate of mild government and more English blood, yet when the occasion required it, he could be an effective leader of men. He filled the space vacated by the ludicrous Stukely and brought wise counsel to bear on the matter of Ireland.

Stukely had straggled to an inglorious end in an African desert. He had led the Pope astray. He had deluded the kings of Spain and Portugal and a host of disaffected Irish, but finally his folly had brought him to a sorry pass. What, wondered Burghley, would be the next hare-brained adventure from the South? Nicholas White, a steady man, would know what was stirring in the wind.

***

'There may thy Muse display her fluttering wing
And stretch herself at large from East to West;
Whether thou list in faire Eliza rest,
Or if thee please in bigger notes to sing,
Advance the worthy whom she loveth best,
That first the white bear to the stake did bring.'
E.S.

That second voyage was not a happy one. A skirmish with the savages saw Frobisher wounded in the buttock, by a bone-tipped arrow. The cursed thing was barbed and had to be cut out. How he had roared, and for a godly man, how he had seared the ears of those who attended him, with a fine array of oaths. The pain did nothing for his temper and acted as an ever-present reminder of the loss of his five men. It nagged at him when he walked the deck. It prevented him from sitting. He brooded.

His men had learned to plunder the traps set by the native people. They took birds and hares. They gathered eggs from the cliffs and from the foreshore. They learned to distinguish the eggs from the stones of the beach, marvelling sometimes at how well the nests were concealed in full view. They kept constant guard against the treachery of the natives, against their ruses to lure the ships' boats ashore; their disguises and attempts to appear as the missing Englishmen.

What he had to show for his efforts was two hundred tons of ore and the horn of the unicorn seal. Sometimes these creatures appeared in groups of twenty or more, holding up their long horns like a phalanx of pike men. Frobisher found one of the long, helical horns on the beach, six feet of wondrous ivory. It would be a gift to amaze Her Majesty.

Not a great return on her continued investment, he brooded. No Frobisher Strait or Queen Elizabeth Strait to the Southern Ocean. His name would not resound like that of Columbus or Magellan. If history were to record him it would be as a drudge, a labouring man who risked his life to make others wealthy.

It might mention that he brought more infidels to entertain the gawpers in the Bell Savage Inn. Conyers, the agile Cornishman, had taken another man, along with a woman and her small male child. They intrigued Frobisher by their impassivity. It was as if they had turned in upon themselves. They lodged together in a small space below decks, but no conversation passed between them. Frobisher had them brought on deck whenever the natives appeared on the shore or circled at a distance, in their little boats. He tried to signify that the three would be restored to their people if the five crewmen were produced. It was all in vain.

The great white bear swam past the ships on its daily expeditions. It swam majestically, pushing the water back with massive paws. It eyed the Englishmen with indifference.

What a trophy, thought Frobisher. What an event it would make in the pit at Paris Garden! The Earl of Leicester would pay dearly for the creature. His badge showed such a bear, muzzled and tethered, holding a ragged staff, a cropped and mutilated tree. History would record Frobisher as a showman, a provider of animals for the circus. He shifted his weight. His arse was paining him. Cold had got into the wound. Six inches of snow lay on the hatches. The shrouds were slippery with ice. He looked at his little fleet lying at anchor, faithful *Gabriel* and poor battered *Michael*.

He stood on the deck of *Ayde* his flag-ship. He was Admiral of the Northern Seas and Governor of the Arctic lands.

It was time to go home, away from this place of treacherous people and more treacherous tides, of hawsers severed by ever-moving ice and skies clouded by swirling myriads of birds.

He gave the order for a volley of ordnance, to let the people know that he had it in his power to destroy them all. He signalled to his captains to up-anchor and set a course for home.

On the twenty-ninth of August, in a rending North East gale, William Smith, master of *Gabriel,* was lost overboard. The boatswain held him for as long as he could, but William, a decent and loyal man, slipped through his fingers.

***

Nicholas White replied that he would be happy to welcome to Ireland his lordship's friend, Mr. Spresor, the illustrious poet.

***

With tattered sails and sprung planks, Frobisher's flag-ship anchored off Lundy. The anchor came home. She staggered, low in the water, into the haven of Padstow. Frobisher was of a mind to discharge the ore there and then, but he hesitated. Better to effect repairs, wait for word of his other ships and make another attempt to round Land's End, before winter set in. He spoke to the young man at the tiller.

"What do you think, Nicholas Conyers? You know these waters."

"Anything is possible, Captain," smiled Conyers. He was pleased to be back in familiar surroundings. "Our ship is more seaworthy than a millstone."

It was by no means an encouraging comparison.

"A millstone?"

"Aye, sir," replied the young man, seeing his captain's puzzlement. "Our saint, Saint Piran, sailed here from Ireland on a millstone."

Frobisher laughed, infected by the Cornishman's good spirits. "A saint on a millstone! More Popish superstition. Pray God we will do better then that. An Irishman sailing on a millstone." The image amused him hugely.

Conyers lowered his voice. "Another thing, Captain," he looked around, noting the curious loungers on the quayside. "This saint found a big black stone and made it his hearth- stone. Didn't the heat draw metal from the stone?"

Frobisher was immediately interested. Conyers had a way of drawing out his story for dramatic effect.

"Metal?"

"Aye, Captain, metal. This Kiran was the father of our Cornish tin mining."

"Ah, tin. I hope we can do better than tin."

Conyers appeared to be affronted.

"Tin has made many rich here in Cornwall and has put bread on the table for many a family."

Frobisher nodded. "I grant you that, young Nicholas. Kiran, you call him. I thought you called him Piran."

"Indeed. In Ireland they called him Kiran. A great saint, he was. His name changed when he crossed the sea." He shrugged.

"A sea-change. You have been to Ireland then?"

"I have Captain, but never set foot ashore. I hear it is a fearful country."

Frobisher nodded absently. "Indeed." He was thinking of the times that he had chased Spanish and French merchantmen, in his *navis praedatoria,* along that island's southern coast. Simpler times, in many ways.

Conyers was thinking of home and the days he had spent chasing rabbits on Bodmin Moor. He even thought of jumping ship, but he was no longer a village boy, tilling fields and excelling at the country sports. He was a hardened seaman, serving under a great captain, who nevertheless, deigned to speak to him and ask his advice. The sea had changed him also. He could not go back.

***

Sir Francis Walsingham called Michael Lok to account. Lok made the long journey upriver to Hampton Court. He had his figures ready. He marvelled at the great clock over the gate. He noted the time of high tide at London Bridge. He was confident.

Walsingham questioned him closely. He was impressed by the assays, despite his natural scepticism.

"Do you see any impediment to the work of your refiners, Doctors Burcott and em . . ." He looked at his notes "Kranych?"

"They are one and the same, Sir Francis. This is the learned Burchard Kranych of Germany." Walsingham sucked in his breath in irritation. He altered his notes.

"He works in collaboration with Dr. Jonas Schutz, also of Germany. Can we trust these foreigners? Can they keep a secret?" Walsingham's natural suspicion of all things foreign was evident. "You have another, an Italian. I have reason to believe that he was playing the alchemist, adding a little of his own gold in the hope of preferment. Do they work well together? Are they supervised?"

"Indeed they are, Sir Francis. My good friends, Dr. Dee and Sir William Wynter, keep a sharp eye on the proceedings. They mediate in all disputes."

"Disputes? What disputes?"

"You see, Schutz finds great difficulty with the smoke. His lungs are weak. He absents himself for days at a time."

"The smoke. I see. I hear that you yourself have taken up that filthy Spanish habit of tobacco. It will destroy your health."

Lok was taken aback. He smoked only in the privacy of his own home. It was true what they said about Walsingham. He had eyes everywhere.

"And what of the other, this Burkitt? Does he also complain of the smoke?" Walsingham was impatient of excuses, mere justifications for failure.

"No, Sir Francis," Lok assured him, "although he does suffer a little from gout, this Burchard."

Walsingham's voice was low and steady, concealing anger. "Tell me at least, that they agree on the methods and the findings. I care not about the spelling of names, so long as they do their job."

"There is some dispute, I grant, about the position of the bellows. Dr. Burchard has strong views."

"One moment," said Walsingham, making another note. He paused. "I strongly urge you to resolve any such disputes, or I will personally show them where I shall insert the bellows."

It sounded like a vulgar joke, something a clown might say in the street or on a wagon at a country fair; something to get a guffaw from villagers and raucous peasants. But Walsingham was no idle jester. Lok trembled inwardly, afraid of failure and the retribution that would certainly follow.

"Perhaps," said Walsingham after a long pause, letting his warning sink well in, "perhaps I should leave it to Captain Frobisher to encourage them to greater vigour. I understand that they go in mortal dread of his anger."

It was true. They trembled at his very name. They feared his return form the icy seas. Nothing would satisfy Frobisher other than the predicted forty pounds of gold to every ton. Impossible, but it must be done, either by science or alchemy.

"You must build bigger furnaces."

"I, Sir Francis?"

"Aye, aye, bigger and better furnaces, with a bellows for each of them if necessary."

"But the expense, Sir Francis. Who would pay?"

"Why, the Company of course. You see to it. Levy the shareholders."

Lok cleared his throat. "The charter, Sir Francis. There is the matter of the charter."

"Enlighten me." Walsingham sat back in his chair.

"The Company of Muscovy, as you know is a joint stock company and holder of a royal charter, whereas we of the Company of Cathay have not been granted such a favour. This, as you appreciate, exposes individuals such as myself, to liabilities."

Walsingham nodded. "I appreciate your predicament. I have raised the matter with Her Majesty and as I have high regard for you, I will take you into her thinking. The Company of Muscovy deals in furs, amber, mere trinkets, however profitable. They are no more than merchants."

Lok was silent. He had given many years to that company. It had made him prosperous.

Walsingham spoke earnestly. "You however, are charged with a greater responsibility. You have revealed new lands, new peoples. You have found riches. Nothing in this world moves without gold. It were irresponsible of Her Majesty to hand all this to a group of grasping shareholders. She has appointed a Royal Commission, comprising of some of the chief men of the Privy Council, including myself and Lord Burghley, to oversee this work. In due course you will submit your accounts to the Commission and all will be paid in full. You will not be the loser for this service to Her Majesty."

Lok closed his eyes. He wanted everything to disappear, the Secretary, the council room, the Company and its shareholders. He wanted to go home to his wife and family. He wanted to hear his unruly children running about the house. He wanted his dinner and a quiet pipe, by his own fireside. The Secretary was still speaking. Lok opened his eyes.

"Captain Frobisher has left Bristol with two of his ships. The other is making its way down the east coast. He brings more than two hundred tons of ore. He will be in the river within a few days."

Lok felt a great weight lifted from his heart. Two hundred tons at forty pounds of gold per ton. Eight thousand pounds of pure gold. God be praised. The King of Spain, he thought with a smile, would be coming to Her Majesty, cap in hand, for the favour of a loan.

The lord of the Americas, conqueror of all the naked Indians, might even come, cap in hand, to the Company of Cathay and its secretary, Michael Lok, for a few pence to tide him over. He laughed aloud.

Walsigham watched him shrewdly. "You are amused, sir?"

"No, not amused. I rejoice at your good news."

Walsingham nodded. "As do I," he murmured. "As do I."

Lok blinked. He saw in his mind's eye, the globe as one of his wife's celebrated plum puddings. Nutmeg and sugar sauce flowed down from the top. There was a sprig of holly at the North Pole. He had a long spoon in his hand. Captain Frobisher sat opposite him with a similar spoon. Somewhere around the Arctic

Circle, Captain Frobisher was excavating a mine. He extracted raisins and peel. He piled nuts and other fruits on his plate. He foraged for the little gold and silver charms hidden within. He smiled in delight at this treasure. Lok could smell the delicious odour of spices and strong wine. Christmas had come early to Michael Lok.

Walsingham was concluding the interview.

"And payment for the crews. Christmas is near. I leave everything in your capable hands, Michael Lok. I have every faith in you."

Michael Lok was not listening. He nodded assent to everything. Eight thousand pounds of pure gold, wafting its way almost to his very doorstep. He was anxious to be gone, to flit downriver to Morttake, to share the good news with his friend John Dee. He realised that he was hungry.

Walsingham did not invite him to dinner. He could see that Lok was anxious to be about his business. Commendable. He dismissed the hungry man. He knew that pipe smokers fidgeted like that; that they fled from company in unpredictable ways. With a bleak smile he wondered if the threat of the bellows had propelled him on his way. He breathed deeply and began to review his notes. Her Majesty would find all this very enlightening.

Chapter Eleven

As the wherry approached the bridge, Frobisher looked up. There was something different about the outline. He frowned. He gripped the gunwale in some alarm. He was never at ease in a small craft. He liked to walk about. The ebb was carrying them at great speed towards the centre arch. He heard the rush of the cascade. John Dee, sitting on the after thwart, giggled with excitement. It was forty years since he had shot the bridge. There was a saint to look out for him on that occasion. Saints were scarce enough in these latter days. The watermen backed water, checking their progress. They worked in unison, waiting their chance. Michael Lok swallowed hard. He would have preferred to walk.

"Are you not swimmers, gentlemen?" John Dee was in great good humour. He was like a schoolboy on an unexpected jaunt.

Michael Lok shook his head. Frobisher stared grimly ahead. He had the mariner's contempt for swimming. It merely postponed the inevitable, prolonged the agony. If the Fates decreed that you must drown, better to get on with it.

"No, I am not," he replied curtly. He did not wish to drown, if only to deprive the onlookers of their moment of excitement. He realised what had changed. The heads had moved. No longer did they adorn the summit of the drawbridge tower. In fact, the tower itself was lower, stunted, festooned in rickety scaffolding.

He looked about. There they were, black beads on pins, on top of the southern tower, the gateway to Kent and Dover. What was afoot? Nothing remains the same.

The current caught them. The oarsmen pulled mightily. The wherry slid down the watery slope. The bridge flashed past. The long prow dipped for a moment, in the turmoil on the downstream side, then rose triumphantly. The watermen pulled again. The workmen on the tower, the loungers on the bridge and housewives at the windows of the narrow houses, waved and cheered. Some few recognised the great explorer, Captain Frobisher. What a thrill it was to have seen him, supreme in his element, master as always, of the situation.

"I shall send you my book on the art of swimming." Dee was chatting on. Whatever about swimming, reading was an even less attractive prospect for Frobisher.

"Keep it," he snapped, annoyed that he might have betrayed fear. He changed tack. "What work is this on the bridge?"

The watermen were raising a short mast and spar with a simple sail, a lateen, noted Frobisher. The men fumbled, nervous under the scrutiny of the great sea captain.

"It is to be a house, good sir, a palace you might say," said one of the men. He tightened the stays and the breeze filled the sail. "There will be none such in the world, they say. It is to be made in the Low-Countries and shipped over in pieces. They say that it will fit together without nails, like a good chair." He prattled on. "There will be sundials and weather vanes. It will be a sight to behold."

Frobisher took the sheet from the waterman. He liked the tug of the sail. He braced himself. It would be a pleasant run down to Greenwich and thence to Dartford to put the fear of God into the men working on the construction of new furnaces.

"You are correct, my good friend," said John Dee. "Its golden towers will shine over the entire city. In fact I have supplied a motto for the sun-dials."

"A motto?" Michael Lok relaxed. He was beginning to enjoy the outing.

"Time and tide stay for no man." It was succinct and apposite, given what they had just accomplished and the urgency of their business.

"It gives me an idea." Frobisher was thinking aloud, watching how the wind plucked at the sail. "Port a little," he said to the waterman on the sweep oar. The sail steadied. Frobisher smiled.

"A house in sections. For our third voyage. We can build winter quarters in the Arctic, our first settlement."

He had great plans for his next voyage, a treasure fleet, a colony of miners and soldiers, a clergyman to preach to the workers and even to the infidels.

"How does the infant?" he asked, emerging from his train of thought.

The heathen man and woman were a disappointment. They both died shortly after coming ashore, but the child, survived. He had left it in the care of John Dee. Dee was interested to find out what language the child would speak. Could it be raised to become a Christian, even an Englishman or would it revert to the condition of a wild creature, like its kinsmen? A wet-nurse had been obtained and John Dee went daily to observe his little Caliban. The creature was as interesting as any beetle or tadpole. He quite liked the idea of educating this odd little fellow. He thought that perhaps he should take a second wife.

Michael Lok sat in silence, turning figures over and over in his head. One hundred men and vittle for an entire winter. Fourteen or fifteen ships. He prayed that the ores, the familiar black and the newly imported red, would yield a steady stream of gold from the Dartford furnaces, irrespective of where the bellows might be.

Frobisher was humming, enjoying his day out. The ebb carried them smoothly along. The sail fluttered. He checked it again, as he might govern the mouth of a lively steed.

"Time and tide," he mused aloud. "I like it. Time and tide stay for no man."

***

It was an irresistible fleet, fifteen of sail, that rounded Cape Clear in June of the following year, the year of grace, 1578. It took with

it the Queen's good wishes for a successful voyage and a new
settlement of Englishmen in that gold-rich region. God Himself,
was with them, in their watchword: 'Before the World was God'
and in their answer: 'After God came Christ, His Son.'

The ships spoke to one another by day with flags and
pennants, by night and in time of fog, by drum and trumpet. The
orders were clear: no swearing, duelling or drawing of weapons;
no dice or filthy communication between the men; prayer twice a
day; four hour watches. A man of God, reverend Mr. Wolfall, left
wife and family, in order to take care of the souls of the men and
bring the news of salvation to the heathens.

Nothing could go wrong, except for storms, fog and, after
Greenland, ice, floes and bergs of driving ice to try men's souls.
Hour after hour they fended off the ice. They heard the timbers
groaning. Oaken knees popped and shattered. The barque *Dennis*
folded like a book and sank in the time that a man might tell one
hundred. The crew escaped in boats and onto the ice. God's grace
ensured that all were saved. However, God neglected to save the
sections of the winter house that had been stowed aboard *Dennis*.
The cold and bedraggled survivors contemplated a winter in
dwellings no better than the squalid burrows and caves of the
despised heathens.

By mid-Summer they raised the mouth of Frobisher's Bay, but
a savage tide carried them south, despite all their efforts. A new
land came up to larboard. It seemed a fair land with abundant
game and wild-fowl. The native people came forward to trade
furs and dried meat. Frobisher was wary. He kept his distance. A
hideous storm scattered the fleet, with some ships standing out to
the open sea and others taking temporary refuge in the lee of the
moving icebergs. The storm relented, with no loss of life or ships.
They battered their way north and came together towards the end
of July, near the site of the gold workings in Frobisher's Bay.

There was no time to lose. The miners worked long shifts in
the endless daylight. Armed soldiers stood guard against attack.
Some rags of English clothing found in an abandoned camp,
finally persuaded Frobisher that his five men were gone forever.

The memory of the Queen's welcome at Windsor, warmed
him. There would be a knighthood and rich rewards. The Earl of

Leicester had been especially gracious. He questioned Frobisher closely and invited him to dine at his house in The Strand. He made him a proposition, two hundred pounds for the great, white bear. Two hundred pounds, the extra little golden charm inside the pudding.

Also at that table there was an arrogant young lawyer and captain of horse, Walter Raleigh. Frobisher recognised a kindred spirit. Raleigh spoke of the Americas and a city of gold. He spoke of Irish rebels and how they must be curbed. He spoke of a fleet to settle Newfoundland. The Earl was hospitable. He let the young man talk. He consulted the other guest about Ireland. Frobisher remembered him vaguely, a young poet in search of a theme. Some of the poet's supercilious nature had changed.

He had hardened into a man of strong opinions. Frobisher surmised that he had seen something of the world. Ireland, the poet insisted, was England's Achilles heel. With climate, landscape and primitive society, it was a breeding ground for treason. Add to that the influence of Rome and Ireland became a powder cask ready for the fuse.

The Earl nodded. He was more interested in the white bear.

"I could very likely obtain one from the Muscovy traders, but I desire a bear from your new and fabled land, this land of wondrous creatures and fearsome cannibals. Two hundred pounds, Captain Frobisher, free-on-quay at Deptford."

The cage was ready, secured to the deck of *Ayde*. He relished the thought of getting to know the creature, of feeding it from his hand. It would withstand the hardships of a voyage better than the wretched calibans of the previous years. The English winter would be kind to it. Frobisher mused that he was by nature a showman. He liked to impress. He loved the applause of the crowd. He would up-stage the ranting players of the theatres with his bear. The groundlings would forsake the dreary tragedies and garrulous comedies of the stage and flock to see true drama in the bear-pit.

He assembled his hunting party of twenty men armed with pikes and in case of emergency, firearms. They carried nets and chains. They set out with two ships' dogs, a merry band embarked on a day's sport.

They found their quarry on a long shingle beach, engaged in devouring the carcase of a seal. They circled warily with pikes and nets at the ready. The bear continued with its meal. It looked about, seeming to realise that the men intended harm. It tossed its head. Its muzzle was stained with blood, belying its amiable expression.

The men realised the enormity of the task. They noted the size of the paws and the claws as big as grappling hooks. They hung back. Frobisher urged them on. They were not so merry now.

The bear charged. The circle of men bulged at one point, but it did not break. One man slipped on the wet stones. The bear opened a terrible gash on his thigh. The man held his pike in front of him as he lay. The point pierced the animal's breast. It pulled back and the pike fell from the wound. Blood stained the white fur. A weighted net fell over the beast's head and body. It threshed and bellowed. Men closed in to save their fallen companion. They thrust and jabbed.

The bear rent the net and lunged at his tormentors.

"Careful," shouted Frobisher. "I want him alive."

But the men could not hear him. Fear and fury took hold of their senses. They lunged and stabbed. Blood spouted from many wounds. The animal broke through the circle, casting men aside like so many flies. It lumbered away, seeking higher ground. It was not difficult to track it. It stumbled on bloody paws, until it came to an area covered in snow and there it fell.

Frobisher came panting to where the men stood around the dying animal. They were looking sheepishly at one another. Several clutched at fresh wounds. Their captain looked, crestfallen, as his investment expired before his eyes. He gestured for a musket and put the muzzle close to the animal's forehead. The bear's eyes were open. It looked up at the captain. It sighed.

Frobisher hesitated. He fired. The bear jerked in a final convulsion. The report echoed among the rocks, with a terrible finality. Frobisher's shoulders sagged. He handed the musket back.

"I will take no more bears," he said softly, to nobody in particular. He set off down the slope following the scarlet trail through the trampled snow. A deep melancholy came over him. He returned to his ship and gave orders for the cage to be dismantled. He went below and wrote up his journal. The Muscovy traders could have the earl's money and all the applause.

The bear made good eating, although many found the liver not to their taste. It lay heavy in the belly, requiring numerous visits to the place below high-water decreed for easement.

The skin, pierced by many pikes, was left to the skuas and the quick, darting foxes. It was a pity, in such a cold place, to discard such a pelt.

The soldiers built the walls of a dry-stone house, but lacked the timber for a roof. They planted peas and corn, thinking to see how they would fare the following year. They thought of the future. Mr. Wolfall's Communion service was the first of the Reformed Faith on the North American continent. He had no doubt that, little by little, the faith would creep forward, by means of the native people, until it drove the Popish practices of the Spaniards back into the sea. He thought that he would bring his family on the next voyage and win people to God by the example of a Christian household. He would build a church in the wilderness, a church with a bell and a steeple. He had heard that the country people loved music and were fascinated by the sound of bells. He gave thanks that he had been given the opportunity to serve.

The ships sat worryingly low in the water. It was difficult to refuse another bucket of ore, another hundredweight, another ton. Frobisher reasoned that as they were heading south, it would make sense to jettison some of the sea-coal in the holds, keeping just enough for cooking. The rest he put ashore for use by the colony in future years. This disclosed a dilemma. The iron hoops on the beer barrels had rusted, through contact with the coal. The staves were sprung. The beer had leaked down into the bilges. Bad as the beer had been, it was better than water. They looked at the prospect of a long and dangerous voyage, with nothing but rainwater to ease the thirst. The cooper was set to work, cobbling together enough barrels to hold water from ice and snow. There could never be enough.

The captains met to agree articles for the return voyage. All ships were to keep close to the Admiral, if possible. If threatened by an enemy, all maps, cards and journals were to be thrown overboard, in order to protect the secret of the mines. Most importantly, all shovels, crow-bars, pickaxes, spades and tools of any kind, the property of the worshipful Company, should be collected, or accounted for and delivered into the keeping of Michael Lok. Sailors must turn out their pockets and hand over, even the smallest pebble to their captains. Everything was water-tight, except for the heavily laden ships.

On the last day of August they staggered away from Frobisher's Bay. They could see the native people rising from the rocks and going to investigate the work of the strange white men with the big eyebrows. Their little boats appeared from nowhere, the low sun glinting on the insect-wing paddles.

The Arctic sent them a farewell storm, a parting shot, battering the fleet and scattering it to all points of the compass- card. Ice closed the door behind them. They limped southwards, carrying their treasure home, to lay it at the feet of their great Queen, as a cat might bring the gift of a mouse to its master, always in the hope of reward.

Chapter Twelve

There was always smoke rising somewhere in the distance, evidence of Black Tom's remorseless drive against the rebels. As the light faded, the hills of Iveragh were dotted with fires. *An Tiarna Dubh*, the people called him, with a shudder, the Black Lord.

Nicholas White, Burghley's sporadic correspondent, was glad that he was on the other side of the water, strolling on Inch Strand, with the low tide making a mirror of the sand. The declining sun dazzled his eyes. He was sickened to his stomach by the relentless savagery of the Crown forces. The splendour of the scene did nothing to raise his spirits, nor did the manners of the two men who accompanied him, William Pelham, the Lord Justice of Ireland and the other, Mr Spresor, Spenser, whatever he called himself. Nicholas always confused the names. Pelham was a soldier, a brawler, a military engineer by his own say-so. Spenser was present in his capacity as secretary to the newly arrived Lord Deputy, Arthur Grey, the Fourteenth Lord Grey de Wilton.

Nicholas had some inkling as to why there was bad blood between Grey and the pugnacious Pelham. It was said that Grey still harboured a grudge against Pelham for a wound received at the siege of Leith, many years previously. He was not slow to say that Pelham's inept siege-works had exposed him to enemy fire.

Pelham, for his part, took grim satisfaction at the mauling that Grey had taken at the hands of the O Byrnes of Wicklow soon after his arrival in Ireland.

For his own part, Nicholas had old grudges to settle against Fiach MacHugh OByrne. As seneschal of Wexford and Carlow, he had suffered from the lightning raids of the Wicklow men. He deplored rebellion and disloyalty, but every day he saw how the Crown forces stoked the fires of hatred. He believed in his heart that there was a better way. The Irish always said 'It will be worse before it gets better.' There was no evidence of things getting better.

The FitzGerald lords had raised their people, for the second time in a decade, to overthrow English rule and reinstate the Catholic faith, James FitzGerald, the fanatic, and his cousin, the slippery Earl of Desmond. The net result was devastation, a wasteland, heads on pikes, women and children violated, crops destroyed and towns left to the wolves. There was a young man with the army, Walter Raleigh. Nicholas knew him by sight, a half-brother to Sir Humphrey Gilbert. Gilbert, one of fifteen brothers, had fought his corner from childhood. In the previous rebellion, it was Gilbert's practice to make an avenue to his tent with the daily cull of heads. Nothing so cowed a man as the sight of the heads of his kinsmen, his neighbours, his wife and even his infants, laid out in two neat rows, as a gardener might set out a path of decorative stones. It was a stratagem that always worked, although surrender to Gilbert was no guarantee of safety. This Raleigh had the look of his older brother.

Nicholas poked at the wet sand with the toe of his boot. He would have liked to go barefoot but it would not have been dignified. He stooped, picked up a cockle and placed it in a basket. The others walked about in silence. That was a relief. The poet did not realise the risk he was running in crossing Pelham. The hunt for cockles had brought a lull to their discussions. They stooped and picked, with murmurs of satisfaction. Along the beach they could see other figures doing likewise. The army was camped near the road but the supply wagons had not yet come up. Every man had to shift for himself for an evening meal. The men were probing the wet sand with pikes and halberds. Nicholas relied on his great toe. The peacefulness of the scene made him sad. He looked forward to his meal of cockles, the essential taste of the sea, the inevitable grit. He would have liked some oysters or even mussels, but there were none to be had. Tomorrow they would move out to the stronghold at Dingle and through the blackened cornfields of Corcaguiney, to the fort at Saint Marywick. He wanted to see the spot at which the rebel, James FitzGerald had raised the holy flag, as the people called it. James had relied on the absurd Stukely, a by-word for instability, but Stukely was no more. James's headless body hung on a gallows in Kilmallock, a target for musketry.

It could be a theme for tragedy, if they were not all so stupid. Nicholas felt no sympathy for men whose grandiose dreams brought nothing but grief. It could be a theme for a ballad, if Mr. Spresor could draw his mind away from shepherds and their infernal piping. He shared something of Burghley's distaste for the poets.

Spenser was arguing again. He had drawn a map in the wet sand. He stood with a cane in his hand, pointing like a schoolmaster. Pelham stood looking down at the map. He had his hands on his hips and his head back. He was breathing loudly, like a restive horse.

It was a passable map of Ireland, Nicholas admitted. The poet had some grasp of the subject. He was speaking as a strategist.

"No, Sir William, with respect, you are mistaken."

Pelham snorted. This insignificant clerk was lecturing him, one of the highest in the land, a farmer's dog barking at a mighty stallion.

"Lord Grey had no option but to strike at O Byrne."

He jabbed his cane at Wicklow. "From here O Byrne threatens Dublin." He jabbed again. "He threatens all the towns of south Leinster." He drew lines radiating out from the mountain stronghold. He put the cane behind his back, gripping it in both hands. He stood with legs apart, awaiting Pelham's reply.

Nicholas waited for the explosion. There was some merit in what the poet had pointed out, but Pelham was not a man to be lectured. Indeed he would sometimes take a wrong course, because of a personal dislike or antipathy towards the speaker.

"Indeed," said Pelham softly, rubbing his chin.

Spenser was encouraged to expand his theme. He drew again, a sketchy England and beyond that, Spain and France. His map took him into the shallows of the now advancing tide.

Nicholas looked at Pelham. The Lord Justice raised his eyebrows with just the ghost of a smile. Spenser was splashing through the shallows, still talking, anxious to drive home his point before the sea could drown his grand strategy.

"So, just as Wicklow is the Achilles-heel of Ireland, so is Ireland the weak point for England's safety."

He drew some lines suggesting great fleets advancing from Spain and France. "Ireland must be pacified, not just for its own good, but for the safety of England."

He looked from one to the other. "That's all," he declared, waving his cane. "It is a matter of life and death." He shrugged. They made no comment.

"Gentlemen," said Nicholas, "I shall wash these and have them raw. That way I shall taste the sea." He laughed. "They will look at me, these little yellow cockscombs and I will bite off their heads."

"Little yellow cockscombs, indeed," mused Pelham, looking at nobody in particular. He waded into the water and swilled the sand from his catch. He took out his knife and prised open a big, fat cockle. He regarded the creature in its jester's hat. A pert little cap. "I am sorry, my friend, but my need is greater than yours."

He bit the meat from the shell and chewed with relish. The sand crunched between his strong white teeth.

Spenser looked into his basket. He reckoned that he might trade them for some bread and cheese.

Across the water the fires glowed in the gathering dusk, stars against the darkness of the mountains, casting their reflections on the glassy waters of the bay. There was a hint of smoke on the breeze.

***

The wagons came up early in the morning, with a great drove of cattle. The countryside was stripped of anything that might sustain the rebels. It seemed that the vacillating Earl had broken cover and declared his hand.

Nicholas pondered. Was it vainglory or pure madness? Did the Earl look upon his wretched people, scrabbling for cress in stagnant pools, with the green stain of grass on their lips, their infants no more than a rickle of bones and did he think them a match for the Lord Deputy with his three thousand veterans? Nicholas could make no sense of it.

He knew that the Earl stood on his dignity. The Earl was proud of his lineage, four centuries of FitzGerald lords in Desmond. He numbered old English and native Irish among his vassals, but his vassals did not trust him. In all the wars and disputes, he had a name for congratulating the victor and abandoning the vanquished to his fate. He demanded loyalty but gave precious little. He left it to his courageous and loyal wife to extricate him by her gentle diplomacy, even by abasing herself, from many a predicament. This time however, she had come too late, an hour too late. The Black Lord refused Fitzgerald's oaths of fealty to the Queen. The Earl of Desmond was proclaimed a traitor. There was a price on his head.

Nicholas brought up to date his inventory of castles still in the Earl's possession. They were few in number. Who needed castles anyway in a country of mountains, forests and bogs? What fool would lock himself in a castle in an age of artillery?

There was a note among his papers, from Sir William Pelham. It was an angry note. He took great offence at the tone adopted by the Lord Deputy's secretary, Mr. Spenser, a jackanapes mimicking the behaviour of a gentleman, a dinner table warrior, a paper strategist, who had never heard a cannon fired in anger. He had gone, he wrote, to Dublin to tell Lord Grey de Wilton precisely what he could do with his sword of state. Her Majesty, he added, had employment for men of experience and parts, in the Low Countries. He would serve no longer in a country fit only for mastiffs and thieves. Nicholas sighed. Why mastiffs? He put the note aside. Ireland was a country that drove its rulers to choler and distraction. Mastiffs were bred to pull down a bear at the stake. The word described his troops to perfection. Ah! things would get worse before they got better.

Nicholas made an excursion through the pass from Dingle to Saint Marywick, in the company of some officers and the opinionated poet. He wanted to see the fort on the cliff, where the rebellion had begun. *Dún an Óir*, the Irish called it, the Fort of Gold, some ancient story of fairy treasure. The country reeked of age and legends.

Their guide told them of the saint who had left his mountain, 'that one over there', to build a boat of skins and sail to a blessed land far to the West, near the edge of the world. There had been saints everywhere.' They saw their curious dwellings, bee-hives of stone where holy men, steeped in superstition, sent up a column of prayer to Heaven both night and day. It availed them nothing. The holy men were wiped away.

The clouds boiled over the saint's mountain. Light and shade flitted over the waters of the broad bay, the bland and inviting strand, the headlands, sharp as axe heads. Huge waves hurled themselves at the sentry cliffs, draping them in veils of white. Any man standing on one of those cliff-tops would have been swept away. It was a safe and tranquil haven, but to get there was to run a perilous gauntlet.

The carcase of a ship, lay aslant on the strand. Its spars and gear were stripped away. Its planks and strakes had been plundered. Light shone through its gaunt and weedy ribs.

"What ship is that?" asked Spenser of the guide.

The man laughed. "That is one of Captain Furbusher's ships. *Emmanuel of Bridgewater*. Loaded with gold, she was. I mind the night she came ashore, God help her." He liked to talk. "We took the poor wretches to Dingle and put them on board ship for Dublin. Captain Newton was the master. He was in a terrible state. He kept babbling about the gold and the voyage through the ice. Lost half his crew, he did, to sickness."

Spenser nodded. "It was a dreadful voyage with a most unhappy outcome."

"I think," continued the guide, "he was most afeard of Captain Furbusher."

"Frobisher," said Spenser.

"Aye, Furbusher. We knew him in the old days. By rights they say, he should have hung for a pirate. He often put into Dingle.

A fierce man out." He recovered the thread of his yarn. "Anyway, this Captain Newton kept asking us to guard the gold. 'Guard the gold,' he kept saying 'or Furbusher will have my life.' He was never paid for his ship either. I heard that his sailors were never paid for their toil."

They dismounted and began to walk, leading their horses, up the long scarp to the Fort of Gold.

"It is funny that she should run aground here," remarked the guide. It was a strange coincidence indeed. "I have some of the gold." The guide laughed. "Any fool could see at a glance, that it was no gold. We took it for sea-coal, but divil a spark could we get out of it." He laughed again. "Fools' gold."

Nicholas was intrigued by the story. He had heard talk of the expedition to loot the treasures of the Arctic. Lord Burghley had mentioned it in correspondence. Burghley knew the ins and outs of the business, the alchemists and refiners who had fallen out over it. He knew of Her Majesty's displeasure at losing her investment and the terrible rows between Frobisher and his erstwhile friend, Michael Lok. He was informed by Walsingham that the two German mountebanks, Jonas and Burcote, Burkitt, some foreign name, had expired from fumes and gout. The whole affair was a shambles.

Michael Lok had tripped over piles of tools in his private rooms, until such time as he lost his house to creditors and was forced to throw himself, his wife and fifteen hungry children on the charity of relatives. Even from the Fleet Prison, he kept up a stream of correspondence, demanding more than the three pounds in every hundred awarded to him by the Commissioners. A shambles! Yet Frobisher resumed service with Admiral Wynter. He was strangely, still a public hero.

They examined the fort. It was a poor excuse for a stronghold. Perhaps in times gone by, some local chieftain found it sufficient to pen up a few cows at night, safe from wolves and envious neighbours, but it would not serve for long against artillery. The breastwork, here and there augmented by black stones from the wreck, stretched out onto a narrow blade of rock, so narrow that a man could lose his footing. There were some small burrows dug into the rock, poor shelter from the rain and no shelter at all from sea-borne ordnance. It was here that James FitzGerald had raised the Papal flag and strained his eyes seawards in expectation of Stukely's fleet. But Stukely's mouth was stopped with sand and Moorish heathens flaunted his standards in derision.

"I think we may say, with some certainty, Mr. Spenser, that this chapter is now closed." It was fitting, thought Nicholas, that this crumbling earthwork, degraded by time and by the relentless sea, should be the footnote to his invoice of FitzGerald castles on the westernmost tip of Ireland.

But Spenser was entranced by the beauty of the scene. He gazed at the sailing clouds, the changing colours of the sea as the shadows drifted across, at the headlands, momentarily veiled like brides and then unveiling. The poet stirred inside him, the clerk, the functionary, silenced for the moment. It is a faerie land, he thought, a place where one might find a portal to a magical realm. He imagined that he could hear the voices of ancient Druids, the chanting of holy monks, the poets singing the praises of a great faerie queen. That was it! *The Faerie Queene,* his theme. The wind was free of the taint of war. It blew unhindered from the Blessed Islands of the West.

"By the time we return to our rendezvous with Black Tom," said Nicholas, breaking into his reverie, "the Earl will no doubt be in chains. His lands will be confiscated. There will be rich pickings for the vultures. You might even get a castle or two for your services."

It was a rude awakening, yet shreds of his dream stayed with him. A castle of gold and silver. Where had he seen that? He could be happy there, free of travelling, united with his wife and family. There he could write his vision of a faerie kingdom and its great queen and earn his just reward.

"Stick close to Lord Grey," said Nicholas. He winked. "The game is on the hazard." He nudged Spenser in the ribs. "Play your cards right. It were better that the country be settled by poets than mastiffs." He chuckled at some private joke.

Spenser frowned. He was obviously missing something. The import of the words nonetheless, was clear. The poet receded. The calculating man of affairs took his place. He must look about, keep his eyes open; keep his cards close and he might yet get his castle of gold, his *Dún an Óir.*

Chapter Thirteen

Don Sebastiano di San Giuseppi saw the whole venture in simple terms. He landed at Saint Marywick, in late summer of 1580, with a strong and compact force, furnished with munitions and supplies for a winter campaign, to drive the English armies from all of Munster. The Earl of Desmond's task was to join him with his risen people. Papal arms and Papal money would dislodge the heretic English from Ireland for all time. The kings of Spain and Portugal were willing to associate themselves with the business. The Pope's son would be generous to those who set him on the throne of Ireland. From the Northern Isles to the Pillars of Hercules there would be rejoicing at the restoration of the true faith. The Pope had not yet had time to draw up a definitive agreement of terms, but who would doubt the word of the Holy Father?

Don Sebastiano landed his force with high hopes, eight hundred men with supplies for five thousand. He was surprised to find English forces in the area. He was not to know that Lord Grey's officers had surveyed the land only a few weeks previously, or that a poet had dreamed his dreams on that rocky headland in the last golden days of summer, just before the topmasts had begun to peep above the horizon. Already he was bottled up in the bay by the prompt action of an English fleet. His best option was to strengthen the fort on the hill and await the arrival of the Earl with his rebel Irish army.

He reckoned without Black Tom who had choked off the entire peninsula at the Eastern end. Fatally he reckoned without Arthur, Lord Grey de Wilton, stung by his recent reverses in Wicklow and thirsting for a signal victory. It was September. The nights were drawing in. The gales of the Equinox cast some of his vessels onto the rocks. Others were taken by the insolent English forces that had come up to pen him in. The men were restive. They played at dice. They quarrelled. They muttered about mutiny. They contemplated selling their services to the English lord. They were practical men who fought for pay, not loyalty. All day they watched the English fleet on station beyond the mouth of the bay, beyond the three peaks, those languid, sleeping, Three Sisters. They strained their eyes, watching for the advancing Irish army. Each day the Irish priest said Mass. It gave them comfort to know that God favoured them against the heretics. They scowled at the Irish gentleman and observed his woman as she moved about the camp. They brooded. They saw great flocks of geese slanting in from the sea to feed in the marshy fields below.

September slid into October. Rain lashed the tents. Firewood became scarce. The water in the little pond was vile. The first frost appeared, riming the stones of the rampart. Wine was rationed. Surely the Earl must come soon with cattle and corn, to lift the blockade and lead them on to victory. The Atlantic winds battered at their shelters. They hunched in cold and wet and waited for deliverance.

Don Sebastiano consulted his officers. He favoured marching out bravely and putting their strength to the test. Some suggested a lightning march to Dingle, seize what ships they could and leave this accursed country behind them. The Irishman, Plunkett, knowledgeable in the ways of his people, favoured a march to the East to link up with the Earl. The handful of Irish allies in the fort, listening to the discussion, knew that they were already doomed.

***

The decision was taken out of their hands. They heard the drums of a mighty army massing on the long scarp below them. They saw the English fleet coming into the bay. They observed great guns being swung ashore. They knew that hell was about to open its jaws to devour them.

Lord Grey was in expansive mood. He looked around the table. They were an impressive group, experienced and wise, like Sir William Wynter, Admiral and latterly Commissioner for smelting, although that venture had not proved to be his finest hour. There sat Richard Bingham, a man of energy and strength, obviously capable of great accomplishments. There were young men eager for glory, Ned Denny, his eager young cousin, Walter Raleigh, Captain Mackworth, brave men, born of good families, connected to the highest in the realm. He was confident that they would do well in the action to come. It was Ned who had first complained that service in Ireland was akin to that demanded of mastiffs. He lamented that any glory gained in Ireland, would be obscured in the fog and mildewed by the rain of that miserable place. It was Bingham who always argued that the best way to conquer Ireland was to use Irish mercenaries. Money well invested.

"I can assure you, young Ned," Grey called across the table, "that any glory you gain at the Fort of Gold, will be trumpeted throughout all of Europe. Am I not correct, Captain Frobisher?"

Frobisher had come ashore reluctantly. The affair of the gold was still a sore point between himself and Admiral Wynter. The wreck of *Emmanuel of Bridgewater* lay on the beach, a reproach to him every time he looked at it, a skeleton at the feast. He wished that Captain Newton might have had the decency to come ashore anywhere else along that jagged coast. He knew that Grey, for all his affability, was needling him, sharing a joke with the supercilious young men. He scowled and shrugged, impatient to begin the cannonade. His orders were to come in close and lob mortar-bombs right into the fort. He was to bring fire to bear on the extension of the parapet that ran along the sliver of rock and blast the cowering defenders from their burrows. That was his kind of work. He had no time for the banter of young dandies, too far advanced in their cups.

Grey gave a toast to success. He hailed his secretary, the poet, calling for a few lines to spur his young men on.

"Mr. Spenser is the man of words. He will set our spirits aflame."

Spenser raised his cup in reply. He was sparing in drink, not sure of his standing among the privileged young officers.

"My lord," he demurred, "I am a studious and retiring soul. My verse is the product of long hours of contemplation. I cannot rhyme extempore. Would you have me celebrate your impending triumph in maimed and limping metre?"

They laughed and thumped their cups on the table, calling for a rhyme. Spenser looked about. He coughed.

"This is a piece, then, as yet unfinished, a battle between virtue and evil." He smiled modestly. He shrugged, offering it for what it was worth. "Sir Satyrane and a proud Saracen knight. Ahem!

'Therewith they 'gan, both furious and fell
To thunder blows and fiercely to assail;
Each other, bent his enemy to quell,
That with their force they pierced both plate and mail, And
made wide furrows in their fleshes frail,
That it might pity any living eye.
Large floods of blood adown their sides did rail,
But floods of blood could not them satisfy,
But hungered after death: both chose to win or die.'" E.S.

He paused and looked around. There was silence. The men looked from one to another. Raleigh began to tap the table with the fingers of his left hand: tap, tap, tap, then with the cup in his right: knock, knock, knock, until the others joined in, with a rattling fusillade of applause. Spenser felt his face reddening at the unaccustomed attention. Lord Grey raised a hand for silence.

"Gentlemen," he began, inclining his head to Spenser, "I would wish for more but it is late. Our friend has caught, in a few lines, the very essence of our trade. I would fain know the outcome of this dire conflict, but we must wait. I know that it will be a great work. Our task tomorrow will be bloody, but we have the consolation of knowing that, like Mr. Spenser's knight, we fight on the side of virtue and loyalty against treason and foul rebellion. Let our swords be keen and our hearts brave."

He looked around approvingly. They were ready. They toasted the Queen, holding their cups on high. They cheered.

"We will carry our trench to within yards of their sorry rampart. Our guns will destroy theirs. We will take them by assault within three or four days."

"And what then, my lord?" queried Raleigh.

"I shall treat them according to the laws of war. Of course if there be any rebels in their number, I shall have to make an example of them."

"And the others, my lord?" Raleigh persisted.

"We shall see," replied Grey. "Now let us finish our dinner and drink to success."

There was one among them, John Cheke, whom Spenser remembered from university. He remembered him as a hasty and ambitious fellow, but no great student. He recalled him at the dinner table, heated and rancorous in dispute, fond of his ale. The officers rose and stretched. There was work to be done in the morning. Spenser found John Cheke standing at his shoulder.

"You have come far, Spenser," remarked Cheke. It was more a challenge than a renewal of old acquaintance. Spenser acknowledged him with a curt bow.

"Still scribbling, I see." Cheke had that sardonic smile that Spenser recalled so well, the smile that masks the hostility of the dull-witted when faced with a superior mind.

"Be a good fellow," said Cheke, clapping him on the shoulder, "and fetch me another cup of wine."

Spenser flushed again, this time with anger.

"You mistake me, sir. I am secretary to Lord Grey."

"Of course. Of course. My apologies, sir," said Cheke, still smiling. "You have indeed come a long way."

He turned his back, leaving Spenser seething. He had forgotten how much he had disliked Cheke. A word, a look, an arched eyebrow can bring back the hurt and the hatreds of youth, just as a perfume or a fragment of song can transport us back to some sunny childhood day, some love, some escapade. It was something to ponder.

***

All that long night the pioneers continued their work, carrying their trench forward to within three hundred paces of the fort. They planted two culverin opposite the Italian guns. In the morning the culverin opened fire on the enemy positions. Ships in the bay, came close inshore, manouevering under the cliff to get under the cannon fire from the fort. Nevertheless, several had their topmasts carried away. Men on deck and in the rigging, fell victim to musket and arquebus fire. Frobisher sent his bombs into the fort and onto the ridge, as a skilled tennis-player lobs the ball onto the penthouse roof. With mortars mounted on both larboard and starboard bows, he kept on the move, coming within range and falling off, to devastating effect.

The Popish forces replied very gallantly, but by mid- morning, their two best guns had been destroyed. They continued their musket fire from the parapet, keeping the English heads down. The parapet showed signs of damage. A cold drizzle began, continuing until darkness.

Ned Denny and his company took the watch. The pioneers began again, cutting through heavy clay, occasionally encountering rock. They moved forward at an angle, changing direction, as a ship tacks against the wind. Closer and closer they came to the rampart, despite frequent, desperate sallies by the enemy, fierce hand-to-hand clashes in the darkness. Italians and Spaniards vied with one another in deeds of courage. Ned Denny's men fought furiously, driving the enemy back behind the imagined safety of their wall.

Grey, unmindful of his experience at Leith, prowled the trench. At daybreak he was within a hundred yards of the fort. He could hear the defenders arguing within. An encouraging sign. Musket balls whistled overhead and slapped into the parados. He kept his head down. In a lull in the fighting he called upon Don Sebastiano to strike his standards and accept terms of surrender. He waited. Tension gathered. John Cheke, by his side, could not wait. Impatient to see the arrogant flags hauled down, he peered over the parapet. In a sudden fusillade, a heavy arquebus ball took away his helmet and one half of his head. He fell, lifeless, at the feet of his commander. Grey had him carried back to the surgeons, to no avail. The cannonade resumed.

Grey retired again to confer with his officers. He had two duties to perform, one pleasant and one melancholy. In Her Majesty's name and in the presence of his leading men, he conferred a knighthood on young Ned Denny for conspicuous gallantry. It was not true that service in Ireland went unrewarded. He spoke movingly of his grief at the death of good John Cheke. Spenser noted the two contrasting events in the journal. He could not deny the small spurt of satisfaction he felt at the news of Cheke's death, but he did not write that down. Neither could Raleigh deny his chagrin at the fact that Denny, his older and more successful cousin, had been advanced before him on the field of honour.

After some deliberation, Don Sebastiano sent out the priest, the Irishman, Plunkett and the woman. They had become an embarrassment and an encumbrance to him. He wished to represent himself and his men as honest soldiers, holding no brief for traitors or rebels.

Grey wasted no time with the three prisoners. On low ground, about a thousand paces from the fort, well within sight of the defenders, he directed that a gallows be constructed. The two men were hanged, disembowelled and then dismembered. The defenders could see the smoke rising from burning entrails. They trembled. They, who had seen the horrors of war for many years, trembled in their windy refuge on the cliff edge. The woman was given to the soldiers for their diversion.

After this brief lull, the firing began again. It went on into the night. The gunners on land and sea had perfected their range. It went on all the following day and through the next night. There were no more sallies from the fort. Raleigh paced up and down the trench, hoping for a chance to distinguish himself as Sir Edward Denny had done.

The invaders were pent up. They abandoned hope. Don Sebastiano sent an emissary under a white flag, to sue for terms. He asked for safe passage for his men, out of the country. He offered himself as a hostage for their good conduct.

"The surrender will be unconditional," responded Grey. "Surrender in good faith and you will be accorded the courtesy due to a defeated enemy."

The emissary returned to the fort. He noted as he went, the thousands of soldiers drawn up for the final onslaught. He was sick with fear. He clung to the shred of hope afforded by the words of the Lord Deputy.

"My lord," asked Raleigh, "have you considered how we shall cope with these prisoners? They are well supplied, as I understand."

Grey frowned. "What is your point, Captain Raleigh?"

"I am thinking of the expense. We hold their ships as legitimate spoils of war. If we return the ships to them we weaken ourselves. We cannot spare men to ferry them home. If we merely give the ships back to them, who is to say that they will not return, replenished and rearmed? The Earl, as far as we know, is still in the field. Would you set these men free to wander about, afflicting the country people?"

Grey rubbed his eyes. They were red and gritty from powder smoke.

"I see. I have been pondering that myself. What do you think, Mr. Spenser?"

"I am merely wondering, my Lord, what you owe to these men. Are they true soldiers of any Christian prince, or are they simply adventurers. Are you in fact, bound to them by the laws of war?"

Grey sighed and shook his head. "It is a nice legal point, I admit. Captain Raleigh, your thoughts, if you please."

"There are some seven or eight hundred of them, as far as we know. Imagine the havoc they would wreak if we set them free to roam the country. Can you take them into the Queen's service, hardened Papists as they are? No, you cannot"

Grey walked a few paces away from them with his hands behind his back, then turned again. "You set me a conundrum, gentlemen. I have given my word, the courtesy due to a defeated enemy."

"To adventurers, my Lord, as our friend so astutely observes." Raleigh inclined his head to Spenser. "Adventurers in league with traitors. Let us say that this time their investment has not paid off."

Spenser observed how tenaciously Raleigh held to his line of reasoning. Was Don Sebastian any more deserving of terms than the priest or the Irishman, not to mention the misfortunate woman? In his canon, women were to be revered, protected. No knight had come to her defence. No god had intervened. He pondered the gulf between the poetic ideal and the harsh reality.

Raleigh spoke softly. "Would you come to his aid if he had lost all his gold on the stock market, or thrown it away at the card table or even in some absurd quest for gold?" He snorted derisively.

"Let me think about this for a while. I thank you, gentlemen." Grey was perplexed. Battle is more straightforward than diplomacy. "In the meantime, Captain Raleigh, I appoint you to keep close watch on the fort. At the first sign of trouble, open fire again. It would greatly simplify matters if they were to fight to the death."

He dismissed them and retired to his tent.

***

Frobisher went ashore. He walked on the beach. The business of the fort was obviously concluded. He stooped at a stream that issued from the marshy country below the headland. He washed his hands and drank some of the sweet water. He washed the powder stains from his face, ridding himself of the smell of brimstone. He had had enough of this place. He wanted to go home, to mend his fortunes, to salvage something from the wreckage of the Company of Cathay. There might yet be venturers who would revive the quest for the Passage to the Indies. No. That was nothing but a wild-goose-chase. Better still, the Queen would find employment for a skilled captain where there were decent prizes to be taken.

He walked as far as the wreck. The ribs seemed to grow out of the sand. The rib-cage was filled with a mound of stone, his ill-fated ore. It was the black ore with the glittering specks that had put him in mind of the night sky. It had all been a dream, a madness. It had destroyed some and sullied the names of others.

It had exposed him to intolerable ridicule. At first it had been such a clean thing, brave men against the Arctic; the unpolluted air; the strange beasts; courage and loyalty. His madness had cost the lives of many, whether by sickness or bad management. It was some small consolation that his seamanship had never been called into question. He admitted to himself that, on balance, he had presided over a disaster. The Papists make use of the excellent evasion of penance, whereby they step aside from guilt and responsibility. He had no such stratagem. He would stand before God on the great last day and explain how duty had warped to overwhelming greed.

It saddened him to see the wreck of a good vessel. Like a willing horse, it had gone beyond its strength. He walked around, touching the timbers. He rapped his fist on the wood. The timbers rang. Soon enough they would be gone too.

"Ah, well," he said aloud. "Ah well."

He spotted something in the withered grass of the sand dunes, something white. Something white and red. He plodded through the yielding sand. It was a body, more a carcase of what had once been a woman, naked and torn, bruised and twisted as if her limbs had been shattered. He looked down at her. Already the beetles and pismires had found her. He felt shame. She might well have been a mother, a wife, a life-companion to someone who had failed to protect her.

He scooped out a shallow pit in the sand and pulled her into it. He arranged her limbs in a last gesture of decency. They had indeed been shattered as if by a blacksmith's hammer. Her eyes were still open. He could not shut them. He asked her forgiveness. She looked up at him from her grave. He covered her eyes with the sand. He went back and forth to the wreck, bringing lumps of the ore to build a cairn over the body. She would never know how costly her tomb had been. He said 'Our Father,' not knowing the protocol for the burial of Papists, yet feeling that some words should be spoken. 'For Thine is the Kingdom, the Power and the Glory…' She might meet him in the Hereafter and blame him if he said no words. No living person could hear him, but still the words were important. Our words bind us, he reflected, to lord and monarch, to lovers and even to business partners. We break

them or twist them at great risk. A word is enough to hang a man
or to ennoble him if he keep it.

***

"Captain Raleigh," said Grey, "I put all matters today under your
direction."

This was his opportunity. This day would send his name all
over the world.

"You have my word, my lord. All will be done as you desire."

Grey nodded to him. He looked away. He gazed out to sea.
The spray was breaking over the distant headlands, pure and
white in the November sunshine.

Raleigh sent his companies to supervise the surrender. He
ordered the defenders to come out in orderly fashion but not in
military formation. He insisted that they trail their standards in
the mud, bright silks trodden into the mire. They were a glum lot,
with nothing to say for themselves. They looked at the ranks of
soldiers hemming them in. The soldiers jeered and mocked their
extravagant, mud-spattered attire. Don Sebastiano yielded his
elegant sword to Raleigh. He was led away.

His men stacked their weapons as they came out. Surrender
was complete and without guarantee. They felt naked without
the means to defend themselves. The piles of swords, pikes,
arquebuses, muskets and armour grew. The English soldiers eyed
the loot. Feathered helmets with chased ornamentation. A man
would cut a fine figure in a helmet like that.

There was another Irishman. He stood out from the foreign
soldiers, in his long and shaggy mantle. He carried on his shoulder
a bundle of withes. He threw the bundle in disgust, beside a stack
of firearms. He spat. Raleigh objected to his insolent air.

"You there," he called stepping in front of the Irishman. He
drew his sword. "What have you got there?"

"What do you think?" replied the man. He spoke good
English. "Have you no withes in England? They are sally gads,
sir, to make baskets."

"For what purpose, my fine fellow? Are you going fishing?"
Raleigh put his head to one side. He smiled.

The man laughed. He shrugged. "To truss up English heads. I see plenty around me." He spat again.

The soldiers looked on with interest, waiting to see how Raleigh would respond to this defiance. The foreign soldiers trudged on. This was no concern of theirs.

"Well then, my friend," said Raleigh, "let us begin with yours." He swung his sword in a broad arc, partly severing the Irishman's head from his shoulders. The blade lodged in bone. Raleigh wrenched it free. The man fell on one knee in his own blood. Raleigh completed the task with a quick, descending stroke. The head rolled away. The body buckled. Raleigh kicked the head to one side, sending it bowling into a puddle. He looked at the blood on his gauntlet. He had begun.

***

Frobisher went back to the stream. He washed his hands again. He sat down. He heard trumpets and drums, a ceremony taking place. He watched geese picking at bright green weed at the edge of the tide-line. This is Martinmas, he thought. This is my birthday. I should be at church. There should be goose for dinner and good cheer in the hall. He thought of Mary Lok and her generous table. I have been in the world for forty five years. I am almost an old man, he reflected.

The geese rose, all together, startled by the noise. Frobisher had never heard anything like it. The hairs prickled on the back of his neck. He felt goose-bumps all over. It was the noise of some terrible beast, voices cheering, laughter mingled with drumbeats. It swelled and swelled. It bayed, filling his head like a swoon, driving out all other sound. The waves were silent, mere painted scenery. The sound roared about him like a hurricane. He closed his eyes. He knew.

He wanted no part of it; no loot; no plunder of garments or armour; no vaunting over an abject enemy; no power or glory. He longed to be amid the ice, pitting his courage against the elements. Up there the world was clean. He ran a handful of sand through his fingers, a cascade of shining grains. He looked at the stream. It cut cliffs and bends like any great river. It created a world. It fanned out, striving towards the sea. It had done this for thousands of years since the world began, every day drowned by the tide but reasserting itself, rebuilding its little world of bends and sand-bars, as the tide retreated. Every day the same task, the same rhythm.

But it was changing. A tinge of rust, a stain, coloured the pebbles in the bed of the stream. He knew. He knew that the stain was leaching out from the fields and from the marsh, where the beast was completing its work. He remembered the bear. The stream changed from rust to crimson. It reached the sea. A plume of red spread out into the bay. It would go all around the world.

He got wearily to his feet, old before his time. He saw a boat putting off from his distant ship. The oarsmen pulled towards him in good order. He waded out to meet them.

Pacata Hibernia

Ireland Pacified

1581-1590

Chapter Fourteen

'To the most renowned and valiant Lord, the Lord Grey of Wilton, Knight of the Noble Order of the Garter

'Most Noble Lord the pillar of my life,
And Patron of my Muses pupillage,
Through whose large bounty poured on me rife,
In the first season of my feeble age,
I now do live, bound yours by vassalage.'
E.S.

Spenser paused. It was a delicate matter. His fortunes, for the moment, were linked to Grey. All was success with Grey. He could sit in the Earl's stronghold of Kilmallock, the Earl's impregnable capital, and call the great men of Munster to heel. Wind whistled through gaps in the stonework, accentuating the emptiness all about. There were no cries of market vendors or cattle lowing in the streets on fair day, only the chink of harness and the tramp of marching feet. It was a hollow victory. The houses stood open to the mountain wind. Lord Grey had conquered a desert.

But the people did not come in to bend the knee. They could not. Their knees could not bear them upright. They starved on the hillsides and in the great forest of Arlo. Their bones jutted through their skin. They wrapped themselves in rags and grovelled in ditches and thickets for anything they could eat. They laid their children in shallow graves, graves not deep enough to keep them from the jaws of wolves. The covert was as thin as it could be, but the people could not come in. The cold wind blew.

The winds of displeasure had begun to whistle around the Lord Deputy. The story of *Dun an Oir* had spread throughout Europe. It was a stain on England's escutcheon. Had it been a few hundred Irish, it would have been different, a few hundred rebels in a far away land on the edge of the world. Europe would have shrugged its indifference, but these were men from the most powerful Catholic countries in Europe. This massacre was a crime that cried to Heaven for vengeance.

Spenser's muse looked down from Parnassus. She saw Lord Grey departing under a cloud. She urged the poet to look to the rising power. She poured sweet inspiration into his fertile mind.

'To the right noble Lord and most valiant Captain, Sir John Norris knight, Lord President of Munster . . . '

'Who ever gave more honourable prize
To the sweet Muse, than did the Marital crew,
That their brave deeds she might immortalise
In her shrill trump, and sound their praises due?
Who then ought more to favour her than you
Most noble Lord, the honour of this age,
And Precedent of all that arms ensure?'
E.S.

Norris's star was in the ascendant. It was a bargain. Spenser would 'eternise' his name in preference to that of Grey. The Irish beggars always offered prayers in return for gifts. A poet must do something similar. Norris was a man of outstanding courage, as he had shown in the Low Countries. He was a man of decisive action, with the good sense to perform his slaughter away from the eyes of Europe. The MacDonalds of Antrim had felt his firm hand. They had watched, impotently from the mainland, when Norris's men massacred the small garrison on the refuge of

Rathlin Island. They had seen their wives, their children, their old and sick, hurled screaming, from the cliffs.

Norris was the man to pacify Munster and settle it with loyal Englishmen. He gave ear to Spenser's plans. He nodded in agreement. Spenser concluded his plea:

'Since then each where thou hast dispread thy fame Love
him that hath enternized your name'
E.S.

In the silence of Munster, Spenser's words resounded bravely. No bird song sounded or dog barked. No cow lowed, bell rang or cock crowed. No children played in the way or geese cackled in a haggard. No smoke rose from cooking fires. The wolves slouched through Kilmallock, looking this way and that, with darting, yellow eyes.

***

Her Majesty called again to Mortlake. She wished to convey her condolences to John Dee on the loss of his mother. She wished also to thank him for his advice on the treatment of her toothache. He remarked on how something as sweet as sugar could result in such distress.

"It is a metaphor for life, Majesty," he confided. "It is like love."

She sighed. It was so true. She had given her heart freely but all had disappointed her. John Dee nodded. He knew only too well how her loves had turned to ashes. He checked himself. His scientific mind was running to metaphor. He would end up like one of the poets.

He showed her his latest project, a boy-child of three or four years, a child of the Arctic. The child bowed to the great lady. He doffed his cap like any great lord at court.

"Captain Frobisher left him with me, Majesty. I wished to find out what his language was, what language was innate in him."

She was intrigued. "What did you find, Doctor Dee?"

He beamed with pleasure. "I found that English came naturally to him. It was a wonder. I concluded that English is the original tongue; that all other languages are aberrations, mere sprigs of the parent tree, as it were." Another metaphor. "King Psammeticus of Egypt did the same experiment in ancient times. He sequestered two new-born infants with a nurse, a girl child and a boy, giving the woman strict instructions that she should speak no word to the infants. In time, one of them said 'Bekos', the Phrygian word for bread. I suspect that the nurse was Phrygian herself and could nor resist words of comfort to the infants. My conclusions point to English, as the language of Adam." He nodded in satisfaction. Science and patience bring all mysteries to light.

"You do well, Doctor. It brings me to another matter. These lands of the Arctic. I wish to know which ones I may call mine."

"They are extensive, Majesty. You have the seeds of an empire in North America." He went to his shelf of maps. They were rolled like pipes and stacked in a pile. He talked to himself and scratched his white beard. He drew out one of the pipes and unrolled it on his carpeted table. He weighted the edges with heavy candlesticks although the parchment struggled to resume its cylindrical shape. He always had to struggle with his maps. It was almost a game.

The Queen leaned forward to inspect her dominions. Dee pointed to the places uncovered by Frobisher, a sketchy coastline fading into conjecture. There was the New Found Land, possibly the size of Britain itself, almost the same shape. There was a serrated coastline which he denoted as Labrador and opposite it, the great pendulous bulk of Greenland. There were winds with puffed cheeks and whales spouting fountains in the sea. There were carracks and caravels, the Zona Frigida and the Zona Temperata. There lay Frobisher's Strait, a clear and uninterrupted path to The Indies. There were several speculative islands labelled *incognita,* where ice prevented navigation. It was a prudent stratagem of the cartographer to fill the empty spaces with delineations of things unknown.

"George Best's map, Majesty, based on the most recent intelligence. *Terra nullius*" he explained. "Nobody's lands. No prince or monarch has claimed them.

The Queen was pleased. Dee wondered if he might recommend a specific for sweetening the breath. Her few visible teeth were black. He thought better of it.

She drew the boy close to her. He blinked up at Dee, his supposed father.

"This little Indian boy. I like him well." She patted him on the head. The boy pulled away. He exhaled sharply. 'Pah!'

"I have made extensive enquiries, Majesty. These Indians are known as In-u-it. It means The People. All others they call The Lice."

"They are proud people. What do they call us?"

"We are Krabloonak, the Eyebrows."

The Queen laughed merrily.

"So I am queen of the In-u-it and of The Eyebrows."

"According to the best maps, that is incontrovertible, Majesty."

"The best maps, of course." She smiled at her little joke. "But do they know this yet?"

"In time they will Majesty. Captain Frobisher made it clear to them."

"Ah, Captain Frobisher. He has requested permission to go out to grass. He speaks of his long service and advancing age. He wishes to return to Yorkshire and become a farmer." She paused. "An old war-horse. He will make a poor farmer. I shall give him ample space, but when need arises, I shall rein him in."

We live by metaphors, thought Dee. It was nonetheless, a good metaphor for Frobisher. He would never be a farmer. He would smell salt in the wind. His nostrils would flare. He would stamp his feet and kick down the door of his stable. He would come back. She knew her man.

"To return to these maps. I have devised stratagems of my own. My Lord Burghley speaks of grafting. He propagates his plants by grafting and selecting the best seed. You do not follow?"

"We were speaking of your new realms, Majesty. Are we talking of agriculture?"

She laughed, chiding him gently. "You do not think in poetry, my dear friend. Let me explain. Ireland is a garden, grown rank with weed. The choicest plants, put there in times gone by, have

153

been poisoned and infected. They have fallen away from their allegiance. The prudent gardener must root them out."

Dee listened attentively, beginning to see the thrust of her metaphor.

"For example, I have taken one of the native stock, a man of ability. I have grafted onto him, the manners and attitudes of an English gentleman. I have nurtured him and protected him from the harsh winds of his native land. Yet I shall replant him as an Irish chieftain to lead his people out of barbarism."

Dee waited. "This is ONeill, is it not?" he asked after a while. The Queen was pleased that he followed her line so well.

"It is all grafting and pruning. This young man will be their chieftain and my earl. He has shown himself willing in service against the traitor Earl of Desmond. He will do well."

She patted the boy again. He twisted away.

"Teach him well, Doctor Dee. Some day he may be my pro-consul in the great North Land."

Dee felt a twinge of fear for the child, his little Caliban. Was it not enough that the infant had been plucked from his native soil, nourished in an alien place, only to be transplanted again to a country of which he knew nothing? Confound Burghley, he thought. It was not a matter of horticulture. He had grown to love the child. He had no desire to see him used as a pawn in a game of Empire.

The Queen made ready to depart. She took his hand in an informal gesture of friendship.

"My wise friend," she said. "I have great need of your advice."

Dee thought to himself that it would be good to go away for a while, away from the dazzling brightness of her sun, the powerful magnetism of her person – more metaphors. He wanted to go abroad, to meet men of similar interests, to read in lofty libraries and open the wonders of the world to his little charge. He felt a father's instinct to protect the child. He had no desire to yield this one treasure to his Queen. Disloyalty, treason perhaps, in the great scheme of things. There was a story of a nobleman, whose king was overthrown. His enemies demanded the head of the king's only son. The nobleman gave them the head of his own son as the last service he could render to his king. It was a matter of honour.

John Dee knew in his heart, that he would run away, rather than sacrifice the boy.

He bowed low. The smallest plants in the garden escape the storm, when great oaks are torn from their roots. The Queen was pleased with her call. Her toothache was no longer a problem. A toothache, when it rages, is of more proximate concern than all the territories on all the maps in the world. When it goes, hope and determination return again to the sufferer. Joy becomes a possibility. She boarded her barge. The oarsmen pushed off. The current took her away.

***

The reports came in to Burghley. Black Tom wrote: 'The unhappy wretch, the Earl of Desmond, wandereth from place to place, forsaken of all men. The poor Countess lamenteth greatly the folly of her husband, whom reason could never rule.'

He was seen with a priest, two horsemen and a serving boy. They were making their meal from the carcase of a horse. The Earl was weeping.

Mad Maurice, Viscount Roche, keen to prove his loyalty and dressed in English costume, led his men in pursuit of the Earl, into the mountains of Sliabh Luachra. They managed to seize four oxen, some bottles and other stuff. They found the priest's sacred vessels. The Earl and his pitiful few followers, escaped into the birch and holly woods on the low-lands. They lay low. One or two faithful kerne came to his assistance. It was winter. Winter always seemed to take a hand in adding to his sufferings. He sent his men out to forage. He made his Confession to the priest. He felt that his final hours were upon him.

The men returned elated, with clothing and food. They drove forty cows and nine horses. They laughed about their success. The Earl immediately ordered a return to the mountains. There they would regain their strength. His people would come to him. In the spring they would emerge, to take back all that had been lost.

***

Eoin Moriarty heard a voice calling from the darkness. His dogs began to bark. His serving men rose with him. They took weapons and went warily into the night. Eoin knew the voice, that of his brother-in-law, Maurice, from another branch of the Moriartys at Cahir-na-Feidh. This must be bad news, at dead of night.

It was a cruel story. The Earl of Desmond's men had taken his livestock and stripped their cabin of everything, even their garments, leaving them naked and shivering, himself, his wife and children, in mid-winter.

He begged for help. "The Earl's men!" He could not understand it. "If they had asked, I could have given them whatever they needed. I would have given it for ancient loyalty. I followed him in the old days. This was unmannerly of him." His teeth chattered. "I would have given it gladly. God blast him for an earl. He is no earl." He wanted revenge.

Eoin wanted an end of it, the alarms in the night, the English harrying and burning. He had reached an accommodation with the new power, in the person of Sir Edward Denny. Some kind of normality was returning. It was time to finish it. He swore under his breath. All bonds of loyalty had been severed by the Earl himself. He buckled on his sword-belt and took up his mantle. He knew where to go.

So died the Fifteenth Earl of Desmond, his head struck off by a former liegeman, one who had lost faith. So ended a line of noble knights, powerful men of war who had held the conquered land for four centuries. The Earl was taken in a squalid cabin. He pleaded for his life. His strength was gone.

There was no fairy music at his passing. No note was struck, in the silence of the fabled mountains. No god came to his aid with magic harp to put his enemies to sleep. There was only the sound of the infant Blackwater, drawing its first strength from the dreeping woods and the dark hillside.

Chapter Fifteen

Munster, without its head, was in effect, *terra nullius*. The circling vultures spiralled down to take their share of the carcase. They tore it to shreds, lumbering away to enjoy their new lands, their forests, their fields devoid of crops or cattle. Burghley was generous to the young men of war. Ned Denny cleaned the dung and filth from the castle at Tralee. He put the jackdaws to raucous flight. He engaged his former soldiers to work the land. He installed his wife, the new Lady Denny, in suitable style. He looked about at the ruinous state of the country and began to go into debt.

Walter Raleigh divided his time between the Court, where he had become Her Majesty's new favourite, and his forty thousand acres on the lower Blackwater. He liked his tight little town of Youghal. It had walls, lately renewed to withstand a siege and a port to feed it, if any siege were to come about. He planned his colony in the Americas. He named that place Virginia. The compliment was not lost on Her Majesty.

She forbade him to go with his half-brother, Sir Humphrey Gilbert, he of the avenues of heads, on the ill-fated expedition to the New Found Land.

Raleigh shed few tears at the loss of Gilbert in a great storm. He danced with the Queen and praised her musicianship.

"When the jacks are up, murmured Lord Oxford, watching the ingenious mechanism of the virginal, "the heads are down."

His companions sniggered. The Queen's fingers stopped. The music died.

"My lord" she said icily. "You have something to say?"

The noble lord made a dismissive gesture. "It was nothing, Your Majesty, just a comment on the intricacy of the instrument and how skilfully your fingers govern it."

His companions lowered their eyes, all sniggering silenced. Raleigh watched silently, noting their names. He knew what they were thinking, that he, an upstart, had displaced some of the great nobles of the realm. The snigger cost them their places at Court.

Raleigh gained some more monopolies, quarrying and mining. He prospered, without handling either pick or crow- bar. As for the enquiry into the events at *Dún an Óir*, he maintained forcibly, that he was following the orders of his superior. Without discipline there would be chaos. The shadow fell on Lord Grey alone.

He peopled his estates with hard-working men of Devon. He set them to clearing briars and whitethorn from overgrown fields. He felled some forest. He directed the digging of saw-pits. He stockpiled timber in drying sheds. He antagonised some surviving Irish landowners. He fished long reaches of the Blackwater, marvelling at the abundance of salmon. Life was good.

***

At Goose Hill, near his birthplace in Yorkshire, Frobisher made a wretched attempt at farming. His hay was damp and mouldy in the stacks. His animals were sickly or inclined to wander. From the top of his hill he could see nothing but more hills. There was no bright line on the horizon. At night he gazed at the stars.

A delegation came, cap in hand, from Methley and Oakenshawe. They put it to him that his land stood on a goodly seam of coal. They wanted to mine his coal and experiment with using it to smelt iron. They sketched a prospect of endless wealth dug directly from his fields.

He felt panic rising in his breast. Piles of black stones and the sulphurous reek of furnaces. Endless wealth. He had been there before. He sold the land on the spot, to the self-deluding fools. Coal and iron as a vision of the future. He could not wait to get away from them.

***

Spenser kept his sinecures. He was Clerk of the Chanceries in Dublin and Commissioner for Musters in Kildare. These posts brought in a small income, with no specific duties attached. It was not enough for a man of some consequence. It did not give him the freedom he craved to complete his work. He kept his eyes and ears open. His diligence was rewarded. He received his castle with three thousand and twenty eight English acres of prime, well-watered land. He remembered the castle, gold and silver in the light of a setting sun. There was some justice in the world.

The late Earl had once owned this castle, Kilcolman, built on a rock near the church of some long-dead saint. The Earl had lorded it over all this country, its lake, its shining river, its placidly grazing herds. Now it was Spenser's turn.

It came with responsibilities. He must build twenty four houses for twenty four honest English families of the Reformed Religion. He must set them to work and collect their rents. He must keep good order and pay his own rent to the Crown.

There were some outlying buildings, a tower house or two, some disputed plough-lands, nothing that could not be settled by reasonable men or by a word in the right ear. He took possession in high summer. His wife and two children seemed happy enough with their new home. There were some Irish servants who struggled to understand their mistress's instructions. They were not stupid as such, but it was exasperating to have to explain the simplest instructions again and again.

Machabyas did her best. She pined for the city, for the noise of traffic and cries of vendors. She missed the playhouse and the easy society of old friends. She tried hard. Her husband was happy. He wrote incessantly. The poetry flowed from his pen. He was convinced that his work, glorifying the virtues of chivalry and of the great Queen far away in London, would bring preferment and some day, a place at Court. She did all that she could to speed the work.

The castle was draughty. He took to wearing his Irish mantle indoors and out. He developed a persistent and irritating cough. However, his work bore him up. It was a pity that the man who had given the coat to him was proving to be a difficult and litigious neighbour.

Mad Maurice, Viscount of Fermoy, lived no more than four or five leagues away at Castletown. He was particularly sensitive about rights-of-way and boundaries. With the arrogance of four centuries of English occupation, he resented and despised the new English. The sweepings of England's prisons, he said, worse than the native Irish. The Irish, wild and all as they were, had some pedigree. They had their laws, their stories, their music. The new English had nothing to distinguish them but their strange accents and their greed. The worst of them was that condescending poet at Kilcolman.

***

Spenser walked his land. He sat by his lake. There were many water birds to charm him, stately swans, a raft of ducks, a piping moor-hen, a warbler clinging to a swaying reed. There were geese and black-headed gulls. He noted a heron, motionless among the water-flags. It could have been made of pewter. It waited and waited. It struck. A frog struggled in the sword-like beak. The heron swallowed the hapless creature with a convulsive movement of its long neck. A lump passed down the long gullet, the frog, one moment alive in its native element and the next moment... He shuddered to think of it.

He felt the sun on his face. At last he lived in a place where shepherds could be at ease. He imagined the presiding nymphs of the lake disporting themselves in the shallows. He pictured mysterious goddesses bathing in his shining river, Awbeg, the little river, which he renamed Mulla. He invented names for all the features visible from his castle, especially Old Father Mole, the highest of the distant hills. Mole was the father of many streams.

He watched over them, directing them in their courses and finding suitable marriages for them, as any careful father would. It would be no stretch of the imagination to see the ancient gods alighting on that hilltop to rest, to hunt in the forest or pursue their amorous dalliances. Spenser felt that he had at last been blessed. He had come home, like a wandering shepherd, to regain his strength.

Some cattle came to drink at the lake. They snuffled and gathered around him. They moved closer and closer, hemming him in. He wished that he had thought to bring a staff. He stood up, spreading his arms wide and shouting. They stepped back in a little dance, but recovered their curiosity. They moved closer, staring at this stranger who had landed among them. He became alarmed.

'Stood all astonied, like a sort of Steeres;
Mongst whom some beast of strange and forraine race,
Unwares in chaunce, for straying from his peeres.
So did their ghastly gaze bewray their hidden feares.' E.S.

A cowherd set upon the beasts with an ash-plant, driving them away from the water and from the apprehensive poet. He lashed about at their rumps and gave a mighty roar. Spenser recovered some of his dignity, gathering his mantle around him.

"I am grateful to you, my good man," he said. "I should have carried my staff."

"Aye," replied the man eyeing him with open curiosity. "They are half wild." He let another roar and waved his stick. The animals scampered away nonchalantly, tossing their heads.

Spenser observed the man. He was of small size and wore a long, shapeless garment that fell below his knees. It was of rough wool, dyed the colour of the country, moss and bracken, earth and saffron. The man went barefoot.

"I am Uaithne, your cowherd. I am part of Kilcolman."

"You speak the English tongue," replied Spenser in some surprise.

"I do," said the cow-herd. "I speak whatever language is needful."

"A rare gift," said Spenser tolerantly. "I did not see you approaching. You are almost invisible in your cloak of green."

"Not green," said the cow-herd, "*Uaithne*. Sometimes men see only my shadow. That is how they know I am about. Uaithne is my colour and my name."

"Well then, Uaithne, talk to me as we walk along. You may tell me about my new land."

"Yours while you hold it." Uaithne looked at him sideways. "You hold it with a piece of parchment. Others have held it with steel. But they are dead. Some day you also will go."

Spenser bridled at his tone. "But while I live, it is mine. You are mine and those steers and all those fields and woods. See that you remember that."

Uaithne shrugged. "It makes no differ to me. I have food and shelter. I have my music and my poetry."

Spenser stopped. "Your music? Your poetry?" He laughed. "You are a poet?"

"I am that," replied the little man. He tapped his temple with this forefinger. "All in here. No need for paper or parchment."

"Aha!" He had heard tell of these rustic poets, poets of poverty and cow dung. Madmen, strumming their stunted harps. "And a musician also?" This could make for diverting entertainment, something to make Machabyas laugh on a winter's evening.

"I am," said Uaithne, with a note of pride. "I have sung the great earls, the warriors, even the gods. Long before your day."

"How long?" There was an ageless quality about the fellow that intrigued him.

Uaithne shrugged again. "Who can say? A thousand years. Maybe two."

"Two thousand?"

"No, two. I do not count them. I just am."

Spenser laughed aloud. The fellow was definitely mad. "Are you a good cow herd? That is the important thing."

"And that's a thing," said Uaithnne. "Your cattle should be on the hills in this summer weather."

Spenser shook his head. "No" he said firmly. "I have set my face against boleying. Those months on the mountains turn mens' minds to rebellion and theft. My cattle are safer in my fields. I will not have rebels for servants."

Uaithne gave his characteristic shrug. "There's good pasture on the mountains. A pity to waste it. You may regret it." He spoke not out of solicitude, but out of respect for the old way. Without boleying there would be no fires at *Bealtine*. There would be no merry-making at *Samhain* when the cattle came down again. Old rhythms would be disrupted. The spirits of the dead would wander the night in confusion, straining to hear the sound of music and dancing.

"You will have no hay," he warned. "No hay for the winter and no cheese from the mountains."

Spenser dismissed his concerns. "All will be plough land. We will dig like Adam in his garden."

Uaithne looked sideways again at his new master. He could not see him digging.

"I have heard some Irish music," began Spenser, changing the subject. "It is not without some merit."

"There has been little to sing about, this many a year."

They walked in silence. The long grass was still damp from the dew. They came close to the castle. It stood on an eminence, surrounded by a wall and outer ditch. It threw a long shadow in the early morning sun.

"Where did you learn your music, my good fellow?"

"From Dagda Mór himself."

"I see. And who is Dagda Mór, if I may ask?" He knew that *mór* meant big or great. Every local princeling and brigand appended *mór* to his title to give himself some importance.

"He is the All-father of the Dé Danann people. He is the greatest of the gods."

"I ... see," said Spenser, nodding slowly. "You learned your music from a god. I look forward to hearing this divine music. Your poetry too, of course." He spoke with exaggerated respect.

"You heard me once before in the hall of the lord Roche, but you were too sick to appreciate it. You were shivering by the fire, a miserable sight to behold."

Spenser remembered the night. It was a jumble of confused impressions. Rosalind had been there and Raleigh. There was some jingling music and chanting. Raleigh had sung about the gallows. Rosalind had lain beside him. She wrapped a heavy cloak around him to drive his fever out.

"Anyway," said Uaithne, in an offhand manner, "my poetry is only in the Irish tongue. English ears could not appreciate it. I will not rhyme in English – although I could if I wished."

"Of course. Of course. I would greatly desire to hear it." He smiled to himself. "I am something of a poet myself." He spoke modestly.

"I know," said Uaithne. "I have heard. Scratching away with pen and paper. Shepherds and nymphs, my lord Roche says."

"So my fame has spread as far as Castletown." He was stung. Roche was a bumpkin caught between cultures. He was not going to make himself ridiculous, defending his work to a cowherd. The greatest men in the realm praised his work. The ladies of the Court, the Queen herself, read his verses with delight.

"He says you have the wrong gods."

Uaithne was matter-of-fact. He had not read the Englishman's poems, for the good reason that the god had neglected to teach him letters. "The wrong gods for our woods and mountains. Foreign gods." He snorted at the absurdity.

Spenser laughed. "Does he indeed? The Viscount, I take it, is learned in the Classics. I must consult him in future, before I dip a quill into ink."

He bit his lip, concealing his fury.

Uaithne continued airily. "Aye shepherds. All the shepherds I ever knew had dung up to their elbows. Half mad they were from standin' to their flocks. Divil a one of them could twist a tune on a pipe. Talked of naught but wolves."

He sketched no idyllic scene. In time however they would learn that the advance of English civilisation would bring stability, prosperity and a much-needed refinement of manners. Good roads would serve to lift the general intelligence of the people. Spenser was happy to wait, to press on with his great work and see the Viscount and his ilk disappear into well-deserved obscurity.

Machabyas, from her window in the central tower, watched her husband in conversation with some stranger, a small man in a shabby garment. They were laughing. She knew that he would come in and go straight to his desk, some new idea beating at his brain. She hoped that soon he would be finished, that they would go to London to engage the printer, that he would see sense and release his family from this dank exile.

They were parting on cordial terms. Her husband made an elaborate bow. The small man touched his forehead. They separated, her husband making for the gate, the little man merging into the colours of the meadow. There were yellow weeds and thistles, lending their bright colours to the field. The small man disappeared. That was another thing. He should put labourers to work pulling out those yellow weeds and cutting down the thistles before they could ripen and send their downy seeds drifting on the breeze, to poison other fields. She resolved to mention it to him when the storm of inspiration abated.

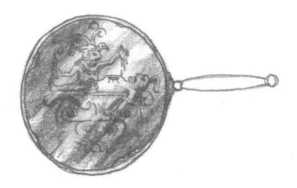

Chapter Sixteen

Captain Frobisher sought out the family of Michael Lok. He had no obligation to do so. He still harboured resentment against his former partner. There were debts outstanding, mariners still unpaid. A man like Lok, with so many children depending on him, had no business venturing his house and everything he possessed, on what proved to be a wild-goose- chase. Even a card player will keep something in hand.

Lok was still in the Fleet Prison. Frobisher had heard that Lok's wife went several times a week with food to keep him alive. She took it from what she bought with her wages as a lowly washerwoman. She always found her husband working on a map. He was drawing North America on a polar triangular net. He was allowed paper and writing implements. He showed her his progress every time she called. He was excited by his creation. This could be the key to restoring his fortunes. There was nothing but talk of colonies. Explorers need maps. She pitied him in his squalid lodgings, amid the straw. He worked among shambling cell-mates with only a beam of light from a high window to illuminate his labours. He was still writing his letters to Burghley and Walsingham. He showed extraordinary recall of every farthing spent on the expeditions and their unhappy outcome. He itemized everything.

She repeated all this to Captain Frobisher. She did not blame the captain. She was willing to close the book on the whole affair. She did not expect the great lords or the Queen herself, to take the slightest interest in her misfortunes or the fate of her hungry children. Deep down, she wondered if he would offer her some coin. The thought offended her, but she knew that she would swallow her pride and accept. She could not afford pride. She knew that he had taken in her circumstances with one glance around the poor, run-down habitation. He came directly to the point.

"I have some money," he began. She flinched. "I sold some land." He gave a dry laugh. "I sold it to some mad speculators who seek their fortunes in digging coal."

She made no comment. It all sounded familiar. She would not be investing.

"I have a command," he continued. "Life on shore does not agree with me."

Her mind raced. Had he come to take some of her children to sea? Was he about to suggest emigration to a new land overseas? She was too old to build a new life among savages. It was as much as she could do to retain what life she had.

"I have invested in a property in King Street in Westminster."

Perhaps he needs a washerwoman. Perhaps he was proposing something less respectable, something indecent. She pictured her skinny and importunate brood, their eyes wide with longing and anxiety.

Whatever the captain proposed, she knew that she would accept.

"I intend running it as a lodging house. To that end I need someone to manage it. I thought of you."

He seemed anxious. Her head spun. He was waiting.

"It is a good premises."

She had no doubt of that. A good address. Beef at three farthings a pound. Pepper at four shillings a pound. It was a long time since she had bought beef. A leg of mutton, one shilling and sixpence. Some unscrupulous butchers tried to pass it off as lamb. She looked at the red, cracked skin of her knuckles. She clenched her fists, hiding them in her apron. Captain Frobisher would demand a strict accounting. Candles at fourpence a pound. She began silently to weep. She had always gone in fear of this man, this bear, this harsh-spoken brawler. He spoke again, awkwardly. "Do not distress yourself, Mistress Lok. If my offer offends you, you have my apologies. I merely thought . . ." He rose to go.

She shook her head. She wiped her eyes with her apron. She smiled.

"No, no, Captain Frobisher, I accept and gladly. I accept and thank you."

"Ah!" he said, relaxing for the first time. "I thought of you before any other. In truth I often thought of your generous table, when I was amid the ice."

She looked at him. There was no hidden meaning. He loved her food. His money had found a safe haven. This venture would not fail.

"What of your husband? Will he raise any objections?"

She looked at the floor. Fifteen shillings for a load of rushes. She shook her head. "He is too taken up with correspondence to notice what I do." She smiled. "He knows not what rope holds the mast." She had often heard him say that.

Frobisher nodded. "I will expect strict accounting. It makes for better friendship."

He held out his hand. She took it in both of hers. It was a mighty paw. She wondered momentarily what work this hand had done. He looked at her chapped knuckles.

"We have a bargain, Mistress Lok," he said. There was no undue familiarity. She was glad of that.

***

In The Mitre Tavern in Cheapside, Frobisher met with the newly-minted knight, Sir Walter Raleigh. This was the place to encounter the leading wits of the city. Frobisher did not account himself a wit, but he had been told that Raleigh had considerable knowledge of the Americas. It was possible that Raleigh could acquaint him with business opportunities in that region. He would surely be able to tell him the latest news of the activities of the Spaniards.

He had lost touch with the lucrative trade of privateering during his stint as a farmer.

He found that Raleigh shared his antipathy to Drake. Drake was the hero of the hour. He had all the luck, a golden touch. The Spaniards, playing upon his name, called him The Dragon. They had felt his fiery breath in Panama and all along the Pacific coasts. By comparison with Drake all other captains were diminished. Drake was the man to be cultivated. He was the man to be emulated. And envied.

Raleigh told him the gossip of the city. He laughed at the story of John Dee, lately fallen under the influence of an Irish mountebank, one Edward Kelly. Kelly took his orders directly from an angel that appeared in Dee's mysterious skryving mirror. Kelly had the gift of seeing the angel and hearing his voice. Dee, who had peered at the mirror for years, straining with all his powerful intellect, to catch a glimpse of the future, was fascinated by the Irishman's rare gift.

Raleigh laughed loudly at the irony of the situation. Kelly had no ears, yet he could hear voices from the spirit world. Dee, the most learned man in Europe, heard nothing. Kelly, a common thief and trickster, had lost his ears in the pillory, yet Dee respected him beyond all scholars. There was worse. Kelly had brought with him his wife, a slattern, and her equally obnoxious sister. Under the angel's instruction Dee had taken this contemptible creature to wife.

Each morning the angel Uziel, by means of the mirror, conveyed his instructions to Kelly. Dee abandoned his swimming routine, but Kelly saw to it that he still had his restorative draught of liquor. Sometimes at night, the angel directed that they exchange wives. Dee had scruples about this behaviour, but Kelly explained that to devote himself to one woman, would distract him from the serious business of divining. The angel assured Kelly that they were on the brink of finding the elusive philosopher's stone. It was all very amusing. Fools and dupes flocked to Mortlake to finance the great quest. Kelly kept the books. Sometimes, it was reported, he communed with the angel in bed, with wife and sister-in-law beside him.

Some word of these merry goings-on had reached Her Majesty's ears. She was not impressed. She wrote to Dee, instructing him to put his house in order. Frobisher guessed how Her Majesty had heard the story. He did not see the funny side of it. He was distressed to hear of a good man brought low.

He engaged two watermen to convey him to Mortlake. He marvelled at the wondrous house on London Bridge. The heads were still there, on bristling pikes, guarding the southern entrance. He watched the watermen pulling on the oars. The rhythm pleased him. The houses and palaces glided by. He stepped ashore at John Dee's stairs and walked up to the house. Some workmen were lounging in the outhouses, laughing and joking among themselves. There was an air of neglect about the run-down garden.

The child opened the door. Frobisher knew that this was his little Caliban. The child looked up at him, with black, penetrating eyes. His dark hair fell in a fringe. He held the door wide.

John Dee greeted him effusively. Too effusively it seemed.

He stumbled over his words.

"You come in happy time, my good friend. Happy time."

"I trust I find you well, Doctor Dee."

Frobisher spoke formally. The man was deserving of respect and must learn again to respect himself.

"Excellent well." He clapped his hands in delight. "I have had great news. A prince of Poland has invited me to work in his palace. He will finance my quest for the stone. It is almost within my grasp." He beamed. "I cannot fail now."

Frobisher grunted. He had seen that wild joy in Michael Lok. Lok had a treasure in his house, but he never listened to her. Doctor Dee was astray in himself, with nobody to guide him home.

He insisted on pouring a drink for Frobisher. The child watched in apprehension. It frightened him when the adults drank the evil-smelling liquid. He made himself small and inconspicuous.

"The child?" queried Frobisher. "Will you take him with you?"

"Of course. Of course." Dee almost cackled. "It will be an essential part of his education. I cannot be separated from my

171

little Caliban." He patted the boy on the head. "This is a wise little fellow. I cannot be parted from him." He laughed.

Frobisher had seen enough. He finished his drink.

"I wish you well, Doctor Dee. Take good care of him. I entrusted him to your care and you will render an account to me."

Dee looked at the captain through bleary eyes. The laughter died on his lips.

In the corridor Frobisher encountered the furtive Kelly. It was obvious that the creature had been listening at the door. Frobisher took an instant dislike to the man. The eyes, too close together, the hair combed down on either side to conceal his shameful mutilation.

"Ah, your honour, sir," said Kelly with an obsequious bow. "Your honour, sir. I was just about to call on the Doctor."

Frobisher blocked his way. "A word, sir, before we part."

Kelly's eyes darted hither and thither.

"I am Martin Frobisher. I give you a friendly warning. If harm should come to the boy or to Doctor Dee, on his travels, I shall hold you entirely to blame."

Kelly straightened up, affronted.

"Enough of your play-acting. I know you for what you are. You may consult your angel if you wish, but I can tell now what the future holds." He lowered his voice to a menacing, reverberating rumble.

"Believe me. I am a man of my word. Already you have lost your ears through your own efforts. I shall complete the task. Every extremity of your body. With my own hands I will cut them off. I will leave you your eyes so that you can see how people mock and laugh. You will be exhibited in a basket to the common multitude. You will be my finest exhibit."

Kelly trembled. He knew this man's reputation. Without the aid of the skryving mirror, he saw clearly what the future held. His agile wits and brazen confidence would be no match for the conqueror of the Arctic, the slayer of the great white bear.

"You understand me, sir?"

Kelly nodded wordlessly. He understood very well.

The child went quietly to the room where the virginal stood. It was dusty from long neglect, but finger-marks showed where he had often handled it. He touched a key and put his ear to the wood. He heard the wondrous sound vibrating within, a pure note, fading, yet true, taking him far away to a strange pace. The note died. He struck a different key. A new note called to him. He closed his eyes. The sound took him away, away over rooftops and hills, over the sea that John Dee had told him about, to a world of white and crystal, a world with strange curtains of light and glistening stars. The note died. The vision faded. He opened his eyes.

"What do you do here?" It was Kelly, come to investigate. "You should not be here."

The child shrank from the man. He watched him fearfully. He had often felt the back of Kelly's hand.

"Out," commanded Kelly. He raised his hand. "Out," he said, standing in the doorway. He feinted as if to strike. He laughed as the little boy ducked and sidled past him, with arms raised to ward off the blow, but strangely, Kelly did not strike. The boy ran.

The garden beckoned, in the bright sunshine. He wanted to watch the swimming creatures in the stone trough, especially the beetles that mimicked the labour of the watermen on the river.

***

The cowherd, Uaithne, had become a distraction to Spenser. The man talked a great deal of nonsense, but it was pleasant sometimes, to sit by the lake and hear his stories of a different world. On those days, Spenser went on horseback. There were more cattle. His stock was rising. The peace and Uaithne's skilful husbandry, were paying a dividend. Some of his houses were occupied by wary settlers. The ploughlands promised a decent harvest.

"Did I ever tell you about the Pooka?" asked Uaithne.

"No you did not. Is this one of your gods again?"

"No," snorted Uaithne. "Not a bit of it. He is a fairy giant."

"Ah!" Spenser waited.

"He is the one that did all the work in the old days. Nights. He came every night to harvest the corn or milk the cows, or whatever. He would grind the corn and take none for himself. He took no payment."

"A useful man," nodded Spenser. "We could do with him here."

"He comes no more."

"And why is that?"

"Well you see, the lord of the castle, Castle Pook, wanted to pay him for his kindness."

"I know Castle Pook. I have a tenant there."

"Well anyway," went on Uaithne, "didn't he wait up one night and didn't he see the Pooka labouring away in the field and he dressed in rags?"

Spenser wondered if he was expected to answer.

"So he felt sorry for him. He caused a fine suit of clothes to be made for the giant and he brought them himself to the mouth of the giant's cave."

"And was the giant pleased?"

"Pleased? Indeed, he was." Uaithne scratched his nose. "But he came no more to do the work."

"Was he not grateful to the lord of the castle?"

"I'll tell you," said Uaithne with a wry smile. "After a few weeks the lord went quietly to the cave. He crept inside. No man had ever done that before." He lowered his voice, enhancing the drama.

"And the giant captured him?"

"No, not a bit of it. Wasn't the Pooka there before him, admiring himself in a big looking glass, all dressed in his new finery? He never came to work again, for vanity."

"Ah!" Spenser was not sure of the moral, but the story stung his conscience. It was not enough to live in a castle of gold and silver. He too had work to do.

The tenant of Castle Pook replied in peremptory terms to Spenser's demand for rent. He pointed out that his family had held that castle for more than two centuries, paying rent to no man. He further pointed out that a repeat of such insolence, could have unfortunate consequences for its author. Spenser consulted his deed of grant. The matter was clear and straightforward. He was the owner of Castle Pook and all its surrounding lands. He had the word of the Queen herself, through her Lord Deputy and the Lord President of Munster, Sir John Norris, his good friend and protector.

He communicated this intelligence to his churlish tenant. The matter distracted him from his poetry, but he could not let such arrogance go by.

Chapter Seventeen

Machabyas considered her position. She was, in her own estimation, confined in a prison. She lived in a castle in the middle of a great plain. From the highest battlements, she could see the rim of mountain that surrounded her, graceful, undulating hills, luring her to go there and pace upon the high places. There were, further away, huge up-thrusting wedges, purple and orange in the varying light. At dawn they seemed to edge closer, but in the misty rain that came too often, they drew back, lurking on the horizon, as if watching her, waiting.

She feared the forest that clad the lower slopes. The forest went on and on, beyond her mountains, blending into the Glen of Arlo, where only wolves and thieves sojourned. She knew this because she had read one of her husband's poems about the rivers and the gods.

'And tell how Arlo, through Diana's spites
Being of old the best and fairest Hill
That was in all this holy island's heights
Was made the most unpleasant hill of all.'
E.S.

He wrote incessantly, often rising from the table at mealtimes to go to his study in the tower. He wrote on affairs of state, of which she understood little. He corresponded with old friends from Cambridge, on matters relating to poetry, to philosophy, to translation. He showed her the letters and, with a certain pride, his answers. She made a concerted effort to follow the arguments but after a page or two, her mind wandered. He would shake his head at her inattention to the finer points.

On Ireland he was consistent. There was a recurring theme: give them twenty days to come in and submit. If they fail to do this, follow them closely in winter time, when the woods are bare. He was not a hunting man but he fixed on a metaphor, 'when the covert is thin.' Harry them in winter time and there will be little work to do with them in the summer.

She understood that he was in the forefront of a struggle for the survival of the English nation, civilisation and the reformed religion. She knew that it galled him to be confined, as she was, in this remote place, this frontier outpost. Enemies could descend upon them at any time, from the sea or from the dark and menacing forest. On the rare occasions that he noticed her apprehension, he assured her that Ireland was under the strong hand; that she had nothing to fear. Yet she did not go, like Diana, to walk upon the hills or bathe, sweaty and hot from the hunt, in the cool waters of Molanna

> 'and after on the soft
> And downy grass, her dainty limbs to lay
> In covert shade, where none behold her may.'
> E.S.

None, except for the foolish god, Faunus, who conspired with the river nymph, to hide and spy upon the goddess in her nakedness, bathing after the exertions of the chase. The covert, however, was too thin to conceal the miscreant. He was dragged forth and beaten until he revealed which of the nymphs had colluded with him. Then he was clad in deer's hide and hunted through the woods with shrill outcry. Molanna they oppressed with stones and rocks, yet she escaped and found her way to the bed of Funshin 'and both combined, themselves in one fair river spread.'

Machabyas thought it strange that he peopled the landscape with gods and nymphs. Yet the forest was dark. He admitted it in the curse that Diana laid upon Arlo and its surrounding mountains…

'Since which those woods and all that goodly
Chase, Doth to this day with Wolves and Thieves abound
Which too, too true, that land's in-dwellers since have found.'
E.S.

That last line was too long. She read it again, beating out the rhythm. There was something odd about it. She looked back. Why had she not noticed? It was everywhere, at the end of each passage of verse, as if he were reluctant to let go. He was a strange one, at one point advocating the submission or extermination of the Irish and at another, peering through the bushes at a goddess bathing in the river. She wished that he would peer at her in that way, but he had become too busy.

***

It was incongruous. He invited the cowherd to come and entertain them on a cold and blustery winter's night. The man had made an effort to tidy himself up a little. He wore rawhide boots, with the hairy side turned inwards. He wore a mantle trimmed with wolf fur, not unlike the one her husband affected on occasions. He carried a harp in a skin bag. He ate and drank copiously.

The children sat by the fire, Sylvanus, a boy of some six years and the little girl, Machabyas, named for herself. Their faces glowed in the firelight. The cowherd unwrapped his harp, a small crooked thing, crudely made, with strings of gut. The children looked at each other, restraining with difficulty, their giggles. Her husband frowned at them. He nodded to the man to begin.

"Before I play for ye, I must tell ye who I am. I am Uaithne."

Her husband nodded again. "I know. Now begin, in God's name."

She smiled at him. It was kind of him to arrange some entertainment. It was not quite the playhouse or the yard at the Bell Savage Inn, but she was grateful.

"I am Uaithne," repeated the cowherd testily, pursuing his point, "harp of the great god, Dagda."

Her husband was smiling. He actually winked at her. There was more absurdity to come.

"When our people were beset by the Fomorians, I was taken into captivity in the heart of Sliabh Luachra."

"Mountains to the west of here," whispered her husband, leaning sideways. "Go on."

Uaithne bristled at the interruption. He needed no prompting. His voice took on a sharper edge.

"I was carried by the Fomorians, into the heart of Sliabh Luachra." She noted how he stared at her husband, demanding silence. "The Fomorians were the worst people that ever came into Ireland, worse even than the English."

Her husband clicked his tongue and nodded tolerantly.

"They would accept no gold or cattle to ransom me. They did this to spite the god, Dagda, to take from him his music. But did he stand for this? No, he did not. Did he not come among them, all alone, to seek the return of his harp? He carried no weapon. He took me from the wall and struck my strings." He lowered his voice to a conspiratorial whisper. His eyes were wide with urgency. "There, in the dún of the Fomorians, in the heart of the mountains, he played for them the three musics. He cast a spell on them".

Her husband was growing impatient. "The three musics? What are these three musics?"

Uaithne took a long, deep breath. He sighed. "They are *An Suantraoi*, the music of sleep, *An Geantraoi*, the music of joy and *An Goltraoi*, the music of grief."

"Well then, let us hear them."

She knew that Spenser had tired of the preamble. She was afraid that he might rise and go back to his study, shattering the mood.

"If you please," she murmured softly, eager to hear what happened.

The cowherd lifted his harp. Light gleamed on wood polished by long handling. She noticed for the first time, the length of his fingernails. The nails were none too clean, the legacy of his trade.

"A little taste of each," said Uaithne. His fingers began to fly over the strings, caressing and plucking. The room filled with merry sound. The flames danced in the hearth. Some servants crept noiselessly into the hall. They stayed in the shadows, beyond the candlelight, looking from one to another in wordless delight. The music ebbed and flowed, inviting them to dance. The children beat their hands on their knees, looking to their parents expectantly. They waited for the nod to get up and dance. Spenser jigged his foot in time, pleased with the unfamiliar rhythms. Uaithne stopped abruptly.

"*An Goltraoi,* he announced. "At this the Fomorians sat down and wept for their manifold crimes and the terrible things they had done to our people."

He began again, slow and plaintive, the music of loss and grief, the sadness of the world, failure and exile, the anxieties of parents. The plangent notes spoke of children lost in the darkness, wild beasts howling in the forest, the approach of death and what might come thereafter.

Machabyas felt a bleak melancholy descending all about her. She acknowledged that she had seen dreadful things and had yet, turned away. She had seen the people crawling out of the woods, crawling because they were too weak to stand, let alone walk. There were children with enormous eyes and the distended bellies of famine, legs like those of little birds. She had witnessed the hurt and incomprehension in the eyes of the parents. She sat by her fire, while outside, the wind culled the poor wretches on the long acre. It was wrong. She began to weep. She wept for the world and for the fear that hemmed her in on all sides.

"Enough of this," her husband said, clapping his hands. "Enough of this gloom."

Uaithne looked at him. He struck one last chord. It hung in the silence of the hall. He stayed his hand.

"*An Suantraoi,* he said quietly. "At this the Fomorians fell into a deep slumber. While they slept, the great god, Dagda, set me free and carried me back to my own people."

He began again, a gentle strain that reached into tired minds, relieving them of their anxieties. It invited weary bodies to lie down and sleep. The children yawned. The music washed about them. The servants, unbidden, sat on forms by the table, resting their heads on their arms. Some closed their eyes. The notes sprinkled gently over them.

Machabyas yawned. She wanted to sleep but the music of grief was still in her head. She had seen a truth, stark in its simplicity. It would be treason to blot it out in sleep. She could not let it slip away. The melancholy stayed with her.

Her husband coughed, to bring an end to the proceedings. The cough caught his breath, as often happened.

"Enough. Enough," he exclaimed, waving a hand. "Your music is tiring us. Let us sit for a little while and then perhaps, you will regale us with your story."

Uaithne laid his harp aside. He took a draught from a cup that he had placed near the fire.

"Ah," he mused. "My story. Ye would not believe my story."

"We like stories, do we not, dear wife?" He was insistent.

She said nothing, knowing that he would get his way and that the little man wanted to talk.

"I can tell ye my story but will ye hear it?"

They waited. The children slept. Uaithne gazed into the fire.

"When the All-father, Dagda, took me from the Fomorians, he set me free from the wood, to go far afield as a man, spreading his music and telling the story of the world."

"He set you free from the forest?"

"No, no, the wood. He set me free from the wood of the harp. I am the spirit of the harp." Uaithne was exasperated. The Englishman was slow of understanding.

"Ah, I see." Spenser smiled again. Machabyas shivered, as if a spectre sat at her hearth. She wanted this man to go.

"When did all this happen?" her husband enquired. He was enjoying the rambling nonsense. It proved something to him about the Irish. He caught her eye and raised one eyebrow. It was a thing he did when comment was superfluous.

"I told you. In the past." Uaithne shrugged. The Englishman was a plodding fellow, wanting chapter and verse.

"So where are your people now?"

She wondered if the prospect of rent had drifted into his mind.

"When the Milesians found this island, they made war on us. They came in their ships. They carried iron. We could not hold them back. After a great battle, we agreed to divide the island between us, one half for the Milesians and the other for the People of Danann."

"Which half belongs to your people? Are you loyal subjects to Her Majesty?"

Uaithne laughed aloud at the idea.

"The upper ground went to the Milesians and all under the earth passed to us. Yeer quarrel is with the Milesians. We can wait until both of ye are finished."

"My quarrel is with the rebellious Irish, above or below the ground. I know no Milesians." The cowherd's story made no rational sense. It was ironic, he reflected, that Uaithne was the only musical shepherd or cowherd he had encountered at close quarters. There was no perfume of Arcadian wild flowers about him. In fact, the closer he drew to the fire the more the true essence of this rustic swain became obvious. The reality of a herdsman's life differed, in some details, from the life of the shepherds of his poems. It was something to ponder, the ideal versus the hard grind of the real world.

"They will come back," said Uaithne, breaking into his thoughts. "They are like the *seabhach*. They hover. They watch. They wait and wait and then, they stoop."

"The *seabhach*?"

"The hawk, the little pooka of the wind. That is their cry in battle. '*A sheabhach! A sheabhach!*'

It sounded like 'Havoc!'

"They will come back when they are strong again. They will swarm out of the Forest of Arlo."

Machabyas flinched. The fire was a gleam of comfort in the surrounding darkness. She hunched closer to the flames. She thought of the wretched people of the woods. Their fires were too meagre to give comfort, just enough to maintain life.

Uaithne put aside his other-worldly manner, the bard, the seer, whatever he affected to be.

"Ye would do better in a town," he said, with genuine solicitude. "The towns hold with the Queen. Get the safety of walls about ye." He took up his harp and put it into the leather bag.

Her husband rose, bringing an end to the evening's entertainment. He offered some coins to the harpist. The man declined them with graceful courtesy.

"As a fellow poet," he said, bowing. "Perhaps you will return the favour some day." He tucked the harp under his arm and turned to go. He paused and faced them. "When ye hear the *seabhach*, take yeerselves away from here. Lose no time. The Milesians will come for ye."

He left the circle of light and the flickering glow of the tapers. He merged into the shadows.

Machabyas looked at her husband. He seemed disturbed. He coughed his nervous cough.

"I shall write to the Lord President and request that a detachment of troops be stationed in the area." He laughed softly. "We cannot have our settlement disturbed by the ramblings of a raggedy minstrel."

He put his hands behind his back and paced about. His feet crunched on the floor rushes. Dust rose from them, irritating his throat. She should have directed the servants to fetch fresh ones. They took advantage of her. He noticed the servants snoring at the table. He rapped his knuckles on the board to rouse them and send them scampering. Lazy Irish, taking every opportunity to loaf about.

Sir John Norris undertook to send ten men to be maintained by Kilcolman, billeted either in the castle or in the houses of the settlers. Good Englishmen and true, recently arrived from Chester.

Machabyas felt some of her apprehension diminish but the melancholy of *An Goltraoi*, remained with her. It stayed with her through the harsh winter days and nights and even into the following spring and summer, although white thorn clothed the woods and birds sang in the forest. It stayed with her when the leaves turned to gold and red and carpeted the woodland ways. It was with her when the wind flailed the last tattered survivors, leaving the branches naked against the sky. The trees, it seemed to her, raised their hands to Heaven, pleading for relief. Her food tasted like ashes. She admitted that she hated Kilcolman more than any place in the world.

***

'Into a forest wide and waste he came
Where store he heard to be of savage prey,
So wide a forest and so waste as this
Nor famous Ardeyn nor foul Arlo is.'
E.S.

In her husband's mind his fears always returned to Arlo. Even the death of Phillip Sidney put him in mind of the wild Irish of Arlo. That place was the source of evil and danger.

Alas for Sidney! He lent his leg armour to a friend and suffered for it. The soldiers of his godfather, King Phillip, brought him to battle in the Low Countries and caused his death. It was a cruel, lingering death. Death hovered over him for twenty six agonising days. Death skulked in the shadows of his darkened chamber. He was thirty three when he died, the age of Christ.

So, died the flower of his generation, poet, athlete, soldier, courtier. A legend sprouted from his bier, his courage and his generosity to a common soldier: 'thy necessity is yet greater than mine.' The last drops of water. There were signs in the sky. All nature mourned his passing, as it had mourned at Calvary. It was mid-winter.

A great nation mourned also. A black-draped ship brought his body home. Thousands upon thousands crowded the river bank to see his coffin arrive. The delay had lent a terrible solemnity to the occasion, a significance more profound than the death of a young man. Four months it had taken to bring him to Saint Paul's Church. The world had time to realise what had been lost, a hero, a youth, the best hope of his generation. There was a funeral to rival that of any monarch, a state funeral for a realm in grief.

There were fifes and solemn drums. There were poor men to the number of thirty three. There were officers and soldiers trailing weapons and standards. A page, carrying a broken lance, rode Sidney's jousting horse. There followed his fearsome barbed horse, his catafract, a beast to strike dread into any onlooker, a thunderbolt in battle. Earls and barons rode by, conscious of the importance the occasion bestowed on them. The Lord Mayor and his retinue, curbed their restive mounts. Citizen volunteers, draped in bandoleers of shot, carried their weapons in the crook of the elbow, chatting like gentlemen returning from a day's fowling. The Company of Grocers, resplendent in their livery, nattered and looked around. Onlookers craned their necks to catch a glimpse of the famous Sir Francis Drake.

The massive bier passed along, borne by fourteen yeomen. Family and friends held his banners aloft. The chief mourners, like monks of old, hid their features in cowls. Five heralds carried his symbols of knighthood, his spurs, his gauntlets, his shield, his coat-of-arms. One carried his helmet, with its boar crest, perhaps a porcupine, maybe even a hedgehog. It was difficult to tell at a distance. A noble knight was laid to rest. The multitudes wept. The choirs sang. The eloquent churchmen spoke at length. The soldiers in Paul's Churchyard, fired a double volley in martial farewell.

***

All this Spenser heard at second hand. He was confined to his bed by ague and pains. It grieved him greatly. He grieved for his friend and patron. He grieved that he had not been there:

'Whilst none is nigh, thine eyelids up to close
And kiss the lips like faded leaves of rose.

That was not strictly true. Sidney's wife had been there to render those last offices. In fact, the wise world was already whispering that, had he been able to forebear from carnal knowledge of her, his wound might have had a chance to heal. His garrulous chaplain let it be known that Sidney had entertained doubts about Salvation, that he had spoken of his fears, that he found his greatest hope in the love of his lady.

Spenser set to work. It made him feel better. The flower, Astrophel, grew out of her grief and his own, the star-shaped flower, red and blue,

> 'And all the day it standeth full of deow
> Which is the tears that from her eyes did flow.'
> E.S.

The words flowed from him. *The Faerie Queene* was set aside. Although Poesie reputedly died with Sidney, Spenser breathed new life into it again. The shepherds, Lycon and Colin, stepped forward once more, with a pastoral eclogue. There were gods, shipwrecks, stars obscured. Albion wept incessantly. Animals, plants, birds spoke an elegy on the loss of the Lord Governor of Flushing. There was an epitaph depicting his pedigree and Another of the Same. There was no doubt about it. The death of Phillip Sidney was a sad business indeed.

Machabyas found occasional diversion in reading the manuscripts. He made no objection, although he never solicited an opinion. This one however, was too sad. It was too long. He was weeping for his erstwhile friend, yet he could not see that she, his wife, was falling to pieces before his eyes. She suspected that some of his grief was for the loss of a rung on the ladder of advancement. She read him well. She wondered if she would merit an elegy, even a sonnet from the rustic shepherds, when her time came.

When Spenser was appointed Clerk to the Council of Munster, her situation deteriorated even more. He was constantly away from home, in conclave with his associates, the great men of the land, cobbling together a master-plan for the confiscation and pacification of Ireland. Dreams of a prosperous and peaceful tomorrow led them on, as fairy lanterns lead the unwary at night, into treacherous bogs and fens. It distressed her to sit with her children, her fellow prisoners, little caged birds, trying to teach them their letters. She thought only of escape.

She walked about the countryside, her skirts always soaked from the long grass. The people looked askance at her. Her human value dwindled. She became a by-word, a joke. There were some who pitied her, even the Irish, a *duine le Dia*, a person already with God. She stopped talking. Her husband was engrossed in his work. He functioned on two levels, the poet lost in a dream of chivalry and the ambitious, climbing man of affairs. She strayed further and further away from him.

Chapter Eighteen

For the first time in his life, Spenser had armed men at his command. They were a sorry lot, the dregs of a train-band, scooped up from some English shire, drunkards, jail-birds and semi-invalids. There were some obviously not in their full wits. The Mayor of Chester had been relieved to be rid of them. As soldiers they were a joke, the scorn of the countryside. It was no wonder, the settlers said, that the English generals relied so heavily on their Irish mercenaries.

Nevertheless, Spenser had hopes for them. He made it clear to them that it was thanks to him that they had arses in their pantaloons and a roof of sorts, over their heads. They owed their living to him. If he turned them out, they would get scant charity from the country people. If they fell into the hands of the wild Irish...well, they had a fair idea of what would happen. They were trapped just as much as Spenser's distracted, wandering wife. It was in their interests to show a semblance of courage and martial vigour. They took to swaggering.

It caused no end of amusement to the powerful nobles of the Council, to see Spenser arriving at the head of his little regiment of rogues, vagabonds and sturdy beggars, with sundry dogs trotting at their heels. He had not the wherewithal to provide them with mounts. They marched untidily and foot sore.

***

Sir John Norris, Lord President of Munster, concluded that the spectacle was not consistent with the standing of an English gentleman. Worse still, it might encourage the disaffected Irish to think that they could take liberties. He resolved to put some steel into Kilcolman, just as soon as funds might become available. He resolved to do a lot of things, when funds became available. It was a constant worry, a nagging irritation, rising eventually to a crisis.

He rubbed his hand across his brow. The scheme of settlement was fraying at the edges. Raleigh complained that cattle were disappearing from his fields. He fumed at the fact that his tenants were inclined to abandon their homesteads, letting the thatch rot and the roof-trees fall in. They left their fields to gorse, brambles and summer blizzards of thistledown. Mr. Wayman, a prominent sheep-master, wrote incessantly about the depredations of thieves and wolves.

Of all of them, strangely, Spenser was the most determined. It was perhaps, Norris pondered, that the poet lived in a world of ideals. He could not settle for less. Norris knew, (Spenser had told him) that he was engaged on a great work, an epic theme, a celebration of all the knightly virtues. It extolled the glory and wisdom of their great Queen. Norris also knew that Spenser harboured ambitions to be an important man at Court. Everything Spenser did was a stepping-stone to something greater.

He appreciated Spenser's view of the situation in Ireland. Few saw it as clearly, a choice for the recalcitrant natives, capitulation and peace with prosperity, or war and annihilation. It was a kindness of a sort, to put the options so starkly. His massacre of the MacDonalds of Rathlin, was a microcosm of what had to be done, a rooting out of weeds to prepare the land for tilth and pasture. It was strange, he mused, that a soldier such as he, hardened in many campaigns, should be at one with a poet.

***

Not that Spenser himself had the military power to put his plan into effect. On his way to Cork, he was overtaken by his old benefactor, now adversary, Maurice Roche, Viscount Fermoy. Mad Maurice rode at a gallop, unaccompanied by his usual troop of horsemen. Spenser heard the hoof-beats. He halted and looked around. His men slouched at ease, shifting from one foot to the other. There was no threat here.

Spenser turned his horse, curious to know what new complaint had moved his neighbour to pursue him so vigorously.

The viscount reined his horse in. The beast was in a lather of sweat. It panted furiously. Spenser noted how his neighbour had got old and corpulent. His face was red from his exertions. A pestilential fellow, with some new grievance. Spenser damned him to hell in his mind.

"Mr. Spenser," began Roche, without preamble. "You must return home at once."

"I am required in Cork for a meeting of the Council."

"God blast you, man. Your poor wife is dead." He had intended breaking it more gently, to make a supreme effort at sympathy and civility. At times such as this, men should put aside their enmities. He wiped his forehead with his bonnet. The feather in the bonnet was bent in two.

It was as if a fist had clutched at Spenser's heart.

"Dead? How can this be? I left her in good health early this morning. How can this be?"

Poor Machabyas, he thought. Unhappy woman. Discontented woman. But she was in good health.

"I am sorry to have to tell you this. She was found in the river." Roche's horse stirred. He checked it more firmly than was needful.

"Where? Where?"

Roche coughed awkwardly. "At *Poll na Marbh*," he said softly, "just downstream of where my river meets the Blackwater. I am truly sorry for this trouble to you and yours."

"I thank you sir, for your pains. I shall return immediately."

Roche nodded and turned his horse. There was no need to labour the details. She had been seen falling from the cliff, a high Tarpeian rock of jutting limestone. *Poll na Marbh,* the Pool of the Dead, was a swirling vortex below the cliff. The witness, the wretched hag who dwelt among the tombs of the friary, had seen her. She told how the woman's garments bore her up a while, as she went round and round. She said that she had heard the poor soul singing. Then her garments drew her down into the brown depths of the great river. The wretched hag, who had seen suffering all her life, had been moved to tears. Roche himself had been moved by the story, moved by pity and to anger. He wanted to strike this man, this cold, inflexible husband, so caught up in his own vision, that he could not see what was obvious to strangers.

He nodded and took his leave.

Spenser knew the grim, forbidding place. It lay upriver from the castle of Renny, a quaint little castle of the Fitzgeralds, part of the confiscated Desmond lands. He had, in his own mind, a legitimate claim on it, disputed of course, by Viscount Roche. This was not the time to be thinking of that. It irked him that Roche referred to 'my river', the Awbeg, that he had, himself, rechristened 'Mulla', 'Mulla mine.' 'Mulla mine, whose waves I whilom taught to weep.' He liked the line. He supposed that he should weep for Machabyas, but no tears came. He rode homewards with his men trudging behind him. They loitered and slouched. He pricked his horse, urging it into a reluctant trot. He left his regiment to make its own way home.

***

Sir Walter Raleigh came to commiserate. Had Machabyas not snagged on a submerged tree, she might well have travelled all the way to his town of Youghal. Her story travelled in her stead, a poor distracted woman, singing her last song as she was drawn under the surface of the hastening river. It was evidence to some, an omen, that the settlement was cursed, that it could never take root in the alien soil of Munster. It prompted a number of struggling families to take the decision to pack their few belongings and leave. Spenser was obliged to fill their places with Irish tenants, surly Papists, skulking away to Mass on the Sabbath, muttering about the retribution to come, upon the return of the old order.

Raleigh complained of the same problem, his hooded eyes masking his disappointment. He brought more disturbing news than the gradual failure of his settlement. Walsingham's network of informants reported a great fleet gathering at Cadiz. It was surmised that the King of Spain intended lifting his armies out of the Low Countries and shipping them across the Narrow Sea, bringing devastation to the Protestant realm of England. The Queen had no force that could withstand such might, either on land or sea. He explained that he was returning to Court to dedicate himself to the safety of his monarch and of her nation. He urged Spenser to come with him.

Spenser declined. "My work is not yet finished," he explained. It would, he reflected, be ironic if his epic poem, glorifying Elizabeth, should be completed just as King Phillip was accommodating himself to new lodgings in Richmond or Westminster. It would be more than ironic if a Spanish army, leagued with Irish rebels, should entrench themselves before Kilcolman's walls.

Raleigh noticed his rueful smile. "You laugh, my friend. Does the prospect of a Catholic armada not terrify you to the bone?"

"My troops will send them packing," replied Spenser.

Raleigh guffawed. He had seen Spenser's troops. They had roused themselves to challenge him at the gate, but he was in the courtyard before they could decide on a course of action. The absurdity of the idea lightened the mood.

"You could revise your work quickly, changing all the names to Spanish."

Spenser smiled. "That is a thought. I could install a popish priest here and dress like some hidalgo." He paused. "If you can spare some time," he began again diffidently, "perhaps you would look over the manuscript."

Raleigh raised a hand. "Please, you must remember that I have some pretensions to being a poet. If your work is as good as I suspect it to be, I may be stricken with envy. I may well denigrate it to the point that you will abandon all hope of success and consign it to the fire. In this way I can prevent comparison with my own humble rhyming, or indeed, I may steal your ideas and represent them as the children of my own fertile brain."

"Aha! I see your devious plan," said Spenser, smiling again, "but nonetheless, I will hazard that, if you will stay a day or two. Kilcolman can be a very quiet place."

Raleigh could see the hunger in his friend's eyes. He understood his need for some kind of validation, some recognition from a kindred soul, some human warmth in his solitary quest. He assented. Spenser left him with the sheets of manuscript.

He took his children to fish in the river. Mulla abounded in white trout. He showed them how to tie dubbes to wands and let them lie on the water, like the flies of summer. They caught nothing. It was pleasant, nonetheless, to lie on the riverbank and watch the children splashing in the water. They paddled in the shallows and peered under the water-plants, exclaiming now and then at some exciting discovery. It came to him that he had been a sort of absent father. Now they had nobody but him.

He sat them down on the grassy bank and told them the story of the fox and the kid. The mother goat told her son to bar the door when she went out and open it to nobody.

'But most the Foxe, maister of collusion
For he has vowed thy last confusion.
For thee, my Kiddie be ruled by me
And never give trust to his trecheree.
And if he chaunce come when I am abroad
Spar the gate fast for fear of fraud.'

He wagged his finger at the children. They listened wide-eyed, fearful of the catastrophe to come. They knew, even at their tender age, that gates should be secured. They had heard their father berating his slovenly soldiers. They knew that bad people lurked in the woods. They feared for the kid.

Of course the fox arrived, not as a fox but disguised as a peddler, with a basket on his back, 'a trusse of tryfles.' His head was bound with a kerchief. His foot was wrapped in a bandage, his poor, weary foot. He limped. He groaned. He lay down outside the door and bewailed his sorry state. He put down his heavy burden.

The kid peered through a chink in the door. The fox, spying him, showed him a mirror. It shone like a jewel. The kid desired this wondrous thing above all else in the world, above his own safety. He forgot his mother's warning. He opened the door. The fox entered.

Spenser's voice dropped to a note of sepulchral doom. The children were transfixed.

The fox, he intoned, opened his basket of knick-knacks and turned them out on the floor. The children trembled with anticipation, like the baby sparrows tremble, waiting to be fed. Everything tumbled onto the floor, except for a bell. This he left in the basket for the curious kid to discover.

'Which when the Kidde stooped down to catch,
He popt him in and his basket did latch,
Ne stayed he once the door to make fast
But ran away with him in all haste.'
E.S.

The children gasped. They shivered at the thought of what happened to the victim. Spenser was pleased with such an appreciative audience. They put away their fishing wands and walked homewards. He let them walk barefoot like the country people. They found wild mushrooms and gathered them into their bonnets, saying 'by your leave,' to the invisible fairies. The children laughed at such silliness, but they looked around all the same.

"You have to be polite to the fairies," he warned them. "They were here first and will be here long after us." They laughed again and frowned at the idea. They were unused to their father engaging in frivolity. The day was good. He reflected guiltily that he had never shared a day like that with Machabyas.

***

195

Raleigh was almost lost for words. "I shall stay until I have read every line. I demand that you come to London and register this at the Stationers' Company. This poem...." He tapped the bundle of manuscript. "This poem will throw open the doors of the Court to you. I am consumed with envy and admiration." He clapped Spenser heartily on the back. He raised his voice as if introducing him to an audience. "We have found our Petrarch, our Virgil."

Spenser's head spun. He looked for sarcasm but there was none. It was joy to hear that in his rural backwater, he had produced something of great merit, merit enough to move this cynical, hardened man of affairs, to rapture.

They talked long into the night. He told Raleigh of his fishing expedition. They had caught no fish but he had caught something else, something that he had not suspected, a thing that could have been lost forever. With his story of the bell, he had caught hold of his children, just before they slipped away forever. That story was told about Frobisher on one of his expeditions, how he had lured an Indian with a bell and lifted him by main force onto his ship. The fairy giant had been led astray by his own image in a mirror. Images, knick-knacks, observations. His mind teemed with them. He could forget nothing. His only relief was to put words on paper. Raleigh understood. The mention of Frobisher darkened his mood.

"She forbids me to go to sea. She keeps me mewed up," he snorted. "I live in her fantasy of love. Frobisher is free to cruise the ocean with Drake. He can harry the Spaniards in Panama and the Azores. To my shame, they rescued my poor colonists in Virginia, while I was mincing about the Court, bowing and scraping. Virginia," he sighed, "a fiasco, as the Italians say and it looks like Ireland is going the same way."

"No!" protested Spenser, vehemently. He shook his head.

"Have you any idea of the value of their prizes?" demanded Raleigh.

Drake and Frobisher were still on his mind. Spenser shook his head again. He understood his guest's frustration.

Raleigh leaned forward and peremptorily, tapped Spenser on the arm. "I will tell you how to catch fish." He smiled at Spenser's puzzlement. "There is a bird in the Indies, a big, black bird with a forked tail and wings like scimitars."

Spenser waited. He was picturing the bird. Scimitars. Pirates of Barbary.

"With a red throat, a flag of danger. A sinister looking fellow. That is who I long to be"

Spenser frowned. Raleigh laughed at his confusion.

"Yes, a bird. I have seen him attack the fisher birds. He flies over and under them, swooping from the skies like an acrobat." He moved his hand, in imitation of the bird's manoeuvres. "Never letting up, afflicting them with his wings, until they drop their catch. He takes the fish in mid air. It is a sight to behold. Such mastery of his element!" He sighed. "She has put me in command of her land forces in the south and west" He shook his head in disgust. "I am too precious to be allowed go to sea."

"And you long to be a pirate bird on the western ocean?"

"With all my heart."

They sat a while in silence. Spenser shifted in his seat. "Do you ever think of *Dún and Óir?*

A log subsided in the fire. Raleigh growled. "What was done there was necessary. They were condottieri. They knew the risks."

"I know," agreed Spenser. "Sometimes terrible things are necessary. But they are terrible nonetheless. They engender great hatreds. They leave a stain. I saw that stain. From the fort, I saw it. It spread and spread. The water could not wash the deed clear of blood. It stained Lord Grey and still does."

Raleigh sat upright, prepared, as the author of the deed, to take offence. Spenser stayed him, raising his hand.

"Let me tell you a story." His tone was conciliatory. Raleigh sat back again. He looked into the fire. Spenser continued.

"When we were marching towards Dingle, we stopped at the castle of a well-disposed nobleman. He invited us to stay the night and partake of his hospitality. When he sent for wine, he learned that his wife had opened all his casks, uncorked all his bottles and flooded his cellar with his finest vintages. She would not, she could not, offer comfort to any Englishman. The nobleman struck her in anger and embarrassment. He struck her on the head, with the door-stop. He left her lifeless in a pool of wine."

"Did Lord Grey not remonstrate with him?"

"No. It was a matter between man and wife. I think, though, that he understood her hatred and her husband's fear. He doubted his own authority. He was not the most decisive of men, as you recall."

Raleigh nodded in agreement. He drew a sharp breath through his teeth. "Indeed."

"You were present at the enquiry." Spenser felt that he deserved a story in return. He was curious.

"I was. He was charged with breaking faith. They tried to taint me also, but I proved that I was merely following orders. To do otherwise would have been mutiny, a crime against good order. The realm stands or falls on order." He laughed sardonically. "It probably helped that I had come to the attention of the Virgin Queen. She could not allow a judgement against her new lap-dog." He took a long drink. "Ah, well. If I cannot bring her Spanish gold, I can bring her an even greater treasure."

"What might that be?"

"You, my good friend. You and your work. I shall bring you to Court, if the Spaniards permit me. See if I cannot secure a place for you."

A loud commotion in the courtyard, interrupted their conversation. They hurried down the stairs and out into the darkness. Raleigh drew his sword, ever ready for a fight. A dispute had broken out between Spenser's men and Raleigh's Irish mercenaries. The Englishmen were getting the worst of it. They were backed up against the door of their lean-to shelter. Those already within had barred the door against the rearguard. They shouted encouragement to their fellows, but declined to come to their assistance.

Raleigh waded in, using the flat of his sword to drive the two groups apart. He swore in both Irish and English. They backed away from his fury. Peace, of a sort, was restored. Raleigh was panting like a hound.

"God's curse on them", he said, laughing. He had enjoyed the exertion, but it was clear to all that he would tolerate no further broils. "They are curs, all of them," he added under his breath to Spenser. "You must show them who is master."

Spenser understood the pent up rage that had almost cost him his men-at-arms. He wished that they were gone from him, but he needed them, as a farmer needs scarecrows among his crops. If the Irish of the forest came close enough, they would see that Kilcolman was defended by men of straw.

He felt his spirits rise, infected by some of Raleigh's strength and vigour. Raleigh could prise open the gate long barred to him, provided, of course, that his impetuous spirit did not lead to some precipitous fall from grace.

Raleigh was laughing. "Did you hear the coward calling from within? 'Remember thy swashing blow, Cedric. Remember thy swashing blow.' Bear thy swashing blow in mind, if the Spaniards land at Cork." He went back inside, chuckling at the humour of it all. He returned to the manuscript. Spenser took a candle and went on tip-toe, to look at his sleeping children.

Chapter Nineteen

John Dee came home to Mortlake a chastened man. The Polish prince had run out of money. No base metal had transmuted to gold. A stint at the court of the Emperor had proved fruitless. The Imperial patience soon ran out. The two slatterns found more enticing and profitable company elsewhere. Kelly, condemned to prison for theft, leaped from a high window and tumbled down a steep glacis. His fertile brain was no use to him on this occasion. His two legs snapped above the knees. His gaolers promptly took him up and hanged him. They had to hold him under the armpits. They let him sag like a puppet on his shattered legs, deriving great amusement, until the noose took his weight and the trapdoor fell open.

Dee was free of his incubus, but burdened by shame at his own gullibility. His house had been ransacked in his absence. His bookshelves were empty. His only hope was a summons from the Queen. He looked about at the wreckage of his home. The local people had denounced him as a sorcerer. There was nobody in the world to help him save his little Caliban. He patted the boy's head.

"We must go, cap in hand," he said. "We must beg our bread at the palace gate." He savoured the drama of his situation, the

Prodigal returned. She might still have need of him. He found some paper and wrote a letter of deepest contrition. He lamented the loss of his library.

With his last few pence he sent a messenger to Richmond. Within hours a waterman arrived to convey him into the presence of the Queen. He went, stiffly to his knees. She looked down from her seat of power. She saw an old and tearful man and his servant, the infidel boy.

"We are pleased, Doctor Dee, to take you back into our good graces. We hope that your future behaviour will be more in keeping with your advancing years."

Dee inclined his head even lower. He had no words. The courtiers looked on with interest. Her Majesty's mood could go either way.

"We wish to speak with Doctor Dee in private." She swept them from the room with a curt gesture, all save Lord Burghley. She did very little without his advice.

"You may stand, Doctor Dee, she said graciously. Her tone was softer. John Dee got slowly and painfully to his feet. His gown was still stained with the dust of travel. The boy remained kneeling. He winced and rubbed his knees unselfconsciously, rocking from side to side to ease the pressure. The flagstones were hard and cold.

"Rise, child," she commanded, "and attend upon your master."

The boy stood up. He rubbed his knees again. He groaned. He caught Lord Burghley's eye. He thought, for an instant, that the great lord had winked at him. He stood upright and lowered his eyes.

"Your books are safe with us, Doctor Dee. We have taken them into our keeping. You have given us great trouble. No doubt, some few volumes have escaped our attention."

Dee looked up at her in profound gratitude.

"As you have proved yourself unfit to care for such a great treasure, we have decided to purchase them for the sum of four thousand pounds."

Lord Burghley clicked his tongue. It was a great deal of money. Dee's eyes opened wide. He gazed up at his saviour.

"You may consult them here at Court at any time."

He nodded his gratitude.

"But you will have an opportunity to repay us."

Dee bowed again.

"You may not know that the Spaniard has gathered a mighty fleet to afflict us here in our island."

"I had not heard, Majesty." He spoke for the first time. "I am only lately arrived home." His voice was hoarse and shaking from his recent fear.

"We are aware of your travels, Doctor. However, to your service. When the Spanish fleet enters our waters, we direct that you raise a great tempest to dash their ships on the rocks, or sink them in the profoundest depths."

He felt the sweat break out on his brow. His confidence had been badly dented by his failure on the Continent. He had spent half a century searching for the secret. By now he should have been established, unassailably, as the most influential scholar in Europe. A storm was a tall order for a man who had become the subject of mockery.

"I shall do all in my power, majesty, to fulfil your wishes."

"Not wishes, Doctor. Our command. You will raise a storm when we require it."

He bowed again. He knew the price of failure. There were still heads on the bridge.

"Your young servant? We take it that he is a Christian child."

"He is, Majesty. I saw to it myself. I instruct him daily."

"Good. You will remain with us until this crisis is past. He will stay to fetch and carry and sort your volumes. You may leave us."

Dee bowed low and backed away from her presence. The boy did likewise, watching his master and trying to keep in step. It was a game. He grinned. Dee frowned at him, warning him to behave. He was in no mood for games. The snow- swept plains of Poland began to look more attractive to his recollection. He was caged. He must perform. He must find some powerful magic in his books. He wondered how Kelly would have handled the dilemma. But Kelly and his angelic master were not around to help him. The skryving mirror had gone missing. The angel, Uziel, kept his own counsel.

***

Time and tide stay for no man. It took the Great and Fortunate Armada almost six weeks to reach the Channel. Gear and rigging were already showing signs of wear, after battling the rough weather of Biscay. As for the tide, it bottled up the English fleet in Plymouth, while the crescent of Spanish ships lay off-shore, bobbing about like so many geese. They followed orders. King Phillip forbade any deviation from his master plan. The High Admiral, Medina Sidonia, had no experience of the sea. There were those in the fleet who had fought the English on the high seas and among the islands of the Indies. They wanted to go in after them and destroy them on their moorings. That was not provided for in the plan.

The tide turned. The English came out like terriers. They knew those waters. They tacked up-wind of the Spaniards and began to herd them into the Narrow Sea. They nipped, like sheep-dogs, at the two horns of the crescent, driving the Spaniards in upon themselves in confusion. It became obvious that the smaller English craft were more agile than the lofty Spanish galleons. Their gunnery was faster and more accurate. They saw how the Spaniards struggled to reload, swinging men over the side, with charges and shot to replenish the guns, a precarious operation in calm water, impossible in foul weather. The dangling loaders fell prey to musket and arquebus. The English gunners laboured in the relative safety of the gun decks.

Frobisher revelled in his command, *Triumph*, the largest ship in the fleet, with a complement of five hundred men. It was a far cry from his little *Ayde*, with which he had tried to conquer the Arctic. By night he kept his eye on Drake's stern lantern. Drake was the bell-wether, as Admiral Lord Howard had decreed. Wherever he led, the fleet must follow.

The Spanish crescent began to fray at the edges. A massive explosion tore out the stern of *San Salvador*. Drake could not resist his instincts. He fell upon and captured *Rosario*. When darkness came, he snuffed out his lantern and took *Rosario* into Plymouth as a lucrative prize. The English fleet went astray in the night.

Frobisher cursed his commander heartily. The pirate in Drake would always assert himself. The Spaniards edged away, always eastwards, towards their rendezvous with the army. The westerly wind freshened to a half gale. They anchored off Calais, feeling acutely the lack of a deep water port. The army was not there. There were no barges for the invasion of England.

They shuffled along the coast to Dunkirk, keeping in close formation. Still there was no army. They moved further east to Gravelines. The anchor chains rattled. The rigging sang. The wind tugged and buffeted at the high stern castles. The English stood off and pounded them. At night they sent fire ships drifting with the wind to spread alarm and destruction. The English were always up-wind. The gale strengthened from hour to hour.

The Spaniards raised anchor and made a break for the open sea. A fierce running battle ensued, as Lord Howard and his dogs hunted them northwards. It went from running fight to rout, from rout to blind panic. The Spaniards headed for Scotland and a circuitous escape route back to Spain.

Their charts were inaccurate, the longitude lines being misplaced and misleading. They fought the great ocean current, not expecting to find it so far north. The men were sick and hungry. They had ample supplies of ammunition, but no use for it. The tempest battered them onto the jagged lee shores of the Western Isles and Ireland.

***

John Dee heard the music in the chimney pots. He heard it in the banging of doors and in every whistling, draughty window. His heart sang to the sound of the tempest. He smiled to see great ladies tacking across the courtyard, clutching their cloaks about them and clinging to their elaborate head gear. The extravagant ruffed collars of the courtiers and gentlemen, flapped about their ears, giving them the air of fighting cocks in high rage. He delighted in the gulls that struggled in the upper air, stationary for a time, looking this way and that and then off, off, sliding down the wind. Crows hurtled about the sky like scraps of black rag. Unseasonal leaves scurried on the pathways, piling in corners or whirling like sprites, where two draughts met.

The watermen took sanctuary in the taverns, spending next week's earnings. The river plucked at their boats, where they hung on moorings.

Although his feet were cold, his heart glowed. The skill had not deserted him.

"I did it," he said, beaming on little Caliban. "I shall teach you all my art."

The boy hunched his shoulders. He was intimidated by all his master's dusty books. He knew, however, that these books contained great knowledge and power. He wanted to know many things but, most of all, he wondered how he had come to this place.

"When you are older," was Dee's unfailing answer, "I shall tell you everything. For now be content to know that your home is the home of the lodestone and the geese. Soon they will arrive on this wonderful wind." He clapped his hands in glee. "This wonderful wind! We shall go to my lord Bedford's fields at Covent Garden to greet them."

It had become a ritual with them. The boy loved to hear them in the autumn as the evenings closed in. They came like shadows, in a perfect pattern, their necks outstretched to catch the first sight of their winter feeding grounds. He had missed them during their time in Poland and Bohemia. There were geese aplenty there but they were not his geese. Some day, he promised himself, he would follow them to their summer home. It should not be difficult to follow them. They made broad arrows in the sky. He knew also that the lodestone would keep him on the right course. There was strange magic in the lodestone.

A door slammed somewhere in the palace. A voice scolded. Dee looked up from his book. His eyes twinkled above his bushy beard.

"Yes!" he exclaimed, raising his clenched fists in a gesture of triumph.

***

Juan Martinez de Recalde, commander of the galleon, *San Juan de Portugal,* knew those treacherous waters. He recognised the towering bulk of Mount Brandon and the headland of the Fort of Gold. He knew the Sleeping Sisters. Eight years previously he had escorted an invasion force to that spot to place some papal by-blow on the throne of Ireland. Winter pains troubled his bones. He was not happy to see those jagged cliffs or the white, climbing surf at their base. He was even more unhappy to find himself forty leagues further to the east than he had calculated on his chart. He was less than pleased to find himself responsible for the remnants of the Biscayan squadron, one companion warship and a vessel seized from some surly Scottish herring fishers.

He took the desperate decision to ride the tidal swell through a small gap at the eastern end of the Great Blasket Island, his hull mere inches from the reef. The surge lifted him and carried him into safe anchorage in the lee of the island. His companions followed, timing their dash to the cresting swell.

They hung there for several days, conscious of activity on shore. No boats put out to welcome them or sell them fresh food and water. They were under no illusion about the welcome they would receive on shore. Three more ships stumbled into the Sound. Two of them foundered almost immediately.

On shore Sir Edward Denny let it be known that any assistance given to this invasion would be the ultimate treason. Survivors were to get no quarter. Any who made it to shore were to be dispatched immediately and their heads brought to him for reward. He received two hundred. His good wife, happy in her charnel work amidst the blue-bottles and blow- flies, checked the tallies. She held a scented handkerchief to her nose and rolled each head aside with a cane, counting aloud to a tally man. She made sure that her husband was fully reimbursed by the Dublin authorities.

The wind abated and swung around to the south east. Recalde gathered his tattered squadron and took them out to sea.

***

The Queen was pleased with John Dee. She promised that she would give him charge of some important college, where his learning would benefit many. He returned to Mortlake to enjoy the fine days of autumn. He was pleased to see that colymbetes, his swimming master, or at least one of his kinsmen, had returned to the horse trough. He resumed his swimming in the river but he eschewed the restorative aquavit that Kelly had insisted upon. He put his house in order and began to instruct the boy. He felt well. The locals regarded him with greater awe than ever. It became common knowledge that he had used his sorcery to bring confusion to the Spaniards. Obviously it was benign sorcery, conducted, as was pointed out, in the shadow of the church of Saint Mary the Virgin.

Frobisher lodged briefly in his house in King Street. He attended upon Her Majesty, who transmuted him, by the alchemy proper to divinely appointed monarchs, into Sir Martin Frobisher. It was an intangible reward. He would have preferred cash to pay his men. He had not profited, as Drake had, from the pursuit of the Spaniards. It tantalised him to speculate on the quantities of gold lost in the proud galleons that had met their doom on the cruel western seaboard.

It irked him that his old friend, become adversary, Michael Lok, lately released from prison, was living in his house. The man was obviously distracted. He sat all day at his table, writing, writing. He was still demanding fair auditing and honest accounting. He could not let it go.

"Look at this, Captain Frobisher," he said, holding up a sheet of paper. It seemed that he had forgotten their old antagonism. 'Bedding, three pounds sixteen shillings and five pence; boat hire, ten guineas.' I have it all here. Burghley ignores me. Walsingham has turned the other Commissioners against me." He ran his ink-stained fingers through his thinning hair. His voice trembled. "What shall I do, Captain Frobisher? What am I to do?"

Battles long ago. He should let it go. As a good accountant, Michael Lok should write it off.

"Be thankful that you are free." Frobisher spoke with unexpected gentleness. He owed him that. He owed him a roof over his head and some small respect. "Be thankful for your good wife and for your children."

Michael Lok frowned. He struggled with the idea. Write what off?

"But look at this I pray you. A bottle of aquavit, ten shillings. I mean to say."

"Indeed," replied Frobisher. He recalled that same bottle and the comfort it brought him when he was amid the ice. Ten shillings and worth every farthing. He realised that he was hungry. He was conscious of delicious smells rising from the kitchen. He wanted some of Mary Lok's cooking. He stood in sore need of her cooking.

"I have made a map, another approach to the Indies. East about, this time. I am proposing another expedition." Michael Lok searched among his papers. "I will show it to you. I have it here, somewhere." He became agitated. "I know it is here somewhere."

"Ah," said Frobisher, rising. "Yes, yes, of course. In good time. All in good time." His mouth was watering. At that moment he was prepared to trade all the gold of the Indies, east or west, for a platter piled high with Mistress Lok's remarkable food.

"I want you to lead it," Lok called after him.

"We shall see. We shall see" Frobisher murmured, closing the door firmly behind him.

Michael Lok totted up the columns of figures, being careful to carry the farthings, the ha'pence, the pence and the shillings. It came to twelve hundred and five pounds, eleven shillings and eightpence. It should have been twelve hundred and six pounds exactly. He began to search for the missing eight shillings and fourpence. It must be somewhere. It must be. It must be.

The Peregrine

1591 - 1599

Chapter Twenty

Spenser felt the tide lifting him as the ship sailed out of Youghal. He was leaving the wooded Blackwater and the mountains that had become so familiar. He was leaving his children for a while in the company of Raleigh's friends, the affable Boyles. The children were happy to exchange the quiet of Kilcolman for the excitement of a busy port town.

Raleigh pointed to a tower on the headland to the east. It was one of the ancient round, pointed towers, built by the monks in ancient times.

"That is my pharos," he said lightly. "When I see that tower, I know that I am safe. It was once part of a cathedral, in Popish times. Now it is a ruin."

"Is it not always the case?" nodded Spenser. "Do you remember the old woman in the friary? Mutability. It comes to all of us."

"You gave her your cloak. Yes, I remember. Do you still wear the
Irish mantle?"

"Only indoors. In winter. Kilcolman is a draughty place."

"How do you find Lord Roche? Have you settled your differences?"

"Not entirely. I will not tire you with a retelling of our disputes."

Raleigh nodded. "If there is anything I can do." He left the thought unfinished.

"It is a wonder that he has not come after me for the coat." Spenser made light of it. He was too excited to think about grievances and grudges, title deeds and rights of way. He had a printer to see and three books of his great poem to present to Gloriana herself. After all this time, it seemed that everyone wanted to read Spenser.

The prow lifted, responding to the Atlantic swell. The ship heeled in the stiff breeze. Raleigh stretched expansively. He breathed deeply. "Ahhh!" he said. He patted the timber of the gunwale, as he would pat his horse. He gazed towards the horizon.

The gulls fell far behind. Bright gannets dived and rose again, crop-full, spreading their wings, like the phoenix. A merchantman, bound for Youghal, passed far to leeward. It set Spenser's mind working.

'Ye tradefull Merchants that with weary toil

Do seek most pretious things to make your gain..'

It was still a secret, spoken to no one, not even Raleigh, his sponsor and admirer. The merchantman was heading in the right direction, back to Youghal of the yew trees and the safe harbour. Youghal of the welcoming water gate and the massive walls. She might well be walking at that very moment, walking with his children in Saint Mary's Gardens. He pictured her, the young widow, Elizabeth Boyle, her skirts leaving a trail on the dewy grass.

'For lo! my love doth in herself contain

All the world's riches . . . . '

The merchants went far and wide, plundering the Indies, east and west, for rubies, ivory, gold, pearls, sapphires. He enumerated in his mind, all those attributes in which she surpassed the wealth of the world, all those parts of her body that out-shone jewels. He dwelt on her beauty, but it was her mind that had won his heart . . .

'her mind adorned with virtues manifold.'

E.S.

It was an idyllic picture. She walked in the garden, surrounded by the all-encompassing rampart.

He had begun to ponder what his little cowherd had said, 'Ye would be safer in a town. When the Milesians come back, ye would be better off behind walls.' Uaithne had poked his latent fear. He said 'when,' not 'if.' The thought was always there, insistent as a grasshopper on a summer's day. There could be found many good reasons for moving to a well defended town, the welfare and education of his two children, the ease of correspondence with his peers, ready access to the Court, should he be required at short notice.

All very good reasons, but the one uppermost in his mind was the graceful young Englishwoman, in the full flower of her femininity. She was a fortress to be taken by patient siege, breaking down the walls by wit and by love. She had crept into his thoughts and even into his dreams. He had begun to imagine her as his companion in greatness, outshining even the bejewelled ladies of the Court.

He gazed at the blur of coastline. The merchantman had gone about, its sails mere specs of white. He envied them their destination, but reminded himself that he too was bound on a quest, an adventure to equal those of his imagined knights. He thought of his triumphant return.

"What do you think?" Raleigh, it seemed had been telling him some news. "What do you think of his offer?"

"Your pardon, my friend. My mind was elsewhere. His offer? Whose offer?"

"Young Richard Boyle. Insolent young upstart. I met him in his uncle's house, the one where your children are lodged."

Spenser felt the colour rising to his cheeks, as if his thoughts had been laid open to Raleigh. He nodded.

"He is the cuckoo in the nest. He offers to buy my land and my town of Youghal. He has no money, just his sword and his fashionable garb, but he is determined to become wealthy in Ireland. I think he may well do so. He puts me in mind of myself, in a way." He laughed tolerantly. "I dream of the Americas and cities of gold. Young Boyle will pick the bush clean in Ireland and buy us all out. I can see it in him already. A man to watch. You could do worse than cultivate his acquaintance."

"I shall pay more attention to him, but I will hold onto Kilcolman, if you please."

"Ready cash," said Raleigh, leaning his elbows on the rail. His eyes swept the horizon. "With ready cash, anything can be accomplished."

It was as if a cloud had passed across the sun. The thought of Raleigh selling up, however unlikely, selling his port, his river, his woods and castles, cast a shadow over Spenser's dreams of the future. Raleigh clenched his fist. He thumped the rail. "There is so much that I could do. Let him come back to me some day with a sack of gold and we can talk terms." He laughed a dry, caustic laugh. "I might even take the young widow off his hands, for a consideration."

Spenser flinched.

"Should Her Majesty permit me, of course. Everything comes back to Her Majesty." He drew out a pipe and tamped some tobacco into the bowl. "Her Majesty." He poked at the bowl, gathering the shreds of leaves into a nest. "May God bless her," he added, straight faced. "I see the hectic in your cheeks, my friend. Does the sea not agree with you?"

"Perfectly well," Spenser assured him. He wanted to walk the deck and put his thoughts in order. Raleigh clapped him lightly on the shoulder. He went below to look for a spark.

***

"Quickly! Quickly!" With much clapping of hands and bustling back and forth, Mistress Lok prepared rooms for her important guest. She managed her staff, composed mostly of her many children, with cheerful efficiency. Spenser was determined to be pleased with everything.

Young girls in white aprons flitted about, carrying sheets, blankets, table cloths, food. Every surface gleamed from polishing. Boys brought armfuls of logs and buckets of coal. They set up fresh tapers.

"Quickly! Quickly! Our guest is weary from his journey. Put the books there. Open the curtain." She clapped again. "Open the curtain. Let God's good sunlight in. Now, out, out everybody." They fled, leaving a sudden silence. "Master Spenser, you are right welcome." She dropped a small curtsey.

Spenser inclined his head graciously. He approved of her manner. There was nothing obsequious about her. This was a woman used to dealing with people of quality, this Mistress Lok, Mistress Quickly, as he had begun to think of her. With a clap of her hands she could marshal a regiment or a company of unruly players. He liked his new lodging. There was a time when he would have stayed in Lord Leicester's house in The Strand, basking in the glow of Leicester's approval. But alas! Time had ruined the mighty nobleman. Time had allowed his fortunes to lead him on to great wealth and influence, to a point where he was almost a king, a man who had determined the fate of a queen. Time had seen him rise and rise as a general, an arbiter of wars. Yet Time had cast him down again, watching his wealth ebbing away in the blood-soaked ditches of The Low Countries. Time sent the little malignant fly to sting the great lord and lay him low. It was a sombre thought, how precarious life can be. It was worth a poem.

Nevertheless, he was determined to enjoy London in all its variety. He revelled in the sounds of the street. The weather was bright and brisk. There was little fear of the plague miasma, no need to shun gatherings and throngs. He looked forward to his introduction to the Court. He was the traveller, coming home from a far country, after many years, bearing treasures of inestimable value. It warmed his heart to think of it. He brought a vision that would influence how England saw itself and its place in the world. He brought knowledge, wisdom and a pathway to peace and prosperity in Ireland. He could see a day when he would be sitting in council with the gravest men of the realm, or escorting his elegant young wife about the gardens of London's palaces.

***

There was a butterfly, Muiopotmos, the fairest of all his kind, overweening in confidence, innocent in his curiosity. Borne on wings of many colours, he flew higher and higher, looking down on the world and the works of men. He espied a palace with a wondrous garden. He descended. So glorious were his colours that even the ladies of the Court envied him. He tasted of every flower in the garden, but still he was not satisfied....

'Who rests not pleased with such happiness,
Well worthy he to taste of wretchedness.'

In that garden there lurked a foe, Aragnoll, a hateful spider with a net of gossamer. The innocent butterfly became entangled in the ingenious net. The spider sprang forth and stuck his weapon sly into the heart of the beautiful creature, killing him outright . . . 'his bodie left, the spectacle of care.'

E.S.

It was fanciful, but apt. Spenser's works bore him up a while, but the Court was engrossed in its own intrigues, its lewd conversations, tittering in corners, illicit liaisons. Raleigh himself was obsessed with one of the Queen's ladies-in-waiting. He had little time to shepherd an awkward poet through the intricacies of Court life. The poet had to fend for himself.

Burghley was Spenser's Aragnoll. The great man stood always behind the throne. He saw everything. He felt even the least vibration of the smallest filament of his web.

The Queen was pleased with Spenser's offering. She held out promise of great things, of preferment and influence. She knew of his good service in Ireland and had heard something of his survey of the present state of that island. She talked of an annual pension of one hundred pounds.

The spider whispered in the royal ear. "All this for a song, Majesty?"

The phrase became proverbial. Burghley mentioned that Spenser had got his vast and lucrative Irish estates for a song. Burghley understood money. It was he who had delayed payment to the veterans of the sea fight against the Armada, until the wounded had died. It was a shrewd policy, like that of a gardener discarding the weakest plants. A poet stood no chance against Burghley.

Spenser's poems no longer bore him up above the range of common men. His wings were maimed. He began, for the first time, to long for the seclusion of Kilcolman and his familiar fields. The annual pension dwindled to a once-off gift of fifty pounds. It was time to go home.

Raleigh lay secretly with Bess Throckmorton and got her with child. He retired to Sherborne, a house that he had cozened from a bishop, in the days of his ascendancy. He began to plan an expedition to America. He engaged Frobisher to take his best ship to sea and waylay the Spanish treasure fleets. He gave orders to his steward to intensify the production of timber from his Irish forests. The yews of Youghal fell to the axe. The oaks of the Blackwater yielded to the saw-pit and to the cooper's adze.

***

Spenser went home to Kilcolman. He made the best of it. His cattle were healthy and sleek. His tenants paid their rents. His men-at-arms were no more insolent than before. His detestation of Maurice Roche was fed anew by the loss of three plough-lands to the mad viscount. It gave him a reason to go on.

He wrote of a shepherd who wandered far from home in search of fame but returned a wiser man. He lampooned the folly and wickedness of court life in a country ruled by an ape and a fox. He left it to the reader to draw his or her own conclusions.

'For sooth to say, it is no sort of life
For shepherd fit to lead in that same place
Where each one seeks with malice and with strife
To thrust down other into foul disgrace.'
E.S.

He questioned his cowherd about the state of his herds.

"Explain to me, Uaithne if you please, why my cattle thrive while those of my neighbours are prey to murrain and disease."

Uaithne scratched his nose. He looked about. He shrugged.

"I have the skill," he said.

"What skill? Do you use herbs?"

219

"What good would herbs do?"

It irked Spenser that Uaithne had a way of answering a question with another question. He elected to play the game.

"So you have other knowledge? Charms, perhaps?"

"Would I use charms and be damned for a witch?"

Spenser shrugged. Uaithne spoke out of a world about which he knew little. It still rankled that Uaithne did not approve of the Greek and Roman gods. He had gods of his own.

"Would you?"

Uaithne drew a string from around his neck. On it was an amulet, a jewelled caterpillar of silver and amber, articulated like a living creature. He held it in the palm of his hand. Spenser was loth to touch it.

"I put it in their drinking trough. It has the power."

"What is this?"

"It is a connach, but a good one. Made by a monk in times gone by."

Superstition and nonsense, but there was no denying that his animals were healthy. He decided to question the cowherd no further, lest he might appear foolish. Perhaps Uaithne's rustic gods had some power, after all.

Raleigh had assured him that there was money in barrel staves. He sent men to harvest the woods. He directed others to go further into the forest to make charcoal. Smudges of dark smoke rose from the kilns. He busied himself at petty sessions, losing no opportunity to thwart any action taken by Mad Maurice. The viscount retaliated by making his detestation of Spenser known to all his tenants. He punished any of his people who performed even the smallest service for the Englishman or spoke a civil word to him.

The antagonism warmed them both. They feinted, like practised swordsmen, probing for a weakness, a suspicion of treason or corruption, a flaw in a deed. Maurice had tradition and ancient loyalty on his side. Spenser had eloquence and political connections. Broadsword versus rapier. Remember thy swashing blow. The memory always made him laugh.

He found himself smiling more of late. Free from the apprehension of appearing at Court, his spirit found ease and happiness in his work. He no longer desired what he had yearned for all those years. He learned from correspondents, that his *Faerie Queene* was the talk of London and of learned people everywhere. His readers laughed at *Mother Hubberd's Tale*. They shook their heads wisely at the telling description of life at Court.

They let him know that Burghley was discomfited by the tale of the fox and the ape. In fact, he had gone so far as to order the suppression of one poem that came too near the bone. It was success indeed to sting the most powerful man in England to such a petty revenge. It was true. The fly, the wasp and the gnat, the most insignificant of creatures, still have the ability to thwart the lion and the dragon.

It gratified him to hear that Burghley had failed repeatedly to acquire the fields at Covent Garden. It pleased him to imagine that the geese of Covent Garden, might be the same geese that alighted by his own lake at Kilcolman on their way to and from the cold northern lands. He wished them God speed. It was worth the loss of the money to have the satisfaction of resenting Burghley and of soaring above his petty plots and machinations. From his castle at the edge of the world, he could loose his bolts at his enemies. Even the King of Scotland had been stung by the depiction of his mother as the false Duessa. That was no small achievement.

Despite all the personal disappointments, he was confident that he had created a world of magic and heroism, a world that made sense of time and myth, of idealism and destiny. There were no limits to his reach. More books would follow. Kilcolman had indeed become his castle of gold, reflecting its light on the world at large. It needed only one thing more, one successful quest. One conquest.

Chapter Twenty One

The fisherman at Rennie was wary. He kept his boat, in a backwater, a cutting in the river bank. He plied a net on the river under licence from Viscount Roche. He knew something of the animosity between the viscount and the Englishman and had no wish to get involved. However, there had been a dirty little flood. February was contrary. The spring run was late. The Englishman offered gold. He gave assurances that he would soon be the owner of the deserted castle of Rennie and that the fishery would lie in his gift. Moreover, he was a cheerful sort of a man, dressed in a long Irish mantle, like a normal person. He spoke of an adventure. He was not unwilling to take a hand at rowing or portages. There could be no harm in it. The country was at peace, of a sort. It was a long, long time since he had gone below Fermoy. It was many years since he had seen the sea. Spenser assured him also that he would indemnify him against any loss of earnings. The fisherman frowned. This Englishman used the strangest words, just like a lawyer or a scrivener. The fisherman wondered if he had drink taken. It could explain his high spirits.

They made good progress. The exertion warmed them. Spenser coughed, now and again but he was elated by the adventure. His hands blistered through his fine leather gloves but he disregarded the pain. The fisherman was more cautious, fearful that a submerged tree might reach out an arm to upset their craft or punch a hole in its planking. He was glad that they were not using one of the more common vessels of lath and hide.

Spenser employed some loafers at Fermoy to help with the portage around the weir. They were glad of the few coppers and curious to know the purpose of this voyage. He told them that they were engaged in a great adventure to rescue a lady from the castle of an ogre. The men looked at one another knowingly. They considered administering a beating and relieving him of his purse, but there was an air of authority about the man that gave them pause. Moreover, the fisherman was fingering the gutting knife he carried in his belt. They were won over by Spenser's good spirits and friendly demeanour. They chattered volubly in the Irish tongue as they worked and laughed at some private joke. They put their backs into the task and earned an extra groat for good will. The travellers sped on their way.

The willows along the bank showed the stain of the recent spate. The inch-fields were strewn with mud and scattered sedge. The water ran murky and brown. All was peaceful. Towards evening they pulled in to an island in mid-stream, little more than a weedy sandbar. They concealed the boat in some low shrubbery and wrapped themselves up for the night. Spenser looked up at the infinity of stars. They seemed to lean closer, as if concentrating their influence on him alone. He listened to the sounds of the night, a coot, an owl, the river swirling over stones. He felt the beneficence of the stars all about him.

The fisherman slept fitfully, uneasy with these unfamiliar waters. The upper reaches of the river flowed through his veins, but here he was a stranger. He could feel the spring run in his gut, the pull of Moon and tide. He was unprepared. He rose before dawn and took a gaff from the boat. He gathered a handful of pebbles.

Spenser woke to the smell of wood smoke and hot food. There was a fish impaled on a stick slanting over a fire. The fisherman gestured to him to come closer. The morning was dry and bright. The air was sharp. There was birdsong all about. He ate of the fish and drank the peaty water of the river. He washed away all the memory of the city and of the Court, all memory of the sniggering, the women painted like harlots, the stench of fear and civet. He forgot the endless waiting and watching, the supercilious courtliness of the fashionable people. 'Should I have heard of you?' To Hell with influence and titles. He was a shepherd, come home at last to his native fields. The river gods smiled to see him. The nymphs of the forest sang their alluring songs.

They sped down river, pulling heartily on the short, blunt oars. The thole-pins creaked. The water began to gleam with silver fish. The run had started, hundreds upon thousands of salmon, driven upstream by the age-old compulsion. The water boiled around the boat. That chaste goddess, the Moon, Diana, Cynthia, urged on this exuberance of life. He might well have stepped from the boat and walked, dry-shod to the bank, so great was the throng. He saw their wild eyes, their mouths gaping with a terrible urgency. He understood. He also had to press on.

The fisherman was agitated. He was in the wrong place. He became morose. His anxiety was a direct counterpoint to his passenger's elation.

"I will indemnify you," Spenser assured him, but it was not about money. It was a sin to ignore God's bounty, just as it would be a sin to take them all. It was painful to go against his instincts. He pulled harder on the oars. He wanted to be rid of his passenger and begin the long, upstream drag back to his native pools.

They slid past the castle at Lismore. It amused Spenser to imagine Raleigh standing at a turret window, surveying his river and the two Irish reprobates trespassing on his waters. He might well have sent men to arrest them. Raleigh was an odd fish. He might laugh or he might take umbrage. How they would have laughed when Spenser threw back his hood, or not, as the case might be. It was a childish thought. He regretted that Raleigh was away from home, possibly in Panama, where the treasure ships lay. For Raleigh there was always, beyond the horizon, a city made of gold, there for the taking. The Shepherd of the Sea could never be at ease. The Saracen bird, with scimitar wings, could never resist a lumbering pelican.

Just before darkness they came to Youghal. The sea tossed their little craft into the inner harbour. It was a cockle-shell among the ships and wherries. The fisherman looked about in awe. He was a small fish in a great pool. He was amazed at the thought of how vast the world must be. The watchmen, after some close enquiry, let them through the water gate. The fisherman followed closely on Spenser's heels. His eyes darted about, taking in the wonder of the busy streets, candlelight in windows, a rumbling hay cart, a group of urchins chasing up and down a flight of steps. The walls climbed up a steep hill, rising almost to the sky.

They came to her uncle's house. Spenser tugged on the bell-pull. She opened the door. She wore a simple bonnet and starched white apron, over her dark widow's gown. Her eyes opened wide in surprise. Spenser dropped to one knee. He gestured to the fisherman.

"My lady," he said, with an orator's flourish of the hand, "I come to lay my humble guerdon at your feet."

The fisherman placed a sack on the doorstep and tipped out a magnificent salmon. He stepped back, enjoying the interlude. Sir Walter would never miss one fish. By his own lights, he should condone the theft as the natural order of things.

She laughed in surprise and pure pleasure. It was the sweetest sound that Spenser had ever heard, a faerie sound, a wood nymph singing to the Moon. Had she told him to slay a dragon or walk through fire, he would have done so without a thought.

"Mister Spenser! What a surprise! You come just in time for supper. Where have you come from? My uncle will be pleased to see you. He is a great admirer of your work."

It was a promising start. Spenser stood up.

"Bring your servant indoors and this very fine fish." She stepped back to admit them.

The fisherman started. He had never been a servant before. He did not like the idea. However, he could smell supper from where he stood and was prepared to yield the point for the moment. Otherwise he would be an Irishman abroad in an English town after sunset. He would be glad of the safety of Elizabeth Boyle's roof over him.

***

All went well. Her uncle, an affable and hospitable man, wanted to talk about poetry. He longed to hear all the gossip of London. He was in awe of this man who had seen the Queen sitting on her throne. This man, in his house, sitting at his table, had spoken to Her Majesty, had even read some of his work to her.

He was surprised to hear that Spenser was not a devotee of the playhouses. He spoke of Raleigh, a hasty man, a man who never stayed to pick the bush clean, as his nephew invariably remarked. He was a man of extraordinary courage, driving his enemies before him, as he had shown on many an occasion, but then he moved on to the next challenge.

It was an interesting sidelight. Raleigh could turn a hand to anything, on land and on sea. He was a formidable warrior and no mean poet. His weaknesses though, were his talent for attracting enemies, and his rash business instincts.

Spenser walked with Elizabeth on brisk March days. They ambled outside the walls as far as the abbey and the lighthouse. The sea breeze ruffled the curls that showed from beneath her bonnet. There was a healthy flush in her cheeks. She had a ready laugh. She was at ease with him. He was enchanted. He was a boy again, but she was more than Rosalind. This was a woman at ease with herself also and with the world.

He spoke of marriage. Her uncle was delighted. She accepted. She loved his children already. It was perfect. Her uncle decreed that they should marry on June the eleventh next, Midsummer's Day in the Church of Holy Mary.

The fisherman could wait no longer. He asked leave to return upriver. Spenser paid him generously and gave him a safe conduct pass, signed in his capacity as Clerk of the Council of Munster. There was great power in the document, although the fisherman could not read it. He folded it carefully and tucked it inside his shirt. He took his leave. The tide wafted him as far as Lismore and then began the hard work. The fish were still running. They raced ahead of him. He took no rest until he swung, exhausted, into the familiar pool below the castle of Rennie.

***

'Trust not the treason of those smiling looks,
Until ye have their guilefull trains well tried;
For they are like but unto golden hooks,
That from the foolish fish their baits do hide.'
E.S.

He could not help it. His courtship became, in his mind
anyway, a duel, a war, a siege, enslavement, pleasure, pain, all
expressed in sonnet after sonnet. She knew nothing of all this,
her cruelty and pride, his joy in the midst of misery and longing.
She was not to know that future generations would read that her
kisses were like a garden of sweet flowers, her goodly bosom like
a strawberry bed, her paps like lilies ere their leaves be shed, her
nipples like young blossomed jasmines. She could not know that
future lovers would borrow his words to express their devotion
or that other, more envious, poets would parody and make fun of
her vaunted attributes.

There was more, a great deal more. As yet she had no idea that
their relationship was evolving on the lines of the fabled loves of
antiquity. She did not realise that in Youghal, a small Irish seaport,
there lived a beauty to outshine Laura or Beatrice.

'Tell me, ye merchants daughters, did ye see
So fayre a creature in your towne before,
So sweet, so lovely and so mild as she,
Adorned with beautyes grace and vertues store?'
E.S.

She was to find in time, that there were two Spensers, the
sighing lover and lusty husband, set against the stern man
of affairs, Queen's Justice for the County of Cork, Clerk of the
Council of Munster, adviser to the Lord President, Sir John Norris
and constant litigant in defence of his rights.

Ice and fire. It was an image he employed in his sonnets. She,
however, was the ice, untouched by his fiery love. She puzzled it
over. It was not so. The true ice was in her husband, as was the
fire. The sonnets wearied her.

He struggled to keep his mind on his main task, his *Faerie Queene*. He completed three more books and sent them to London. He propounded at every opportunity, his icy plan for starving the rebellious Irish into subjection.

The fire celebrated their marriage. She learned that she loved one Spenser, the man who had found his youth again, the boy who capered on the strand at Youghal and wrote her name on the sand. How extravagantly he had lamented the advance of the tide as it made little archipelagos of the ripple marks and drowned the graven letters in a sudden advance, sending her name back into infinity. There was a significance to everything he saw. All things pass away, but not their love.

> 'My verse your virtues rare shall eternize,
> And in the heavens write your glorious name.
> Where, when as death shall all the world subdue
> Our love shall live and later life renew.'
> E.S.

Could all that be true? Once she woke in the night to find his place in the bed empty and cold. She found him on the roof, looking out over the battlements at the fields and dark woods beyond. He was a man of ice, naked under his mantle. He was barefoot. He stood deep in thought. She came to him and put her arms around him, shocked to feel how cold he was.

"You will get your death out here," she chided, putting her hands under his cloak. She caressed him softly, bringing warmth back to his body. She slipped inside his ample garment, giving her warmth to him. She murmured low sounds, forcing him to respond, to come back to her from his icy reverie. He shuddered.

"Listen," he said quietly.

She strained to hear. There it was, a voice far away in the forest, perhaps even on the hills.

'A sheabhach!' it called. 'A havoc! A ha-a-a-voc!' The wind carried the voice away.

"What is that?" she asked, with a shiver.

"A challenge," he replied. "Some drunken oaf disputes my title."

"What does it mean?"

"The hawk. It is intended to frighten me, but he will not succeed."

"Come inside," she cajoled.

The ice went out of him. He turned to her and pushed her urgently against the stone of the battlements. In the shelter of his mantle he raised her night gown and entered her. She groaned with pleasure. The hard stone pressed against her back. Again and again, in a paroxysm of need and desire. A different poetry, the metre of life. They clung together, gasping. The stars looked down.

Thin and spare, from a great distance, it came again, 'A havoc! Aa-a-a ha-a-a-voc!'

Spenser laughed. "I hope he gets his death out there, the drunken fool." He gathered her in his mantle and took her gently back to bed.

'Let no deluding dreams, nor dreadful sights
Make sudden sad affrights
Ne let house-fyres, nor lightning's helplesse harmes
Ne let the Pouke, nor other evil sprights . . . . . .
Fray us with things that be not.'
E.S.

The infant conceived that night, was christened Peregrine, the swiftest of all hawks, Peregrine, the pilgrim, after his father, who had wandered far but had come home again to all that is precious.

***

"I heard the *seabhach* again, said Uaithne. "Ye would be better off in a town."

"You fear too much, my friend. We have peace at last. Did you not hear that the Dublin parliament has reaffirmed Ireland's loyalty to the Queen? The Irish lords are broken."

"The parliament did not consult me," replied the cowherd sharply. "Do you see those yellow weeds? Do you see the thistledown on the wind? That is how it spreads."

He did not elaborate. "Take your family away from here. I say this because I am a poet also. Even the lord Roche will pay heed to the advice of a poet."

Spenser smiled. He liked the forthright little man. When he said that all the Irish poets and harpers should be rooted out, like the yellow weeds, and hung up alongside the pipers, he reprieved one in his mind. As Queen's Justice he could do that.

The thistledown drifted about them. It rose and fell on a gentle zephyr. It snagged on blades of grass and fell to the ground. It rolled about, joining hands like schoolboys released from the tyranny of the master, scurrying from one place to another, doubling back, lifting into the air for pure joy and landing again to lodge in a place of safety. It made him smile.

***

Sir Martin Frobisher was a troubled man. For most of his adult like he had made war, enduring the long days of waiting, long lonely voyages, pursuits in the immensity of the ocean and then, the ship shuddering to the thunder of cannon, the shouting and alarms. That thunder, at last, made him wealthy. He had a rich wife, a house in London and great estates. Yet something always nagged at the back of his mind. He had never found the passage to the Indies. His three voyages had ended in ignominy and rancour. It was time to make amends.

He went up on deck. His squadron was bombarding a fort, El Leon. The Spaniards had built it to stifle the port of Brest. Their shrewd commander, Don Juan del Aguila, was holding out against English and French armies. Frobisher had lost track of the intrigues and sharp practice that had prolonged this miserable campaign. He knew that Sir John Norris was enriching himself by claiming expenses for five times the number of troops than he actually commanded.

October storms made life at sea more wretched than usual. Here he was again, pouring shot down on the heads of the misfortunate defenders of another windy promontory. What was it, he wondered, about the Spaniards? They kept coming back, like dogs baying a stag. They could not take a beating. It was in their nature. They locked themselves into seemingly impregnable fortresses and invited their enemies to rain fire on them, until all were destroyed or powder and victuals ran out. Then there would be a truce, until reinforcements arrived or supplies were replenished and war began its endless cycle again.

El Leon was a more imposing fortress than Dún an Óir, the one he had blasted to destruction in Ireland. This one had held out for weeks. He knew that, at that very moment, Raleigh with a company of his tin-miners from Cornwall, was tunnelling under the landward walls. Raleigh cropped up everywhere, a sinister bird of war. There was no doubt that Raleigh would profit from this campaign, only to squander the spoils in some other hare-brained scheme. Without the Queen's limited tolerance of her former favourite, Raleigh would descend into penury or worse. The headsman kept his axe sharpened for such as Raleigh.

He beckoned to Nicholas Conyers, now a hardened veteran of many voyages. Frobisher approved of Conyers. The Cornishman's eyes were still keen. He was as agile in the rigging as any man twenty years his junior. A good, God- fearing man, unfailingly loyal to his captain and to his Queen.

Conyers made his obedience and waited.

"Do you know, Nicholas Conyers, I have been thinking?"

Conyers was silent. It came as no surprise that his captain was given to introspection. He had often noticed him standing at the rail, staring apparently, into vacuity. He had noticed him holding a piece of metal, a lodestone, in his hand, turning it one way and another, allowing it to swing on a piece of string. Perhaps it was a charm, an amulet. Perhaps this piece of metal had preserved his captain through many perilous situations.

"The boy, Nicholas Conyers. The Indian boy that you captured for me."

"Aye, sir. Conyers remembered well the infidel woman who had fled from him. He remembered her dark, animal eyes full of hatred. He recalled vividly how she had struggled. She had bitten his hands and scratched his face. In the folds of her garments he had found an infant. It was a poor triumph for a Cornish wrestler to subdue a woman, however fierce and wild. It was not something to brag about, any more than he bragged of being one of those who had brought home the fools' gold.

The broadside erupted under their feet. The ship lurched under the recoil. Plumes of smoke billowed from the guns. Frobisher steadied himself, holding on to a shroud. The smoke drifted about them.

"How was that, Nicholas?"

The seaman was surprised by his captain's familiar tone.

"God save the mark, Captain. Right on target." "Good. Good."

They heard the guns trundling back to the gun ports and the shouts of the gunners.

"We must take him back. We must bring him home."

"Who, sir?"

"The infant. We must restore him to his people."

"Savin' your presence, Captain, he is no longer an infant. If he lives at all, he is a man."

Frobisher nodded. "Of course. So much the better. He will be able to help us find the passage."

Conyers tugged at his ear-lobe. He could see flaws in the plan. He had no desire to revisit the frozen seas and the floating mountains of ice.

Frobisher drew from his pocket the blade of lodestone. He dangled it from its string. The blade turned one way, hesitated, then turned in the opposite direction. The point swung from side to side, as if questing for something. It quivered and settled into one direction.

"Take this," he said, handing the blade to Conyers. "I shall draw up a commission for you. If I do not survive this war, you must take the paper to my wife in Yorkshire. She knows my mind. She will provide funds for you to take that unhappy child back to his people. We will have no luck if we do not do this. He can be the means of bringing them to knowledge of the true religion and loyalty to our Queen."

Conyers took the blade. He laid it in the palm of his hand. Life had suddenly become complicated. Frobisher's plan was vast, touching almost half of the world, determining the fate of a heathen race. Conyers held his tongue. Maybe a Spanish cannon ball would make the whole scheme irrelevant. He wished no harm to Frobisher, but there must be some limit to loyalty and duty. He dangled the blade again. It twitched and settled to north. It felt like a live thing, maybe a fish taking a bait.

"You see, Nicholas Conyers, it knows your mind. Let it be your conscience. Guard it well, Nicholas."

Conyers looked at the splinter of metal. He felt a strange fear. Perhaps there was witchcraft in it, something that might steal his soul. He wanted to throw it into the sea, but feared that Frobisher might ask for an accounting. The captain did not say things lightly.

The broadside roared again. The smoke stung their eyes. They coughed.

"Guard it well and remember my words."

For the first time in many years, Nicholas Conyers wished that he was home again on his native moorland. He was tired of the sea and tired of war. He felt a weight descend upon his shoulders. He saw the woman's black eyes filled with loathing. He wondered how he would introduce himself to her son.

Sir John Norris sent word that he required two hundred sailors from Frobisher's fleet, to fill up his numbers and join him in a final assault on the fort. The tin-miners had done their work. The charges were ready to blow.

Chapter Twenty Two

Frobisher was called to his own final accounting, where nothing in a man's life is overlooked. He fell, while leading his men into the breach of El Leon. A ball from a Spanish arquebus, tore through his entrails and lodged against his spine. They carried him back to his ship.

The ship's surgeon probed for the ball. He was a man of skill and experience. He worked quickly. The patient groaned. Nicholas Conyers and two others, held him down. The surgeon located the ball and drew it forth in a welter of blood and faeces. It put Nicholas in mind of the bear. The surgeon dropped the ball into a wooden bucket, with a heavy 'thud'. There were others of its kind already in the bucket, a harvest, a clutch, of leaden eggs. It looked to Nicholas as if the surgeon had done more damage than the projectile. The man stitched and bound up the wound, but still dark blood oozed through the bindings. He looked wordlessly at Nicholas and drew the corners of his mouth down in an expression of dismay. He wiped his hands fastidiously on his apron and moved on to the next casualty.

Frobisher slept a fitful sleep. Nicholas bathed his forehead. He noted that although Frobisher plucked at the sheet that covered him, his lower limbs did not so much as twitch. It was obvious that the ball had torn some vital organ of the spine, some nerve that governed the movement of the lower body, some block and tackle that levered the muscles into motion. Nicholas had plenty of time to think about it.

He heard the capstan squeal and creak and the clanking of the anchor chain. He felt the ship coming alive. Through the stern window, El Leon swung into view. Smoke was rising from the fort. A huge rent appeared in its wall, a cascade of stone, dust and mortar. Men were dying there, or killing. Nicholas was glad to be away from it intact. He wanted none of the glory. He tucked the sheet around his captain's shoulders. There was little else he could do.

At Plymouth they lowered Frobisher into a launch. Nicholas snarled at the sailors for letting the stretcher jar against the ship's side. He sat with his unconscious captain as the sailors rowed upstream to a small, rudimentary hospital. Frobisher was in the throes of a high fever. There was a stench of suppuration. Nicholas stayed with him while the surgeons inspected the wound. It was a hideous mess. They bound it up again, despairing of their art. They left the patient in the care of his loyal servant.

Nicholas stayed beside him. He managed to spoon some water between his captain's lips. 'Starve a fever.' That much of physic he understood. He knew also that Frobisher had not bowels enough to cope with any nourishment.

At night he spoke to his captain of their many escapades, the pursuit and capture of Spanish treasure ships. He promised him even bigger and better game in the future. He spoke of the fights at sea and on land. He spoke of tempests, of the great white land and seas filled with floating mountains of ice. He said nothing about the gold, knowing instinctively that it was a painful subject. He made no mention of the savage people, fearing that he would inadvertently let slip a promise to bring the boy home. He had not spoken the words. Had he given his word, he would have to keep it. A man's word is everything. He compromised. He spoke confidently of sailing once more to find the passage to the South Seas. That should cover the matter of the boy. Drop him off on the way past.

He reminisced about the days when they had patrolled the south coast of Ireland and the western approaches, watching for the Spaniards and sometimes, helping themselves to a heavily-laden merchantman. He recalled the Italian army on the very edge of Ireland, and how they had been bombarded into submission. It was all victory and success. He talked for days and nights, hollow-eyed from lack of sleep, fearing that if he stopped, his captain would cease to exist and Frobisher's responsibility would fall on his shoulders. He looked idly at the lodestone. He dangled it on its string. It always pointed in the same direction.

Frobisher opened his eyes. He looked at Nicholas in the flickering candle light.

"Remember, Nicholas." It was the last thing he said. Was it an order or a question? Was he picking up on the train of reminiscence, like an old friend recalling the adventures of youth? 'Remember the time…..Oh, the sights we have seen…' It was too late to ask. He slipped away during the middle watch, when all the world was dark. Nicholas closed his captain's eyes. He whispered words of contrition into the dead man's ear, as his mother, a half papist, would have insisted. He dozed on the stool.

When he awoke, they told him that Frobisher's soft organs, such as they were, had been sent for burial at Saint Andrew's Church. He was to accompany the body by sea to London for final interment at Saint Giles-without-Cripplegate.

Nicholas knew Frobisher to have been a religious man. He had died in the sure and certain hope of the Resurrection. This presented the simple sailor with a problem. How would the captain travel to Plymouth to recover his entrails from the care of Saint Andrew? Might he appear before God with a great void inside his rib cage? Would he travel by sea? It was too much for a weary man to reason out. His head ached. He wanted desperately to go home.

He had nothing in the world to show for his years of service, except a few coppers, a shard of lodestone and a piece of paper from his captain that he could not read. He knew that if he were to be taken up as a deserter, he would most assuredly hang. There were kinsmen still in Cornwall who would shelter him and give him employment and maybe even listen to his yarns, by the welcoming fireside on cold winter nights.

He had no need of the lodestone. He headed westward along the ever-narrowing peninsula. He avoided the most travelled ways. He kept his head down. He left the sea behind him.

***

Raleigh, fresh from the wars, came to Kilcolman. He came to demand sight of the next three books of *The Faerie Queene.*

"All England demands these books," he said, with mock severity.

Elizabeth was charmed, as always, by his gallantry. She explained that Spenser was from home. The assizes took up much of his time. She directed that Raleigh's men be lodged and fed, taking care to keep them as far away as possible from Spenser's shiftless, indolent garrison. Raleigh spoke sternly to his men. He reminded them that they were on important business.

"You leave your gates ajar, I notice," he remarked.

Elizabeth shrugged. "It has become the practice. My husband says that we have nothing to fear nowadays."

Raleigh grunted. "In England we live in constant apprehension. The country, they say, is crawling with Jesuits. They lurk in every cupboard and under every bed. The Spaniards are poised to send an even greater armada." He laughed. "You really should lock your gates."

She enjoyed his bantering tone. The Spaniard had become the bogey-man, always lurking just below the horizon. She had no doubt that men like Raleigh, would send him packing with his tail between his legs.

Spenser returned late in the evening. He was in good spirits. He was delighted to see Raleigh. They sat by the fire.

"I note that you travel alone. Is that wise?" Raleigh was frowning.

"My soldiers," said Spenser, with a rueful smile, "are nothing but a hindrance and a provocation. I heartily wish that Sir John had taken them with him to Brittany. They are worse than useless."

Raleigh persisted. "But the country people? Do you not put yourself in danger, travelling alone after dark?"

"The country people are under the strong hand. That is all they understand. That is all they ever got from their own lords. Now at last, they bow down to England's law."

"So all is well? I have been abroad for a long time. Ireland is pacified at last? *Pacata Hibernia est?*"

Spenser nodded his head from side to side. "To a degree," he conceded. "The cunning wretches use our own laws against us. It is impossible to empanel a jury entirely of Englishmen. They are too few. They have to neglect their farms. They grow weary of jury service."

"I know what you mean. They are intimidated. A jury of Irishmen will always find against an English plaintiff or the Crown."

"They make a mockery of the courts," agreed Spenser, but at least they accept the principle of English law. I fear it is necessary on occasions, to bypass the law. Justice must sometimes turn a blind eye, in the interest of the common good."

"This is serious matter," interjected Elizabeth. "But you have returned tonight in good spirits. Have you had good news? Sir Walter tells me that we live in constant danger from the Jesuits and King Phillip."

Raleigh smiled, his warm friendly smile, the smile that had won the heart of the Queen.

"Better than hanging a Jesuit, I have secured title to the castle at Rennie." He slapped his knee in elation. "One in the eye for Mad Maurice."

Elizabeth clapped her hands. "Oh, wonderful! It will be a home for our little Peregrine when he comes of age."

"Did the viscount dispute this?" queried Raleigh.

"He has been a thorn in my side since I came to Kilcolman. He invokes old Irish law, the laws of the Brehons. But he forgets that I am the Queen's Justice. Ha ha!"

Raleigh smiled at some inward amusement.

"Moreover, I have scotched all claimants to Castle Pook. I have had a good day."

Raleigh queried the strange name. Spenser was obliged to tell the story of the giant, the hard-working goblin, consumed by his own vanity.

"You must employ that giant in your poetry. I have come here to see your next books."

Spenser was pleased. "I can show you some manuscript copies. The originals are already gone to London, to Ponsonby."

"Splendid!" exclaimed Raleigh. "Have you made an end to *The Faerie Queene* ?"

"By no means," protested Spenser, "but I confess that I have been distracted by my overwhelming love for this lady." He leaned across and took Elizabeth's hand. She blushed with pleasure.

Raleigh inclined his head. "An understandable diversion. You are a fortunate man, my friend. And you, my lady, are fortunate also, to have your beauty eternized by England's greatest poet."

Elizabeth blushed again. She glowed at the realisation of her good fortune.

They talked long into the night. On the following day Raleigh immersed himself in the manuscripts. He was humbled to be admitted to the presence of genius. He entered Spenser's world. He forgot his day to day cares. He read the *Amoretti*, a sonnet sequence detailing Spenser's pursuit of Elizabeth. He read in *Epithalamion*, about the excitement and music of their wedding day and the following night. Somewhat anatomical at times, Spenser dwelt on her physical beauty, but ultimately, giving pride of place to her beauty of mind. Raleigh raised his eyebrows at some of the lines. The physical details lodged disturbingly in his mind. This was an unexpected aspect of his contemplative friend.

He saw Elizabeth dressed as a goddess, a handmaiden of Venus and Gloriana. Cynthia, the Moon queen peered in the window of their wedding chamber. Gloriana, Cynthia. The Queen saw everything. Raleigh also was privy to the secrets of their wedding night. He looked at her in a new light, a merchant's daughter, transmuted by the alchemy of words. He felt a twinge of envy.

He was reluctant to leave their bower of love and happiness, but he had business to attend to. At nightfall he led his men out into the gathering darkness. He looked back at Kilcolman. A light glowed in the tower. Smoke rose from the chimney.

The gate was still ajar.

***

Raleigh made straight for Castletown, where he was warmly received by Viscount Roche and his gracious lady. They sent food and drink to Raleigh's men and permitted them to come within the shelter of the walls. The men lit a fire and made good cheer with Roche's men. All was conviviality and song, a far cry from the times of suspicion and long night watches.

In the hall Raleigh made himself agreeable to Mad Maurice and most especially, to his wife. He complimented them on the many improvements to their castle, the addition of a chimney, glass in the arrow slits. Defence had given way to comfort, as befitted their advancing age.

They questioned him about his many adventures. His life sounded like an old tale of knightly deeds. He told of his voyages and exploits in war, in a self-deprecating tone. Nothing he had done had been for vainglory or personal gain. That famous story about his fight at the ford near Youghal, was exaggerated. He had not challenged a hundred men, to rescue his fallen comrade. It had been only twenty. He was fortunate, he pointed out, to be the instrument of their great Queen. He had lived in the glow of her favour. He quoted the well known doggerel about the rebel, Rory O More:

'So as his raigne endured not long, but tumbled in the myre,
Because he sinde in that he moved our noble Queene to ire:
O lamentable thing to see ambition clime so high,
When superstition's pride shall fall, in twynckling of an eye:
So such is every rebeles state and evermore hath bene
And let them never better speede, that ryse against our Queene.'

Anon.

"Ah, yes," said Maurice, "there is no gainsaying the poet." He sighed and looked into the fire. "Rory was left to bewail his fate in the forest, with none but wolves for company. According to the poet, even the wolves wept with him."

Raleigh nodded. He clucked his tongue in that universal note of disapproval and regret. "It is a crude verse but true, nonetheless." He laughed softly. "And to be commemorated in such jangling rhyme, an indignity worse than death."

They smiled together at the observation. Lady Roche rose stiffly. She took a bottle from the table and refilled their cups. She stood by the fire.

"Thank God," she declared, "for a hearth and a roof over our heads, this chilly night."

"There will be rain later," added Raleigh.

"I know," she replied. "I feel it in my bones. I suffer grievously from the pains." She clapped her hands. "But enough of my complaints. Tell us of London, the fashions, the playhouses, the talk at Court." Her eyes shone in the firelight. Raleigh was a being from another world, a glittering world of wit and music. It was as if a comet had swum into their firmament and paused to shine its beams on their quiet backwater.

"Ah, yes, the playhouses. You should go to London."

She dearly wished that she could go, but her husband had grown fond of his quiet life. No more campaigning. No more ambushes in dreeping forests or long marches in pursuit of rebels or hereditary enemies. He liked to hunt a little and fly his birds. He liked to pursue the white trout in his river, but he complained often about the damp air.

"When I was last there, I attended *The Tragedy of Richard III*. A remarkable piece. You should make a shift to see it some time. A monster; a bottled spider; abortive rooting hog." Raleigh leaned back, putting his hands behind his head. "The funny thing is, I quite liked him. Unapologetic evil. I enjoyed his wit. A murderer of children. A Macchiavel on England's throne. Strange. I liked him."

Lady Roche held her cup in her two hands. She watched the flames dancing in the hearth. "My grandmother knew him. She danced with him on the night before Bosworth Field. She always spoke of how nimbly he danced. She liked him very much." She sighed. "I should like to dance again."

Maurice's voice rumbled in his throat, a note of dismissal. Dancing had always seemed to him a frivolous waste of time. He was glad to be past it, but pleased to see his wife so charmed and courted so gallantly.

"Come with me to Cork," said Raleigh, "and we can make merry and dance all night, if you wish."

Maurice held out his cup. Life had grown dull for her. She hungered for society.

Raleigh teased. "Of course, you must not tell Her Majesty of your grandmother's liking for Richard Crookback. She might put you in The Tower as a dangerous rebel."

They laughed, all three, at the absurdity of the idea. They spoke of family histories and the complexity of genealogies. Maurice dismissed his tenuous connection to the late Earl of Desmond.

"I sent one hundred and thirty nine cows to the army that hunted him down. I have a letter from Her Majesty, thanking me for my loyalty and pardoning me for any crimes or misdemeanours committed in my name or by my men. If crimes they were." He paused. "I was party to that sorry pursuit of the Earl. She confirms all my titles. I am secure here on my rock, as the Roches have been for centuries."

"Not quite all," said the lady. "There is the matter of Rennie and Mister Spenser." It was an unfortunate remark.

Mad Maurice exploded with rage. He dashed his liquor into the fire. A gout of flame shot upwards from the logs. Spittle flew from his lips.

"Spenser!" he cried. "Spenser! That conniving, cozening, creeping…" His rage overcame him. He struggled for words. "That sleeveen!" He fell back on the Irish tongue for his most contemptuous insult, a man of no honour or morality; a watcher and loiterer; one with the denigrating remark that maims a better man; a cheat. In short, a sleeveen, a lick-spittle who leeches onto men of influence and power in order to line his own pockets. A parsimonious man who never showed an open hand to another. There was more. He paused, gasping for breath. "That sleeveen," he added at last. His eyes blazed with hatred. Even the mention of Spenser's name had spoiled a perfect evening.

"I take it that you are no friend of Mister Spenser, then." Raleigh smiled. He watched his host over the rim of his cup.

Maurice took a deep breath. He refilled his cup. He laughed. "What leads you to that conclusion?" He wiped his mouth with the back of his forearm. His wife signalled to him to be silent. He avoided her eye.

"I accept that he is a man of some influence, the Queen's Justice, honoured in some circles as a poet." He snorted. "His cowherd is a better poet. More rooted in his own culture. The real thing."

"His cowherd? What of his cowherd?" This was an interesting line of conversation. It amused Raleigh that England's greatest poet should be challenged by a lowly working man, a villein of the meanest kind.

"He is no common cowherd," protested Maurice. "He is one of The Old People, The Good People, who held this island before the Irish, the Milesians, as he calls them. He was poet and harpist to the old gods. God blast it! He was my harpist, until that reptile, Spenser , lured him away."

"No he did not," chided his wife gently, fearful of another outburst. She was convinced that some day, her husband's heart would burst in an attack of apoplexy. "Uaithne left of his own accord. No man can put a barrier in the way of The Good People." She half-believed the stories of the people who danced around the white-thorn in the moonlight and lived under the raths and mounds that dotted the countryside. No, she did not believe the stories, not there in the light of a crackling fire, but on the road at night, she was not so sure. Uaithne explained that he had lived long enough with the Old English. He wanted to see the New English, the Undertakers, the Planters, with their stumbling, mumbling peasants, who broke the green sod, mangled the ancient forests and pined for England and safety. He wanted to understand them, before the Milesians gathered their strength again and swept them all away. They would become a part of his endless story, his interminable chant of kings and gods and terrible battles.

"So Spenser has offended you?" probed Raleigh.

"Oh, that he has. In more ways than you can imagine." Maurice's rage had subsided. I did him a kindness once, a kindness I now regret. I should have left him to die."

"Ah, no. Ah, no." murmured his wife. "That would not be in your nature."

"But he also, had shown kindness to the wretched woman in the friary," Raleigh remarked. "I told you about that."

Maurice conceded the point. "I grant you that. That was before his soul was warped by greed and cruelty. And lack of good manners." His voice shook. His wife stared at him, willing him to leave off.

"I have always found Edmund Spenser to be a most courteous and loyal servant to Her Majesty. Whatever he possesses was confiscated from incorrigible traitors and rebels. Whatever he has achieved was through his own native genius." Raleigh's tone was gentle and reasonable.

Maurice turned the cup in his hands. He grunted. "It is not that. It is not even the land." He grinned rather sheepishly. "He comes here with his chest full of Greek and Latin gods. He peoples our woods and rivers with nymphs and satyrs. They fornicate in every forest clearing. Licentious creatures, the product of diseased imaginations. God's breath! We lack the weather for that kind of behaviour."

Raleigh laughed aloud. It was a terrible crime to inflict those naked, capering creatures on the Good People and the Pookas of the Irish countryside. Roche joined in the laughter, admitting the ludicrous nature of his complaint. The tension in the hall eased. His wife left the mantle shelf and sat down again.

"So you could forgive him for the land and for his opinions of your country, but cannot accept his gods."

"May God forgive me, but I hate the man. I wish him no joy in his possessions. But more than that, I detest his drivelling poetry. Shepherds piping day and night! How can anyone thole this endless stream of nonsense? Give me the cowherd any day."

Raleigh laughed heartily. "I shall noise your opinions abroad among the wits of London. Your cowherd must have his day in the sun."

He rose and stretched. He drained his drink. "But now, we must be on our way."

"What, in the middle of the night?" The lady was shocked. She was disappointed that such a pleasant evening was ending abruptly.

Raleigh bowed. "My lady, it pains me to have to leave this hospitable house, but I must ask you to fetch your travelling robes and allow me to escort you to Cork."

Roche was on his feet. "What villainy is this? He looked around for a weapon. In the shadows of the hall he saw armed men. They stood silently. How had he not observed them before?

"What villainy is this?" he demanded again. "You are a guest in my house."

"And honoured to be one, sir. Which is why I consider it an honour to escort you and your lady in safety to Cork." Raleigh bowed again.

"Why now? For what reason? This is no time to be on the road." Roche looked at the shadowy figures.

"There have been certain accusations laid against your honour. Accusations of treason. I count them as nothing but idle malice but they must be answered without delay. Please make yourselves ready for the journey. Your horses await you."

"You sir, are the traitor," snapped Roche. "I will have your head for this."

"Please understand, sir, that I do this out of regard for you and your lady. The roads are dangerous. At night we may escape the attentions of the rebels, the Milesians, as your harpist might say." He smiled bleakly. "We shall keep to the bogs and the mountain paths."

"There are no rebels in my country," expostulated Roche. "I am a loyal subject to Her Majesty, as will be proven. You will rue the discourtesy of this night."

"It pains me greatly to put you to this trouble, but I assure you, it is for your own good." Raleigh spoke softly but there was no room for argument. His men stood all about. Roche's servants were unmanned by the cordon of steel.

The viscount threw on his riding cloak. He draped a heavy coat around his trembling wife. He chucked her under the chin.

"We will ride out together to meet these enemies," he said. She raised her chin defiantly.

"Where you go, I go also." She blinked back her tears. She looked at Raleigh with withering contempt. He looked away, a sleeveen in any man's language.

Chapter Twenty Three

Damn the man, thought Lord Burghley. He rubbed his eyes. He was tired of dispatches and he was tired of Ireland.

"Damn the man," he said aloud. The poet was correct. Burghley accepted that, after all his years in Ireland, Spenser might know a thing or two. It galled him to admit that Spenser's way was the only viable way. Ireland must be broken, dismantled and put together again in an orderly and civilised manner. This dispatch was no rambling poetic fancy. It was a closely argued and costed, scheme for the destruction of the clan system and the imposition of English law throughout the island. It recommended the appointment of the Earl of Essex, with an overwhelming army and the establishment of strategic garrisons encircling all disaffected areas, especially Ulster.

He turned his thoughts to Ulster and to O Neill. His horticultural metaphor came back to him. O Neill was the seedling that he had nurtured in a sheltered arbour. He had fed and watered this plant, protecting it from frost and parasites. He had hardened it off in the war against the Earl of Desmond. O Neill had given good service in Munster against the rebels, crushing his own kind as ruthlessly as did the English. But O Neill had grown rank with arrogance and power, in his native Ulster. He had grown into a vile weed, spreading seeds of rebellion throughout Ireland. He had even offered the throne of Ireland to the King of Spain. The poet was accurate in his assessment. O Neill and all his kind must either be rooted out or Ireland must be abandoned.

He directed his lawyers to examine every title and every right claimed by O Neill. They came up with one that tickled his lordship's bleak sense of humour. O Neill, like all his forebears, claimed the rights to the fisheries on the Bann and sundry other rivers. They valued their eels and salmon. They guarded them jealously, taking refuge in the fog of the ancient Brehon laws. Those rights had descended to O Neill from ancestors who had lived before The Saviour came down on Earth.

The cunning lawyers explained how O Neill's overweening pride could be dismantled by little and little. All fishing rights had devolved to the King after the conquest of Ireland in the year of Our Lord, 1172. The Irish chieftains themselves had so sworn. It would be the sport to remind him that he could not dip a line in the water, or trap the smallest elver, without Her Majesty's permission.

Burghley rubbed his hands in satisfaction. He well knew that the small indignities could serve to put an enemy in a rage. In choler, the judgement of even the coolest man is impaired. In rage, O Neill would make intemperate utterances and rash decisions that would bring him ultimately to the block. Burghley looked forward to pointing out to Her Majesty, that her insolent subject was fishing her pool, without a by-your- leave.

He had once examined a poacher who had fished a stream on his country estate. The rascal, in fear, had admitted that he 'pegged' the stream with pebbles, urging the fish to a place where he could lift it swiftly with his gaff. The poacher explained that he threw the pebbles to plop in an encircling ring, dissuading the fish from trying to escape, driving it to where he wanted it. Burghley likewise, would plop garrisons around O Neill's lands and gaff him when the time was right. He would cut off his head and eviscerate him, like any fish. It would take patience. He had plenty of that. The poacher had taught him a useful lesson, but he had hanged the rogue anyway.

He decided after some deliberation, to overlook the real or imagined mockery in Spenser's tale of the ape and the fox longing for power and influence. Spenser, unwittingly, had described his own disappointments.

'For I likewise have wasted much good time
Still wayting to preferment up to clime,
Whilest others always have before me stept,
And from my beard the fat away have swept.'

The jest returned upon the jester. Yet the poet had keen eyes and good understanding. It was said that his young wife, she of the lilies and ripe strawberries, had mellowed him and softened his caustic tongue. Burghley decided to recommend to Her Majesty that she appoint Spenser High Sheriff of the County of Cork. The poet could wear the lion's skin, wield the lion's mace and swell with a little borrowed importance.

'First to his gate he 'pointed a strong gard,
That none might enter but with issue hard;
Then for the safeguard of his personage,
He did appoint a warlike equipage.'
E.S.

Burghley laughed at the recollection of Spenser's lines. He did not like to admit it, but Spenser had allayed his suspicion of poetry. It was a powerful medium. He read it as a guilty pleasure, but with an eye to its usefulness.

The ape appointed a palace guard of Griffons, Minotaurs, Dragons, Crocodiles, Beavers and Centaurs. Spenser's variegated men-at-arms were almost as strange, drunkards, lunatics and vagabonds. Burghley had heard Raleigh's description of Spenser's military might. 'Remember thy swashing blow.' Raleigh could set the table on a roar. To Raleigh, everything was for sale, even loyalty to a friend. He liked the taverns and the gossip of the street as much as he enjoyed the rarified atmosphere of the Court. Burghley had heard tell of a wondrous lizard that could change its colour to blend with the background. Raleigh had that gift.

He signed his recommendation to Her Majesty and stamped his seal upon it.

***

Don Juan del Águila y Arellano loved maps. Maps were the eyes of every army. With his maps and charts he directed his fleet and his land-forces, whether in North Africa, the Low Countries or France. He knew every harbour fortress. He built not a few.

He saw England's weakness in the west. Cornwall, long and narrow, dissected by many inlets, was vulnerable to a sea-borne invasion either from the north or from the south. It could be taken and held along the line of any of its rivers, amputating the long leg by which England stepped far into the Atalantic. The Isles of Scilly would make a haven for his ships, whereby he could choke off England's commerce. Better still, he could waylay the fleets of Hawkins and Drake, returning from their raids on Spanish strongholds in the Americas. He could take Plymouth with ten thousand men and sit, like many-headed Cerberus, guarding the entrance to The Channel.

He showed his grand strategy to his captains. He showed them also, the harbours of southern Ireland. There were deep- water bays and promontories crying out to be fortified. He indicated Kinsale and the headland, shaped like a key, another Cadiz. His men would like Kinsale, where the maidens went bare breasted in the summertime. He could use Kinsale, with its deep harbour and good holding ground.

He spoke of the restless Catholic population, pleading day and night for the Catholic King to send succour and of the powerful Catholic lords who would rally to The Cross, as to a crusade. His spies and captured fishermen told him how Cornwall groaned under impositions and levies. The people, lately Catholic, would not resist a Spanish force. It was time to begin the next phase of the holy war. He sent four galleys and two companies of *arcabuceros* to invade Mousehole.

***

Raleigh was furious. As Lord Lieutenant of Cornwall, those three days in July were a stain on his honour and a reproach. He had discovered in recent years, the difficulties of being an absentee proprietor. The Spaniards had burned three villages and a Protestant church. They had spared another, in which Mass was sometimes said, a distinction not overlooked by the country people.

He rushed troops into Cornwall but the Spaniards had already embarked. They left behind them the smouldering ruins of Mousehole and a great many surly Cornishmen, as resentful of the tardy English as they were of the invaders. Don Juan had left a gage, a marker, a challenge, to say that his men would be back.

The Spaniards were everywhere, elusive as mice, in The Channel and in the Atlantic. There was no end to King Phillip's money and no limit to his ambition. Another, more powerful armada fleet was building in the Biscayan ports. It was time, insisted Raleigh, to let slip the dogs.

Drake and Hawkins took their fleets to Panama, where they could sever Spain's jugular. They could stem the flow of treasure, on which King Phillip's power stood.

Raleigh and the Earl of Essex made a daring raid on Cadiz, returning the courtesy of the burning of Mousehole. They held that port, causing massive disruption to the King's plans. For a brief time, King Phillip found himself bankrupt. It was stalemate.

The tide of events moved in favour of the Catholic cause. In April, some few ships in great distress, returned to Falmouth to report that both Drake and Hawkins were dead. England was deprived of its fiercest watchdogs. Raleigh and Essex hoisted sail for home. The King's preparations resumed. Don Juan del Águila y Arellano unrolled his maps anew.

In October, the King's mighty armada set out once again, for England. Whether by God's grace, or by the machinations of Doctor John Dee, a fearsome tempest, a Protestant wind, fell upon the fleet, off the misty cape of Finisterre, permitting only a few surviving ships to limp, bootless home and weather- beaten back, to their Galician havens.

Raleigh and Essex, returning in tempers as foul as the weather, from an abortive ambush of the treasure fleet at the Azores, were sick with shock to learn of England's narrow escape. They had no doubt that the King would try again. And again.

***

Dismayed by the rivalries between the factions of Burghley and Essex, Spenser occasionally retreated to the quiet and solitude of Rennie. He walked in his orchard. He sat under an oak tree, wrapped in his mantle, looking upriver. The oak was a colony filled with birdsong, labouring beetles, diligent pismires and scurrying creatures. It came to him how fleeting life is, in comparison with the oak, how irrelevant the business of men is to all the creatures that inhabited the oak, the birds, the flies that swarmed in the sunbeams. He thought of poor Machabyas and her terrible fall from the height. He offered a prayer for her soul and for himself, who had neglected her.

He wrote. A torrent of verses poured from his brain. He wrote to Burghley and to Essex. He upbraided them in carefully chosen words. Their rivalry was meat and drink to King Phillip. It left the unrepentant rebel, Fiach MacHugh O Byrne, able to play them both for fools. It had always been Spenser's contention that Wicklow was a running sore. O Byrne infected all Leinster with treason. He leagued himself with O Neill in Ulster. He communicated with Spain. O Byrne was a mountain sorcerer. Taken in his most flagrant treasons and blatant murders, he had the ability to sue for pardon and get it. Both factions agreed that O Byrne, old and sickly as he was, should be prevented from joining in an alliance with O Neill. Spenser insisted that just as he had savaged the army of Lord Grey de Wilton, many years ago, O Byrne would defeat any half-hearted attempt to curb him. He had to be crushed without quarter.

He rode, one day, to the ruined priory. It prompted thoughts of delightful melancholy. It was there that he had conceived his theme of *Mutabilitie*. The river still sang. The reeds swayed. Birds darted in the willows.

The old woman was there also, wizened and shrunken as the Sybil. He knew her story: the widow of a nobleman drawn into rebellion in pursuit of a hopeless cause. In the place of servants and loyal liegemen, she had only her cats. It was said that the cats sometimes brought her their prey, a vole, a leveret. He thought of that other old woman in her palace by Thames side. He was no longer her scrawny cat, bringing his offerings to her doorstep. He had lost faith in her and in his great enterprise. He was losing faith in himself. All was changed.

He gave some bread to the wretched creature.

"You are still here," she said in a cracked and wheezing voice. It was more a question than an observation, almost a challenge. "It will not be for long." She bent low, clutching the bread and scuttling behind a tomb. He hoped that the sun gave some warmth to her bones. He felt the chill of her words.

Nothing lasts. He wanted to question her, as he might have questioned the Sybil herself. But Sybils speak in riddles, playing on mens' foolish vanity. It was better to confine her to the world of poetry, a world in which he was, for the moment, still king.

He walked among the ruins. Everywhere there were stones inscribed to long-dead Roches, stones encrusted with ancient lichens, orange and grey, the life of a man or woman, reduced to a few graven letters. The melancholy began to settle upon him.

Something was missing. On previous visits to the priory he had always felt a frisson of excitement at the possibility of an encounter with his old adversary, Mad Maurice. He was trespassing. Trespass should produce a thrill of apprehension, the possibility of conflict or pursuit, scrambling through bushes or over boundary walls with the angry shouts of the proprietor fading further and further behind. That was all gone. That was for laughing boys now. Mad Maurice was a broken man, in both body and spirit. Raleigh had seen to that, dragging the elderly couple over mountain and bog, at dead of night. At Cork he had supervised their interrogation and close examination. There was nothing to reveal. They were no traitors. It cost them their health to prove it.

Spenser was ashamed to think that he might have had a part in setting Raleigh on. He had no love for Mad Maurice or for his kind. The Old English looked down upon the brash new settlers. But still, Roche had been kind to him once.

He returned to the old woman. He slipped off the rough mantle. He was no longer entitled to wear it. He was not entitled to enjoy Roche's kindness any longer. For a second time, he tried to relieve her misery and his own inchoate sense of guilt.

She clutched the garment to her. Her eyes glistened, but she was far beyond tears. She put her face into the wolf-fur lining of the hood. She inhaled the warmth of his body.

"Go away from here," she whispered. "Leave this place." Her fingers were like the talons of a bird.

He was not loth to leave her there, among the graves. He resented that her poverty made him so melancholy. The day had grown colder. He was anxious to return to Rennie, to a fire and a glass of wine to dispel his sense of foreboding.

***

Nicholas Conyers stooped under the low doorway. The servant stood to one side.

"Mister Nicholas Conyers," he intoned with a distinct note of disapproval.

There was no doubt that the Cornishman, dressed in shabby clothes, all dusty from the road, was an unprepossessing sight. His shoes were worn down at heel. His toes peeped through gaping toecaps.

The lady studied him closely. She was a small woman with the quick movements of a wren. She had been reading at a table by the window. A tapestry covered the table. The window panes cast a pattern of diamonds across the cloth. She beckoned to Nicholas to come closer. He stepped into the light of the window. He held his hat in both hands. He waited for her to speak. She put her head to one side.

"So, Nicholas Conyers, you have condescended to join us." He was not sure of her meaning, but guessed that she was asking for an explanation. He cleared his throat. He drew the crumpled paper from inside his shirt.

"A letter, milady, from Captain Frobisher."

He held it out to her. She plucked it from his fingers and tilted it towards the light. One edge of the paper was torn into serrated teeth.

"Hmm, hmm," she murmured as she read. She touched the jagged edge. She took a folded page from her book and spread it out, flattening the fold with both hands.

"Now, let us see." She matched the torn margin of her page to the seaman's letter. The indentations conformed exactly. She nodded.

"It must be a rugged road from Plymouth to have taken you all this time."

Nicholas hung his head. She could have him taken up for desertion and hanged at Wapping as a warning to others. She could have him impressed back into the service, the thing he had most tried to avoid.

"Well?" She looked up at him, waiting. Something about her told him that she would be satisfied with nothing less that the truth. A great weariness overcame him. He swayed. She gestured to the servant to bring a chair. The servant did not approve but he brought it anyway, with ill grace. Nicholas sat down. His shoulders drooped.

"It was the war, milady. I grew tired of it. I wanted to go home."

"I see. And what of your duty?"

"My duty was to Captain Frobisher."

"Sir Martin," she corrected.

"Sir Martin. My duty ended when he…" He made a gesture with his hand. "I went back to the moors. I worked as a shepherd."

"So why then, do you come to me now?"

"The war followed me home. I stood with Master Godolphin in the fight at Penzance. Eight of us against four hundred Spaniards." There was a note of pride, by God, in his voice. He had stood with Master Godolphin against the enemy. Few could claim that. "They invaded my country."

Absently she pushed the two papers together again.

"As we have invaded many. There will always be war. You are a man of war, Nicholas Conyers. Your spirit drives you to seek employment again."

"No, milady. I was reminded of my duty to the captain." "Who reminded you?"

"The lodestone, milady." He drew the string from around his neck. He dangled the blade, allowing it to spin. The servant stepped forward, but the lady raised her hand to stay him. The lodestone twitched like a live thing and settled, quivering, in its wonted direction.

"It reminded me of the captain,"

"Sir Martin."

"Sir Martin, beg pardon, milady. It reminded me of my captain, Sir Martin and his last orders."

"I understand that you tended him in his final days."

Nicholas nodded.

"That was kind of you." Her voice softened. "I am grateful."

Nicholas said nothing. He was not accustomed to the notion of gratitude. He turned his hat in his hands.

"My husband told me that you are a great runner." She laughed softly. "But it has taken you more than two years to run from Plymouth to London."

Nicholas coughed. "I went first to Yorkshire, milady. They told me that you had removed to London, to this house by London Stone." He felt foolish.

"Even so. London Stone, where all the world begins."

He realised that she was teasing. She leafed through her book. "Now, listen to this. Do you read the poets, Nicholas Conyers?"

He shook his head.

"You do not read?"

He shook his head again. He felt a flush rising in his cheeks. She began.

'In wrestling nimble and in running swift,

In shooting steady and in swimming strong;
Well made to strike, to throw, to leap, to lift,
And all the sports that shepherds are among,
In every one he vanquished everyone.
He vanquished all and vanquished was of none.'
E.S.

"Does that not describe you, Nicholas Conyers?"

He sat up, straightening his shoulders. "I cannot swim, milady. I am a sailor."

She nodded. "Another of your sea-going superstitions. Now, to come to my husband's wishes. I too must honour his instructions, his orders. Have you found the heathen child? Are you prepared to bring him home? Are you ready for this wild-goose-chase?"

"Indeed, milady I am not." His frustration poured out. "I have been to Mortlake as the cap....Sir Martin, directed. The house of John Dee is empty and boarded up. The gardens are overgrown. The slates are gone from the roof. It is a sorry sight."

"Have you no news of the boy?"

"A man watering his horse at a trough, told me that the Doctor no longer lives there. The boy is now a man. He told me that the boy had long since, joined with a cry of players. He complained mightily about the filthy water. He said the master always saw to it that there was clean water in the trough. Something to do with sorcery, he said. He complained that his horse was often sickly from the foul rainwater."

"What do you think of all this?"

"I think he should get off his arse and fetch a bucketful from the river, lazy sod."

She laughed aloud. "No, no, no. I mean about the heathen boy and a voyage to the frozen lands."

"I beg your pardon, milady. I do not know. If he has fallen among the players, I fear that he is lost. I am told that they are masters of impurity and all the vices. Sons of idleness. Always in debt. I would be afeard to go among them." He looked at her helplessly. "What do you advise?"

She saw an awkward countryman, with big, strong hands. He was a man who had braved many dangers. His hands had done cruel work. Yet those hands had comforted a dying man. She understood his fear of looking oafish in a world of wit and licentious sophistication.

She picked up the lodestone and let it swing. It found its pole, its lodestar.

"You captured him, Nicholas Conyers and you must set him free, if that be his desire."

"And my duty to the cap...Sir Martin?"

"I am Sir Martin's heir. I am, therefore, your captain, until your duty is discharged."

Nicholas struggled with this notion. It must have something to do with the serrated piece of paper, some legal hocus-pocus that bound him from beyond the grave. "You will go to my house in King Street and take lodgings with Mistress Lok. When you are suitably washed and brushed and fit to be seen by polite society, you will accompany me to Bankside, to seek out this Caliban. Pray God that he be not sunk so far in depravity as to be beyond redemption." She seemed to smile a little at the thought, which surprised Nicholas. "If he will not go with you, I shall find you other employment. I shall need protection from those incorrigible rogues in the playhouses anyway. Go now. The servant will conduct you to Mistress Lok."

The servant sniffed. Nicholas shrugged. He had few options or prospects. It was as good a plan as any.

"Take no notice of the old man in the smoky room. He is still prosecuting a private war against your captain."

Nicholas rose to go. He hesitated. "The poem, milady?"

She smiled again. "Oh, it is not about you. It is about poor Phillip Sidney."

"Sir Phillip," interpolated the servant. He was concerned that standards should not be allowed to slip in the house of Sir Martin Frobisher.

She gave him a withering look.

"Sir Phillip Sidney, she said. "It is the work of Edmund Spenser, a man of exquisite sensibility."

"Why would he write about shepherds? I was a shepherd once." He shook his head in puzzlement. A poet must be mad to waste his time writing about shepherds.

"Never mind," she said brusquely. "Go about your business and try to move a little more speedily in future."

Nicholas touched his forehead with his bent forefinger. "Aye, milady." He was prepared to go wherever Lady Frobisher and the tide of Fortune, might take him.

Chapter Twenty Four

'Lastly came Winter cloathed all in frize,
Chattering his teeth for cold that did him chill,
Whil'st on his hoary beard his breath did freese
And the dull drops that from his purpled bill
As from a limbeck, did adown distill.'
E.S.

Spenser enjoyed his encounters with Uaithne. The cowherd showed scant respect or deference to his master's high office. He offered his opinions baldly, without preamble, a mish-mash of legend and prophecy, a fatalistic view of the world. He claimed to have seen it all. Down all the ages, he had seen the great people rise and fall, their cities prosper and decline into decay. For all their power and glory they were doing no more than cobbling together a means of surviving from day to day. Those bare stones standing in circles on the hilltops, were once the abode of mighty kings and Druids. Some day, mused Spenser, he would write down the stories of this comical little man, Uaithne, both bard and seer, with a drop permanently depending from his frost-nipped nose.

"I will leave this place soon enough," the cowherd told him.

Spenser felt a twinge of regret. Change disturbed him, even the loss of an illiterate labourer. He would miss the little man and his undoubted skill with animals and, worse still, he would be put to the inconvenience of finding a replacement from the dwindling number of English settlers. What use would a cowherd be who kept one eye on the forest, in constant fear of attack? What use a man who would let the beasts stray, rather than venture after them into the green gloom of the woods?

"Why must you go?"

"I have seen enough here. You also will go. Your settlement here is cursed."

"You refer to the war of ONeill in the north? You do not understand. The great Queen has armies enough to crush ONeill and all other rebels. There is no need for you to flee."

Uaithne gave a scoffing laugh. "Flee, is it? I might just go home. Will they not come with harrows and spades to destroy the crops and starve the people again? Will they not fell the woods and burn the roofs over the heads of the people? And will the Irish learn to love your Queen and will there then be peace?"

"All that would not be necessary if the people were not led astray by their treacherous lords."

Uaithne returned to his original assertion. "This English settlement is cursed. You know that the soldier, Norris, is dead?"

"I have heard that. A great soldier. A hero of many wars. He died in his brother's house in Mallow. He died, poor man, of gangrene."

"Gangrene, is it? Did you know that the spirits of all those he hurled down from the cliffs, came by to curse him in his last hours?"

"I did not. This is all superstitious nonsense. Sir John was a great soldier." Spenser was irritated that he was arguing with an ignorant servant.

"Or that the Divil himself came to claim his soul?"

"You are a foolish man, Uaithne, to pay heed to the gossip of servants." Spenser had heard the story. He had heard it repeated by those who should have known better. There were some who saw it as an omen. A dark man had been seen entering the sick man's chamber at dead of night. In the morning Sir John was dead. His head and the upper half of his body had been turned backwards, twisted, they whispered, so that he could look back at what he had done in life, instead of looking forward to the bright hope of the Resurrection. It was proof, to ignorant minds, of whatsoever they needed to prove.

"He died in great pain, God help him." Spenser, the rational man, had an explanation. "He was contorted by anguish."

"The Divil mend him," replied Uaithne. "May his heels kick at Heaven."

A silence descended between them. Spenser racked his brain. The silence was awkward. As is always the case in Ireland, he fell back on the subject of the weather.

"It is unseasonably cold. There was frost last night."

"Don't I know it?" replied Uaithne, wiping the drop from his nose, with the back of his hand. "It is the *garbh shíon.*"

"The what?"

"*Garbh shíon na gcuach.* The harsh weather of the cuckoo. It holds the spring back. I warned you. There is no grass growth and we are almost out of hay."

"Do what you can," directed Spenser. "There will be grass anon."

"Aye, anon. And then the Milesians will return. I warn you. When I go, the cattle-murrain will return also." His hand went to the cord around his neck. He touched the amulet.

"Jesus wept!" exploded Spenser. "Have you no cheering news? Do you not know that ONeill is compassed all about? That Fiach OByrne is humbled? Can you see no bright future for Ireland and her misfortunate people?"

Uaithne made no reply. He sniffed and pulled his cloak around him. He shrugged and turned away. Spenser watched him go. Uaithne, steadying himself with his staff, was Winter, presaging doom. Some day, he promised himself, he would enforce respect from the little man, even if he had to beat the insolence out of him with his own staff.

He returned to his castle. Elizabeth met him in the courtyard. She was upset.

"They are fled," she said.

"Who?"

"Your soldiers. Your men-at-arms. They have gone and they left the gate open, as usual."

Spenser laughed aloud, maybe too loudly. "The Divil mend them," he said. The laughter caught his breath. He coughed violently, bending over and placing his hands on his knees. He wheezed for breath. "Damned cuckoos," he gasped. "We are better off without them."

She looked at him in puzzlement. She was agitated. "But what shall we do? We must have some protection."

He stood upright again. "We will hang out more flags. We shall make a show of power." He spoke grandiloquently. She was not reassured.

"I am serious. We must have protection."

"We could run away," he went on. "We could go with Uaithne to the west, to the mountains of Sliabh Luachra and live under the ground with his Queen of Faerie."

"I will not listen to this." There was a high colour in her cheeks, roses upon lilies.

He laughed, shrugging off her anxiety. "Mutabilitie," he said. "We must change with the times. He coughed again. "Damned cuckoos," he muttered.

She walked away from him, then turned and came back. She would not meet his eye. "I have read your survey of Ireland. It frightens me. If people read it, they will hate us all, you, your wife, your children, all of our settlement. You will spread the seeds of hatred for generations. I beg of you to destroy it." She clutched his arm. He turned her face to his. He wiped a tear from the corner of her eye.

"My love," he said gently, "I do everything for you and for our children. You know little of the world. Some things are difficult, but they must be done. Anyway, the manuscript has gone to London."

She turned from him, taking her fingers from his arm. The cold blast of the cuckoo chilled his blood.

***

Owen, son of Rory OMore, knew only warfare. He had many hurts to avenge. The story of his father, alone in the wilderness, with only wolves for company, haunted his childhood. There was treachery. There were massacres of his people. The shame of his father's surrender to Lord Deputy Sidney, humiliation before the high altar in the cathedral in Kilkenny, burned inside him and kept him from his sleep.

He learned his trade from his kinsman and foster-father, Fiach MacHugh OByrne, harrying the insistent English in the hills and glens of Wicklow, burning and making prey, even to the walls of Dublin. ONeill, in Ulster, heard of the young man's fame. He approved. Men of such ability and motivation, were useful to him.

OByrne sent him out from Wicklow, like a projectile, against the English of the boggy midlands. Owen swept them from their settlements, bottling them up in the fortress town of Maryborough. He gave no quarter. Even his distant cousin, Black Tom, favourite of the aged Queen, was wary of him. ONeill, High King of Ireland in all but name, directed the young man south towards Munster, ordering him to pull up the English settlement by its shallow roots and drive the foreigners into the sea. If any man could do this service for him, it was Owen MacRory OMore.

***

It was no great walk to Saint Giles's church. Nicholas Conyers followed the directions, delighting in the colloquy of London's bells. There was a rhyme that he had largely forgotten. 'Brickbats and tiles. When will you pay me?' Something from a dimly recalled childhood; his mother dandling him on her knee. 'Oranges and lemons.' Impossible to imagine. She had great hopes for her boy. The noises of the street surrounded him. It was all new.

Cripplegate. He found the church. There were cripples aplenty. This could have been his fate, a wayward shot, a fall from a yard-arm, a sword-thrust from some blood-thirsty foreigner. The Almighty had favoured him, sparing him the years of sitting by church gates or on street corners, enforcing alms from indifferent passers by. He did not have to exhibit maimed limbs, to win their pity, limbs lopped off or mangled in the service of Her

Majesty. He still had health and strength. He dropped a coin into an outstretched hand. He had money in his purse, courtesy of the captain's widow.

"God shield you, friend," said the squatting beggar.

He stepped inside the gloom of the church. He had one scanted duty yet to fulfil. He walked the aisles, peering at the monuments of great men. He could not read the inscriptions. There was no need to. He spotted the bust of Frobisher from a distance. He recognised the features as they had been in life, strong and determined, the lifeless eyes gazing towards some eternally retreating horizon. He noted the unicorn in blue and gold. He thought hard. Frobisher's unicorn was a fish, was it not? There were gryphons on the shield.

Nicholas stood erect, making his obedience, touching his forefinger to his forehead. He thought of the time they perched together in the swaying crow's nest, the time they descried the New World, with the ice growling all around. He could hear the ice knocking against the hull and the ship echoing to its keel. The world was pure and gleaming then, filled with promise. He felt better for having paid his respects. The question of the Resurrection came back to him. How much of Frobisher lay in the tomb? What of his internal organs? It was a question for more learned minds than his.

He became conscious of a figure standing beside him. It was an old man with a few wisps of white hair covering his pate. Even in the half-light of the church, Nicholas was struck by his deathly pallor. There was the sour, metallic stench of tobacco on his breath. Nicholas stepped aside, yielding his place before the monument. He observed the gaunt and spectral fellow. The old man clutched a sheaf of papers. He muttered under his breath. The breath rattled in his chest. He shook the bundle of papers.

"I know my rights, Martin Frobisher. I will have my due."

The stone figure made no reply. The eyes stared into infinity.

"God curse you, Frobisher. I will be paid."

He shook the papers again, as if he might constrain the bust to yield up the money, not by prayer, as is the way with beggars, but by curses and threats.

Nicholas was tempted to intervene, to put a stop to this disrespect to his captain. He did not, however, wish to become involved in an unseemly tussle with a lunatic, a bedlam, especially in the sacred precincts of a church. That would be a contest he could not win. He stood quietly until the old man departed, muttering and wheezing.

He looked a last time, at his captain. He remembered his voice, calm and steady, even in the midst of the storm. He recalled his great strength and courage; his loyalty to his crew; how he had gone, again and again, to seek his missing companions in the frozen waste. The captain could well have sent those two hundred seamen into the breach at El Leon under some other officer. He could have observed their fate from the safety of his ship, but he insisted on leading them himself.

Nicholas too, had a duty to perform; one last order from his dying captain. He went out into the sunlit street. The bells began again.

'When will you pay me?' Was that not what the old man had been asking? Perhaps he too had been touched by the disaster of the gold. It was an unfortunate business altogether. He, himself, had not yet been paid for that last voyage. He had written that off, as they say, many years since, although he had never written it down. It possibly lurked somewhere in some dusty ledger known only to clerks and calculating men. They had the skill to write it down, to write it up, write it in and eventually, write his money off. He shrugged. Writing remains where memory fades. It might well rise to the surface some day, an unlooked for bonus, a piece of flotsam from the wreckage of the Company of Cathay.

'When I get rich,' said the bells of Shoreditch. 'When will that be?' queried another. 'Boom, boom, boom, boom, boom,' said the great bell of Bow.

***

It pained Spenser to think of leaving, even for a brief period. Elizabeth insisted. She wanted to be in Youghal, safe behind its walls, until the present troubles blew over. She wanted to be safe and warm in her uncle's house. The rebel army could hurl itself against the walls of Youghal, like the waves of the sea, but inevitably it would be swept away by a mighty undertow. She knew that Youghal had been sacked by a rebel army long ago, when the Irish lords were strong, long, long before her family had settled there. It was ancient history. The Queen would never allow Youghal to fall to the rebels again. The townspeople knew the importance of trade. The Queen would send Sir Walter and his fleet. The rebels, themselves, would not destroy so valuable a town. The future lay in the security and prosperity of the towns.

She wished to walk in the comfortable streets and hear the chatter of merchants. She wanted to taste the wine of Portugal and hear the rumble of casks on gangplanks. She longed to hear the tread of soldiers, the clink of their equipment, the shouts of their officers and the cry of the watchman in the night, telling the town that all was well.

Spenser gathered his papers. He tapped them into a neat pile. It was the part of his life over which he had complete control. He sent knights out to encounter dragons and come, triumphant, home. He pitted them against Paynim enemies and sorceresses. He could direct a wasp to grieve a ferocious lion and distract him from his prey. What general would not wish to have that power; to marshal the hordes of stinging insects to afflict his foes? The thought appealed to him. They could visit plagues and fevers on entire armies in the night. In the morning the camp would be strewn with dead and dying men. Cooking fires would dwindle to ashes. Tents would gape open to the wind. It was a dream. It could never happen.

He put the papers in a satchel to travel with him, three more books of his epic work, the children of his brain, almost as dear to him as his living offspring, his issue, his progeny—the language of deeds and lawyers. *Per stirpes*, from the living stem. The Spensers had taken root in Ireland. They would grow and grow in wealth and power. His name and his great poem would grow. His confidence in the project had come back, taking him by surprise with the urgency of the enterprise. Books ten, eleven and twelve would follow in due course, the templates of chivalry and just rule. Already they seethed in his brain. The towering oak of his poetry would overshadow, overawe, the upstart scribblers of London, the briars and weeds that tangle the forest floor. He secured the thongs of the satchel and placed it on the table, ready for the morning. He rested his hand upon it for a moment. He frowned and took his hand away. He shivered.

He went out onto the battlemented roof. The wind was still from the east, a dry, carping wind that found every crack, every unglazed arrow-slit, every unshuttered window, a wind that would follow a man into his bed. He could not sleep. He could smell smoke on the wind. He could see pin-pricks of fire on the wooded hills. The charcoal burners were having difficulty in keeping their kilns tamped down. The wind was reducing their labours to ash.

He mused on the nature of fire. No wonder some heathen races worshipped it as a god. It warmed and comforted the body. It offered safety in the darkness, keeping wild beasts and malevolent Pooks at bay. It broke out at times in rage, as all gods do, consuming everything in its path.

John Dee had shown him once, a mirror of shining stone. It had come to him from the Americas, where savage people gave their own children to fire. Spenser had seen nothing but a dusky reflection of his own face. John Dee admitted to the same experience. His associate, Kelly, the gifted Irishman, had seen things though, feathered priests on high platforms, tearing the hearts from victims, infants, men and women, spread out on altars of stone. The arms of the priests ran red with gore. Their teeth showed like those of ferocious animals. They held the grisly offerings aloft, before hurling them into a flaming brazier.

The multitudes bowed low, beating their foreheads on the earth, mothers and fathers, brothers and sisters, crying out in gratitude that they had been spared and that their sacrifice would bring prosperity and plentiful crops.

Kelly was a man of rare gifts. He could explain life as a cycle of growth and decay, of sacrifice and renewal. It was strange however, that this seer, this mystic, had not descried his own ignominious end. It was a question that had puzzled John Dee for many years.

Elizabeth came to him.

"I have ordered horses to be ready at first light." She did not touch him. She did not put her arm through his, as she had been wont to do. She did not open her robe and offer her white body to his touch, as had been their way in previous times, long, long ago. Too long, it seemed.

"I must curb the activities of those charcoal burners. There will be no trees left. I will see to it immediately we come back. *Céard a dhéanfaimíd gan adhmad?*"

"What did you say?" She looked at him strangely. She could just make out his profile in the dim light.

"What will we do without timber, firewood, roof-trees?"

"What indeed?" His detachment disturbed her. It was no time for philosophical discussion.

"Ships to bear us up in the rolling ocean?"

She made no answer.

They heard it again, carried on the wind, a voice from the dark, encircling forest.

"A Ha-a-voc! A Ha-a-a-vo-o-o-oc!" The hawk was coming.

Chapter Twenty Five

There was a story of Darius, King of Persia, who once took a notion to conquer the Scythians. When the two armies stood in battle array, facing each other, a hare started up from the field between them. It darted hither and thither, looking for a way to escape. A troop of Scythian cavalry spurred their horses in pursuit, with wild yells and halloos. The great king was filled with dismay that the Scythians so scorned his mighty host. They would chase down a hare before battling the greatest army ever assembled. Darius gave the order to turn about, leaving the windswept plains of Scythia for the luxury of the cities of the south.

Bleary eyed from lack of sleep, Spenser watched a hare starting forth from the trees on the margin of his home field. The short deer, the Irish called it, all legs and ears. He did not like hares. To eat them, he had heard, induced melancholy. Skinned and dressed for the pot, a hare looks like a severed arm. He watched how it dodged this way and that, like a snipe in flight. He marvelled at its speed. The Irish of course, are descended from the Scythians. This he had ascertained from wide reading in ancient books. The thought gave him a cold feeling in his breast. He saw crows rising from their city in the treetops. It was too far away for him to hear their raucous protests. The crows circled, no bigger than gnats.

He went down into the courtyard. Three horses, saddled and ready, stamped their hooves impatiently. There was a pack-mule laden with bags, an ill-favoured beast, a horse inexpertly put together, perpetually resentful of its barren state. No hope of progeny. A grudge against the world.

Three things, the Irish said, *triúr gan riaghal*, three things without control, *bean, múille agus muc*, a woman, a mule and a pig. He kept the observation to himself. The pigs were loose in the yard. They rooted everywhere, startling the horses. The horses snorted and shied from them. The mule ignored them, pondering its grievances. It regarded the haste and flurry with baleful eyes.

Elizabeth emerged from the doorway dressed in a heavy travelling robe. She carried her youngest, Peregrine, in a fold of her garment. She mounted by the block and sat astride, holding the child in front of her. She held him tight. She said not a word.

Uaithne arrived, gasping for breath.

"Come, come," he said urgently. "There is no time. They are here. He seized the reins of Elizabeth's horse. Young Sylvanus sprang into the saddle. He tugged on the lead rein, jolting the mule into motion.

Spenser mounted slowly. His joints were stiff. He resented the journey ahead. His daughter, Machabyas, sat behind him, her arms about his waist. Uaithne ran before them, through the open gate.

The pigs followed in a riot of joy, scattering in all directions across the open fields. Spenser's cattle cavorted about, alarmed by all the activity. Uaithne turned southwards towards the lake. The geese were gone. Beyond loomed the encircling forest.

The cattle scattered, fine healthy bullocks, Spenser's particular pride. When all his neighbours' animals wasted and pined, the cattle of Kilcolman throve. The cows gave good milk. He had the best cowherd in the world in Uaithne.

He noticed that Uaithne carried a leather bag strapped to his shoulders. Why would he bring his harp with him at this early hour? The bag jounced up and down as the little man broke into a trot.

Great God! His satchel. His manuscripts. His immortal progeny. They were still on the table in the hall. He resented the haste that had caused him to overlook them. He reined in the horse.

"My manuscripts. I must go back for them."

Uaithne grasped the bridle. He pointed.

The woods to the East seethed with armed men. They surged through the undergrowth, trampling new pathways and brushing the low-hanging branches aside. They moved with grim intent. Their harness rang. Their spears glinted. The crows flapped overhead, fearful for their young in their high, swaying, bundles of straw and twigs.

They came to the margin of the woods. They saw a field full of livestock, pigs, cattle, fine sturdy beasts, chickens pecking among the weeds. Beyond, stood a castle, silver and gold in the early morning sun. They saw to their left, a small group of riders making all haste towards the forest margin. They spurred their horses in pursuit. The riders reached the trees and disappeared from sight.

***

Owen Mac Rory's men were hungry. Since leaving the forest of Arlo there had been nothing but hard riding and butchery. There was not an English farm left standing in their wake. Everywhere they went they brought havoc, corpses hanging from trees, torn women and girls, crouching in the ruins, whimpering and gazing with mad incomprehension at what had once been their homes. There were infants impaled on stakes, wizened trophies of victory. Their spears were decked with obscene mementoes of rape and murder.

Owen Mac Rory O More left no seed to grow, no child to become a man to go seeking revenge, no woman capable of bringing forth a son who would bow the knee to the tottering English Queen. His vengeance was complete, except for a few fugitives in the forest. They could go. They could spread the news of his great victory. They could make the people of the coastal towns tremble at what was to come.

He called his men back. They fell with glee upon the livestock. They laughed like boys, as they chased the pigs and chickens about the place. They herded the cattle into a small enclosure, selecting some for the cooking fires. They exulted in their victory.

They found papers in the castle and used them to set the building ablaze. It burned merrily. The oaken beams crackled. Pine furniture exploded, as ancient resin took light. Upper floors collapsed in the inferno. The roof imploded, sending a towering column of smoke and flame into the sky. Sparks flew like a myriad of stars, wondrously bright against the smoke The ruin was complete. The army feasted and took their ease. The Milesians reigned supreme.

Uaithne led them by winding paths through the forest. He walked with great sureness, his hand on the bridle of Elizabeth's horse. The child dozed in the shelter of her robe. Spenser found himself checking incessantly that Machabyas was still there. Her grip was light on his waist. He feared that she might slip from the horse, out of weariness and fear. He squeezed her hand and made reassuring noises. Sylvanus constantly looked behind and tugged the lead rein. Of all of them, the mule was the least fatigued. It whickered and snatched at the weeds on the forest floor.

The forest sang to them. New growth gave a green tinge to the sunlight that shafted down upon them. Thrushes sang their fluting songs of spring and fertility. Doves murmured their repetitive inanities, always the same, 'hoo hoo – hoo, hoo hoo – hoo'. The cold had gone out of the wind.

This was the Greenwood, of which he had often written, where knights and ladies sought shelter from storms; where goddesses and their attendant nymphs, disported themselves; where shepherds contended, one with another, in contests of music and rhyme. Today however it was a place of refuge.

Uaithne raised his hand. They halted, listening carefully. There were no sounds of pursuit. They could still smell the smoke. Uaithne gestured them forward. He patted the horse's neck. They plodded on.

Spenser looked at the trees. He had catalogued them, the birch for arrows, 'the ash for nothing ill.' The oak over- towered them all. It was the king of the forest, but the tensile ash was his favourite. It could do so many things. But he had said all that before. With a cold chill he realised that he had come to the end of poetry. The children of his brain, his best verses, were even at that moment mere scraps of charred paper, circling like crows in the sky, over the ruins of Kilcolman. He could not start again. He could not sit down like a journeyman poet and seek to plagiarise the work that had once sprung joyfully from his brain. He could not imitate himself, like a base actor on the stage, parroting the words of a better man. The great enterprise, the celebration of a faerie queen, was a mocking dream. He admitted again, that he had lost faith in all that he had praised. Cynthia, surrounded by sycophants, had become a crone, desperately trying to hold back age with face-paint and gorgeous jewels. The gods had sat in judgement on top of Arlo Hill and had found that Mutabilitie rules everything. It overcomes Nature, Power, Beauty, the gods themselves, even Love. There is no stability.

For no reason at all, he remembered the investors in the Company of Cathay. He would have put money into the venture, had he not been an impoverished scholar. Those, who had given their money, lost it. Some became embittered. Others wrote it off. One or two went mad. The wise ones had given merely pledges. Their fingers had not been burned.

'Write it off,' whispered an inner voice. 'It is gone. It was all a delusion.' It was true. The flames of Kilcolman had consumed only paper. The knights and ladies, the castles and courtiers held no reality for him any more. Better to let the fire make a clean end of everything. He had no wish to become a scarecrow figure, stumping the streets, tugging at sleeves, telling strangers how Cynthia had neglected him, had betrayed him by growing old and withered.

He thought to offer this revelation to Elizabeth, but she rode like one in a trance. He laughed softly. Uaithne looked at him. He nodded. It was as if the cowherd understood. He tugged more urgently on the reins.

Spenser gave him a wry smile. He felt for his daughter's hand. She was still with him. That was all that mattered. He patted her hand. He kicked his heels into the horse's flanks. The forest sang.

The sunlight slanted down. The nymphs, the knights, the piping shepherds, the faerie ladies were no more. He wrote them off.

***

Owen Mac Rory called his huntsmen to him. They came all three, with their dogs, gaunt rangy wolfhounds and a mournful looking sleuth-hound.

"It appears that we let a big one get away. I want him back."

Owen held some charred papers in his hand. They had floated down from the heavens. "This is the castle of Spenser, the High Sheriff. I want him back. Oh ho, I want him back." He rubbed his hands. He smiled in his beard. He had heard nothing but ill of Spenser.

The huntsmen saluted their chieftain. They patted their dogs and grasped their mighty bows. They loped away, calling some marksmen from the feast. The dogs bounded ahead. The lead huntsman sounded his horn.

Owen Mac Rory crumpled the paper, some gibberish rhyming stuff, and cast it aside.

***

Before noon the fugitives came to the river.

"Owenduff," said Spenser, hoping to break the silence between himself and his wife. "Blackwater."

She looked at him and made as if to say something. She checked herself. She was not interested in a linguistic disquisition. She looked at the racing water in despair. She looked upstream and downstream. There was no sign of a ford or better still, a bridge, no kindly sandbar reaching out to help them across.

From far away in the forest came the sound of a hunting horn and the deep-throated belling of hounds.

Uaithne led them on. They came to the pool where the fisherman was wont to moor his boat. It was still there, concealed in the river osiers. There was no sign of the fisherman. The oars were still on the thole pins. They clambered aboard. Sylvanus clutched the reins of the three horses. The mule refused to budge.

It dug its hooves into the river mud and the soft leaf-mould. It tossed its head and snorted. It rolled its eyes. The dogs were coming closer.

Spenser took the oars. Uaithne pushed the boat out into the stream.

"I take my leave of you," he said abruptly. He slapped the horses, urging them into the water. Their hooves sucked in the mud. They shied and reared in protest, but as the river took them, they began to swim. They swam wide-eyed, with heads straining forward, like little wanton boys learning the art for the first time.

"But the dogs," called Spenser. He tried to keep the boat steady against the current.

"Dogs, is it?" came the reply. "Go across. It is time for me to return to my home place." He raised his hand in farewell. Spenser pulled towards the other bank. The boat moved diagonally across the current. The horses snorted. Spenser prayed, not to the Almighty, but to the spirit of his poor drowned, demented wife. 'If you are still here; if your soul still haunts this river, forgive my coldness and neglect. Bear your children up in this flood.' He prayed silently and pulled harder on the oars.

Looking back over the heads of the swimming horses, he saw the mule, still with the bundles on its back. He saw tall dogs bounding from the trees. He heard their voices. He saw Uaithne standing among the reeds. Run, run, he urged silently. He watched as Uaithne held out his hands. The dogs fell silent. Their tails drooped. They crept towards him in all humility. He pointed towards the trees. The dogs bounded away. Soon, their voices sounded again in the forest, fainter this time and fading away. The hunting horn called again and again, dwindling into the distance. Spenser looked back. Uaithne was no longer to be seen.

Instinct took over. The boat glided into the reeds. The bedraggled horses struggled onto firmer ground. Elizabeth climbed out. She still clutched her child, with fierce determination. She looked up at the mountain slanting over them.

"We will go over the mountain," she said. They were her first words since their flight had begun.

Spenser stood on the gunwale of the boat, tilting it so that the river filled it. It settled among the tangled roots of the reeds. He knew that eventually, the hunters would retrace their steps. He wanted to keep the river between his family and the dogs.

They walked their exhausted horses through the trees. The ground began to rise. The trees gave way to gorse and then to bracken. Spenser made to take the child from Elizabeth, but she would not release him.

Onward they toiled, upwards towards the crest. Linnets whirred in the yellow gorse. Loose stone rolled and slipped underfoot, but they could not stop. A keen-eyed watcher from far below, might see them moving as specks on the mountainside. They climbed, in constant dread of the hunting horn. The little boy whimpered from hunger. Elizabeth held him closer, making soothing noises. Sylvanus took his sister's hand. They bent to the mountain. They took short steps. Their legs ached. Their breathing rasped.

The earth below became shrouded in shadow, but still they climbed in sunlight, insects on the mountain top. The river faded to dull pewter, a scribble amid the darkening forest.

They crested the mountain and threw themselves down to rest. They were in a place of great standing stones, the ruins of some ancient city of the Druids. The place was sombre, suggesting unimaginable time, perhaps from before the Flood. They were too weary to speculate. The stones cast long shadows, longer and longer. Darkness soaked up from the ground, creeping up the standing pillars until the amber light fled, even from their tips. Darkness enveloped everything. The fugitives slept.

Chapter Twenty Six

Nicholas Conyers was somewhat disillusioned. He had assumed that the captain's wife had merely to click her fingers and the authorities would send men scurrying throughout the city to locate this heathen savage and bring him before her. Instead, she had provided Nicholas with garments of tawny serge. He wore shoes with buckles on them. Silver buckles. He was uneasy in the clothes of a gentleman.

However, he was beginning to become interested in the players. She brought him to The Swan, crossing the river by wherry. He learned to hand her from the jutting prow of the boat and steady her gait on the river steps. She reminded him of his mother. She corrected his speech. Some nights they went to Blackfriars, where the stage was indoors and lights illuminated the action. He always walked a pace behind her, as befitted a servant.

There was a great deal of talking. The actors might come forward and share their innermost thoughts with the spectators. It struck him as odd that the other characters did not seem to hear. Usually they spoke in a limping kind of verse. It was strange. They went to the Bell Savage, where Captain Frobisher had once exhibited a heathen savage. A caliban, the proprietor recalled. That was a long time ago, when the captain's pockets were empty, his shoes were down at heel. The calilban had died. The people still kept coming though, for a few days anyway. He knew of no calibans nowadays. He showed them where poor Sir Thomas Wyatt had rallied his last few followers. He sat on that bench there. He was one of those poets too. Not very practical. No, he no longer held plays. That had been his wife's idea. The yard used to be thronged in the afternoons. There was money in it, but truth to tell, he had grown tired of all the talking. He suggested, Whitefriars, The Curtain, The Red Bull. No, the one in Shoreditch, The Theatre. That was what they called it. He laughed. "For a crowd of poets they didn't come up with much of a name, did they? The Theatre. I ask you!"

He had a great deal more to say. He advised Lady Frobisher to keep her hand on her purse. "Rogues, all of them." She thanked him for his advice.

"I have my man here to protect me," she said, nodding towards Nicholas. He blinked. He was beginning to understand his role.

She always seemed to know the people in the theatres. Everyone greeted her as a valued patron. They saw a great many plays, sometimes in sunshine and sometimes in rain. She had a regular place in a cubicle to one side of the stage. The actors were protected by an awning, the Heavens, they called it, but most of the spectators stood in the open air. They showed their approval by loud applause and their disapproval with equal candour.

More and more, he was drawn into this world. He stood behind her ladyship's chair, not sure whether he was there as a guest or as a bodyguard. Sometimes he felt like a pupil.

He saw a hunchback king, a murderer, propose to the widow of his victim. He admired the fellow's nerve and marvelled at his argument. The hunchback interrupted the funeral. He knelt before the bier. The corpse, they said, bled in the presence of its killer. He pleaded. He cajoled. The young widow weakened. She capitulated. The funeral moved on. The hunchback smirked at the audience. Nicholas was disgusted, but he marvelled at the language.

Murderers came to dispatch two little boys. They debated the morality of the deed. One put forward the merits of the case. He outlined the advantages. He was a short, squat fellow, with a dark and villainous face. His companion weakened. His conscience gave way.

'Where is thy conscience now?'

'In the Duke of Gloucester's purse.'

W.S.

The audience gasped. One guffawed. Nicholas put his hand to his dagger. He stepped forward to intervene. The lady put her hand on his sleeve. She whispered.

"It is play acting, Nicholas."

He stepped back, embarrassed by his foolishness. He had forgotten. He hoped that the spectators had not noticed. There was no need to fear. They gazed in horrified silence at what ensued.

It is mere play-acting, Nicholas assured himself. He had seen worse deeds in war. Nevertheless he was moved, almost to tears, by the plight of the little boys. He hated the hunchback king.

Another time there was a gross, fat man who insulted a prince. He led the boy astray, corrupting his morals, to the great distress of the aged king. This was a man of no honour, a cheat, a coward, a man who never paid his reckoning. He planned a great career for himself when the prince should ascend the throne. He would be the hangman and enrich himself on the property of those he hanged. The audience loved him. Nicholas despised and loathed him. It was more evidence that the theatre corrupted the morals of the people.

Yet he was moved to pity another day, when the new, young king turned his face away from his old companion.

'I know thee not, old man. Fall to thy prayers.'

W.S.

The theatre was shocked to silence. Nicholas scratched his head.

The landlady, the bawd, at another time, described the death of the old man; how she had struggled to keep some heat in his body; how she had felt his feet. They were cold. She felt his legs, onward and upward and all was cold as any stone.

Nicholas felt a tear trickle down his cheek. It ran into his beard. He sniffed and wiped it aside with his sleeve. It was ridiculous. It was mere play-acting. Mere words. The players were clever with words. They played upon his feelings, as if on an instrument.

As for instruments, there was always a player with tabor and drum. Sometimes there was a fiddle or rebeck, played with varying degrees of skill. There was another, a kind of box on legs. Nicholas, standing behind her ladyship's chair, could see the mechanism, when the player opened the lid. The player struck levers that lifted a series of pegs. The pegs seemed to snag on strings inside the box, to make a pleasing noise, a very ingenious device.

He came to recognise the various musicians. The drum and tabor man, sent armies into battle. Nicholas felt cheated that the armies marched off-stage. He heard their martial tramp. It would have been more exciting to see a band of soldiers accoutred for war.

However, he learned to see them in his mind's eye. The man who played the elaborate box was the short dark young man who had murdered the princes in the Tower. He was the servant who remembered his swashing blow. This remark always drew laughter. He laid about him, with a great wooden broadsword, often throwing himself off balance. He fought like a bumpkin, an ungainly oaf. The young, pacing gentlemen of that play, circled one another with rapier and dagger. They stabbed to murderous effect.

Yet the bumpkin returned in courtly clothing, to provide music for a ball. He played softly in the inner stage, while the people of quality danced and two young lovers touched palms and spoke for the first time. Nicholas was transported to a grand palazzo. He strained to hear every word. He had never imagined that love could be spoken in poetry. He marvelled at the delicacy of the player's touch, as his fingers struck harmonies from the box. At the end, he wept openly at the cruelties of fate and chance that had laid two young people in the darkness of the tomb. The sombre music reverberated in the gloomy crypt. The audience applauded.

"You are moved, my friend?" asked Lady Frobisher.

"I know not why, my lady. Is it not mere play acting?" Nicholas wiped his eyes. He grinned to conceal his embarrassment.

"Indeed," she agreed. "The theatre is full of surprises. It finds things in us that lie unsuspected in our hearts."

She went across the stage to congratulate the players. They bowed to her. The ladies curtsied. Not ladies either, but boys with heavily rouged cheeks and wigs of tow. They fooled nobody, least of all Nicholas, who had seen them at close quarters and yet, and yet. He checked himself sharply. Boys with wigs and painted cheeks. Hold on there, Nicholas. But yet, his heart had gone out to the star-crossed girl.

Lady Frobisher was speaking to the man in charge. He was nodding. He looked towards Nicholas. He beckoned. Nicholas walked across. He had never stood on a stage before. He gazed about. The spectators had left. Footsteps rattled on the gallery stairs. He wanted to seize the moment, to speak to the theatre, to let his voice boom out, to be recognised and acclaimed as the coming force in the world of the players. He tripped and recovered his balance. The man, the manager, smiled.

"It can do that to you, the stage. You can lose control of your tongue and your limbs. Your hands grow large as hay- forks. You know not where to put them."

Nicholas nodded. He felt like a true bumpkin.

"I have spoken to Master Will about your quest," said Lady Frobisher. "He has enquired abroad and may have some news."

"Ah, yes," said the man. "To find a heathen savage among the companies of players should not be difficult. They are all heathens, my friend and no more savage people could you meet. They will rend one another for a good mention. They will tear one another to pieces to get a leading part. Their feuds run bitter and deep." A ghost of a smile played about his lips.

Nicholas suspected mockery. They were playing with him. He felt his anger rising.

"But, wait," said the manager. "I know your story. It likes me well. An infant, taken in a barren place, who grows to be a man and is revealed to be a long lost prince."

Nicholas was disturbed by this new slant. Was he the villain of the piece? He relapsed into truculence.

"I have a commission from Captain Frobisher."

"You have. You have," said the manager gently. "We have deceived you for too long." He looked across to where the murderer, the bumpkin, was dusting off the musical box. Nicholas noted the elaborate pattern of the inlay, silver against ebony. It was a thing of great value.

"Caliban," called the manager. "This gentleman wishes to speak with you."

"Anon, Will," said the young man. He continued to dust the instrument. He blew upon the levers and pegs. He flicked the rag over them. He closed the lid. The strings twangled within. He stroked the dark wood. He approached. He bowed.

"How may I be of service to you, sir?"

His voice was gentle. Nicholas removed his cap.

"This is Nicholas Conyers," said Lady Frobisher. "He sailed with my husband to the frozen lands."

"I have heard this story so many times from good John Dee," replied the young man. "He has told me of my people and how they make their home where no other people could survive. He always told me to be proud. Even Captain Frobisher could not live in the land of my people, but I survive in his. I have made it mine."

"And you shall conquer it, young Caliban," said the manager. "Would you go back to the Arctic seas, if the opportunity came your way?"

The young man pondered. His dark eyes glinted. He shook his head. "I would be as a plant from some tropical country, rudely thrust into frozen soil. No, I have found my world. It is music and the stage. I would not change it."

They stood in silence. The manager watched Nicholas closely. Nicholas coughed. He shuffled his feet.

"I ask your pardon, sir," he began. "It was I who took you from your people." He hung his head.

"And brought me to this place of wonders. There is no pardon necessary. We must go where Fortune takes us. I pray that she may be as kind to you as she has been to me."

Nicholas took the lodestone from about his neck.

"The captain gave this to me to give to you. It is from your country. If you decide to go there, it will guide you."

They gazed at the shard of metal. It jerked on the thong.

"It seeks always the Northern Star, the one true element in the firmament," said Nicholas. He checked himself, surprised by this flow of words. Where had that come from? Master Will gave a little nod of approbation, closing one eye. He liked the phrase

"I will not go there. I honour my people. They gave me life and courage. I think of them often, but I cannot go back. You have found your heathen savage. I will live my life among these hairy people and bring music to their warlike souls."

He laughed. He held out his hand. It was warm and strong. Nicholas took it gladly.

***

The girl, Machabyas, passed in the night, there on the mountain-top. The dew lay on her brow. A spider-web covered her features. Dewdrops hung on the web, like jewels. Her heart had stopped from terror and weariness.

Spenser awoke. He looked around at the looming stones. The sun had reached only their crests. The air was cold. He saw the girl, with a veil over her face. Rosalind! No. He scrambled to her side. He saw the spider, Aragnoll, the murderer of his butterfly. He brushed the web away. He held her to him. She was cold. His voice choked in his throat. He called her name. Nothing came but a terrible animal noise. He was in a nightmare. He wailed and rocked her back and forth. He had no words.

Elizabeth came to him. She knelt beside him. She put her arm around his shoulder. "No, no," she moaned, over and over. The baby cried. Sylvanus stood, looking down the slope. He clenched his hands.

They scraped a shallow grave in the thin mountain soil. They laid her on a bed of heather and covered her with a cloak. He wished that he had kept his Irish mantle to keep her safe. He gazed a last time, on her face. He brushed her hair with his fingertips then drew the cloak over her features. How often had she played

'Peep' with his mantle? The oldest game, a game of eyes meeting and hiding, then meeting again. A game of enduring love.

They covered her with heather and bracken. They piled stones over her, dark red and jagged. Sylvanus struggled with the largest stones. They made a cairn to keep her out of the reach of scrabbling wolves and carrion birds. They took their leave of her. She remained, in the company of the ancient Druids and maybe even the Good People, a daughter of Ireland, in that high place of tombs.

Chapter Twenty Seven

"So now, Nicholas Conyers," began Lady Frobisher, "circumstances have changed. You are released from your obligation."

Nicholas waited. His course had changed suddenly, as if his ship had broached in a half-gale, throwing pots and pans and crewmen all about below decks. The sails flapped and fluttered aloft. The words were filled with air. He could hear the sails above him. Words. All his life he had used them, a small handful of words relating to his trade. He had never thought about their power until he heard the players. He drew his mind back to what she was saying. Steady as she goes. Stay, stand. Strong words. Stop. He resolved that he would learn to read words.

"*The White Bear.* I must conform to my husband's wishes. Are you interested?"

"My lady, I do not understand."

"I was saying, while you were day-dreaming and gazing out of my window, that I have a ship in need of employment."

"I have left the sea, my lady. I will stay on land."

"No, Nicholas. You have strayed from the sea." There it was again; stay, stray. One little flick of the tongue and a whole new meaning to the sound.

"You are day-dreaming again. Loafng. Listen to my proposition. You are a seaman. You will never be anything else. Loafing around playhouses and street corners."

'Loafing,' whatever the word meant, it was the definition of an idle fellow, a wastrel who kicked his heels at street corners, whistling through his teeth. He stood up straight and threw his shoulders back.

"You will learn to read. You will study navigation and cosmography. When the winter is over you will take my ship to sea. Do you agree?"

Nicholas nodded assent. He heard the imaginary sails crack open. They snapped open. They billowed full of wind. They bellied. They boomed.

"Then make your mark, Nicholas Conyers." She pushed a sheet of paper towards him. He was unsure as to where he should put his x. She turned the sheet around. The letters at the top were bigger. He dipped the quill in the ink jar and made his mark. He realised that that little cross bound him to her. What power then, lay in the many other marks that covered the page?

"Very good," she said, sprinkling sand over the ink. "I will have no back-sliding. You will go to my good neighbour, John Speed, a good tailor but a better maker of maps. He will instruct you in everything you need to know."

No back-sliding. No sneaking, slithering, slipping, snivelling. He was a schoolboy again. He could not wait to learn letters, to nail down words, to find out what learned people saw in books.

***

In Mary Lok's lodging house in King Street, Nicholas found a secluded room, little more than a cubby hole. There was a table and some stools. The light from the window was good. He studied his books, following the letters with his index finger. The print was easier than hand-written material. All the letters were a standard shape. The double s threw him for a little while. On its own the s did sterling work. Combined with other letters it suggested many things, a sneer, a sly fellow. There was something of the snake about s. Coupled with another s it became more like an f. He liked the way c threw a grapple across to t, whenever they met. They all linked together to make a meaning. The process delighted him. The days grew colder. Guests came and went. Nicholas worked on.

The old white-haired man from the church, lived in an upper room. He carried with him the constant stench of tobacco. It was not long before he discovered where Nicholas studied. He took to disturbing him. He enquired about his studies and his objectives. He was delighted to hear that Nicholas was a sailor, that he was interested in cosmography. He brought bundles of maps to the table in the little room.

"This one I drew myself," he said proudly.

It was a good map. It showed the Americas. Nicholas was astonished to see how far north he had sailed with Captain Frobisher.

There were sea monsters and winds with puffing cheeks. There was writing, but not in the English tongue. He realised that he had a long way to go in his studies.

"You might be interested in a proposition," said the old man. "See here how the sea is open, here along the top of Muscovy. A ship could sail along here, all the way to the Indies. And then..." He left the thought unfinished. His eyes glowed. His finger lay on the kingdom of the Great Khan, the realm of Cathay. The fingernail was stained yellow. "And then..." Endless possibilities.

Nicholas became a fugitive in the house. He read his books in the comforting warmth of the kitchen, oblivious to the clatter of pans. He struggled with writing and ciphering. Mary Lok would leave a bowl of warm soup at his elbow, only to find it later, cold and untouched, as Nicholas immersed himself in his work.

There was another man in the house, not much older than Nicholas himself but he walked with a stick and coughed a great deal. Sometimes he sat by the fire in the parlour, with a shawl about his shoulders. Mostly he kept to his room.

He was a man of great importance, Mistress Lok said. She always urged great haste in seeing to his needs. She was proud to have such an important person in her establishment. He had come over from Ireland on weighty business. He conferred with the Earl of Essex in that great house on The Strand. He was not to be disturbed. It worried her that the gentleman ate so little. She chided him about it. She suggested that his abstinence pained her personally. She begged him to eat, just a little, for her sake. He would smile his wan smile, with a faraway look in his eyes and make an effort.

It pained Nicholas too to see food wasted. He enjoyed Mary Lok's cooking. She put meat on his skinny frame. He figured that if he stayed too long he would be too fat to go back to sea. Too fat to wrestle or run. Too corpulent – a nice round word – to climb to the crow's nest or dangle below the futtock shrouds.

Still the fire was inviting, as winter tightened its grip. There was ice along the banks of the Thames. The watermen blew on their hands.

He read by the light of the fire, tilting the page towards the flames. Sometimes he would look over the top of the book, at the man sitting opposite. The man disturbed Nicholas's generous soul. He seemed to have the sorrows of the world on his shoulders, as well as the shawl that made him look like a hunchback. His eyes were sad. The firelight played on his features. He caught Nicholas's furtive look once or twice and acknowledged him with a smile, more of a wince than a smile, the merest recognition that he was there.

"What do you read, sir?" The question startled Nicholas.

"A book," he replied and felt immediately foolish. "A book my tutor gave to me."

"Your tutor?"

"It is a long story."

The man leaned forward, placing both hands on the knob of his cane. "I have some time still. I would hear your story."

Nicholas was surprised. He really had little to tell but he told it anyway, a plain tale of a boy running away from the drudgery of a hill farm; a life at sea under the leadership of a great captain; sea fights with French and Spanish mariners; long arctic days with strange people and wonderful sea beasts; floating mountains of ice; gold in abundance, that was not gold and yet it drove men mad, just like the real thing. There was that running fight against the Invincible Armada. There was not much to tell, in truth.

"And the book? You are a scholar?"

Nicholas laughed softly. "I am put to school with John Speed. He gives me books to read and charts to study. I have become moderately good at the mathematic."

"So what do you think of the book?"

"There are some things that I like, but a great deal I do not understand." He was emboldened by the man's interest. He thumbed through some pages. "Now listen to this. This is good. This is a dragon." He read.

'His crest above spotted with purple dye,
On every side did shine like scaly gold,
And his bright eyes glancing full dreadfully.
Did seem to flame out flakes of flashing fire.
And with stern looks to threaten kindled ire.'
E.S.

"Now that is good. I can understand that. I can see the dragon but . . ." He felt that he had said too much. He was overstepping some mark.

"But?"

"Well," said Nicholas, "then he goes on, page after page, gods and heroes and what not. I could make no sense of it."

"I see."

"I mean it is a poem about a gnat that stings a shepherd and warns him about the dragon. Why does he not come to the point?" Nicholas pronounced the g, the ge-nat.

"Ah, but he does. He shows remorse for killing the gnat. He builds a great monument."

"That I can understand," persisted Nicholas. "But all the rest? I ask you!" He liked that phrase. He had picked it up from the man at the Bell Savage. 'I ask you!' The plea of a reasonable man, against the absurdities of the world.

"I know," said the man. "He does go on a bit. But his remorse is true. Yes indeed. He knows remorse."

A log rolled in the fire. Flakes of flashing fire flamed out. They flickered. The two men looked into the little inferno at the centre of the hearth.

"You are a kind and decent person," said the man, after a while in pensive thought. "Might I prevail on you to accompany me to Ludgate? I am not too steady on the frost. I have some business there."

"It would be no trouble at all, sir. It is no more than a cock's step away." Nicholas was grateful for the conversation. This was obviously a man of learning.

"Less than half an ass's roar." The man laughed gently. "In Ireland they measure things differently."

Nicholas put the book aside. It was time for dinner. He rose to go in. He paused. "I will go with you to Ludgate, on condition that you tell me your story, as I have told you mine

"There is precious little to tell," replied the man. He remained seated. He gestured towards the book. Nicholas handed it to him. He went to the door and looked back. The melancholic man was holding the book in his hands, but had not opened it. His fingers touched the embossed leather of the spine. He was staring vacantly into the fire.

Nicholas drew close to the table. He licked his lips. Mistress Lok placed a platter of fragrant stew in front of him.

"I saw you having a great talk with Mr. Spenser about his poems. That will do him good. Cheer him up a little."

Nicholas put down his spoon. Blackness swam in front of his eyes. He felt the heat rising to his cheeks.

"Jesus Christ in Heaven!" he swore. "Do you mean Spenser the poet? The man who wrote that book?"

"None other. It is a privilege to have such a great man under our roof. Now eat your dinner and let me hear no more swearing."

Nicholas took up his spoon. He picked at the food. He went over in his mind, again and again, what he had said. No, he had said it was good. Very good. That scaly dragon, unfolding like the links in a chain. Yes, he had spoken of some few reservations. Too many gods. Too many strange names. He was sure that his remarks would prove helpful to the poet in time, help him to refine his thinking. Oh Jesus Christ in Heaven! He picked again at the food, pushing it about the platter. A g on 'nat'. The man had said 'nat', I ask you!

He stood up and went back into the room to explain, to apologise, to reassure the poet that he meant no disrespect, that in fact his poetry was quite good, very good indeed, excellent. In fact he should write more.

The poet's chair was empty. The book lay unopened on a stool. Nicholas swore again under his breath. He went back to his dinner. There was no point in wasting good food. No swearing, Nicholas. No back-sliding, Nicholas. Read this book, Nicholas. He longed for the open sea and the surge of the ocean rising beneath his keel.

***

They made their way, on the morrow, to William Ponsonby's establishment off Ludgate. It was more than a cock's step, because Cheapside was blocked by wagons carrying oak beams. The lead wagon had shed its load. The drivers were trying to make the horses go backwards. They chucked on the reins. The horses, although shod with frost-nails, slipped and skittered on a thin film of ice. The drivers cursed and swore. They clicked their tongues and tugged on the reins. The horses rolled their eyes and snorted in protest.

Nicholas was alarmed by Spenser's breathing. With every step he could hear a rattle in his companion's chest. With every stagger or slip on the ice, Spenser had to pause, until his breath returned to him. Sometimes Nicholas had to steady him by a firm grip on his elbow.

Ponsonby made them welcome. The work was well in hand. He produced a bundle of sheets and placed them on a table. Spenser bent to examine them. Nicholas peered over his stooped shoulders. There were numbered pages of print, four to a sheet, but facing in different directions. The numbers were not in sequence. Nicholas wondered if he should draw their attention to the problem. It was a very odd way to make a book.

It was not poetry. There were no narrow columns of verse, no wood-cuts or floral capitals. It looked like a conversation between two characters from a play, but they spoke too much, even for players. There was a title page mixed up with the others. *A Veue of the Present State of Ireland.*

Nicholas saw the phrase 'reducing that salvage nation to better government and civility.' He wondered what a 'salvage nation' might be. Perhaps some nation that had been lost and had been recovered.

Spenser was speaking. There was some kind of altercation.

"All of it. I will not publish." He was emphatic.

"But I have been to some expense. I must pay Singleton for the printing and the paper." Ponsonby was dismayed.

"I shall reimburse you. You need have no fear of that."

Ponsonby was relieved, but argued yet.

"It is a very fine dialogue, closely argued. Why will you not go on to publication?"

"Because I will not." Spenser sat down on a chair. The argument was distressing him. He rubbed his brow.

Nicholas caught the publisher's eye. He shook his head in warning. Ponsonby took his meaning.

"Let me get you a cordial, some wine perhaps. You should not be abroad in the streets with that cough."

"Indeed, we have been all over. Have we not, Nicholas?" Spenser spoke ruefully. He was not looking forward to the return journey.

Ponsonby poured three glasses of a strong wine of Portugal. The wine glowed like ruby in the glasses.

"Your health, Mr. Spenser," he said, raising his glass. "And you too sir," he added. "I did not catch your name."

"My apologies," intervened Spenser. "My infirmity has rendered me boorish. This is my good friend, Captain Nicholas Conyers of *The White Bear.*"

"Your servant," said Ponsonby, raising his glass again to Nicholas, in salute.

Nicholas looked at Spenser in surprise. He beamed with pride.

"Captain Conyers is a fierce warrior against Her Majesty's enemies on the high seas." Spenser took a sip of the wine. It eased his breathing. He looked at Nicholas with the ghost of a smile. "I must warn you William, that he wages war also on bad poetry and slovenly poets. He will have none of it. He holds with the new men and the players. You must be careful of what you publish from now on."

Nicholas made no reply. He felt that he would be out-manoeuvred and out-gunned in any discussion with these two men of words. He downed the wine. It warmed his gizzard. Captain Frobisher always said that. 'Warm your gizzard.'

"Indeed I shall," said Ponsonby amiably. "But to return to our discussion. What has moved you to withdraw from publication?"

Spenser sighed. "I have had enough of Ireland. Anything I say will add fuel to that fire."

"But so much work. Why throw it away? The argument is convincing."

"That is why I do not wish to publish it."

Ponsonby shook his head. He tried again.

"When the Irishman reads this, when he sees the garrisons all around him, he will choose obedience and law over annihilation. Even the Irishman will think of his family. You do him a kindness."

"The Irishman, as you say, will not read Spenser, in his forest hideaway. He will raise his children to resist, to carry on after him. I know the Irishman. There is only one solution and I do not want it to bear my name. I do not want to be remembered in the same breath as King Herod."

"It would not come to that, my friend." Ponsonby gathered the papers. "When did you reach this conclusion?"

"My wife has begged me not to put this out. She opened my eyes. But if you must know, I came to this realisation while standing on a mountain-top, looking down on a land of surpassing beauty. My daughter spoke to me."

"Ah," said Ponsonby lightly, "so you came down, like Moses from Sinai, to dash your tablets to pieces."

"Something like that," said Spenser, rising to his feet. He leaned upon his cane. "Your arm, Captain Conyers, if you please."

Nicholas stepped forward.

"What then shall I do with all this paper?"

"Make spills to light your infernal pipe. I know that you have become thrall to it. Better to ignite the vile weed than to inflame the Irish." He laughed a short dry laugh.

"I should not laugh," he said lightly. "It filches my breath away."

He took Nicholas's arm. "I shall send to you, William." He flourished his cane. "But for now I shall leave the stage."

"Be careful," warned Ponsonby. "The streets are blocked. They are moving The Theatre across the river. They say that they will build a stage for all the world. They are calling it The Globe." He spread his arms in oratorical fashion, mocking the vanity and presumption of the players. "The Globe! I ask you." He rolled the sheets and put them carefully, on a high shelf. He paused for a moment in thought, then tapped the roll of paper, pushing it further in, out of sight, for the time being.

They went out into the street. The frost had retreated. The wagons had moved on. The Theatre had migrated to its new home.

"We must follow them, you and I, Nicholas, and see what these fellows have to offer to the world."

"Indeed," replied Nicholas. He held himself proudly erect. He walked with a new confidence, with the hobbling poet on his arm. Just two words, 'Captain Conyers,' the idle coinage of a poet's brain, had made the difference.

***

They betook themselves to Blackfriars. At least the stage was indoors. There were lamps. The press of bodies took the chill from the air. Outside all was winter, but inside, the hearts of the groundlings and of the gentle folk in the gallery, burned with patriotic fervour.

'O for a Muse of Fire'

Spenser shifted on his seat. He leaned forward, taking in every word. It was many years since he had attended a playhouse. He had tired of their ranting, their licentious bawdry. This was different.

'Then should the warlike Harry, like himself
Assume the port of Mars; and at his heels
Leash'd in like hounds, should famine, sword and fire
Crouch for employment.'
W.S.

He was gripped from the outset. He knew what the prologue foretold. He knew those hounds. They strained at the leash. Proud horses printed their hooves in the receiving earth.

Nicholas sat, replete with the pleasure of anticipation. He had seen it before. He had a tendency to nudge his companion, drawing attention to the good bits. He became restive during long legal argument. To him it was fine for Henry to invade France for whatever reasons he chose. He was the king.

Spenser's legalistic mind enjoyed the exposition of Henry's entitlement to the Crown of France. The law is everything. It was a good case, if one held one's fingers crossed. It was a better case, because the groundlings hated the mincing, arrogant Dauphin, a sleeveen as the Irish might have described him. He was not so sure about the truculent Irishman, Macmorris. The garrulous Welshman, Fluellen, was played by a small dark-skinned man, far too young to be a hardened veteran. Welshmen can be dark skinned with equally dark eyes and a great flow of language. Nicholas nudged him in the ribs.

"Caliban," he whispered, with a kind of proprietorial pride. "I told you about him." He looked at Spenser sideways, making sure that he appreciated the wonder of it all. "He is not Welsh, you know."

Spenser had guessed as much. It was all play-acting, the fields of France, the broken walls of Harfleur. All in the words and in the mind.

The arrogant Dauphin boasted of his steed, the paragon of horses.

'I will trot tomorrow a mile, and my way shall be paved with English faces.'
W.S.

Spenser was back again on the brink of Ireland. The fields were paved with faces, Italian, Spanish, Portuguese, their dead eyes staring up unseeing at the flying clouds. *Gort 'a Gearradh,* the Field of the Cuttings, *Na Gorta Dubha,* The Black Fields. It was Uaithne who had told him the Irish names. Uaithne claimed to have been there, to have seen it all. Another of his outrageous yarns. Spenser had not argued with him. If Uaithne had been there, his head too would have fetched a bounty.

Nicholas nudged him again. Three soldiers were debating the justice of the king's cause. If the king's cause were just, then the soldiers themselves were justified in whatever they were called upon to do. If the king fought in an unjust cause, then the soldiers were still justified by their obedience to their king. It was an argument that would stand up on that terrible Day of Judgement

'when all loose legs and arms chopp'd off in battle, shall join together at the latter day.'
W.S.

That was a question that had always perplexed Nicholas. He imagined a veritable blizzard of heads and severed limbs, on the last day, flying in all directions, seeking out the scattered components in battlefields and oceans all over the world and fettling themselves for judgement.

Spenser took no comfort from the soldiers' argument. Every man must face his own guilt.

The theatre fell silent. Nicholas nudged him again. Damn the man, I am not asleep.

"This is good," whispered Nicholas. "This is good. What would it be to fight for such a king?"

'He that outlives this day and comes safe home,

Will stand a tip-toe when this day is nam'd'
Spenser felt the hairs rising on the back of his neck. 'And gentlemen in England now a-bed,
Shall think themselves accurs'd they were not here, And hold their manhoods cheap whiles any speaks That fought with us upon Saint Crispin's day.'
W.S.

The audience cheered and clapped. Nicholas stood and applauded. The player king basked in his moment of glory. Spenser felt the bile of envy rising in his gorge. This painted player in his rumpled robe and gimcrack armour, was England. He could rouse a nation with his words. In all his books, with all his knights and heroes, his gods and nymphs, Spenser had never achieved such a reaction. No gentle reader, sitting by his hearth, would rouse himself to battle at Spenser's words. No man would hazard his life as a result of reading his elegant and polished lines. The only nation that he would ever rouse and bring together, by the power of his words, was Ireland. He knew that his solution was no solution. Fortunately those words would never be published. Ponsonby would light his pipe with them. Perhaps some fishwife might find them and use them to wrap fish at Bellyn's Gate. He pictured the fierce eyes of mackerel and haddock, slippery eels, their toothed mouths agape as they spoke his words. They chattered about him, their chins wagging up and down, a chorus of demons.

The theatre swayed. It revolved around him. Sheets of paper swirled in his vision, lofted by the wind. He slumped sideways, falling against Nicholas.

Kindly hands lifted him and bore him downstairs. The cold air revived him a little. Voices were whispering.

'Spenser. Spenser. It is Spenser the poet.'

Curious eyes regarded him. He was the centre of a most unwelcome drama.

The manager and the author got wind of what had happened. They came out, full of solicitude, dismayed that so distinguished a guest had taken ill in their house. They offered to send for a carriage, but Spenser waved the idea away. The author extended his hand. "I am honoured, Mr Spenser, that you came to our poor entertainment."

Spenser took his hand. "The honour is mine, good sir. I have seen the future. I may put my quills aside now and depart. I too am thrall to Mutabilitie."

They shook hands.

Nicholas took him home through the icy streets. They walked like men who had drunk too well. Nicholas helped him upstairs to his room.

"Quickly, quickly," cried Mary Lok. "Fetch a warming pan for Mr. Spenser. Quickly, quickly." She clapped her hands. She bustled to the kitchen to prepare some warm, spicy wine.

Nicholas laid him on the bed. He pulled off Spenser's shoes. He stopped short of undressing him. He knew how a man could resent too much help. It robbed a man of his dignity. He could become an enemy. Nicholas piled the bedclothes over him. Spenser regarded him with a wan smile.

"Ah, Captain Conyers," he said, "it is time for shrift."

"No, no," protested Nicholas, "but if you wish I could send for a priest."

"No priest," murmured Spenser. "You are a captain. You have power of life and death over those who serve under you. You can join man and wife together. You can make terrible war."

Nicholas wondered where all this was leading.

"I venture that you can hear the confession of one poor wretch, better than any priest. You might even absolve him, like the Papists do."

Mistress Lok came back with the wine. She carried a note and a purse.

"This came today from Essex House."

"Open it, Nicholas," directed Spenser.

Nicholas spilled twenty gold coins onto the bedspread. Spenser picked them up and let them fall through his fingers.

"What does he say? Read the letter, Nicholas."

Nicholas broke the seal. He looked at the cursive writing in momentary panic. He focussed and then unfocussed. The less he concentrated, the sooner the shapes appeared. It was easy. He read.

"He sends his compliments and begs that you will not be disturbed about money. He will quit all your debts. He sends this small token to tide you over." Nicholas spoke cheerfully. This was good news.

"The tide, Nicholas, is running against me. I ask you to go to the Earl and thank him for me. Return the money and tell him that I lack the means to spend it."

It was a lot of money. Nicholas replaced it in the purse. He drew the drawstring and tied it with a seaman's skill. He jingled it, weighing it in his hand.

"You will feel better in the morning. You will go to the Earl yourself."

"Ha, ha," said Spenser softly.

"Nicholas and I will make you comfortable," said Mistress Lok. "Nicholas, undo the points."

This was somewhat different. A woman's work. He could lend a hand. He thought of how he had ministered to Captain Frobisher in his final days. He took some pride in his gentleness. Spenser would not resent his care.

Spenser plucked at the covers.

"Tomorrow, Captain, you must sit with me and hear my story. I will tell you of green fields and the bright rivers of Ireland. I will tell you of the woods and all the wonderful variety of trees."

"You must rest now, Mr. Spenser," insisted Mistress Lok. "Nicholas, do not tire him. Watch with him a little while." She went out. Her shoes sounded on the stairs.

Spenser clutched Nicholas by the sleeve. Fingers long and small, not the calloused hands of soldier or seaman. Delicate hands that had done no murder.

"I shall tell you of my crimes, Nicholas and you shall grant me absolution. Enter it in your log. 'This day I granted forgiveness to one wretched poet, for giving away a child of his own blood, for murdering his wife, through cold neglect, for leaving a daughter to perish on a mountain top.' Oh, Nicholas, my crimes are manifold. I have condemned hundreds, nay thousands to die. There is not water enough in your ocean to wash the blood away."

"Ah, no, no, no," protested Nicholas. "You are a gentle soul. Sleep now and in the morning you will feel better." He patted Spenser's hand, awkwardly. He was not at ease with such confidences. In the morning, he resolved, he would buck him up, bring him to see the Earl, get some hot food into him. He tucked the covers about the poet's chin. He took his leave. Spenser's eyes followed him to the door. Nicholas turned again.

"Write it down, Nicholas. Write my shrift into your log." He tried to smile. Nicholas raised his hand in farewell. He went downstairs. He needed a drink and time to sit in quiet reflection.

The old man found him in the kitchen.

"Is Mr. Spenser asleep?" he asked. "I hear he has come into some money. I want to talk to him about a business venture."

"Tomorrow," said Nicholas patiently. "Tomorrow will be time enough."

On the morrow, Mistress Lok found that Spenser's sad spirit had fled. She wept. "Cold, cold" she sniffed. "What a poor, gentle man he was. And so cold. So cold. God bless him. Cold as any stone."

She closed the shutters on the windows facing the street.

***

It was no funeral to rival that of Phillip Sidney, but due respect was paid. Pre-eminent among the mourners was the young Earl of Essex. This was only fitting, as he paid the costs. The oaken coffin was lined with lead. A troop of poets lifted it from the hearse. They struggled manfully to bear it into The Abbey. They were aware that they were carrying the last remains of English Poesie on their shoulders. While Spenser lived, English Poesie had danced and clapped her hands. Now she was dead, without strength enough in her fingers to lift a quill, a feather.

They laid him beside his master, the great Geoffrey, the man who had depicted in his time, all England, from the highest to the lowest. The poets filed past. They threw elegies into the tomb. They broke their pens and cast them upon the coffin. They would write no more.

It was the place to be, that bleak, cold morning, the place to be seen. It was an opportunity to catch the eye of some wealthy patron. In paying tribute to the master, they filched a little of his glory. They became part of his legend.

"Mere play-acting, Will," confided Jonson in a stage whisper. He nudged his companion in the ribs. His companion motioned him to silence. He was moved by the solemnity of the place, the soaring Gothic arches, the drone of prayer, even the incessant coughing of the congregation. How many kings had left their bones among these stones? He thought of Chaucer and April days, of sunshine and laughing pilgrims. He thought of Harry Bailey and his bagpipes, leading them to the tomb of the holy blessed martyr. He longed for birdsong and green fields.

"I'm for The Mermaid and a hot pie," whispered Jonson. It was not such a bad idea.

Nicholas stood quietly near the door, while the great ones left. He mused on the poor man in the tomb. It was too late to hear his story. He could do no more than conjecture. There was some suggestion that he had left his children behind him to perish in a fire in a castle consumed by flame. No, Spenser would never have done such a thing. There was a new widow now in Ireland, a country of many widows. The poor man had begun his confession, but had been granted no time to finish it. That would do. Nicholas's Cornish mother remained a Papist in a patchy sort of way, until her dying day. She had told him that absolution depended not on the power of any priest, but on the repentance of the sinner and a firm purpose of amendment.

On those Popish grounds, the poor man was quit of his debts. He murmured a makeshift prayer for the poet.

He went outside. The lords, gentlemen and ladies, were waiting for their horses and carriages. The poets were making themselves agreeable. The wind, sharp and cold, had set in from the east. He could smell the river. He was sure that he could hear, in the distance, the thunder of the cataract under the bridge. The tide had turned again. The river was racing for the ocean. He was hungry. It was time for Deptford, a platter of oysters and *The White Bear.*

Epilogue

Bess often passed the idle hours in perusing her husband's papers. She discussed them with him, his journals, his maps, his *History of the World*, fantastical voyages and fights at sea. All so long ago. So many things had changed. She recalled their first meeting. She was little more than a child, a bright and eager new arrival at Court. He was the Queen's favourite, expert in dancing and wit. How they had loved, hiding their shining eyes from the Queen, lest she should read the truth in them. Raleigh's eyes were closed.

The Queen was old and dried up. She snaffled Bess's golden boy. She held him on a short rein. How they had stolen from her presence and made love in anterooms, even in Her Majesty's private apartments. There was a baby, Damerie, a beautiful boy. The plague took him almost at once. Or was it witch craft? The Queen's mother was a witch, they said.

"God hold me in my wits," she exclaimed. "It is forty four years since they put you in The Tower. You never cared what rope held the mast. You squandered your Irish estates, those fields and woods, those shining rivers. All is peaceful now in Munster. Edmund Spenser was right. He showed the way. Ireland will never see war again. That man, ONeill, was shattered at Kinsale, with all his Spanish cronies. He buggered off, as you used to say, to Rome, with all the money he could wring from his unfortunate followers and lost it all, on a slippery Alpine path.

Do you know that I approached Richard Boyle for compensation? I said that you had made an improvident sale. He laughed at me. He sat in your house in Youghal. He lorded it in your castle at Lismore. He angled for your salmon. He angled for more than salmon." Her voice was bitter. She had never liked Richard Boyle, the Great conniving, Earl of Cork. "Do you know what he said to me?"

Raleigh made no reply. She grasped a fistful of his shrivelled hair. She shook his head. He did not blink.

"He said to me, he said 'Madam, your husband never learned to pick the bush clean, before moving on to the next. I am the gleaner.' He said it, as if it were something to be proud of. He is the scavenger who follows the army. He is the one who strips the corpses of brave men, the dog that gnaws on their bones."

She sighed. Raleigh grinned, as if dreaming of those days. The battles, the Indian prince all dusted with gold. He had walked on the tombs of kings in Panama, tombs filled with gold and emeralds, unbeknownst to him. He knew it now. It was too late to go back. He had seen the warlike women of the Orinoco, but he had never found El Dorado, the gilded city on the lake, the gilded man.

"Gold," she said. "It drove you all mad. Do you remember your quarrel with Frobisher over *Madre de Dios?* There was enough for both of you, but yet you had to snarl like mastiffs, over the division. I feed the birds on my lawn in the mornings. I squander my bread, but their need is yet greater than mine, as they say. They alert one another to the food and then, they squabble over the crumbs, although I have enough for everyone. I chide them. I tell them to share, but still they fight. They encroach, one on another's empire."

His teeth were still good, though yellow. She tapped his silver tobacco box. She peered at the inscription. Her sight was fading. *'Comes meus fuit illo miserrimo tempore.'* 'It was my companion during that most miserable time.' That vile tobacco. "Where was my companion? You may smile, but it is true. You are a bird, an eagle, perchance a pirate bird. You never could rest when you espied a prey. God hold me in my wits, but my love for you has cost me dear. You lost my brave boy on the Orinoco. You let him slip through your fingers."

She gazed at him. Twenty nine years she had carried him with her. She was beyond anger. She was beyond tears. She remembered only the love that she had felt for this golden warrior, this eagle, this poet, this glorious fool.

She took his head in her hands. She stroked his straggling locks. She kissed his brow. It was cold. She kissed his parchment lips. He made no response. All passion fled.

She opened the velvet bag and placed his head inside. She gazed at him a last time, then gathered the folds about him. She drew the string and tied it with a bow. It was time to send him back to his tomb to prepare for the Resurrection, for the day when they would be together again, for evermore, embarking on the great adventure of eternity.

***

'But could youth last and love still breed,
Had joys no date, or age no need,
Then these delights my mind might move
To live with thee and be thy love.'
W.R.

A NOTE ON ORTHOGRAPHY

Spellings have been modernised in the quotations, only when the sense might be obscure. Spenser delighted in archaisms which may have appeared quaint to his contemporaries. To a modern reader they could prove impenetrable.

Poets
E.S. Edmund Spenser c. 1552-1599
P.S. Sir Philip Sidney 1554-1586
W. R. Sir Walter Raleigh 1554-1618
W. S. William Shakespeare 1564-1616
Q.H.F. Quintus Horatius Flaccus. 65 BC-8 BC

TIMELINE
1550
Birth of Spenser 1552
Birth of Raleigh 1554
Company of Muscovy 1555 Coronation of Elizabeth I 1559 1560
Birth of Shakespeare 1564
First Desmond Rebellion in Ireland 1569-1573
Company of Cathay 1575
Frobisher's voyages 1576, 1577, 1578 Spenser's marriage to Machabyas.
Shepheardes Calendar
1579
Drake's circumnavigation of the world 1577-1580 Second Desmond Rebellion 1579-1583
1580
Massacre at Smerwick Plantation of Munster
Spenser at Kilcolman *Books I II III of Faerie Queene, Astrophel*
Funeral of Sir Phillip Sidney Execution of Mary, Queen of Scots.
Drake's raid on Cadiz
1587
THE ARMADA 1588
1590
Spenser one year in London Made Queen's Justice for Cork 1591
Married Elizabeth Boyle *Amoretti, Epithalamion*
1594
Wrote *A View of the Present State of Ireland in the Present Time, Books IV, V, VI of Faerie Queene*
Death of Frobisher.
Rebellion of O Neill, followed by Nine Years War 1594
Loss of Kilcolman Death of Burghley 1598 Death of Spenser
Birth of Cromwell 1599 1600
1601 Don Juan del Águila, O Neill, O Donnell, defeated at Kinsale
Death of Queen Elizabeth I End of Nine Years War 1603
Accession of James I Peace with Spain Flight of O Neill and O Donnell 1607 1610
Plantation of Ulster
King James Bible 1611
Deaths of Shakespeare, O Neill, Galileo, 1616

Hugh Fitzgerald Ryan

Execution of Raleigh 1618
1620
Charles I 1625
Cromwell elected to Parliament 1629
1630
A View of the Present State of Ireland published 1633
1640
Peregrine Spenser reported impoverished in the Barony of Fermoy
1641
Rebellion in Ireland 1641 English Civil War 1642
Death of Elizabeth, wife of Walter Raleigh 1647
Execution of Charles I 1649
Cromwell in Ireland 1650

309

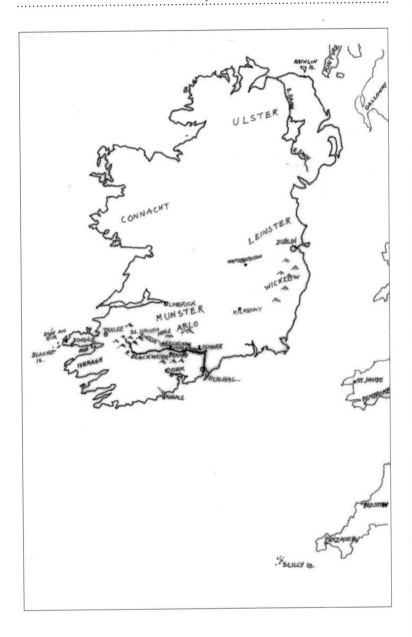

Printed in Great Britain
by Amazon